(un)like a Virgin

Lucy-Anne Holmes

sphere

SPHERE

First published in Great Britain as a paperback original in 2011 by Sphere
Reprinted 2011 (twice), 2014

A CIP catalogue record for this book is available from the British Library.

ISBN 978-0-7515-4760-3

Typeset in Caslon by M Rules
Printed and bound in Great Britain by
Clays Ltd, St Ives plc

Papers used by Sphere are from well-managed forests and other responsible sources.

MIX
Paper from
responsible sources
FSC® C104740

Sphere
An imprint of
Little, Brown Book Group
100 Victoria Embankment
London EC4Y 0DY

An Hachette UK Company
www.hachette.co.uk

www.littlebrown.co.uk

For my beautiful sister.

Chapter 1

My name is Gracie Flowers and I'm an estate agent. But before you say, 'Oh, bloody hell, you're not, are you?' let me defend myself by saying that I'm not like all the others. For starters, I'm nice. For seconds, I can't lie. Like, really can't lie. When a client asks other estate agents if a four foot by five foot kitchen is small, they'll say something like 'Oh, no! It's far from small. It's compact and demonstrates a remarkable use of space. You'll get all the mod cons in there.' If a client asks me whether the five foot by seven foot kitchen is small, I'll choke and say, 'Yep, tiny. Try to swing a gerbil in there and you'll dislocate your arm. You'll be keeping your microwave in the living room.' You'd think these qualities would be a hindrance when selling houses, but they're not. They're really not. I'm an astonishingly good estate agent, and no one was more surprised about that than me. Well, maybe my mum.

Ken Bradbury, my boss, the owner of the London chain of estate agents, Make A Move, says that I'm the best female estate agent in London. And although I always say, 'Ken, you sexist toad, lose the word female,' I'm as chuffed as a pub patio ashtray to be respected for what I do. What's even weirder than the fact that I seem to be peculiarly brilliant at selling houses is this: I absolutely love being an estate agent. Choosing a home is a massive decision in people's lives and it's me, Gracie Flowers, who's there making sure they don't mess it all up. I match the person to the house, so that they can create a home full of love, dreams and happy memories. And I also get to nose around other people's homes, which can be very enlightening. It's the best job in the world. Why we're as popular as bankers I don't know.

There is a bummer, though, and it's a big old builder's bummer. I have to work on Saturdays. So when normal people are lying in bed all snugly and drooly, dozing and deciding where to go for breakfast, I'm wondering if I can get away with just one more eight-minute snooze and whether I have any clean pants for the day.

I wake up in the same way, at the same time, every Saturday. It's not by an alarm clock. I don't need an alarm clock. This isn't because I'm a perky early riser. Far from it. It's because I live in the noisiest flat in London. My Saturday wake-up call is as follows:

7.42 a.m. – The freight train from Portsmouth to King's Cross thunders, no roars, no lacerates my eardrums, as it travels along the railway line a few feet from my bedroom window.

7.54 a.m. – Another freight train; the longest of the week. It lasts for nearly two minutes and sounds like the Red Arrows are doing a flying routine inside my pillow.

8.03 a.m. – The third alarm call comes when the men in

the glass shop below me arrive and turn Capital FM on. Very loud.

8.14 a.m. – Another freight train.

8.15 a.m. – The men in the glass shop below me start smashing sheets of glass.

For some reason the combination of smashing glass, the freight train and the crackling of Capital at around the eight fifteen mark arouses my boyfriend, Danny. It tends to be at about this time that I feel his erection on my bottom.

When Danny makes love to me later in the day he can be quite adventurous. However, when he makes love to me in the morning he seems to think that flapping his penis onto my bottom constitutes foreplay. Erotic. Now I like sex, but if I have to be honest, at eight fifteen on a Saturday morning I prefer to snooze. I normally lie still and hope that he'll stop, which is what I'm doing now. It's not proving very effective, though. He's just shifted his weight and moved his penis onto the other bottom cheek. Damn!

I lie still and let him do it anyway. He doesn't normally take very long in the morning.

'Danny, baby, be careful, I'm not taking the pill at the moment,' I mumble into the pillow. I forgot I needed to go to the doctors and get another prescription for my contraceptive pill. That was stupid, Gracie. Stupid.

I've been going out with Danny Saunders for ten years. He asked me out two days before my GCSEs started. Actually, technically they'd already started as I'd completed my French oral the day before. This means I should be able to say, 'Excuse me, where is the nearest bank?' in French, but I can't. I haven't the foggiest. Anyway the bulk of the exams, the two a day for about a fortnight, were still looming at this point.

I didn't know much about Danny when he stopped me in the corridor and proceeded to cough and look at his feet for a few minutes before eventually saying, 'You know this shit prom thing, do you want to go with me?'

I knew his name, though, Danny Saunders. I thought it was a nice name: friendly, blokey, approachable and pronounceable. I knew he was clever – he was in all the top sets – I was aware that he was pale and into computers, and I was definitely familiar with his height. 'Bloody tall,' I called it. It turned out to be six foot three. But that was about all I knew.

I kept myself to myself at school. At that time my mum and dad were the Torvill and Dean of the ballroom dancing world. They'd won the World Ballroom Dancing Championships for seven consecutive years, but all this was before *Strictly Come Dancing* and ballroom dancing's subsequent rebirth of cool. And this was Kensal Rise Community College, where you were only cool if your dad was a DJ or in prison. 'Your dad's a gay lord,' people would say to me, if they bothered to say anything at all. Hence the keeping myself to myself.

I was therefore surprised to be asked out to the 'shit prom thing'. I looked at Danny Saunders with the nice name closely and noticed that he was at least a foot taller than me, lean and broad-shouldered. I was also pleased to see that he was wearing a Ramones T-shirt. My dad had a Ramones T-shirt, and at the time my dad was my hero. I looked into his deep-set brown eyes and nonchalantly said, 'Yeah, OK, why not?' But inside I was thinking, Phwoar, Danny Saunders is fit.

I'm not thinking that this morning, though. I'm thinking

something else entirely. The eight seventeen passenger train hasn't even gone past and Danny is grunting and lolloping off me like a roll of old carpet. But that's not the worst of it: I can feel something gooey down there.

'Danny Saunders, you arse!' I screech, punching him in his annoyingly concave belly.

'Aw, Grace, babe. I totally forgot,' he pants.

'Plonker!' I hit him again.

'Can't you get that morning-after pill thing?'

I sigh, sit up and wipe my eyes like a tired child. I'll have to get the morning-after pill thing. Thank you, Danny, for pointing out the bleeding obvious. A baby definitely isn't in my plans for the foreseeable future. But the busiest weekend in the modern world is facing me and God knows when I'll find the time to fit in a trip to the pharmacy.

But I mustn't worry about that for the moment, I think, smiling to myself as I get out of bed. I have a big – no, very big – morning ahead.

Chapter 2

I have a feeling that my bathroom routine is different to most people's. I can't be certain, but I've never met anyone who showers as quickly as I do. Danny tells everyone I shower as though an armed militia is beating down the door. I don't have the heart to point out that it's a ridiculous analogy, if it even is an analogy. I never did get my English GCSE.

If an armed militia were banging down my door I would hardly be in the blinking shower. I would either be trying to squeeze my bottom out of the small bathroom window or I'd be standing in the middle of the bathroom in a formidable Lara Croft stance, armed with a plunger and an aerosol, ready to punish the swines for hurting one of my precious doors. I own my flat. Not that I call it my 'flat'. Because it's not a flat. It's a maisonette. I stripped and sanded all the doors myself and spent hours in Homebase gazing at shades of white before painting them all purple. I love my doors.

The reason I shower quickly is because I like to have time

to talk to myself in the morning. I don't know what I'd do without my morning pep talks. I got them from my dad. My mum likes to start the day with fifteen minutes of yoga, and when I was little I would get in her way and interrupt her karma, so Dad used to lock me in the bathroom with him and entertain me. He would set me down carefully on the toilet lid and I'd look up at him and listen as he shaved and talked to himself.

'Good morning, Camille, looking very fine, may I say,' he would start, smiling at his reflection. I would giggle. 'Now then, you handsome devil, what have we got in store today? Oh, the Clydesdale Cup. And are we going to win it? Oh, we are. Good, good. We're going to keep the control in the cha cha cha, aren't we? Not like the last time when we nearly catapulted Rosemary into the judge's lap. Although he would probably have enjoyed that, wouldn't he, the filthy toad?' Then he'd wiggle a few cha cha cha steps. 'Camille, don't dance and shave, I have warned you. It can get bloody. So, winning the Clydesdale Cup, what else? Oh I know! I'm going to sing a song with my beautiful birthday daughter, Gracie. What shall we sing?'

Now, as the bulk of these mornings happened when I was between the ages of three and eight, one might expect us to be singing 'Twinkle Twinkle Little Star' or 'Old MacDonald Had A Farm' together. But no, by the age of four I knew all the words to 'Wichita Lineman' by Glen Campbell. At five my favourite song was 'No Woman No Cry' by Bob Marley. My sixth year was quite prolific because we covered a lot of Bob Dylan and the Beatles; and I was singing most of the major Motown hits by the time I was eight.

'Up tight. Everything's all right!' I shouted. It was the morning of my eighth birthday and I was in a massive Stevie Wonder phase.

'Gracie,' my dad said, clocking my enthusiasm with a smile, 'the time has come. Today is a very important day because I'm going to introduce you to someone very special. Someone very special indeed. A woman with a huge talent. A beautiful, deep, rich voice like you, Amazing Grace.' He called me that a lot. 'A woman with the courage of her convictions. A woman who worked tirelessly for the rights of black people. A Goddess. Gracie Flowers, may I introduce you to . . . the one, the only . . . Nina Simone.' And he walked over to the cassette recorder on the bathroom windowsill and pressed play. That was the first time I heard the song 'Feeling Good'. 'It's a new dawn, it's a new day. It's a new life for me and I'm feeling good.'

I was eight and watching my dad who loved me mouth the words to this wonderful song. He mimed being a fish and a butterfly and I laughed in delight – quietly though, as I didn't want to miss a word – and I remember feeling good.

That Nina Simone day was exactly eighteen years ago. And I'm feeling pretty good this morning, too, despite the semen situation.

'Happy birthday, Gracie Flowers, how you doing?' I say to my reflection. 'Whoa, not pretty. That'll be last night's tequilas. Concealer, where are you?' I say, delving into the cosmetic detritus by the sink. I do completely love my flat, however, its standard of cleanliness may not always attest to this fact. It's generally a complete tip on Saturday because, if I tidy at all, it will only ever be a rushed, haphazard attempt on a Sunday.

'So, Gracie Flowers, let's get down to business,' I say after

I've smudged away my tequila shadows. 'You've got a lot to get through today. You could get giddy after the announcement, and there may be champagne, so practise what you want to say.'

I stand back from the sink slightly and take a deep breath. I imagine Ken Bradbury saying, 'It is with great pleasure that I give the job to Gracie Flowers.' Then I start to perform.

'Oh my goodness,' I gasp, putting my hands over my mouth in mock surprise.

I have to giggle. I'm so rubbish at acting.

'Oh. My. God,' I try in a higher register. It's better, but not much.

'Argh! No way!' I screech, which is dreadful.

I have a problem. It's fairly obvious to everyone that I'm going to get the job of Head of London Sales. I've been the company's top negotiator ever since I became a negotiator, and Ken Bradbury himself pretty much told me the job was mine. 'My decision works very well in your favour, Gracie,' he said and then he winked. It couldn't have been clearer. So this is all really just a formality because Ken likes to have a big Saturday-morning announcement whenever there's a new appointment at Make A Move. He thinks it encourages a healthy rivalry amongst the team. I've been to loads of them and it's very important to act surprised. I saw one bloke simply nod and go up and shake Ken's hand. No gasp, no tears, no witty but not vulgar expletive. We had one word for him: smug.

At Make A Move there is only myself and my good friend Friendly Wendy in the entire company who are of the fair and delicate sex. The rest of the employees belong to the sex that read the *Daily Star* and like to throw office equipment at each other's heads. 'Men' is the technical term for them, although Friendly Wendy and I prefer to lump them under the more appropriate term, 'dickheads'.

The bloke who nodded when he got his promotion eventually became known as Smeg. It started out with the odd quip: 'Is this ssssmug yours?' And, 'Would you like a ssssmug of tea?' But substituting the word mug with smug offered limited comic value, so in the end he became known simply as Smug which in turn became Smeg – and Smeg stuck. Ken Bradbury's nickname originated in a similarly organic manner. At first he was known by his initials KB, then these got changed to KY, and now he's simply known as Lube.

I mustn't look smug when they announce me. Smeg's left now and it's his job I'll be taking over. I really don't want to be called Smeg 2. Or Lady Smeg. Or Little Lube. If I'm given a nickname at all I want it to be Lady Boss.

I clear my throat and try again. This time I opt for soft and gracious.

'Oh my goodness, Ken, thank you,' I say, in a way I hope will sound quietly overawed. 'I won't let you down, I promise. I love Make A Move. I started here over five years ago, answering the phones on Saturday mornings. And here I am now being given this amazing opportunity. What an honour! I owe so much to you, Ken, for your support and guidance. I'm going to ensure that Make A Move is the only estate agent in London that people want to use.' Ken will love that bit. 'And I'm going to whip your arses, boys,' I add, with a scowl at all the blokes.

When I finish my little speech, my heart is pounding. I stop and look at my reflection in the mirror. I look like the same Gracie Flowers: a five-foot short arse with long blonde hair that never stays in its ponytail. I'm still chubbier than I want to be, but I feel amazing.

I've worked so hard for this day, and now it's here. I did it. I walk, as though on air, over to my five year plan, which is laminated and framed on my bathroom wall. I kiss it and walk to the windowsill, pausing for a moment to wince at my cactus. I'm sure someone once told me that cactuses were unkillable. They got that wrong. I press play on the CD player and listen to 'Feeling Good' by Nina Simone.

Chapter 3

I didn't always want to be an estate agent. Like most little girls I wanted to be a singer. But then, like most little girls, I grew up.

I remember the moment when I was first drawn to the job, though. I was twenty and I was at home with Mum when the doorbell rang.

'Grace, I haven't got my face on, will you go!' my mum shouted from upstairs. Those were her words exactly, I know because I recall thinking how even when she had her face on she made an excuse not to answer the door. My mother hated answering the front door. She wasn't lazy, but she'd started to hate seeing people – or people seeing her, I wasn't sure which.

I opened the door and a tall young man in a suit stood on the doorstep before me. I don't remember the details of his face, but I know that it was handsome and that I regretted answering the door in my leggings and Dad's old Ramones T-shirt. I was going out with Danny at the time, but I was still twenty with plenty of hormones, and the man before me had put those hormones in a Magimix and whacked it up to full speed.

'Hello. So sorry to trouble you.' He sounded posh, like Conservative party posh. 'I couldn't help knocking on the door. It's just that this house is so beautiful.'

I smiled at the strange, handsome, posh man. I agreed with him. My childhood home was beautiful, although people didn't usually knock on the door to tell us.

We were just off the busy Chamberlayne Road, but our house felt like a sleepy idyll away from the mayhem. That's because it doesn't sit next to the other houses on the road, it's perched behind them, hidden by trees. There's a tiny driveway, which most people miss, which leads you to our house. It doesn't look like the other houses nearby, either, which are all three-storey red-brick Victorian monsters. Our house is made of grey stone, similar to the stone you find in Bath, and it's square with two floors and a porch with a little Gothic turret.

The posh man stood in the porch and looked up at the carved stone arches above him.

'Beautiful,' he said again.

I pointed at the floor beneath his feet.

'What's this?' He said, stepping aside.

'It's a gravestone,' I told him. 'The man who built the house buried his wife there so that every time he walked into the house she would be with him.'

'A love story,' the man murmured as he stared at the stone.

'Hmm. Although, according to the Christians her soul would have burned in hell because she's not buried in consecrated ground.'

He looked up suddenly. 'Is the house haunted?'

I paused for a moment, unsure of what to say. If you asked my mother she would say the house is undoubtedly haunted, but in my honest opinion I've never noticed any otherworldly activity. And believe me, I was definitely on the lookout for it.

'Not really,' I said.

He laughed. 'Is there a garden?'

'Yeah.'

'Is it gorgeous?'

'Yeah, there's a fig tree and a pear tree and a silver birch, and the birds really love it. It gets sun in the afternoon and evening, so you can sit out all day. We've got a swing seat under . . .' I stopped myself. I was sounding like a plonker talking about trees.

'Gosh. Sounds lovely. Listen, I'm an estate agent. Don't get out the garlic,' he said, which I thought must be some strange posh-person expression. 'If you ever wanted to sell this house—'

I stopped him then.

'We'll never sell it. Sorry. It belonged to my dad's parents and they gave it to him. It's always going to be in the family.'

'Oh, right, good,' he said, and he turned and walked away.

It was that strange posh man's visit that put the idea in my head. I wasn't doing much with my life at the time – you might say I hadn't started living at all – but all that was about to change, because shortly afterwards I walked into all the estate agents on the Chamberlayne Road to see if they had any vacancies. Everyone I spoke to was completely unimpressed by my lack of qualifications, except for Lube, who said, 'I need an office dogsbody on a Saturday. Key duties are answering phones, making the tea and getting bacon sandwiches. I'll give you a month's trial.'

I was still on trial and living at home when I wrote my five year plan. As you might expect, people have taken the mickey out of my plan over the years. They say I'm obsessive, but I prefer 'driven'.

I wrote my plan on my twenty-first birthday, exactly five years ago to the day, in fact. It was a glorious day and there wasn't a cloud in the sky, not even a wispy one. I sat on the swing seat in the corner of our beloved garden with my favourite book, *The Five Year Plan: Making the Most of Your Life*, and a notebook. I listened to the silver birch sway and rustle and I thought and wrote carefully for two and a half hours. Oh, and I hummed and sang 'Mr Bojangles'. I only remember that because at one point I got carried away and my mum shouted out of the window for me to 'Please stop singing that damn song'.

The words I wrote that day are now on the bathroom wall of my maisonette. This is what they say:

Gracie Flowers – My Five Year Plan

Thinking big, aiming high

One year from today I will have:

- A full-time job at Make A Move doing anything
- Saved £2,500

Two years from today I will have:

- Been promoted to sales negotiator
- Saved £5,000

Three years from today I will have:

- Become the best-performing sales negotiator in the branch
- Saved £10,000

Four years from today I will have:

- Become the best-performing sales negotiator out of *all* the Make A Move branches
- Have bought my own place (even if it is a shoebox without a lid)

Five years from today I will have:

- Been promoted to Head of London Sales
- Be living in my own place

And today, on the very last day of the five years, I have achieved this. 'And I'm feeling good,' I sing along with Nina. Then I hear my phone ringing and suddenly I don't feel quite so good. It's my mum. I know this because the ring tone I have chosen for her is 'Flight of The Valkyries'. The de de der ders perfectly prefix whatever ominous announcement she's about to impart.

'Morning,' I say into my mobile.

'Grace. Oh good God, Grace, turn that off, please.'

I pause the stereo. My mum used to love Nina. My mother loved Nina right up until the point that I started to love Nina, then she drastically went off her. She maintains that my Nina Simone period was one of her most challenging as a mother. I knew my mother was vexed when she was called away from rehearsing the cha cha cha to meet my primary school teacher. The school was worried about me.

'So, Grace, what do you want to be when you grow up?' my teacher had asked me, just as she had asked all the other boys and girls.

'A big black lady,' I immediately replied. My teacher didn't know how to respond, so she told the headmistress, who called my mother. Seems entirely unnecessary, if you ask me, she could have just broken the news to me herself.

My Nina Simone period came straight after the Stevie Wonder and Motown phase, so it's no surprise, when you think about it, that at eight years of age I wanted to be black. I would cling to black ladies when we went shopping and ask them to sing to me. I even wrote to *Jim'll Fix It* asking him to make me black, though I never heard back. I've stopped all that now, but Mum still has a thing against Nina.

'Grace, happy birthday.'

'Thanks, Mum.'

'Now, your father doesn't want you to wear purple today, Grace. He has a very bad feeling about you wearing purple.'

'Oh, God,' I sigh. Purple is my favourite colour. Half my wardrobe is purple and my purple flowered baby doll dress is the only thing that's clean at the moment. I think about ignoring the request, but I'll be seeing my dad later so I can't.

'OK, fair enough,' I relent. 'He's starting to get a thing about purple, though, Mum, and it's weird.'

'Don't blame me.'

'No, right, well I'd better go. I've got the announcement at nine thirty.'

'Well. Let me know how it goes.'

'Will do. Love you, Mum.'

'Yes, yes. Bye.'

'A mother's love.' I sigh after I've ended the call. That reminds me. I cannot forget the morning-after pill today, I think, as I leave the bathroom to find something not purple to wear.

Chapter 4

'Isn't that what you wore to my hookers and pimps party?' Friendly Wendy asks as soon as she sees me. I can tell she's surprised because bits of the bacon sandwich she's eating have just easyjetted out of her mouth and landed on my exposed cleavage.

'Oh, give us a bit of that,' I pant, looking at her sandwich. She hands it over and I bite into it. Delicious. I love bacon sarnies. I'll never be thin.

'So is this the sexy Lady Boss look?'

'Hardly. I was wearing my little flowery purple dress, but my dad had a bad feeling about purple.'

'Again?'

'Yep.'

'But your dad used to love purple.'

'Aren't they the clothes you were wearing last night?' I ask, clocking Wendy's walk of shame. I'm sure she was wearing that outfit in the pub last night. Wendy makes a bad attempt at looking coy, but I'm having none of it.

'Yeah, you've still got nacho goo down the top. That'll be a nightmare to get off,' I mutter, scratching at the crusty stain.

'Oh, er, Grace, I wouldn't do that if I were you.'

'Urgh! Wend!' I say, jumping back immediately. 'So who was he then?'

'Freddie's friend Martin.'

'As in Freddie, the man you fancy above all others? You slept with his mate?'

'Do you think I won't be in with a chance with Freddie now?'

'I can't say for sure, but I think it would be a wise move to stop sleeping with his friends.'

'Hmm, but I feel it's getting me closer to him.'

Wendy finds it very difficult not to shag people, hence the nickname, Friendly Wendy.

'I feel a bit sick,' I tell her, looking around our office, which is currently crammed with all the men from Make A Move's five branches – the men I'll shortly be whipping into shape in my role as Lady Boss.

In truth, I quite like this sick, nervous feeling, when you have to hold your breath and clench your bottom because your whole body is gurgling in anticipation. Does that make me weird? Probably.

I used to experience it much more frequently than I do now. When I was young I sang in competitions. Not because I had pushy parents – far from it – the singing competitions were all my idea. Well, my idea via a girl called Ruth Roberts, who I went to primary school with. Now she *did* have pushy parents. Her parents were so pushy she'd done a demo of 'Walking On Air' and sent it to record labels by the time she was nine.

Ruth Roberts was my sometime best friend from the age of five to eight. I say 'sometime' because she was the sort of girl who would be arm in arm with you and calling you her best friend one day, then the next she'd ignore you and tell your classmates you had nits. Ruth Roberts sang in competitions and I liked singing, so I begged Mum and Dad to let me have a go, too. I did my first one at the age of eight and I loved it. Dad drove me to Milton Keynes and we sang along to Nina Simone in the car and had toasted teacakes dripping with butter in a Little Chef en route. I can't tell you how exciting it was – my mother doesn't allow butter or yeast-based products in the house.

I sang 'Castle On A Cloud' on stage in front of four judges, numerous parents and hyperactive siblings – and I won. I didn't expect to win. It was only when Ruth Roberts eyeballed me on the way to pick up her second-place rosette that I started to feel this gurgly sensation in my tummy for the first time. I beat thirty-two other girls, four of whom also sang 'Castle On A Cloud'. We had a celebratory Burger King on the way home. Dad and I swore not to tell my mother and discussed what song I'd sing next time. It was one of my best days. Not *the* best day, but it's absolutely up there. The only problem with the day was beating Ruth Roberts as she never spoke to me again.

'There's Lube.' Wendy nudges me and I hide the bacon sandwich in my desk drawer and stand up straight. 'Oh my goodness, KEN. Oh my goodness, KEN,' I repeat to myself. I must, must, *must not* call him Lube after the announcement.

Ken Bradbury walks buoyantly into the office. He's a short man with a wide, cheeky-chappy face and a close crop to hide his receding hairline. He dresses a bit like Jonathan Ross: expensive suits that always look a fraction too tight, teemed with a garish tie. Today it's purple. Good call, Ken. He's followed in by another man who looks familiar. He must be a new recruit from another branch. He's tall and very handsome. Wendy has obviously clocked him, too, because her elbow is poking my rib in excitement. For once I agree with her fit-man-o-meter. He is very gorgeous. Tall, tick. Dark, tick. Handsome, tick. Full marks. And that, as any lady knows, is rare.

'I think he might need some special Lady Boss attention,' Wendy hisses. I smile.

'Here you all are. My team. My men. My empire,' begins Ken. I love Ken, but he does think he's Julius Caesar.

'I can smell your hunger and it smells magnificent,' he says, taking a deep breath. Strange, I thought we smelled like rank, hungover people myself.

'Now then, a big day. Head of London Sales, as we all know, is the big cheese. You get a bit of commission from every sale made in the company. You do the hiring and firing and whipping into shape. You motivate, you lead, you inspire.'

My knees start to shake.

'Now, today's appointment is exciting. This person is one of, if not *the*, best in the business.'

Whoa. My stomach is doing cartwheels.

'I would like to introduce you to John St John Smythe, your new Head of London Sales,' he announces proudly, and the tall, dark handsome bloke steps forward.

Oh my goodness, I'm going to faint. My breath catches in my throat and suddenly it feels as if all the air in my body is leaving me. I've come over all woozy, like a woman in a corset drama. I reach out for Wendy, but she's staring open-mouthed and doesn't expect me to lurch at her. I fall into her with a yelp and she stumbles into the man to her right, who drops his Starbucks. We both land in a coffee wet patch at his feet. Everyone turns and watches as the man pulls us both up.

'Sorry, Ken,' shouts Wendy. 'It was me. I went arse over tit.' She puts her hand firmly around me to stop me going again.

'You all right?' she whispers in my ear, but I can't answer. I simply stare at the bastard who's got my job and ruined my plan, ruined everything. And he looks at me. And then he smiles, and I recognise him. It's the man who came round to my childhood home years ago and said it was beautiful.

I could cry, and I never, never cry.

Chapter 5

I failed. I failed. I failed. I failed. That's all I can think. Gracie Flowers failed. Gracie Flowers failed. Again.

It's been so long since I last failed that I'd almost forgotten what it felt like. Isn't it lovely how humiliation hunts you down, even when you've tried so hard to build a new identity? The only other time I've felt like this was the last singing competition I did nearly ten years ago. The whole day felt wrong from the beginning. Mum drove me there for a start. We didn't sing Nina Simone for obvious reasons. In fact, we didn't sing at all. We didn't even speak. And we definitely didn't stop for high-fat snacks. There was a bag of peeled carrots in the car. It was miles away – Manchester – and it was the biggest competition I'd ever been in: British Under Sixteen Singer of the Year. The winner got to work with Sony on an album, so it was massive. Singing competitions had always been fun, surreal and ridiculous, and the only way I got through them was by not taking them too seriously. Just sing the song as best you can was my motto. Dad's motto. But this one felt monumental, life-changing, too huge to get my head round. It meant I could leave school and become a singer, and I cracked under the pressure. Exploded is probably a better word.

We all had to sing a hymn or gospel song in the first round and I was due to sing my first song after Ruth Roberts. Ruth took to the stage and started to sing 'Amazing Grace'. I'd heard her sing it over a hundred times before. I used to enjoy listening to it, but that day I just couldn't bear it. It's hard to explain, but it's as though my whole being rejected the song and the competition, so I screamed to block it out. I stood in the wings while a fellow contestant sang and I screamed uncontrollably until she stopped and I was carried out.

In many ways that's more dramatic than not getting the Head of London Sales job, but it felt the same. I'd spent years working towards something only to fail.

'We should probably step out of the bogs,' Wendy says. She has a point: we've been in here for twenty minutes. Wendy's been looking in the mirror, fiddling with her dark bob and adding more black eye make-up. She looks a bit like a bug. A beautiful bug, but a bug nevertheless. She knows it and she's not ashamed. Every time we get invited to a fancy dress party she wears her home-made bee costume. It's an all-in-one black catsuit with a big spongy bee-shaped middle and deely boppers. She always pulls. Wendy can work the bee look like no one else.

I've been sitting on the loo, not saying a word since the announcement. Five years of work and it may as well have gone down the loo I'm sitting on. I failed the five year plan. The book doesn't tell you what happens when you don't achieve what you want. It doesn't tell you what to do when some strange man appears out of nowhere and stands where you should be standing. I'm supposed to be writing my new five year plan this weekend. What's the point? For the past five years I've known what I was aiming for. Now I feel lost. I can't carry on working under this posh bloke. I was supposed to get his job. I had it all planned. What now? Will somebody please tell me, what now?

'Gracie, I need you to speak to me. I mean, I know you're in shock, but you need to speak. How can you sell houses if you can't speak? How will you sing to your dad? I mean, I suppose you could mime . . .' she trails off for a moment. 'GRACIE!' Uh oh, it's her cross voice. The one she uses when the boys steal her printer ink cartridges and take them home. Wendy always gets panicky when I don't speak. 'SAY SOMETHING. SAY ANYTHING.'

'I hate him,' I growl.

'Excellent,' she seems genuinely pleased with my progress. She waits for me to add to it, but I don't oblige.

'On the bright side, at least he's good looking.'

I stare at her and shake my head.

'I need him to leave this job quickly, then I'll get promoted and it won't be all bad. Otherwise he might stay for years. Then what would I do?'

'Grace, come on. It's not that bad.'

'Wend, it is. I'm giving it three months. And if he hasn't gone by then, I will.'

'Where?'

'No idea. Some other company that will have me.'

'But what about Lube? He loves you!'

'No, Wend. He's just proved that he thinks absolutely nothing of me.'

'Grace, that's not true.'

'Wendy, if I was a posh bloke I'd have got the job, but because I'm a short blonde woman I didn't, and I can't tell you how angry that makes me. Do you know what, Wend? I'm going to fight. I'm going to make him sorry he walked into Make A Move. And so are you, Wendy. Help me make his life hell.' I look in the mirror and make a roaring sound.

'Oh, bleedin' hell,' mutters Wendy.

Wendy follows me out of the loo and into the office. The theme tune from *Rocky* is playing in my head. I'm going to sell so many houses this posh bloke will be terrified. I'm going to sell so many houses that Ken will come crying to me about the mistake he's made. I am going to sell so many houses that there'll be nothing left for anyone else to sell.

They've put Posh Boy at Smeg's desk, which is opposite mine. I sit down.

'What's this?' I say frostily. There's a pile of printed forms in the middle of my desk.

'Estate Agent of the Year forms,' says Posh Boy. He's ever so good looking. It's ever so annoying.

'What?'

'You get your clients to fill one in when you complete a sale. There's a prize for the best estate agent business, which I want Make A Move to get, and a prize for the best individual. I won it last year.'

I eyeball Posh Boy. He smiles; I don't. I'm going to win this year, I decide. It's Posh Boy or me. Let the games begin.

Next to the forms sits a lone business card. 'John St John

Smythe – Head of London Sales'. I turn my nose up at it as though it's a dead rodent. I want to toss it in the rubbish bin, but I don't. I'm better than that. I drop it in my bag instead. I'll use it as a toothpick.

The phone rings and he reaches for it, but I am John Wayne when it comes to answering the phone and I get there first.

'Good morning, Make A Move.'

'Am I speaking to the Lady Boss?'

'No, I'm still plain old Gracie Flowers.'

'You'll never be plain, Gracie Flowers. Now then, do you fancy selling me some houses?'

'I'm loving the plural, Bob, what are you wanting?'

Bob the Builder, as I call him, because he is a builder, is my magic client. He has a huge building company and he buys anything that needs renovation. He gets his boys in, makes the property look beautiful and then hands it back to us to sell.

'Right, we've got this big beast on Shirland Road. No one's seen it yet.'

'What's it like?'

'A total shit hole,' I tell him. I said I couldn't lie. 'And there's another stinker that came on last week off the Harrow Road. That would suit you, too.'

I notice Posh Boy looking at me with his mouth open. I bet they don't describe properties as shit holes where he comes from. They probably use terms like 'well-appointed' and 'enviably located'. And don't get me started on 'architect designed'. Architect designed! Who else would design it? A dinner lady? I loathe estate agents like that.

'Excellent, Gracie, that's just how I like them.'

'Right, Bob. I'll come to you. I'm on my way.'

I hang up.

'Wend, I've got an eleven and an eleven thirty coming in to exchange contracts. Can you make sure there's champagne in the fridge and clean glasses? If I'm slightly late for the eleven o'clock, will you keep Mrs Walsh chatting. She's got twin girls, so you can ask her about them. And the wife of the eleven thirty is a lady of restricted growth, so whatever you do, don't use the word midget and try to make sure the boys don't take photos of her on their mobiles like last time. Also, will you ring the Shirland Road man and find out what he'll take. I'll try and get an offer out of Bob this morning.'

Wendy is in her efficient office manager mode and nods curtly as I stand up from my desk.

'Good work.' It's John Posh Boy Whatsit. Could he be any more patronising? 'Grace? Is that your name?'

'Yes.'

'Pleased to meet you.'

I nod.

'Although . . . have we met before?'

I shrug. I'm giving him nothing.

'It's a lovely name, Grace.'

'Thank you,' I say.

'It's my mother's name.'

I don't respond and start to walk towards the door, but I bump into my desk on the way.

'Ow, tits!' I exclaim. Posh Boy laughs. The name Grace has mocked me since childhood.

I manage to sashay out of the door all the same. Estate Agent of the Year, I think, rubbing my newly bruised thigh, I like the sound of that. He's not taking that from me as well.

Chapter 6

When I embarked on my career as an estate agent I was handed a tatty box of index cards and told by Lube to get my 'chops round them'. On each card was scribbled a name and telephone number. Occasionally, there was a note, too, offering a valuable piece of information such as '500,000 max' or 'bloke's a tosser'. On my first day I called every number in the box to find out if that person was still looking for a property. Most had moved four years previously or didn't answer. Out of the whole box of two hundred only two needed my help. However, there was one card that fascinated me. The name 'Robin Duster' was printed clearly in capitals spanning two lines, and below it was a mobile number and a street address. What intrigued me was that the entire card had been circled in biro-drawn stars. Now, the doodles could have been because Robin Duster bored the cheaply tailored suit trousers off my predecessor on the phone, but really, if telephone tedium drove estate agents to doodling, everything in the office would be covered in graffiti. The Miss Marple in me decided that Robin Duster had *earned* his stars, so I set about stalking him.

For three weeks I called him three times a day, but there was never an answer or even a voicemail. So on the Monday of the fourth week I left work and drove to the address on the card. I pulled up on Scrubs Lane outside a single-storey industrial-looking building with no door. I started to suspect the stars denoted my predecessor's suspicion that Robin Duster was a serial killer, so I texted Danny:

Hey, hot stuff, checking out a client. If you never hear from me again, here's the address.

He texted me straight back:

Wish you wouldn't keep doing this, babe. Why don't you get some work singing?

I got out of the car and walked slowly round the building, where I saw a gate propped open by a bag of cement, and a young lad with his top off loading a van.

'What's a nice girl like you doing in a place like this?' he asked.

'Are you Robin Duster?'

'Nah, I wish,' he answered and pointed through the open gate. 'He's in there.'

'Thank you.'

'You can thank me any time.' He winked. I left that job to Wendy, who performed it with aplomb in the bathroom of one of Bob's showroom apartments three years later.

I walked through the gate into a yard stacked with bricks, planks and bloke debris – unwashed mugs, empty Coke cans and old copies of newspapers showing nipples – and at the far end was a partially pulled down grille leading to a brick building. I could hear sounds coming from inside, so I crouched down and entered, imagining my severed limbs being pulled out of the canal by a dog walker in the morning. The building was full of sheets of wood, plastic and metal. A man stood in front of me wearing a visor over his face, combat trousers and a T-shirt, he was holding a whirring, sparking machine that looked a bit like a chain saw and he was cutting a thick piece of kitchen surface material. I spotted a yellow hard hat on the floor and put it on just in case. Whoever it belonged to had a very large head, so it sat quite low on my face, making me feel like a Lego figure. Robin Duster was deep in concentration, so I walked over to a shelf where a radio was playing and turned it off. I don't like the radio.

'Who the hell are you?' the man shouted.

'I'm Gracie Flowers,' I told him.

He turned the machine off.

'Who?'

'Gracie Flowers.'

He pulled the visor off and I tilted my hard hat so he could see my eyes.

'You from the Inland Revenue?'

'Yes. You owe me loads of money,' I said with relish.

His face fell.

'I'm joking.'

'How do I know?'

'I'm an estate agent.'

'Oh, you're not from Smiths?'

'No,' I said affronted. How dare he? 'I'm from Make A Move.'

'What are you doing here?'

'Are you Robin Duster?'

'Yes.'

'I wanted to see if I could find you some properties.'

He laughed loudly.

'I like properties that need work done to them. The more the better.'

'Excellent. Consider it done,' and I shook his hand and left. I still have the hard hat. It sits on top of my filing cabinet at work.

Over the next few weeks, whenever we got something suitable I would print out the particulars, put them in a plastic sandwich bag, take them to his depot on Scrubs Lane and slide them under the gate. I used to add a little note on a Post-it, too. For a long time I used to write, 'Hello, Robin, hope you're well. Thought you might like this.' But by the time I put the eleventh envelope through his door I'd deteriorated to, 'Robin, this property needs so much work it will make you poo your pants and cry for Mummy.' It was the eleventh property and the poo reference that got him interested. Ten minutes later I saw something I never thought I'd see: Bob's number flash up on my mobile.

'Robin,' I sighed as I answered it. 'I do wish you'd stop pestering me.'

'Gracie Flowers. Gracie Flowers.'

'Robin Duster. Robin Duster.'

'Call me Bob.'

'Bob the Builder.'

'Don't you dare.'

'Promise.'

Oops.

'Listen, I'm outside the property you sent me. Good work. Can you get the keys?'

'Give me four minutes. I'm on my way.'

Fifteen minutes later he'd put in an offer, bought me a pasty and told me I was 'OK, for an estate agent'.

So Bob the Builder was a tough nut to crack, rather like trying to crack a Brazil nut by banging it repeatedly against my head for months, in fact, but once cracked Bob turned out to have the softest, gooiest, truffliest centre.

He's a legend and a man of few words, which I admire greatly. When faced with a topic of conversation he won't hurl himself at it and rub himself all over it, like an overexcited dog – or me – he'll simply think, then speak. Genius. His main passions are QPR, fishing and making millions and millions of pounds. Oh, and his hideous girlfriend, Stella. She's not actually hideous, she's stunning, but stunning in the style of a WAG pictured at a funeral in *Hello!*

Stella's with him today because they're going to do some shopping after the viewings. Not that Stella looks like the sort of girl who would want much, maybe just a helicopter and a tropical island.

'Yep, I'll take this one, too,' Bob says. 'Put in at fifty under asking and we'll go from there.'

He's standing in the centre of the run-down room, darting his eyes quickly about him, as he always does when he's thinking. Bob looks like Bruce Willis, according to Wendy. In fact, years ago Wendy forced me to develop a crush on Bob by repeatedly saying things like, 'Imagine those calloused hands travelling up your thigh,' and, 'Think of that strong builders' back as it pumps up and down on top of you,' when no one else was in the office. It wasn't a full-blown crush, and meeting Stella for the first time soon doused it. She's the least warm person I've ever met.

Still, I'd best make an effort. She's currently looking bored and staring out of the window.

'I love your shoes,' I tell her. They're four-inch patent heels in an appropriate blood-red colour. Normally, when girls meet other girls we find a whole shared language revolving around handbags and shoes, over which we can bond, but even that doesn't work with Stella. Rather than do the obligatory, 'Oh, thanks, only twenty-five quid in Dorothy Perkins' retort, she just gives me a look. And what a look it is. She manages to say so much simply by raising her top lip, and the gist of it is, 'Don't speak to me. I will never speak to you. You will never be able to afford these shoes and you would look like a backward child trying on shoes in a tranny shop if you did. The mere fact that I'm sharing air with you offends me.'

I stare back at her. It's such a feat of coldness I wonder whether I should applaud.

'All right, sis, we'd best get on,' Bob says, walking towards me. I think that's why Stella hates me, because I get on so well with Bob and he calls me sis.

'Cool.'

'What do you think got into Lube?'

I shake my head.

'Dunno. He obviously thinks that John St John Smythe is better than me.'

'That name rings a bell. Wasn't he at Smiths?'

'Probably. He's twat enough.'

'I've always got a job for you, finder of shit holes. I'd do you some business cards.'

'Thanks.'

I watch them leave and then I slowly lock up, because for the first time in I don't know how long, I don't want to go back to the office.

Chapter 7

He's so annoying! I've never met anyone so annoying in all my life. He's more annoying than a period. And he's so posh. I didn't think they made people that posh any more. He actually said, 'Yah,' and he wasn't even doing an impression of the blonde one in *Absolutely Fabulous*. And he says, 'Righto,' all the time. Righto?! It's awful. He says something infuriating like, 'Where do I find the headed notepaper?' and Wendy says, because I won't speak to him unless absolutely necessary, 'Second drawer down,' and he says, 'Righto,' as though he's a dotty grandma. And he's not even very good! He hasn't got any new clients and he's been here four hours now. He brings absolutely nothing to the company.

I'm not going to let him get any new clients either. Not only am I John Wayne on the phones, I'm Billy Bob Quicksilver the Firearm Phenomenon Who's Never Missed a Shot in His Life when it comes to the door. You see, at Make A Move the person who talks to the client first gets the client. I get lots of new customers by being first to the phone, but the problem with the phones is that fifty per cent of the calls we receive at Make A Move are made by people who live on a completely different planet. It's not a bad planet. On the contrary, it's a very hopeful planet. These people say, 'Oh, hello, I'm looking for a one, well, two bed preferably. Near Portobello. Seventy thousand max. Has to have a garden,' to which you just have to say, 'Aren't we all, love. Sadly prices in Portobello are proper mental. One beds with no outside space start at about half a million. I know. Ridiculous. I blame the government. Basically, it leaves us with two options. Make a lot of money drug trafficking, or move to Wales.' But what can happen is, while you're educating the hopeful, someone else in the office picks up a 'show me the money' call. But . . . but – and it's a good but – people who walk into the office rarely waste your time. They've looked in the window first, so they know the sort of prices we're talking. They've done the foreplay and they're ready to get it on. That reminds me, I must get the morning-after pill when I go to Sainsbury's. Anyway, this is why I always, always, always – OK, except when I'm on the loo – have an eye on the door.

For example, right now I've spotted a family of four outside, but John Posh Boy Whatsit hasn't. Estate Agent of the Year, my bottom. It must have been rigged, is all I can say. I can't move suddenly or I'll draw Posh Boy's attention to them, so I do my slink across the room to the filing cabinet, followed by the uninterruptible swoop to the door for a, 'Hiya, can I help you find your next home?'

It goes off without a hitch, and before I know it I'm standing in the arch of the front door and the family of four are smiling and nodding in front of me. They look like a lovely family. The mum and dad look young and handsome, there's a beautiful girl of about fifteen, who's humming to herself and smiling, and a brother who appears to be slightly younger and who looks suitably bored with the whole outing. The mother is absentmindedly playing with her daughter's hair, and it's such a tender action it gives me a pang, making me long for a loving gesture from my own mother.

'You have gorgeous hair,' I say to the girl, because she really does. It's long and thick and a gorgeous reddy brown. 'You could do shampoo adverts.'

'So have you,' she says, smiling shyly.

'Oh, ho, thanks.' I laugh. My hair's all right. It's blonde and there's lots of it, but it finds the simplest things, like staying in a clip, very hard indeed. 'How old are you?' I ask the girl.

'Fifteen.' She smiles. I knew it. I could sense it. I remember being fifteen, for a while it was the most magical age.

'Now then,' says the dad in a good deep man voice, 'this caught my eye.' He points at a three bed in the window.

'Hmm.' I smile sadly. 'It's lovely. The only thing is I've just had an offer on it. Like,' I check my watch, 'seven minutes ago. And the would-be buyer has already gone over the asking price. I'm sure it'll be accepted. I can show it; I just think you'll have a fight on your hands. However, I've got two similar properties and I haven't shown either yet. One came on the market yesterday. Similar sort of thing, but with a bigger garden.'

The lady gasps.

'Mum's a garden designer,' the girl tells me.

'Oh, wow!' I smile. 'Well, that's great. I haven't seen it

recently, but I think the garden's in a bit of a mess, so you might have a project on your hands. Funnily enough, the other property is brand new. It's nearly finished, but if you were interested we should talk to the builder; he's a friend of mine and you could liaise with him about what you wanted garden wise.'

'You're good,' the man says.

'Thank you.'

I hope Posh Boy heard that bit.

'No, seriously, you're much warmer than the other estate agents we've met today. Some have been quite terrifying.'

And that bit. I hope he heard that bit, too.

'It sounds silly but I really like my job.' I say that quite loudly.

'That's what it's all about,' says the mother.

'Yeah. You're right.'

'I'm going to be an actor,' the boy says proudly.

'Fantastic. How exciting!'

'I don't know what I want to be yet,' the girl tells me.

'Well,' I say to her. 'What's your name?'

'Emma.'

'Well, Emma, find what you love doing most in the whole world and do that.'

'Do you love doing estate agent work more than anything else in the whole world?'

I hesitate.

'Um, yes. Yes, of course.'

'Do you think we could see those properties you mentioned on Monday?' the father asks.

'Course, come inside. Ignore the posh bloke to the right; he won't be here long.' They laugh. They think I'm joking. 'Grab a seat and I'll get some high-calibre biscuits. Then we'll schedule some viewings and I'll do some brilliant interrogation work to see if we've got anything else you might like.'

'We're the Hammond family,' the mother informs me. Then, all of a sudden, they start singing the theme tune to *The Addams Family*, but replacing the word Addams with Hammond. It's so spontaneous and joyous that when they finish we're all laughing. They're fast becoming my favourite family ever.

They follow me into the office and I just know they'll buy the property with the big garden. I have a sixth sense about these things.

Estate Agent of the Year. Don't mind if I do.

Chapter 8

I don't think it's politically correct to say this, but I love Sainsbury's. I'm in the big one by the canal, off the Harrow Road. I come here every Saturday after work and buy flowers and doughnuts. I've been coming here every week since I can remember. When I was little I'd come with Mum and Dad. It was vital that Dad and I accompanied Mum in order to make the case for food with taste versus food with no calorific value, trying to sneak cheddar and bacon under the five bunches of celery in the trolley. Sadly, family trips to Sainsbury's were a high point in my childhood. They became a bit hectic as Mum and Dad got more and more famous, though, as they used to get besieged by people wanting autographs. A weekly shop took nearly three hours once when I lost count of how many shopping lists and cereal packets they were asked to sign. Nowadays Mum does the shopping online, but I still go in person. Normally I quite enjoy it, but not today.

Bob the Builder put offers in on both the properties I showed him, I received another from a flat I showed last week and I took on that lovely new family who I know I'll be able to sell to. My two completed sales filled out their estate agent forms saying I was the best estate agent they'd ever come across. I should be buzzing, but instead I'm seething inside, and my mood isn't improved by the fact that I'm having to visit the pharmacist in the middle of the store. At least I'm hoping to visit the pharmacist, although he seems to have gone for his lunch.

'Do you know how long he'll be?' I ask the young girl standing at the counter behind rows and rows of Strepsils.

'That depends,' she answers sullenly. She's eating toast behind the pharmacy counter! That can't be EU approved.

'Um, depends on what?' I venture.

'On whether he gets hot or cold food.'

'*Right.*'

'Obviously.'

'Can you help me?'

'Dunno.'

'I need the morning-after pill.'

She looks at me and chews. It's toast and marmite. It looks quite tasty.

'Have a good night, did ya?' She smirks.

'I'll just wait here for the pharmacist,' I tell her. Cheeky cow.

'He must have gone for cold,' she says, nodding towards a man in a white coat who's rushing in our direction.

'She needs the morning-after pill!' the girl shouts towards him.

'Follow me,' says the man. I do and we end up in a tiny back room lined with boxes of tablets.

'She's new,' he says by way of apology.

I smile.

'So when did you have unprotected sex?'

Lovely! I'm talking to a strange man about my sex life. Danny, you owe me one for this.

'This morning.'

'That's fine. You've done the right thing. You have up to seventy-two hours to take it, but it becomes less effective the longer you leave it.'

I nod.

'Now then, can you remember when your last period was?'

Nice! Now we're on to menstruation. Happy birthday to me.

'Um, maybe two weeks ago.'

'Right, well you'll be at your most fertile now, so let's get you fixed up.'

He asks me a few more embarrassing questions before telling me to wait outside for the tablet. This is proving to be a rather rubbish birthday, I think as I walk back out to find the girl attacking a packet of Haribo. She offers me one. I decline and pretend to look at the vitamins on display lest she starts asking me what position we used.

'Here you go,' she says eventually. 'That'll be twenty-seven quid.'

Danny!

'Cool, thanks,' I take out my purse. 'Oh,' I say, looking inside. My cash card isn't there. I search my handbag. Nothing. Where is it? When did I have it last? I definitely had it the previous night when I was in the pub across the road from where I live. Damn! I've left it at the pub. I set up a tab and left it behind the bar. I always do this. I search again for cash.

'I've only got five pounds and about thirty pence,' I tell the girl.

'Sorry, I can't give it to you. You'll have to come back.'

Oh, brilliant, bloody brilliant, I think as I walk away. Some posh bloke has stolen my job and my boyfriend has accidentally impregnated me. Blinding.

'I hate men,' I mutter. I must have said it louder than I thought because a man stacking Mr Kipling boxes looks at me and cowers.

Chapter 9

I finish work at 2 p.m. on a Saturday. I pick up the doughnuts and flowers from Sainsbury's and then, as always, I drive straight to see my dad.

My dad is buried at All Souls Cemetery, which is across the canal from Sainsbury's. Built over 150 years ago because the Victorians were popping off like flies and there was nowhere to put them, it's a beautiful place to be buried. The Victorians went in for big old statues and ornate gravestones to honour their dead and see them on their way to heaven. I wish we'd gone for something more ornate than the plain granite tombstone we got for Dad, but I guess Mum and I weren't feeling that creative at the time. We chose the right wording for the gravestone, though, at least: 'He jumped so high, then lightly touched down.' It's a line from his favourite song. He's buried in a lovely part of the cemetery, in a far corner under a silver birch, which was his favourite tree. Like me, he used to enjoy sitting on the swing seat in our back garden and listening to it rustle.

'She's talking dirty in my ear,' he used to say.

'Slut,' my mum would call the silver birch tree. Mum had a sense of humour then.

My dad died ten years ago this summer. That's one of those facts that makes no sense whatsoever as it still feels like yesterday. I had woken early to revise for my GCSEs and was sitting at my desk with the curtains drawn, working by lamplight, when my dad knocked softly on my door.

'How you feeling, Amazing Grace?'

'I'm going to fail!' I wailed. I was in a proper hysterical teenage panic.

'Gracie Flowers. My little girl,' he said, and he came into the room and sat on the bed and sang to me. He sang softly and it calmed me. Sometimes even now, when I'm feeling stressed I close my eyes and I can still hear him singing to me. I can picture him clearly, too. He was wearing a pale blue shirt and the Levi's jeans he lived in when he wasn't dancing. He was good looking, my dad. I'm not sure if you're supposed to say that about your own father, but he was. He had salt-and-pepper hair and a twinkle in his eye. He was hairier than a lot of the men on the dancing circuit. Mum said it made him more masculine, although he said it was a pain in the behind having to shave twice a day. My mum adored my dad. Everyone adored my dad. He had a meeting that morning in Soho with a television company who wanted to talk about a prime-time ballroom dancing show. He was excited. My dad believed if we all sang and danced the world would be a much nicer place. I was so wrapped up in myself that morning that I didn't even wish him luck.

'I love you, Gracie Flowers,' he said, kissing the top of my head when he'd finished singing.

‘I love you, too,’ I said. Thankfully. I say that because my mum didn’t. My mum and dad had had an argument the night before. I’m not entirely sure what it was about, but I think it was because my mum thought she should have been invited along to the meeting. She was worried they’d want my father to partner someone younger and more glamorous on the show. It was important to her. They’d danced together for nearly twenty years. She didn’t say anything to him as he left the house that day.

Later, I was in the exam. I’d read the paper through, like they told us to, and was just about to start on the first question when a teacher scuttled into the exam hall and whispered to the examiner. The next thing I knew the examiner was tapping me on the shoulder, then she led me out of the room and told me that Dad had had an accident. Another teacher drove me to the hospital, but it was too late. I saw my mum through some glass doors talking to a doctor. Then I heard my mum howl. And it was the worst sound I’ve ever heard.

He was knocked down by a bus. It sounds almost comical. He was on Regent Street, crossing the road, when apparently a fan shouted at him. He stopped, waved and did a dance move, then carried on running right into a bus. Silly sod.

Still, he’s buried in a lovely place. The slutty silver birch whispers in his ear and I come once a week for a chat and a singsong. My mum never comes. She hasn’t been here since the funeral. She hasn’t really been anywhere since the funeral.

When I first started coming I would lie on the ground, knowing that he was there a few feet beneath me, and cry. Then I started to chat to him. I told him all about Danny Saunders, who stood by me. I told him how I couldn’t apply to music college, which was something we'd always spoken about. I explained that it was because I couldn't leave Mum. I told him all about the singing competition I'd entered shortly after he was buried, and how I'd screamed my head off while Ruth Roberts was singing for the judges and how they'd asked me not to enter any singing competitions again and how I didn't want to anyway. Then I ran out of things to say to him because my life seemed to have stopped moving in any direction at all. That was when I started to bring my ghetto blaster down to the cemetery and play music to him. Then the ghetto blaster broke and I started singing to him instead.

One day I came to see him and noticed that there was a new grave next door but one to Dad's. I looked at the fresh soil and the new flowers. There's nothing sadder than fresh soil in a graveyard. You can't help but think of the people left behind and their loss. I sang Dad 'Mr Bojangles' that day. Actually, I didn't just sing, I did a few little dance steps as well. When I finished I heard clapping and a man saying, 'Bravo.' I looked about and saw an older couple, a man and a lady, both dressed in wellies and Barbour jackets. The man was holding a Thermos flask and the lady a bunch of daffodils from Sainsbury's. I know because I'd put the same ones on Dad's grave earlier.

'Bravo,' the man said again.

I blushed. I felt like I'd been caught naked. I'd never met anyone else at the graveyard. No one else ever came to the silver birch corner.

The lady put the flowers on the fresh grave. She was in her sixties, but she was beautiful. She looked like a retired ballerina.

'Lucky you, Mum,' she said to the grave with a smile. Then she turned to me, 'You don't by any chance know the song that goes, "Heaven, I'm in Heaven", do you?'

The man in the wellies and Barbour jacket roared with laughter. I've never heard anything like it. He could literally have woken the dead. I thought we might have a scene from Michael Jackson's 'Thriller' video on our hands.

'She'd love that!' he screamed, and the beautiful lady joined in with his laughter.

Of course I knew the song. Fred Astaire, my father's dancing hero, sings it in an old black and white movie.

So I sang the song and they danced like Fred and Ginger. It was weird and wonderful, and afterwards, they introduced themselves. Leonard and Joan, brother and sister. Leonard opened his Thermos and shared his whisky-laced coffee with me.

'Camille Flowers,' Joan said, looking at my dad's grave. 'A wonderful dancer. It was so sad when he died.' And she hugged me. God, I remember that hug. I closed my eyes and melted into it. It made me realise that my mum hadn't hugged me for years.

We arranged to meet the next week and then the week after that, and now we've been meeting every week for seven years. Leonard still brings his Thermos and I still bring the doughnuts.

I'm not thinking about our history today, though, as I walk to silver birch corner. I'm thinking about John St John What's-his-name taking my job.

Joan and Leonard are already seated in their usual spot, on top of the monument to Alfred George Roberts. He was a textile merchant who died in 1893. We say it was the syphilis what got him, although we don't know that for fact.

'Happy birthday to you!' they start to sing. We've celebrated many birthdays over the years.

'Oh darling . . . ' Joan says as soon as she sees my downcast face. 'Did it not go your way?'

'No! Some posh bloke got it. He gave the job to some posh twat who didn't even work for the company.'

'That's a travesty! Do you want me to talk to the lubricant chap?' Leonard asks as he takes a doughnut from the bag.

'One doughnut today, Len, your blood pressure was up this morning,' Joan instructs him.

'Spoilsport! Now, while we're on unpleasant subjects, Grace, what did you make of that letter?'

'What letter?'

'There was a letter. Did you not get one? A company – oh what are they called, Joan? I had it a moment ago in the car.'

'Something construction.'

'Yes, yes, something construction. But what construction? SJS Construction? Was it?'

'I think it was, Len.'

'Well, anyway, this construction company want the land we're standing on, Grace. They want this corner of the graveyard to build an access road to a big development they're planning.'

'They can't be so arrogant as to think they can build a road through a Victorian graveyard!' I replied.

'Actually, they can. And, in fact, they could. The council would allow it apparently because it only affects a few graves.

Mum's, your dad's, Alfred's here and two others I believe, but the relatives of the deceased have the final say.'

'Oh, thank God for that. They must have written to Mum. I'll write back and tell them where they can shove their access road.'

'That's our girl. Now then, "Feeling Good"?' Leonard enquires.

I walk over to Dad.

'Hi, Dad,' I whisper. 'Not a great day for the five year plan. Sorry.' I pause for a moment, then I start to sing. And like every birthday I'm taken back to the bathroom, when I sat on that toilet seat and Dad first played Nina Simone to me.

Chapter 10

My birthday is on the same day as Danny's dad's. Friendly Wendy is into birthdays and star signs and general superstitious nonsense, and she thinks it's weird that Danny goes out with a girl who's born on the same day as his dad. When I asked her why, she just answered, 'Um, dunno, its just a bit twisted, that's all.' I don't know about twisted, but it is incredibly annoying. Especially since Danny's mum and dad moved to the middle of Wales, because it means I spend all my birthdays on the M4.

We're supposed to be setting off as soon as I've visited my dad, but I've decided to delay things a few minutes.

'Dan.' I call him on my mobile when I'm back in my car.

'Hey, birthday girl.'

'Do us a favour. I left my debit card in the pub last night. I couldn't get that pill thing – it's £27! – can you pop over to the pub, pick up the card for me and run up to Sainsbury's and buy the pill for me. You need to go to the pharmacist in the middle. He should remember me. I've answered all his questions, I just didn't have the money to pay.'

'Oh, Grace, babe.'

'Please, Danny, he said I'm at a fertile point or something and I need to take it quickly. I just need to pop in and see my mum before I go.'

Then I hang up. It's best not to give Danny time to formulate an excuse, and anyway, I'm already swinging into Mum's driveway. I don't even stop to look at my beautiful childhood home. I just jump out of the car and run up to the porch.

'All right, Mildred, how's it hanging?' I say as I cross the threshold. Mildred is the lady who's buried under the porch.

'Mum,' I call as I walk into the hallway. There aren't any lights on, so I flick the light switch. Nothing. Mum never changes light bulbs, although I'm sure she has some. There are bound to be boxes and boxes of them stored somewhere.

The house looks different inside from when I was a child – it hasn't been decorated since then. That's not the difference, though. The difference is that it's crammed with stuff. When I was little there was room to run around or dance in the house, whereas now there are just narrow corridors of space that allow you to move from one cramped room to another. Piles and piles of books, DVDs, beauty potions, make-up, gadgets and fitness equipment are stacked in neat piles against the walls and the effect is suffocating. I've tried to speak to her about it, but she gets defensive. She says that she doesn't nag me about how I spend my money, so it's not fair for me to do it to her. But it's not the money that worries me. I remember at the time of my father's death people saying how clever Dad had been with their money and how my mother would always be well provided for. So it's not about that; it just makes me sad to think of her sitting in a cramped, dark house buying things she doesn't need to fill a void in her life that will never be filled. Mind you, thinking about my mum makes me sad, period.

'Grace, is that you?' Her face appears at the top of the stairs.

My mum is beautiful. Perhaps that's the most frustrating thing. Mentally she may be a fruit loop, but her outer casing is divine. She's short, like me, but whereas I curve in and out dramatically and have a bottom the size of a widescreen TV, my mum is petite all over, like a little bird. My dad used to call her his little starling because she seems to flutter everywhere. She's blonde and she wears her hair in a neat wavy bob, like movie stars in the fifties used to. My mum has been all dressed up with nowhere to go for ten years.

'You look nice,' I say. She smiles vaguely. 'Did you get a letter about the cemetery and people wanting to build a road over Dad's grave?'

Mum's lips tighten and she walks back to the bedroom she came from. 'I don't know,' she says.

I walk into my dad's old study. I try not to look at his old cork noticeboard with all the pictures of us and postcards and tickets to parties pinned to it. Nothing has faded because Mum won't open the blinds in here. It's like walking onto a dark stage where a play set a decade ago is about to take place. His old computer sits where it always sat, looking archaic now. Somewhere in one of the drawers is his old mobile phone. My dad never got to see the iPhone or, more importantly, the iPod. It's funny the things that make you sad.

There aren't any letters, opened or unopened, upon the desk.

'Mum, where do you put the post?' I shout, but as I'm shouting I stub my toe on something underneath the desk. I reach down and slide a heavy cardboard box towards me.

'What have we got here?' I mutter.

The box is full of letters, all of them unopened.

I sit on Dad's swivel chair and rummage through them. The aim is to spot the All Souls Cemetery postmark, but that's soon forgotten when I realise they're all formal, terrifying-looking letters. Many from British Gas show a red letter in the address window. The words 'Urgent' and 'Do Not Ignore' swim in front of my eyes.

'Jesus,' I mutter.

I take the top few letters and put them in my bag. I'll have to pay them for her when I get the chance. I carry on searching for the All Souls Cemetery letter. It's not there. Maybe Leonard was wrong and it won't affect Dad's grave after all.

'Mum!' I shout, walking back into the hallway. 'Mum, I'm off.'

'Oh, bye.'

'Are you sure you didn't get a letter from the cemetery?'

'Not that I remember.'

'You'd definitely have remembered. I'll see you tomorrow, then.'

I wait for her to say something like 'happy birthday' or 'wait a sec, let me give you your present' or 'I love you', but she doesn't. She just stands at the top of the stairs and nods.

Chapter 11

I love my car, even though bits keep falling off her. It was my exhaust last week, and the week before that a wing mirror. The passenger door generally won't open and some of my less agile clients have found it hard to get in the car through my side. She's a Nissan Micra and she was my twenty-second birthday present to myself. She was £650, and even though she's cost me a lot more since then, I adore her. She's red and her name is Nina. The only thing about her that I'm not keen on is the pattern on her seats. They're flecked with yellow and people have commented that it looks like vomit stain that won't come off. People can be so cruel. My favourite bit of Nina is her horn, which I am beeping furiously at the moment because Danny bleeding Saunders is in the pub while I'm waiting outside in the car.

So far we're an hour and twenty minutes late leaving for

Wales. I purse my lips and beep my horn again, then again, and again. God, I love my horn. This is the second horn I've had on this car. I wore the first one out. I'm very proud of that.

My local pub is the best pub in the area. It's called The Festering Carbuncle and is thankfully more pleasant than its name suggests. The Festering Carbuncle is a gastro pub, I'll have you know, and it's run by probably the nicest man alive. In fact, if there were to be a Nicest Man in the Universe competition, I would enter Anton and put all my money on him. I don't know how old he is, but he must be getting on for about fifty because he has a son my age and he's done a host of exciting things in his life. He was a roadie for U2 for years, then, when he left that job, he had a photographic exhibition showing all the photos he'd taken of the band over the years. It was a big success and afterwards other bands asked him to photograph them, so he spent a few years touring with The Rolling Stones, Pink Floyd, Red Hot Chili Peppers and Blur. When he found himself rocked out, he bought The Festering Carbuncle, which in those days really was a festering carbuncle. Anton did it up, put lots of his photos on the walls, employed lovely staff and set about his other passion, which is cooking.

The Festering Carbuncle was one of the deciding factors in me buying my flat. That and the fact that it was the only flat I could afford. I walked into the pub with Friendly Wendy, having just viewed my future home, and Anton was sat on one of the wooden tables with three staff eating bangers and mash. Proper looking juicy sausages, creamy mash and gravy. Wendy and I stood in the doorway, our mouths watering, transfixed.

The pub wasn't even officially open then, but Anton sat us down with them and gave us sausage, mash and mugs of tea, and told us all about the area. As soon as I'd wiped the last bit of gravy off my plate with a slice of homemade crusty bread, I called and put an offer in.

'All right, love, calm down,' a man says as he passes my car while I beep the horn.

'I am a wronged estate agent and it's my birthday. I can't calm down,' I shout back at him.

'Gracie Flowers,' says Anton, walking out of the pub towards me.

The sight of Anton always makes me smile. He's tall. Mind you, everyone's tall to me. I think Friendly Wendy is tall and she's only five foot three and a half. Anton's got a lot of hair. It's got grey in it, but you wouldn't say he's grey. He's still brown. His is a Hugh Grant circa *Four Weddings and a Funeral* style. He's not buff but he's quite fit looking. He takes his dog, Keith Moon, on a long walk everyday and I suppose he must lift barrels and things while he's working to keep in shape. He always wears loose cotton shirts and jeans. He's very comfortable in his own skin, is Anton. He's just simply lovely.

'For you, my darling,' he says and hands me a plate with a bacon sandwich on it. See what I mean! He's lovely.

'Oh, Anton, really? It's my only birthday present!'

'Oh Gracie, I didn't know. Will you be in tomorrow for the karaoke? The first of many, I hope.'

'Oh.' I pause. I loathe karaoke. 'Probably not.'

'Oh well, try to make it. I'll sing you a special birthday song.'

I wince inwardly and change the subject.

'How's Freddie doing?' Freddie is Anton's son, a handsome young lawyer who Friendly Wendy is in love with.

'Ah, he wanted to talk to you about getting on the property ladder. Something like your flat . . .'

'Maisonette.'

'I do apologise, maisonette, would be perfect.'

'Has he got my number? Here take my card. Or . . .' Brainwave. 'He could call Wendy, he's got her number, she could talk him through the properties we've got—'

'I think he wanted to be looked after by the super estate agent that is Gracie Flowers.'

Damn.

'Cheers, mate.' Danny slaps Anton on the back as he bounds past him and round the car to the passenger door.

'Oh, Dan, I haven't fixed that door yet so it still doesn't open. You'll have to crawl in through my side,' I say, climbing out of the car.

Danny folds up his long limbs and clambers into the car.

'I really should get that fixed. It's a nightmare when I have clients,' I mutter.

'I'll be off, Gracie Flowers,' says Anton, and he bends down and kisses me softly on the cheek. Anton always smells nice. The perfect combination of musky man aftershave, olive oil and hops.

I get back in the car and belt up. Danny is already tucking into half of my bacon sandwich, so I take the other half and we set off. Finally.

It's not until we're on the M4 that I remember about the morning-after pill.

'Danny!' I shout him awake. 'Where's my pill thing? I've got to take it.'

'What? Oh, babe. They wouldn't give it to me. It has to be you. I went all the way down there for nothing. Lampard scored while I was gone as well.'

Bugger, I think.

Chapter 12

A Foxtons estate agent would describe Danny's parents' house as 'peacefully located in the beautiful Welsh countryside'. I would say that it's 'inconveniently located in the epicentre of absolutely nowhere'. The nearest postbox is over two miles away. The nearest village – and by village I mean cluster of cottages with a general store and a pub – is nine miles away. When they first bought it and Danny and I came to visit them, we couldn't believe it. We didn't see a soul on the road for ages. It was such a novelty we pulled over as soon as the windy road allowed and had a quickie. It wasn't the most successful sex we've ever had, because at one point Danny got a bit carried away and toppled into a bush. Unfortunately, it was a bush of stinging nettles and he didn't have any trousers on at the time. That was the end of the quickie. He lay on the back seat, moaning with his bum out for the rest of the journey, putting my Boots Protect & Perfect on his arse because he said it was soothing!

We haven't had random outdoor nooky for a while, I think, looking at Danny, who's still asleep. He could sleep through a world war. He's really good looking is my Danny. He looks a bit like that bloke from the *Twilight* films who teenage girls faint over. He's certainly pale, like a vampire, mainly because he works for a company that makes computer games, so he spends most of his time in darkened rooms staring at a computer screen. When Dad was alive he'd always make wild predictions about the man I would end up with, Prince William being a favourite. I maintained that I would only consider Prince William if he learned to play the acoustic guitar. All I wanted from a man when I was younger was that he should be able to play the acoustic guitar. Around the time Dad died he was keen for my future husband to be Will Young – he just missed him coming out. He never met Danny. Sometimes I wonder what he'd think about me ending up with a computer gamer who doesn't play guitar, although, to give Danny credit, he did get his grade one recorder.

'How's work, babe?' I say, trying to ease him back into the land of the living as we're almost there.

'Uh,' he says opening his eyes and swallowing. 'Crap.'

'Why?' I lean my hand across to touch his knee.

'Dunno.'

'Talk to me, Danny. What's wrong? I thought you loved your job.'

'Aw. Nah. Bored.'

'Babe, maybe you need a new challenge. You could try another company or ask for a promotion.'

'Yeah,' Danny says, looking down. He stretches his legs and I move my hand back onto the steering wheel.

'Why don't you read *The Five Year Plan*?'

He turns to me and gives me a sleepy smile.

'Yeah, maybe.'

I smile back and blow him a kiss.

'You won't regret it. You've had the same job for years. You're bound to be bored. You need . . . to think big, aim high.'

'Think big, aim high,' he echoes. 'Grace?'

'What?'

'Mum wants you to sing at the party tonight?'

'Why does she want me to sing? She's never heard me sing.'

'She has. She was going through all the old home videos and she came across our Year Ten Christmas show. Do you remember?'

'Oh, yeah, didn't I sing that Mariah Carey song?'

'You were amazing.'

'And didn't you read some poem?'

'Yeah.' He laughs. 'I well had a crush on you then.'

'Soft.' I smile at him. 'You'd better tell your mum I can't sing.'

'Grace, just sing. You're in the middle of nowhere. It'll be fine.'

'Danny!' I shout. 'No!' I hate to get cross, but sometimes it's necessary. 'I'm not singing, OK. Jesus!'

Obviously we're late. We walk into the living room and everyone already has the ruddy glow of at least two drinks and all the best bits from the buffet table have been devoured. The good thing about Danny's parents' house is that it's cosy and warm with old beams and open fires. Just the sort of place you want to arrive at after four and half hours of driving in a Nissan Micra.

'Danny!' shrieks his mum. 'And Gracie! Look, here she is.'

I love, love, love Danny's mum. In many ways I don't know what I'd do without her. She's more my mum than my mum. I was gutted when they decided to move to Wales. I used to adore going to their house in London. Danny's an only child, like me, and when the four of us had dinner there, it felt like a proper family meal. Mrs Saunders would keep the conversation going with questions and stories, and she was always interested and thoughtful. I love roast chicken, so she'd often make it for me, and when I became an estate agent she would cut out articles about the property market from the paper for me. She would tell us about the charity fêtes and coffee mornings she'd been to, and somehow she'd make them sound fun. She squeezes Danny first, then me. 'Here's Grace,' she whoops. 'Our entertainment!'

Now I may love her, but I'm not going to be bullied into this. I give Danny a steely look to indicate that he needs to save me, but he's already wrapped up in the embraces of his other relatives.

'Happy birthday,' Danny's dad says, wandering over to me.

'And a happy birthday to you,' I reply.

Danny's dad scares me. Not because he looks like Freddy Krueger, but because I see in him what Danny will become. And if I had to pick one word to describe it, that would be lazy. If I were allowed more words they'd be 'lazier than a dead swine'. He is definitely a 'I'll have my dinner in the lounge watching *Top Gear*, love' sort of a man.

'I hear you're singing tonight,' he says.

'Er, well,' I mutter.

'We've got a chap to play the piano for you – Margaret's son, a music something-or-other – where is he?' Danny's dad looks about him, then raises his hand with a jerk in the direction of a youngish-looking man with a beard, who literally runs towards us and puts his arm around me. Blimey, I think, as he nearly winds me with his embrace. The Welsh obviously don't get much physical contact.

'Grace! Grace Flowers,' he says in an English, not Welsh accent. 'Oh, I'm so sorry, you probably don't remember me. Not with the beard. I taught at Kensal Rise Community College. Well, I assisted for a while when I was doing my teacher training course. Music?'

'Oh, um.' Nope, I don't remember him at all.

'Olly Bell. Well, Mr Bell.'

Oh, Mr Bellend. Now it's coming back to me.

'Oh yes, yes, I remember you.'

'I couldn't believe it when Mr and Mrs Saunders said you'd be singing and asked if I'd accompany you. What an honour.'

'Oh, but—'

'We're all so excited.'

'Um, my throat is a bit sore. I'm not sure whether I should—'

'So what are you doing at the moment?'

'I'm an estate agent,' I tell him proudly.

'Sorry?'

'I'm a sales negotiator at Make A Move on the Chamberlayne Road.'

'Oh, God. I'm so sorry,' he whispers for some reason. 'Can I ask what happened?'

'How do you mean?'

'Well, with your singing career?'

'I don't have a singing career. I haven't sung for years.'

He looks taken aback and Danny's dad looks uncomfortable. I look around for Danny to save me, but he's talking to his mum. Whatever they're saying it looks serious.

'Pam,' I say, walking towards them. They both look up at me suddenly, almost guiltily, and I have a fleeting feeling that they've been talking about me. 'Pam, my love, I don't sing any more. Honestly, please, I haven't sung for about a hundred years. I don't want to make a big deal of this, but I can't sing tonight.'

'Oh just a few songs,' Pam begs.

I'm getting angry. Not so much with Pam, more with Danny. He knows I haven't sung in public since my freak-out all those years ago. Why isn't he standing up for me? Why has he put me in this position? I glare at him.

'Oh, go on, Grace. Just do "Son Of A Preacher Man". Dad's dad was a vicar. Go on, everyone will love it,' Danny insists.

'Oh, "Son of a Preacher Man"!' Pam screams, clapping her hands together.

'Yeah, that's all you have to do, Grace.'

'Everyone will love it!'

'Go on, Grace.'

'Dan! No! Jesus!' I say stroppily, then I stomp outside and look up at the stars. It's always raining in Wales, though not tonight, thankfully.

'Rubbish birthday to me, rubbish birthday to me, rubbish birthday to Gracie, rubbish birthday to me,' I sing sadly.

'See, you've still got that voice.'

It's Mr Bellend again.

'Do you know where the nearest pharmacy is?' I demand rather than ask.

'Oh,' he says, seemingly taken aback. 'There's a Boots in Carmarthen.'

'How far is that?'

'Seventeen miles.'

'Will it be open now?'

'No.' He laughs at the concept, then he takes a sip of something that looks like whisky judging by the glass he's holding.

'Damn!' I say vehemently, taking his glass from him and having a slurp myself. Ooh, bit of a burn. It is whisky.

'It should be open tomorrow. It's a slow old drive from here, though,' he adds.

That'll be my one lie-in of the week gone, then. But if I get up and go first thing, it'll only be about twenty-four hours since the accident, so I should be all right.

'Rubbish birthday to me.'

Chapter 13

As a rule I endeavour never to get into arguments. People often assume that because I'm quite feisty, I like a good barney, but they couldn't be further from the truth.

Mum and Dad never argued, either. At least, not that I knew. They often spoke passionately about choreography or the merits of Candarel over sugar, but I never once heard them raise their voices or slam doors. Except the night before Dad died. It was late when I heard them. We'd already said good night and gone to bed. I was lying awake thinking about glaciers and they were in bed chatting. I could hear them murmuring to each other. It was all the same as every night, until suddenly I heard Mum's voice, loud and firm, saying, 'NO!' Then there was the sound of movement in their room and more words being angrily spoken by Mum. I couldn't hear it all but I caught the gist. She was repeating herself a lot. 'What about me?' she kept shouting. And, 'It will be all about the two of you. How do you think I feel? I'll be forgotten.' Mum hadn't been invited to the meeting with the television company, and it sounded as though she was worried they would want my dad to partner someone younger. Wendy thinks this is why I can't bear confrontation. She says that because I heard this row, and then soon after Dad died, I associate arguments with bad things happening. She may well be right because I can't bear raised voices and I hate any form of confrontation. Normally, I'll do anything to avoid it, but today I'm having a very trying morning and am dangerously close to having a scrap.

My day was going quite well, too. I'd managed to unglue my eyes at eight o'clock this morning, which was a feat of unimaginable dexterity as I'd stayed up until 3a.m. doing the washing up with Danny's mum. Not my finest washing-up hour, it has to be said, as I was really clumsy and broke two wine glasses. Then I dropped a bowl of mayonnaise, which I wouldn't recommend as it was very messy. The mayonnaise hit the floor and then began bouncing around all over the place like Penelope Pitstop. I can be a bit of a liability in the kitchen, although I'm not usually that bad, but I do like to stay up and help Pam. The boys tend to conveniently pass out in the living room, leaving Pam and I to open a bottle of port and put our Marigolds on. We normally have a bit of a gossip, but she was quieter than usual last night. I hope she's not cross with me about the singing, or the mayonnaise, or anything actually. I really love Pam.

So this morning I got out of bed, which wasn't as easy as it sounds because Danny's parents' spare bed is so comfortable and its blankets so soft and the room so quiet that you feel like you're lying on a spongy cloud in Heaven (the fictional, spiritual place, not the gay club). Anyway, I managed to haul my tired body up and then crept around like a brilliant burglar getting dressed and washed and leaving the house. Outside, I took a big lungful of fresh Welsh air and got in the car. I had just about managed to convince myself that a nice seventeen-mile drive in the country was what I should be doing first thing on a Sunday morning, rather than basking blissfully in bed. I even kept calm, smiled and waved at the maniacal-looking farmer who made me stop my car so he could walk a gazillion gormless sheep across the road. Calm was still in attendance when I got stuck behind a vehicle that was seemingly being driven by a short drunk person with neither hand on the wheel. My relationship with calm encountered some turbulence when I got to Boots at 8.59a.m. only to find it doesn't open until ten thirty. Ten thirty! There wasn't even a café open where I could get a cup of tea and a bacon sandwich. But I really wanted to make it work with calm, so I dozed in the car. That's not much fun in a Nissan Micra, but I tried. Calm and I were still going steady.

I must say, however, that right now calm is in danger of being brutally dumped in favour of her sister, fury. Because – wait for it, you will want to bonk fury, too – the pharmacist is refusing to give me the morning-after pill.

'Um,' Swallow, breathe; don't thump the woman, Gracie. 'Why not?'

'It's our policy.'

POLICY!

Danny says it's very obvious when I'm annoyed with someone and trying not to wallop them. He says I start blinking like

I've got a bug in my eye and I move my mouth strangely, as if I'm trying to devour my bottom lip. I'm doing that now.

'Why?'

'A pharmacist has the right not to distribute it. If you'd been raped and the police were involved then we would reconsider, but otherwise it's our policy not to give out the morning-after pill.'

'But . . . but . . . it was an accident and surely you've got no right—'

'As I said, we do have the right and it's our policy.'

'Please, I'm begging you. I'm only twenty-five – well twenty-six, but only just – and I can't have a baby at the moment. Please. I know my circumstances and it's not the right time. And pardon me for saying but . . . you're not the person to tell me I should. It's my decision.'

'It's not just your decision. There's the father, your family, his family, God.'

God! That's the sort of ridiculous statement that makes me scrunch my face up really unattractively and stare at her. No one believes in God any more.

'Excuse me, but you shouldn't be having sex if you aren't prepared for the consequences.'

'But everyone has sex for pleasure. What else are you supposed to do?'

As I look at her I realise that actually she might not have sex for pleasure, and anyway, yesterday's two-minute quickie definitely didn't constitute pleasure.

'Sorry. Please.'

'I'm sorry, no. Now, if you'll excuse me, I have to get on.'

'This is sh—' I stop myself. I was about to say a rude

word, which wouldn't get me anywhere. Regroup, refocus, Gracie.

'OK. Right. Fine,' I say, with poisonous pleasantry. 'But if I do get pregnant, I'll bring the baby here and you can look after it.'

With that, I leave.

Chapter 14

Whenever my day's going terribly I always have to meet my mother. It's one of the Laws of Rubbish that my life religiously follows. Today's a case in point. Not only have I been denied birth control and had to drive for hours on a road where one lane was unavailable for use for sixty miles for no apparent reason other than to give hundreds of orange bollards an airing, I now have to endure Sunday roast with my mum. Actually, the roast isn't the bad part. My mum's roast is quite good. She always spends ages preparing the meal when Danny and I come over; she goes the whole Yorkshire pudding and five vegetables hog for us. This is mainly because she dotes on Danny. The cooking is all for him. She will force feed food upon Danny like he's a suffragette on hunger strike, though she'll hardly eat anything herself, so fearful is she of putting on half a pound in weight. She'll also spend the duration of her time at the table trying to dissuade me from eating anything either. I ignore her, but it's hard to really enjoy your food when someone is watching you and commenting, 'Is that five roast potatoes you're having?' and, 'There are hidden calories in horseradish, you know,' and, 'You don't want any more, do you?' in an accusatory tone.

'Oh, Danny, do we have to?' I ask, as I turn the ignition off in Mum's driveway.

'Yep, come on. I'm starving and we're late,' he says, opening the door and stretching his legs.

I don't even take off my seatbelt. I just flop forward and lay my head on the steering wheel.

'I just want to go home to bed,' I whine.

'Not long now.'

'Oh, hang about, what did I do with those letters?' I say, taking off my seatbelt and reaching towards the glove compartment. I open it and pull out the scary letters I took from Dad's study yesterday, then I lay them on my lap, look at them and yawn.

'Nice tonsils,' Danny says, because he always says that when I yawn.

'Nice penis,' I say, because it's my retort. I'll never be a lady.

'What you got there?'

'I got a bun in the oven,' I say in a bad American accent.

'Don't scare me, babe.'

'Oh! Oh! It's kicking!' I joke.

'Don't.'

I don't want a baby, but Danny doesn't have to look so appalled by the concept of me having his child.

'It's OK. I'll get the morning-after pill – or the two-days-after pill as it's now called – as soon as we leave here. There's a late-night chemist, hopefully without morals, on the Harrow Road.'

I pull out the first letter. It's a credit card statement.

'Drop us at the pub first, babe,' Danny says. I hear him but I don't answer, I'm too distracted by the letter I'm holding.

'Uh oh.'

'What?'

'Uh oh.'

'Grace, what have you got there?'

'My mum owes eleven thousand pounds on a credit card – and she hasn't made the last two payments.'

Eleven thousand pounds! That's a car. Or a new kitchen and bathroom. Or a deposit on a studio flat with no outside space in Cricklewood. How is she going to pay that back? It took me years to save ten grand and I work! The estimated interest is over a hundred pounds for last month. It's debt that's getting bigger and bigger, like a genetically modified chicken. I pass it to him.

'Uh oh,' he agrees.

'Are you coming in?' It's Mum calling from the porch.

'Rosemary,' he says, throwing the letter back at me, 'you look ravishing.' Danny always turns into a smarmy maître d' around my mother, but I'm grateful of it today because it gives me a moment to compose myself. I put the statement and the other unopened letters back in the glove compartment and close it.

'Hey, Mum, you look nice,' I say, getting out of the car. My mum gives me the glassy smile that I've become used to over the years.

'Danny, I was wondering if you'd mind changing some

light bulbs for me; you're so nice and tall,' my mum tweets. Not as in online networking; as in flirting. 'And whenever you get a second, I'd be so grateful if you could pop over and do the lawn.'

'Not a problem, Rosemary.'

'I spoke to your father this morning, Grace.'

Whoa. I wasn't expecting that so fast. She normally waits until pudding to drop the 'I've been talking to the dead' lines.

Mum talking to my dead father is a relatively recent phenomenon. It didn't happen when I lived at home, or at least if it did she didn't mention it. In the early days after Dad's death, when we were all a bit loopy, she used to wake in the night and claim to have seen him watching her from the end of the bed. But that only went on for a few months. She's often dreamt about him, and occasionally she would mention the dream, but they used to be the 'I dreamed your dad and I were in Cornwall' type statements to which I would usually reply, 'I've never been to Cornwall,' or, 'Cornwall's supposed to be beautiful.' There didn't seem anything particularly unhealthy about it, until one day about three months ago, she called me at work. Wendy put the call through to me and made an eek face, as she sometimes does when Mum sounds a bit odd. So I picked up the phone and said, 'Hey, Mum.'

'Grace, Grace, I've spoken to your father.'

She made it sound as though she'd been trying to get through to him for ages and the number had been engaged. Her delivery was so matter of fact that I couldn't respond.

'He . . . he . . .' she was starting to sound excited now and couldn't get her words out. 'Grace, you're not to wear purple.'

'Sorry?'

'That's what he said. I heard his voice this morning and he said, "Gracie, don't wear purple." Don't wear purple, of all the things!' She was starting to trail off and sound emotional now. 'Are you wearing purple now?' she whispered.

'Yes.'

She gasped.

'You'd better go home and change then.'

So I did, and all the time I worried that Mum, who for a long time had had a scatterbrained approach to the plot, had finally lost it.

I feel Danny tense behind me. I'm not surprised. He's probably worried I'll get back in the car and he won't get his roast, and it does smell good.

'Oh?' I'm trying to be casual, which I think most people would find tricky under the circumstances. 'What did he say?'

'He's worried about you, Grace.'

'What? About me wearing purple?'

I see my mother's perfectly aligned back go rigid. This is what my mother does to ward off confrontation. She tenses various parts of her body, mostly her back and her jaw, but sometimes you'll see an arm suddenly stiffen or a hand quickly clench. The latter can be disconcerting. The first time Dan saw the hand clench, he ducked.

'No,' she says tightly. 'Sit down at the table, Danny. Perhaps you'd open the wine.'

'Of course, Rosemary,' says Danny. 'Oh, these flowers are nice. Have you got an admirer?'

I glance quickly at him. He's pointing to a large vase of fresh flowers on the table. I haven't seen fresh flowers in this house for years.

‘Who gave you . . . ?’ I start, but Mum ignores me.

‘He’s worried about you.’

‘What’s he worried about?’ I say, following Dan to the table.

‘He thinks you should start singing again.’

I roll my eyes. What is it about this weekend and people conspiring to make me sing? I’ve been quite happily ***not*** singing for years.

‘Why?’

‘He thinks you’re too talented.’

‘Oh, does he?’

‘And so do I.’

‘Come again?’

‘I agree with him.’

‘Oh, of course you do.’

‘Don’t be facetious.’

‘When did he say this?’

‘This morning.’

‘Mum . . . ’

‘Grace . . . ’

‘Dad’s dead,’ I say softly, and I walk towards her and try to put my arms around her, but she’s rigid and I feel like a cow.

‘I did get the letter from the cemetery.’ My mum says the word cemetery so quietly that it’s barely audible. It’s the same way she says all words that are in any way associated with Dad’s death.

‘Oh! Brilliant. Where is it?’

‘I replied.’

‘Oh right—’ I start, but something in the way she looks at me makes me stop. ‘What did you say to them?’

She doesn’t reply; she just walks calmly over to the knife

block and pulls out a carving knife. She's pointing it at me when she speaks. Not deliberately, as though she's about to stab me, but it's still pretty macabre.

'Mum, what did you say to them?'

'I told them they could have the land,' she says, and she starts to carve the beef.

And so another terrible meal at my mother's has begun.

Chapter 15

I drop Danny off outside the pub. The karaoke has started and I can hear two girls murdering Girls Aloud. Not literally. That would be disturbing. I really like Girls Aloud. I don't listen to the radio, so I know absolutely nothing about pop music, but Wendy always buys me Girls Aloud CDs because they remind her of the girl band we formed at school with another girl. We were called Destiny's Baby Sister. I know – dreadful. But we were fourteen, and we were definitely better than these girls in the Carbuncle tonight.

'So what are you going to do?' Danny says. I've let him out my side, and now that I'm back in the car, he's crouching down beside my window.

'About what?'

'About your dad's grave.'

I close my eyes and sigh.

'Dunno.'

'You look shattered.'

'Cheers, smoothy. You won't be getting no action from me. Oh, babe, I've got to go. The pharmacy shuts at ten and I'll just about make it.'

We have a quick kiss and then I drive off.

Sometimes I wish I had a brother or sister. Actually, that's a complete falsehood: I *always* wish I had a brother or sister. I've been playing my own fantasy sibling game for years. I used to fantasise about having a younger brother called Charlie or Rufus, or something quirky like Felix. He would be two years younger than me and would completely adore me, obviously, because I was his big sister, and I would have trained him from an early age to know that I was always right about everything. I would teach him about girls and help him shop for clothes, and spoil him rotten at Christmas. I would introduce him to everyone as my 'baby brother' and that would make him blush a bit because he's quite shy. Mum would adore him as well, which would be good because then we'd have something in common. I'm sure Mum wouldn't be nearly so mental if I had a baby brother.

However, I'm split fifty-fifty between Felix Flowers, the little cutie, or a nice, big, sensible sister who had an amazing ability to sort everything out. Wendy's got the perfect older sister. Her name's Lucy and she's thirty-three, married with two children and she does things for Wendy like email her to remind her of family members' birthdays. She even offers suggestions of what presents to get them. I've modelled my fantasy older sister on her. She's called Alice and would be a maternity nurse. Alice is extremely capable. She would have noticed that Mum had stopped leaving the house way before I did and she would know how to make Mum happy. She would have stopped Mum spending thousands on her credit card, and best of all she would have twin girls, called Camilla, after dad, and Ginger, after Ginger Rogers, and I would babysit them and Mum would love them. And when we were together we would be a big, laughing happy family.

It would be lovely to know there was someone I could talk to about Mum, because I don't know what to do about her. I haven't known for ages. It's become much worse since I left home two years ago. Fifty per cent of me feels guilty that she's on her own, but then the other half of me knows I have to get on with my life. I can't fade away in that mausoleum with her. I did it for long enough and I dreamed of the day when I would get out and breathe and live. It would be easier to deal with if she was nicer to me, but she's not. And I don't know why. I know she doesn't hate me, but I'm pretty sure she doesn't like me. I always get the feeling I've done something wrong, but I don't know what it is.

This issue with the graveyard will be the biggest falling-out we've ever had. How can it not be? She can't give my dad's grave to a building company. What's she on? And how did she get in so much debt? Somehow I'll have to bail her out. The really infuriating part is that if I'd got that job I would be on much more money and would be in a far better position to help her.

'John Whatever Your Stupid Name Is, I hate you!' I mutter as I look for somewhere to park. There's a bus stop outside the chemist, but I'd better not pull in there. In the past, people have commented that I'm anal about driving misdemeanours, but I prefer the term 'sensible'. One of my most largely exercised rants is against people who park in bus stops, because then the bus can't pull in and has to stop in the middle of the road, thus holding up the traffic. My heart beats faster just thinking about it. Anyway, if I were to park at this bus stop and someone who knew me saw my car there, I'd get proper ribbed, like those ultra pleasure condoms, for weeks after. It's about two minutes to ten and I need to find somewhere quickly, so I turn off the main road and pull up in the side street.

'OK, bag, money,' I say, quickly making sure I've got everything. I get out of the car and lock it – no one would actually want my car, but I'd be completely lost without it – then throw my keys in my handbag.

'ARGH!' I scream as something knocks into me. I fall into the car's bodywork with a crash and someone grunts behind me as my arm is wrenched away from me. I try to turn my head to see who's attacking me, but as soon as I do I feel someone's fingers in my hair and then my head is slammed into the car. I feel dizzy, like I'm going to throw up, then suddenly I'm released. I hear running footsteps and look up to see two figures, one swinging my bag as he runs across the road. I take a step forward but my legs buckle as if I've never used them before and I fall to ground. As I steady myself I notice a tear drop onto the pavement. I peer at it. It looks so strange. I haven't cried in years, but as my eyes focus on it I realise it's not a tear. It's blood – my blood. I feel my face. There's a cut at the top of my nose and a big hot bump forming on my forehead.

Someone's taken my bag. Yet again I don't have any money to buy this pill thing. Someone somewhere must be having a laugh. I get up slowly and walk tentatively to the chemist, hopefully they'll take pity on me and let me use their phone to call the police. I reach the chemist, but a metal grille has been pulled down over the glass frontage. It's closed.

'*Ferme la porte*,' I say quietly, which is a bit weird as I didn't think I could remember any French. There's a phone box on the corner of the next block and I make my way, unsteadily, towards it, dial 999 and ask for the police. The lady I speak to sounds concerned that I'm on my own and tells me someone will be with me shortly.

I hope she's right. I really don't want to be here alone. The street suddenly feels very hostile. The bastards might come back. They've got my car keys. They could come back and take my car. There's a spare key at home. I dial 100.

'Hello, operator.'

'Oh hello, I've just been attacked and someone has taken my money. Can you help me? Can you put me through to the pub where my boyfriend is?'

'Yes, we'll reverse the charges. What's the name of the pub?'

'Oh, thank you.'

'What's the name of the pub?'

'Oh sorry. It's called The Festering Carbuncle, London W10.'

'Right, and what's your name?'

'Grace Flowers.'

I hear a ringing tone, then a really loud din and an Australian accent shouting, 'HELLO!'

'I have Grace Flowers on the line, do you accept the charges?'

There's a short pause when I can hear pub noises and then what resembles the amplified sounds of someone retching.

'ANTON!' the Australian voice barks.

There's another short pause and I realise that the retching sound is someone trying to sing Elvis Presley's 'All Shook Up'.

'Anton speaking.'

'Hello, I have Grace Flowers on the line, do you accept the charges?'

'What? Grace. Yes. Yes, of course.'

The operator hangs up.

'Anton, I've been mugged. I'm waiting for the police. Can you—'

'Where are you?'

'You know the pharmacy on the Harrow road. It's at the far end, opposite the graveyard.'

'I'll be five minutes.'

'But—'

He hangs up as a police car pulls over and a policeman and woman get out. I walk slowly out of the phone box, feeling like I've just stepped into an episode of *The Bill*.

Chapter 16

Anton didn't bring Danny or my car keys. His presence here is entirely unnecessary, but I'm so ridiculously glad he's here. He came with his dog, Keith Moon, and even though Keith is the daftest dog on the planet and wouldn't hurt a cauliflower, I feel much safer with him next to me.

It's all happening now. There are three police cars in total. One has stayed with me, one's been driving around to see if they can catch the bastards and the other one has gone back to the pub to get my spare car key from Danny after I'd called him on Anton's phone. He sounded pretty wankered, so I told him not to come. The last thing I need is a drunken Danny smoking rollies and telling me repeatedly how much he fancies a kebab. I can't be cross. I take full responsibility for his drunkenness because he didn't have much to do except down glasses of wine while I argued with Mum this evening.

The first police car radioed an ambulance, so I got to sit in a real ambulance while I was cleaned up. It was very *Holby*

City, although the novelty wore off when they taped a big bulky bandage to my forehead. That's not the worst of it, though. The rest of my face looks pillaged. My chin and mouth are normal, but everything above them is sporting a shade from some grisly Gothic eye shadow palette. At least it doesn't hurt at the moment because the ambulance people 'gave me something for the pain'.

The rest of the time I've been sitting in Anton's racing-green jaguar with Keith Moon on my lap.

'Shall I put the radio on?' Anton asks, reaching for his knob. Not his ooh-er knob, the one on the radio.

'Oh, do you mind if we don't?'

'Do you not like music?'

I chuckle at the thought of not liking music. 'I love music. I just hate the radio.'

'Why?'

'I don't like the randomness. I want to know what I'm going to listen to,' I tell him.

I'm not messed up at all about my dad dying, but there's this one little personality trait that's developed since the accident. I don't think it's that bad and it doesn't make me a complete freak, I just don't listen to the radio, that's all. I haven't for years and years. I know why it is. It's because my father gave me music. Literally. Nearly every day of my childhood he introduced me to a new song. He did it delicately, excitedly, and always with a reverential smile. I loved those daily gifts. When I tried to play Nina Simone to other eight-year-olds they said she was revolting, and perhaps I would have thought so, too, if I hadn't been introduced to her by my father. But then he died and the music started to hurt. There always seemed to be a song coming from somewhere, hurling a new memory towards me, and it made me feel out of control with grief. One minute I'd be functioning and doing fine, and the next I'd walk past a shop and hear the strains of a song he'd sung to me, or we'd sung together, and the sadness would feel like it was strangling me and I'd want to cry or scream or just curl into a ball and hide. Radio was the worst. It was like a trauma lottery. Why would I do that to myself? I haven't listened to the radio since then. 'Do you like music?' I ask Anton.

'Bloody love it.'

'That was a stupid question really, considering that you spent years touring with bands and now do karaoke in your pub.' I gasp. 'Oh, Anton, I took you away from your karaoke.'

'Urgh,' he shudders. 'Some of my favourite songs being massacred by the drunk.'

'Did you sing?'

'I did, yes.'

'What did you sing?'

'Oh, I sang with a friend of mine.'

'What?'

'A Simon & Garfunkel number. Way before your time.'

'What song?'

'"The Sound Of Silence".'

'Oh, I love that song.'

'I have it on CD. No random radio required,' Anton says, reaching towards the stereo.

He puts on 'The Sound Of Silence'. I hear the familiar guitar chords and soft voices of Simon & Garfunkel, and it sounds warm and familiar, like I'm being welcomed back to an old home. Dad loved this song. I've never taken this to the cemetery to play to him. How could I have forgotten it? Dad was going through a Simon & Garfunkel phase the summer he died. Shortly before the accident he drove me to a singing competition in Chester. He had a tape of Simon & Garfunkel playing live somewhere and we sang along to it all the way there. 'The Boxer', 'Scarborough Fair' and a song called 'Bridge Over Troubled Water'. Oh God, I hope Anton doesn't play that one. Dad sang it so beautifully in the car that day, and he played it again when we parked at the theatre, before I had to go in and register. I remember him singing the words: 'Your time has come to shine. All your dreams are on their way'. And as I kissed him and got out of the car, he smiled and said, 'All your dreams are on their way, Grace. Knock 'em dead, Silver Girl.'

It's a bit sick, but I find myself pretending I'm not sitting here with Anton; I'm sitting here with Dad instead. I'm pretending I'm fifteen and we're on our way to a singing competition. Yes, I know that makes me a freak, but I've just had a bang to the head. I close my eyes.

Anton starts to sing along. Wow! He can really sing. His voice isn't dissimilar to Dad's. It's the same key and the same gentle style; he doesn't push the song at you, he just sort of lays it gently at your ears.

I know it's crazy to pretend that a pub landlord is your dead father, but it's also blissful. Oh, so blissful.

The next song is 'Bridge Over Troubled Water' and I can't bring myself to ask Anton to turn it off. Instead I keep my eyes closed as he sings the first lines to me: 'When you're weary, feeling small. When tears are in your eyes, I will dry them all.'

'Your turn,' Anton whispers, in the musical refrain in the middle, exactly as Dad would have done.

'You swine, I get the belter notes,' I would whisper back, because Dad always used to split songs so I got to sing the hard bits.

Anton sings the song just like Dad did, and I feel as if Dad's talking to me. He's saying that things will be all right.

'You shine, Gracie Flowers,' Anton says at the end of the song. But I can't look at him because – and I know this is crazy lady speak – it feels like my dad is saying he's proud of me. Even though I don't think Dad would be. Not really.

'Thank you,' I sniffle back.

Then the police lady opens the car door and a blast of cold air hauls me abruptly back to the present.

Chapter 17

'Oh, Gracie Flowers, it's no use. You look like someone's put foundation on a plum.'

I sigh sadly at my reflection. Covering up the bruises hadn't worked, so I'd put a scarf around my head to hide the dressing and now I look like a fortune-teller with an abusive husband. It's taken me forever to get ready this morning. Even longer than the morning after Wendy's last birthday, and I didn't think anything could be worse than that. I was sick four times.

'Today so wasn't supposed to be like this. I should be Lady Boss, not Scabby Mess,' I groan. 'What to do, Gracie Flowers? What to do? Your twenty-seventh year doesn't seem to like you much. Talk about bad birthday weekend. Although I did enjoy the bit in Anton's car. Now that is sad,' I say, pointing at my reflection. 'The highlight of your birthday weekend was sitting in a car waiting to give a police statement about your assault. Sort yourself out, girl.'

But the truth is, for some reason I loved the time I spent in Anton's car last night. I don't know why, but I felt happier there than I have done in a long time. It's ridiculous. I'm a happy person. I've got Danny, a job, a flat. It must have been those painkillers. I should find out what they were and see if I can get some more.

I step back from the sink, take three deep breaths, straighten my back and look myself in the eye. 'What's the plan?' I say loudly. My bruised face looks back blankly, then my shoulders slump forward because I don't really know what the plan is and I'm tired.

I'm tired because I only had three hours' sleep. I went to Casualty and had my head stitched after I'd made a statement to the nice policewoman. I should have asked the nurse at the hospital if they had any of the morning-after pill, but Anton was with me the whole time and I didn't think he'd want to be acquainted with mine and Danny's problematic two-minute Saturday-morning quickie. So, I still haven't taken that stupid pill and those pesky little sperm are probably having a right old time.

'The plan is to get Posh Bloke out of Make A Move quick. Show him and Lube and everyone that you are the man for the job. Grow some balls, Flowers!' I cringe. I'd hate to have balls. 'That's what you're going to do, Grace, work hard. Work harder than everyone else! WORK HARD, GRACE, AND GROW SOME BALLS!'

My eyes flit to my new five year plan, which is sitting empty on the wall, waiting for me to fill it in. I pick up the felt tip I've left here expressly to write my next mission. I take the lid off.

In one year I will have . . .

In two years I will have . . .

In three years I will have . . .

In four years I will have . . .

In five years I will have . . .

'Will have what, though?' I whisper. 'What will I have done?' And for the first time in so long, I don't know.

There's a knock on the bathroom door.

'Grace, babe, I've got to go.' It's Danny and he sounds desperate.

'Coming,' I shout back, but I don't move. I'm still staring at the blank space I need to fill.

'Grace.' Danny bangs on the door again. 'We cannot leave it to chance that I will be able to keep clenching.' He sounds in pain. I'll have to let him in. I put the lid back on the felt tip and look at my blank five year plan one last time before unlocking the door.

Chapter 18

There are two things in my life that I'm proud of. The first is that I have never been in debt. Actually, let me clarify that, I might have owed the price of a bar tab because I'd forgotten to settle it on the night, like I did at the weekend, or borrowed a tenner off Wendy and paid her back a few days later, but I have never been in debt to the bank or had to pay a bank charge or interest. It's a trait I clearly don't get from my mother.

The other thing I'm proud of is something that's very close to my heart, because I spend a lot of time doing short trips in my car. I have never parked illegally. Nope, never. Not even a quick double park while I run into a shop to get a pint of milk. This is because I believe that if we all start bending the rules on the road there will be travel chaos. Holding such strong beliefs is vexing in London, though. Take today, a tosspot in a Porsche Boxster has parked on the red route outside the office with his hazard lights on. This meant I had to wait for a lull in the traffic to get round him in order to park in my legal spot around the corner. So tosspot Porsche driver has made my slow morning even slower, thus causing me to be late for work. Well, not late, but not as early as I like to be. I love being first in the office, especially on a Monday. It's a chance to put the kettle on and get my head around the week. It works in my favour, too, because lots of potential clients call before 9 a.m., when they're on their way to work and spot one of our signs. And we all know the motto: whoever speaks to the client first, keeps the client.

I get my Make A Move key out and put it in the lock, only to find it's already open. This never happens. I walk into the office. It's him. John Posh Boy Whatsit, and he's on the phone already. He looks even more attractive than he did on Saturday. In fact, he looks sun-kissed. He's probably got a yacht. Rah rah. Pull that rope, Jeremy, rah! A badminton racquet leans against the side of his desk. Badminton. He's such a twat.

'Four bed, you mentioned,' he's saying.

He's only gone and got a four bed already this morning. Four beds are 'show me the money'. I feel like picking up the phone and screaming down the line, 'He doesn't need a four bed. He's probably got a butler!' but I don't. Instead I pick up my phone and dial the number for Transport For London and ask to be put through to their parking department.

'Hello,' I say to the woman. 'There's a Porsche Boxster parked on the red route on the Chamberlayne Road, London W10. Yeah, I know. Tosspot. Driver doesn't deserve a Boxster,' I tell the lady. She agrees and thanks me for my call. I walk into the kitchen to put the kettle on, and when I return, Posh Boy is off the phone and looking flustered. He's flapping about his desk looking for something. Eventually he shakes his jacket, hears some keys, mutters, 'Thank heavens for that,' (because he's so posh), pulls them free, runs outside and gets into the Porsche. When he comes back a few minutes later, he walks straight up to my desk. I keep the straight back of one who has the moral high ground and brace myself for hostility, but his face looks more concerned than anything.

'Grace . . . '

'Do you want tea?' I ask, polite but frosty.

'No, no, I've got a coffee.'

I turn back to my computer. I offered him tea! Why did I offer him tea? That was far too nice of me. Don't do it again, Flowers. Remember your balls.

'Grace,' he says again, 'you don't have to tell me what happened, but do you want a day off?'

It takes me a moment to work out what he's on about, but then I remember the Halloween look I'm sporting today.

'No, of course I don't want a day off.'

My words come out sharply, and when I replay them in my head it reminds me of how my mother talks to me. Now I feel guilty. I'm rubbish at being mean. I need to get better at it if I'm going to let Posh Boy know who's boss. Balls, Grace, balls.

He's still standing in front of me with that concerned expression, and he's trying not to look at my face. I soften. He's far more sensitive than the other blokes who work here. They'll all be like, 'Hi, Mr Potato Head, have you seen Gracie?' I must say sorry for sounding like a cow. I'll feel bad about it all day if I don't. I'll say sorry this once and then I'll get back to behaving as though I have the biggest balls in Britain.

'Sorry, I didn't mean to snap. I was mugged last night.'

'Jesus, Grace, you poor thing.' His voice is kind. Bloody posh but very kind.

'No, I'm OK.'

'Where?'

'The Harrow Road. They only took my bag.'

'But . . . did they? They didn't punch you?'

'No, they sort of pushed my head into my car.'

'Bastards.'

'Hmm.'

'Where on the Harrow Road?'

'The dark bit opposite the cemetery. I'd just pulled up at the late-night chemist.'

'How awful.'

'I'm fine. My face looks worse than it feels,' I lie.

'It's still a lovely face,' he says and smiles. 'And at least you'll be better for our paintballing team-building event in a month's time.'

'Sorry, what?'

'A paintballing, team-building event.'

'Paintballing? Team building?' I repeat slowly, with undisguised disgust.

He nods.

'You seriously expect me and Wendy to run about in the grass getting pelted with paint by a load of mental blokes?'

'You'll be all right,' he says, and starts to walk back to his desk. But then he stops and turns and smiles, a funny little shy smile. 'I'll protect you,' he says, but he mouths the words as though it's a secret.

John Whatsit is flirting with me. Urgh! I feel sick.

'Oh, there's your family,' he says, nodding to the door. I took my eye off the door! He unnerved me with all that 'lovely face' stuff. Lucky they're my people coming in or I might have missed out on some new clients.

God, he's so annoying.

Chapter 19

The second best day of my life was the day I made my first sale at Make A Move. I felt like I was drunk on fizzy wine at lunchtime. I was giddy and smiley and I wouldn't shut up. But it wasn't just me who was happy, everyone involved was thrilled. Lube, obviously, because property prices were sky high at the time and he made a tidy sum from my efforts, but it was the faces on the people who'd sold their flat and the people who had just bought it from them that made it all worthwhile for me. The property was a three-bed garden flat near Ladbroke Grove. The couple selling were academic types in their early sixties, who'd raised a family there but had decided to retire to Chichester and enjoy crab sandwiches and sea walks, and they had sold to a gorgeous young newly married couple who couldn't wait to start a family. It sounds silly, but something about the transaction said, 'This is the right order of things.' It wasn't about the money, it was about a home being passed carefully from owner to owner. It was about love and laughter and memories and hopes for the future.

Funnily enough, this same flat has just come on the market again, and it's this flat that I think will suit my nice family. The gorgeous couple who lived there had indeed started breeding rampantly and now they have three children: toddler twins and a new baby. Nightmare. Talk about never getting any sleep again. Mind you, I can't actually blame the mother because her husband was trip-over-your-shoes, forget-your-own-name handsome. I was selling his studio flat at the same time, and when I turned up for a viewing once he answered the door without a top on. It was so exciting that the next week at the same time I pretended Wendy was a potential client and booked a viewing so she could come and drool over him, too.

I haven't seen the property this time round. I have tried to pop over to take new photos, but understandably Claire – the mother – has been too busy. This is the first viewing and I'm hoping for an offer. You can't get better than an offer on a first viewing, and it would show Posh Boy just how big my balls are. Especially as he's coming along. He's decided he wants to 'shadow me'.

'Grace, yah, I want to shadow you on this viewing,' he said after my family arrived at the office.

'I'll show you how it's done,' I replied.

'Righto,' he answered, and I thought very hard about stapling his tie to the desk.

It's a stupid idea for him to shadow me with this family, though, because it means there are too many of us to get in the car. So now we're all stood in the driveway waiting for him to park his posing mobile.

'Glad you could join us,' I say when he finally appears. 'Hope you didn't park on a red route.'

He gives me an annoyed look, which pleases me greatly.

'Ooh, mind the dog pooh,' I say, deliberately too late. 'Oh, dear. You'll need to wipe that off your shoe before you come into the client's house. We don't want you walking poo through their nice flat.'

Posh Boy finds a piece of grass and starts to stamp the sole of his shoe on it.

'Gather round,' I say to my favourite family. 'I want to draw your attention to this parking space. It belongs to the flat. And as this is West London, let us all take a moment to worship at the altar of that sentence. Your own parking space. I mean, on market days you'll probably have to shoo people away from it and during carnival there'll probably be twenty blokes from Trinidad having a barbeque on it, but it is still *your* parking space and it beats driving around the block for forty minutes before realising that the nearest free space is in Archway.'

'Oh, what a lovely building,' the mum says, admiring the big white stucco-fronted property.

'I know, it makes me think of a Jane Austen adaptation when young ladies come to London to find a husband. They often walk out of houses like these, don't they? This is a great street to live on.'

'Is that a yoga studio across the road?' says the girl.

'Yeah, I think it's a good one, too. They do that hot yoga.'

'Cool.'

'The flat's got its own entrance just to the side here. Are we all together, John?' I call. 'Have you got that poo off your shoe yet?'

'Yes,' he calls flatly.

'Excellent.'

We stand like carol singers on the doorstep and I ring the bell. There's no answer for a long time.

'She does know we're coming, doesn't she?' asks Posh Boy impatiently.

'No, I thought we'd all pop round on the off chance,' I sing, as though he's stupid.

'Maybe you got the time wrong.'

See! See, how annoying he is?

I hear movement behind the door. Thank God. It would have been really embarrassing if we couldn't get in. I listen carefully. I think I can hear sniffing and snivelling. Oh dear, I hope Claire hasn't got a cold. I don't fancy catching it and having to blow my bruised nose. Ouch.

Eventually, the door is pulled back a fraction.

'Hi there,' I say. There's no immediate answer, just another sniff. Finally we see Claire, but she looks terrible and nothing like the carefree former model with the handsome husband I remember from five years ago. In fact, she looks a lot like the baby she's carrying on her shoulder. They both have big puffy red faces and watery eyes. What with my scabby face and her tears we're not a very good advert for the area.

'Oh, Claire, my love. Shall we give you space and come another day?'

She shakes her head and steps back to let us in.

'This is the Hammond family,' I say, smiling and gesturing towards them. 'And this is John, our work experience boy,' I add without looking at him.

We stand in the hallway. All the doors leading off it are

closed. 'Are you sure you want me to show them round?' I whisper.

Claire nods, but she doesn't say a word. At least I don't think the sobbing, hiccupping sound that follows is a word.

Posh Boy looks at me as though I'm the most insensitive estate agent he's ever seen, and perhaps I am. She did sound a little harassed on the phone, but I'd assumed that's what women with young children sound like.

Oh, well, we're here now. I open what I know is the lounge door. Funny how I can remember the layout of all the houses I've sold.

'This is a great room,' I say confidently as I step inside. But then I stop, suddenly, when I see it. It used to be a great room; now it's a mess. And I have a really high mess threshold, so for me to call a place a mess it must be bad. The curtains are drawn, so this normally bright room with patio doors onto the garden is virtually black. There's a small girl on a dirty sofa watching *Come Dine With Me* and eating Wotsits. I can't get my head around how much the room has changed. It used to be a big spacious living area, with a dining area, lounge and kitchen to the side, but now there's a nappy-changing station on the table, which explains the whiff of poo and baby wipes, and there are towels everywhere. Two potties sit in the middle of the room, bizarrely surrounded by six dining chairs. Don't ask. It looks awful and it stinks.

'I think we should leave her to it today,' says Mrs Hammond, the mother of the family.

'Yeah,' I agree.

This is my fault entirely. I should never have shown a property I hadn't seen for five years. Anything can happen in that time – and it clearly has. 'Shall we just have a peep in the garden?' I suggest, hoping at least to salvage one good impression from the property. I've known clients offer on a flat purely because they've loved the garden, such is the desperation of people to have even a square foot of grass in London.

'OK,' Mrs Hammond whispers.

We tramp through the assault course to the patio doors, and I glance at the bookcase, as I always do, searching for a copy of *The Five Year Plan*, hoping to meet another aficionado. I never have yet and today's no exception. I steady Mrs Hammond as she nearly slips on a small puddle of wee, then I try to pull back the curtain, but it won't open. It's caught on something the other side. I tug a bit harder, but then I hear the sound of a child's voice saying, 'No!'

'Hello, there, young person behind the curtain. Do you think we could have a little look at your nice garden?'

'No,' he repeats.

'Please,' I try, tugging the curtain again.

There's some shuffling behind the material until a small boy's head is revealed. There are two striking things about the child. One is a big green slug of snot sliding towards his mouth, and the other is something big and white that's stuck to his head.

'What's that on your head?' Posh Boy asks in a 'talking to an under three' voice.

We all peer at it. It looks like a badly applied bandage, but then, just as I am about to say, 'Oh, did you bang your head like me?' it dawns on me that it isn't a bandage at all. It's a sanitary towel. Thank God it's clean.

This could well earn a place in my top ten crap viewings.

We traipse back to the hall.

'We'll pop off now. I'll give you a call later,' I say gently to Claire on the way out.

She nods and I lead the Hammonds to their car, then I run back to Claire, who's staring into space at the door.

'Are you all right, Claire?' I whisper.

'No,' she chokes. 'He's left me for his masseuse. I've got to sell the flat to get out of here.' She sounds desperate.

I stare at this beautiful, broken woman and I want to hug her, but she's still holding the baby.

'I'm so sorry,' I whisper. And I am. I couldn't think of anything worse. I imagine how I'd feel if Dan left me. I'd be lost. And that's without a load of little people relying on me.

She doesn't say anything; she just begins to cry. Then the baby starts as well. She gives me a sad apologetic smile and closes the door.

Posh Boy's still on the driveway checking the soles of his shoes. He looks up as I pass.

'Well, that was a cock-up,' he says, sounding rather thrilled.

What can I say? Nothing. It was a cock-up, and I wish he hadn't been there to witness it.

Chapter 20

'Shit, man, what happened to you?'

There's no toast or Haribo today, so I have her full attention.

'I was mugged.'

'Shit, man. Where?'

'Harrow Road.'

I should get it printed on a card or T-shirt really.

'No way, man.'

'Is he in there? The pharmacist?'

'He's with someone, innit.' She leans towards me and makes her eyes slitty. 'What did theys look like?'

That's an original question. I'll give her that.

'I don't really know. Young probably, because they were running fast. Two blokes, not that tall. Only saw them from behind. They both had their hoods up.'

'What they take?'

'Oh, just my bag. A big purple bag from Primark. Do you know how long he'll be?'

'Nah. Shit innit.'

'Yep. Yep, it is.'

'Wheres on the Harrow Road?'

'Up by the late-night pharmacy.'

She gasps. 'Were youse getting the morning-after pill and theys take your bag?'

'Yep.'

'That is so shit.'

'Yep.'

'Shit. I'm not supposed to but—'

She pulls a bag of pick-and-mix out from under the desk and offers it to me. I accept, reach in and pull out a wiggly worm. Result.

'Thanks.' I smile.

'I hope it wasn't my brother,' she says, and she's serious.

I don't have a brother, let alone one who might be a mugger, so I don't really know what to say. I make an eek face and hope it will do.

'Your boyfriend's lush, innit,' she says.

'I love wiggly worms,' I say, then I chomp off his head. The worm's obviously, not Danny's.

The chemist walks out of his Tardis with a middle-aged woman. They both spot me and the lady walks to the counter as I make my way towards the chemist.

'We've met recently,' he says, as though trying to place me, and leads me into the Tablet Tardis.

'Yes, I came in on Saturday to get the morning-after pill, but I didn't have any money, and then my boyfriend came in later but you wouldn't give it to him.'

'But you've had an accident since then.'

'Yes, I was mugged.'

'I'm sorry.'

'It's OK.'

'So when did you have unprotected sex?'

'Saturday morning.'

'Have you had sex since then?'

'He'd be so lucky.'

'And your last period?'

'Two weeks ago.'

'Oh, that's right.' Now he pulls an eek face. They really are very handy. 'You're in a fertile time of the month and it's been more than two days since the incident occurred. Emergency contraceptive isn't a hundred per cent effective anyway, so I must warn you ... there is a small chance that, even if you take this, there could still be a pregnancy.'

'Yes. Thank you.'

'We have pregnancy tests here if you're very late or if you feel ... in anyway different or at all pregnant. OK, here's the pill. Just pay Tara outside. Do you have money today?' I'm learning that people are very nice to you when you have a scabby face.

'Yes,' I nod, feeling the thirty quid that Wendy lent me in my pocket.

I walk slower than usual towards Tara. For some reason I feel worried that another freak incident will happen to stop me buying the pill, but I manage to pay her and leave Sainsbury's without either dropping the packet down a hole, a bird swooping down and flying off with it, being mown down by a shopping trolley or hit by a meteor.

'Thank God for that,' I mutter as I settle safely inside my

car and lock the doors. I open the packet and knock the pill back with some water from a bottle under the seat.

'Please, Dad, God, Allah, Buddha and the tooth fairy, I am most definitely not ready to have a baby yet. Please don't let me be pregnant,' I say aloud, and it may sound odd, but I feel quite confident that they heard me.

Chapter 21

After two weeks of constantly checking whether I felt 'in any way different or at all pregnant', I am absolutely thrilled to say that, apart from the scab on my face, the posh bloke ruining my life, my broke mother and my father's grave possibly being dug up and tarmacked over, I feel perfectly normal. Oh, except that Danny is being very weird and distant. I've barely seen him since the accident as he's been working late all the time. I'm assuming that's because he doesn't want to look at me and my disgusting face at the moment, which I can understand. And I'm probably being needy, too, but all I really want is cuddles at the moment. It's strange, but on the plus side I've been working late, too, and am currently whipping Posh Boy's arse until it's pink and sore. On the sales front, that is. Urgh! Anything else would be gross.

'What's up with you?' asks Wendy. 'Why are you pulling that face?'

'What face?'

'That turned-up-nose face.'

'Oh, I was just thinking about Posh Boy.'

'Big crush.'

'Hardly, I was just thinking that I can't stand the bloke.'

'That's denial. It's Massive. Huge. Like a big glass of orange crush but with John in it. Have you had a dirty dream about him yet?'

'Wend!'

'Oh my God. I was just joking, but you have, haven't you? Oh, my frickin' shoes! Tell all now.'

She moves her swivel chair niftily towards me, nudges my client chair out of the way and leans forward onto my desk.

'Hello,' – she puts on an upper-class accent – 'I'd like a penthouse apartment as close to Portobello as possible, money no object. I shit the stuff! Oh, and do you have the particulars on the wanton dream you had about your posh boss?'

'I bloody hate you!'

'You love me. So did you really have a fruity dream about him?'

I nod sadly. As if he's not annoying enough in life, he's entered my dreams as well.

'Oh my God!'

'But I can't talk about it,' I hiss. 'It made me feel proper nauseous when I woke up. And what about poor Danny lying next to me while I had a sordid dream about Posh Bloke!'

'What do you mean, not fair on Danny, blokes get lob-ons all the time for girls that aren't their girlfriends. So what happened in the dream?'

'Just . . . you know . . . stuff.'

'Oh, I know stuff!'

'Wendy, stop it now, please.'

'Was it good? Did you wake up all sweaty and turned on?'

'No, Wend, I woke up feeling ill. But it was weird, I was being chased by something or someone bad, and he was helping me. And we ended up having to sleep in this derelict place on a mattress and then, you know . . .'

'Yes, I do bloody know.'

'That's all you're getting.'

'It's so sweet.'

'It's so not sweet. I feel dirty. I don't like him. He's really annoying.'

'He has a big-time crush on you, too.'

'He does not.'

'Grace, shut up. He does. I mean, most blokes get all gooey round you because you're short and blonde and have big boobs, but his eyes sort of . . .'

'Sort of what?'

'Watch you.'

'No,' I say, but I know they do because I feel them.

'I'm with Danny,' I say firmly.

'I know, and he has girls phoning for him all the time, it's just biology, I guess.'

'Oh my God!' I gasp. A Range Rover with an SJS Construction motif on the side has pulled up outside the office. An old man is in the driver's seat. 'SJS Construction. SJS Construction. I'm sure that's what Len said.'

They're the evil graveyard destroyers. And this chap has parked on the frigging red route! I push my seat away from my desk, smooth down my dress and walk outside. I'm panting slightly. Gracie, don't get cross. I repeat the word 'calm' in my head as I walk towards the car. I knock on the passenger window and the old man opens it.

'Yes?' he barks. I feel about six years old in front of this man. He's huge. His head is nearly touching the roof. He has a big Michael Portillo nose, lots of silver hair and a wide older-man girth that the seat belt is stretched taut over. He's obviously got a lot of money, but something about his face and big gnarly hands tell you he worked very hard for it.

'I wanted to ask you something about the construction plans you have for the graveyard.'

First he groans, then he fixes me with the meanest stare I've ever seen. Whoa! This man looks like a proper bastard. I've never met a proper bastard before. It would be quite exciting if I didn't think I was going to wet myself.

'It will not affect the graveyard.'

'But your company's written to my mother. My father's buried there, and it's his grave you want to remove.'

'Who's your mother?'

'Rosemary Flowers.'

He smiles and opens his arms as though I'm an old friend. 'A lovely woman. I had no idea she was *the* Rosemary Flowers, the ballroom dancer. She still looks as youthful as ever.'

'You met my mother.'

'Yes, I received her letter and dropped by to thank her for her cooperation. We had a most pleasant chat. Nice little windfall for her. You should be pleased.'

'What?'

'The money we're offering is substantial.'

'You're bribing her?'

'No. Offering compensation.'

'Did … did you give her money?'

'No, but we will. When they all agree.'

'They won't all agree.'

'Young lady. You'd be surprised what money can buy. Your mother's looking forward to that money, don't be selfish and ruin it for her. And,' he stops here and smiles again, 'please do send your mother my love.' Then he looks into his rear-view mirror and pulls away.

'BASTARD! BASTARD!' I shriek after him.

'Grace!' It's John, striding across the road towards me. 'What's the matter?'

'Oh, don't get me started,' I say, breathing deeply to calm myself down.

'What?' he says, gently putting his hand on my shoulder. I nearly relax into his touch, but I can't forget that horrible man in a hurry. I wiggle free from Posh Boy's touch and go back into the office for my coat and car keys.

'Grace. What's this about?' He doesn't sound so smitten now he's seen me swearing at a car in the street.

'I've got a viewing,' I say, pushing past him to the door.

Chapter 22

It wasn't a lie. I do have a viewing. A few viewings, in fact, at Claire's flat. Or my unsellable flat, as I've started to think of it. Although I mustn't think that or I'll never sell it. I've never wanted an offer on a flat so much and I've never had less luck getting one. It's not helped by the fact that Posh Boy enquires how I'm doing with it about three times a day.

'Oh, yah, Grace, any luck on that messy three bed?'

'I'm working on it.'

'Righto, keep it up. I would have thought you'd have had an offer by now. Ha, ha.'

Really, one of these days I'm not going to be responsible for my actions and there will be an accident involving a violently thrown hole punch to his groin area.

I feel so sorry for Claire and I want to get her a good offer so she can move out of that place. It holds so many bad memories for her. Her husband was having massages in their bedroom – and saying yes to the happy ending. One afternoon she walked in there to fetch a baby monitor. She said she knocked three times first. I can't believe a man would do that in his own flat while his wife's in the house.

I've only shown the flat once. I've tried to take other clients to see it, but Claire always cancels, gently telling me it's not a good time. Anyone in her position would find it hard to keep her home fresh and tidy for potential buyers to look round, so I've arranged a block of viewings and am going over to help her have a spruce up before they arrive. Today is the big day – six viewings. It's a bit of a risk, I admit, but I'm desperate for an offer, not only to help Claire, but also to wipe the self-satisfied look off Posh Boy's face.

'Grace, hello. PATRICK, PUT THAT DOWN!' Claire says, opening the door and simultaneously taking another sanitary towel out of her son's hand. At least Claire's dry-eyed today – that's a big bonus.

'Sorry.' She sighs. 'He's obsessed with them, so I just give in and let him have them. I've started buying them specially. I'm hoping he'll grow out of it. I'll keep them out of sight when people are here.'

'Hiya,' I say, walking inside. 'Hello, beautiful boy, are you being good?'

'I eees ha sishe.'

I have no idea what he's trying to say.

'Ooh lovely, that sounds like fun,' I exclaim. I look to Claire to translate, but she's started crying. Already. Oh, dear.

'Are you all right?' I mouth.

She takes a big breath and attempts to smile.

'Patrick saw his daddy last night, didn't you, darling?' she says in a crazy, 'I'm trying to be happy' tone that sounds completely on the edge. 'And Patrick's going to have a little brother or sister.'

My mouth drops open as I look at Claire, but then I turn back to the child.

'Oh, Patrick, that's exciting. I wish I had lots of brothers and sisters, like you,' I say, picking him up. 'Now where's your twin sister, shall we go and say hello to her?' I walk into what Lube describes on the particulars as the large multi-purpose living space, but which is really the lounge/dining room/kitchen/playroom/nappy-changing area I secretly call the Room of Doom. Inside I find Patrick's twin sister, Daisy, staring at an old episode of *Murder She Wrote*. I hear Claire sob in the hallway.

'Hello, gorgeous,' I say to her. I put Patrick down and he walks straight over to his sister and belts her with a plastic digger.

'Patrick! You don't hit people.'

Daisy starts to cry. Brilliant. Our first viewers arrive in twenty minutes and she's bawling as the side of her face starts to go red.

'Oh, poppet,' I say, giving her a cuddle. 'Bruises are very in at the moment.' She puts her little arms around me and sniffles into my shoulder. I close my eyes for a second. Baby cuddles are so lovely. When I eventually open them I see that while she's hugging me she's also pinching Patrick. I flick her sticky hand off him.

'Ah, that's nice,' says Claire walking into the room and seeing the cuddle while missing the violence.

'How do you want to do this? One of us could take these terrors out for a walk and the other could tidy if you want.'

Claire's eyes open wide.

'Would you mind?'

'What, tidying?'

'No, taking them out in their buggy for a walk. That would be amazing. The baby's asleep, so it would be peaceful.'

'No, not all.'

I smile at her, feeling sad that she's so thrilled by the thought of fifteen minutes to herself, even if those fifteen minutes involve industrial-level cleaning.

I strap the children into the double buggy and bolt out of the door.

'*Weeeee*!' squeals Patrick.

I hope he's referring to the speed I'm going at and not to actually needing a wee. We've no time for that.

I want to pick up something from the picture framers. It's a present I've brought for Anton to thank him for being so kind on the night of my accident. I've been meaning to fetch it for over a week now, but I've been bottling it as it's a bit wet as presents go. All right, very wet. It's a picture I found in Portobello: a little drawing of a bridge over a rocky stream. That's not the wet part, though. The really damp bit is that I wrote in my best writing beneath it, 'Thank you for being my bridge over troubled water, Grace x'. It's quite unlike me to do something like this. I've never given Danny anything this soft, but I kept thinking about how safe I felt in Anton's car, and then I saw the picture and had a compulsion to buy it. I put it in to be framed, but now I'm worried that because I've had it framed he'll feel he has to display it. I've been getting in a bit of a tizz about it, to be honest. Perhaps I shouldn't give it to him after all. Maybe I'll get him a bottle of nice wine instead.

'Just get the frigging picture and give it to him,' I mumble, striding purposefully towards Ladbroke Grove.

The twins smack and pinch each other for the entire journey, and by the time we get to the framers I'm exhausted and I've only had them for seven minutes. The buggy is too wide to enter the shop, so I have to shout to the bloke, 'I'm picking up a picture, it's a little pencil drawing of a stream and a bridge.'

'Oh the "Bridge Over Troubled Water". For your fella, is it?'

'Um, no. Just a friend.'

The bloke raises his eyebrows.

'Here you go, love, looks lovely.'

I look at it and smile. It may be wet, but it does look nice.

'Thank you. That's great.'

'Very romantic. What did he do?'

'Nothing,' I exclaim.

'I'm joshing you, love. That's twenty quid.'

I give him the money and wend my way back. Now I'm not only worried that my present is wet, but that it may also look like a come on. Who'd have thought giving a present could be so problematic. I'll be sticking to M&S vouchers from now on.

At some point on the return journey the twins stop attacking each other, and when I take a peek at them they've dozed off. Result.

I put my finger to my lips when Claire opens the door, and she smiles and puts her thumb up. I walk in, leaving the buggy in the hall. The Room of Doom is looking positively feng shui.

'Brilliant,' I tell her.

'Excellent team work.'

'Dream team.'

'You've got the knack with the kids.'

I pull a funny face, because all I did was run them quickly along the uneven pavements of West London.

'You're not pregnant, are you?'

'No,' I say. 'Why?'

'Oh, just something my mum used to say. It's probably an old wives' tale. "If you've got a way with the babes, you've got a babe on the way." Or something like that. Coffee?'

I shudder. I don't like that old wives' tale very much.

Chapter 23

Leonard and Joan aren't here. They never miss a week at the graveyard except when they go to Dorset for two weeks every September, and they always tell me beforehand. I don't like it. I've eaten two doughnuts.

Still, I've had a good chat with Dad. What I tend to do in times of crisis is talk aloud about my problems while standing on Dad's grave until I come to some sort of conclusion. Then I state the conclusion loud and clear and wait for a sign. I always take it that Dad sanctions the outcome because my father was pretty canny and I'm sure if he didn't agree with a conclusion formulated on his grave he would let me know somehow, by dropping a branch on my head or getting a bird to poo on me or something.

'So you're saying you're cool with that?' I ask. 'I go to Mum's and open her bank letters with her; we work out how much she owes and then I get a loan and take over paying them off. Excellent. So that's the plan then. And she has to tell the evil SJS Construction people to shove their money right up their . . . Sorry, Dad. So that's it. Done deal.'

I look about me, waiting for a sign of discontent, but the sun moves from behind a cloud to dazzle Dad's grave, the silver birch and me with light.

'Nice.' I smile to Dad. Well, to his tombstone.

'Oh, Grace, Grace, a man came to see us.' It's Joan, looking very flustered for someone who's usually so elegant.

'Hiya,' I say. 'I was worried something had happened to you. Who came to see you?'

'Leonard is just parking. A man from SJS Construction. He visited us at our house about an hour ago. Oh, Grace, he's not a very nice man. He was quite threatening. I said we should go to the police, but Leonard said they'd laugh at us. I don't think they would, do you?'

'What did he say?'

'That we're the only people who've objected. He offered us . . . Well, Grace, he offered us an awful lot of money.'

'How much?'

'Twenty thousand pounds.'

'Twenty thousand pounds! And what did you say?'

'Well, I didn't speak, I let Leonard do the talking while I made the tea. I wish I hadn't made that man tea, Grace. I'll throw away the cup when I get home.'

'What did Leonard say?'

'He said that this spot was magic and couldn't be bought for any amount of money. He said no. He said it for you, too, Grace. He said that we three come here to pay our respects and that that is something that can't be bought.'

'Bloody goat!' shouts Leonard as he appears. 'I knew the chap as well. Not well, but I played cricket with him years ago. He came in like an old friend, didn't he, Joan? Joan even made tea for him! And then he turned, just like that . . .'

'He did, Grace, he did.'

'He of all people should know. He lost his wife years ago now, didn't he? What was her name?'

Joan shook her head.

'Oh, what was it? I had it a moment ago,' blusters Leonard.

'Lovely woman. Terrible when she died. He fell apart.'

'Leonard wrote him a lovely condolence card.'

'Now look what he's doing. This definitely calls for a letter to the *Gazette*. I'll get *London Tonight* onto this. Just you watch me.'

'Relax, Len, think of your blood pressure,' Joan soothes. I get out the doughnuts, but as I'm crossing Dad's grave with them I look up and I see something. There's a car parked on some industrial land across the canal. It's a great big Range Rover. Not just any old gas-guzzling Range Rover, mind, it has a logo on the side that looks suspiciously like the SJS Construction motif. There's a large silver-haired man standing beside it, and he's holding something up to his face. It might be binoculars, but it could also be a camera, so I hold a finger up for his benefit. I feel like a football hooligan, and it's not altogether unpleasant. That must be the land he wants to build on. And he obviously needs an access road down the side of the graveyard and over the canal. I keep my finger up until he gets back in his car.

'Now, then, Simon & Garfunkel anyone?'

Leonard and Joan don't respond, they just stare at me with sad eyes.

'It's all right, I'm going to make Mum change her mind, then the pressure won't be all on you,' I tell them, sounding far more confident than I feel.

Chapter 24

My mother. Now there's a sigh. Where to start with my mother? We used to get on when Dad was alive. To be honest, our lives were amazing when he was here. Life excited Dad. 'Grace, guess what I saw?' 'Rose, you'll never guess what happened!' 'Listen to this, my lovelies!' He would sweep us up in his amazement for the littlest things: a new version of a favourite song, a funny sitcom, a comfy sweater. He found wonder in everything and, as a result, so did we. But when he died and it was Mum and I alone, we didn't find anything wonderful, least of all each other.

I thought she was a princess when I was growing up, though. Every fairy-tale heroine looked like my mum in my imagination. When Cinderella danced with Prince Charming at the ball, it was my mum and dad doing the Viennese Waltz. Light as a butterfly she would cover the floor, her exquisite face lost in a dream, my father revering her as he moved her in his arms. She became the nation's sweetheart, with a manager to organise magazine interviews and TV appearances. She even appeared on *This Morning* with Richard and Judy.

The Rosemary Flowers you meet nowadays couldn't be more different. She hasn't left the house for at least three years. I can't be sure it's not longer than that, to be honest. I think it started the day I had my freak-out at the singing competition. When I say I screamed and screamed, I don't want you to think I made a few 'eek' sounds because that definitely wasn't the case. No, I howled. I howled as though someone was being murdered in front of me or I was being murdered myself. And I ran onto the stage, but only because it was the quickest route to the exit. A man appeared from backstage and caught me, while another ran from the audience to help him. They carried me out as I screamed and someone called an ambulance. I calmed down once we were outside, in the sense that I stopped yelling and started crying. I cried a lot that day – so much that I worried I'd never stop. I haven't cried since.

I don't remember my mother in the ambulance with me, but I do remember her at the hospital, how she dropped shaking to the floor as though she couldn't take any more of what life was offering her. When we returned home from that trip there was an unspoken agreement between us that we weren't terrific socially and that we should probably stay at home for a while. But whilst I eventually got going again, she didn't. She just got worse and worse. Now she sits at home all day, buying things on the internet, doing her workouts and thinking. I sometimes wonder whether I work really hard so I don't have time to think. There's nothing worse than having time on your hands to listen to those nagging voices of doubt inside your head. I'd rather sell houses.

Still, I shouldn't complain, at least I've stopped worrying that she'll kill herself. There was a time when Wendy and I were on suicide watch. It was horrible. Before Dad died my mum used to make her own dancing dresses. She'd go to the fabric stores in Shepherd's Bush market, where she'd haggle and flirt, then she'd come home with rolls and rolls of material and take to her sewing machine for days at a time. I would watch, fascinated, as the creation unfolded on the dressmaker's model. The pulsing bleat of the sewing machine was a regular backing track to my life growing up.

But during the dark years, as I call them, when it was me and Mum at home, she didn't touch the sewing machine. It sat there gathering dust and fluff, another symbol of a life given up on, until one day I came home from Danny's and heard the ghostly sound of the sewing machine from my past. I crept upstairs and into the spare room and there was my mother surrounded by swathes of velvet and silk, all richly textured, but all black. Weeks it took her, longer than any dress she'd ever made, and when she finished the result was chilling. It was by far the most beautiful dress I had ever seen, and I invited Wendy over to show her.

'It makes all those Oscar dresses look scabby,' Wendy whispered when she saw it.

It had a mid-calf-length skirt made of velvet, which was shaped around the hips and ruched slightly at the front, as though there were a train at the back. There wasn't a train, though, just a small kick of material that came from just under the bottom. The silk bodice rose to a heart-shaped top, with side panels of velvet, and she'd sewn row upon row of tiny beads and sequins across the front.

'What's it for?' Wendy whispered.

I shrugged.

'It's not a dress she could dance in. She wouldn't be able to move her legs. She doesn't need a dress to go out in because she never goes anywhere.'

'So what's she going to do with it?'

I froze.

'She's going to die in it.'

Wendy gasped.

'Don't be silly,' she said, but not in a way that suggested I was being silly.

We walked out of the spare room as though in a trance, then we raced through the house, hiding painkillers and sharp knives, convinced that my mother had made this beautiful dress to meet my dad in heaven. The Death Dress, we called it, and we only ever whispered in its presence. It sat on her dressmaker's dummy like an ominous premonition for over a year, then one day I walked into the spare room and it had been covered up by a plastic dress protector. I think that was the day my mother decided to live. Not that she really does live. More like buries herself alive.

These days it's virtually impossible to communicate with her. We do speak – I'm civil; she's vague – but that's it. Today, though, we're having to go beyond that, and it's not easy for either of us. We've been going round in circles for thirty-five minutes according to the cooker clock. We're getting nowhere, and now I've resorted to whining like an eight-year-old.

'***M-u-u-m***,'

'Grace, I don't want to hear another word on the subject. I'm accepting this man's kind offer.'

See! She's impossible.

'It's not a kind offer. How can it be a kind offer? It's a place I've gone to every week to be close to Dad.' My voice cracks, making us both recoil. I used to be so good at not crying, but for some reason tears keep popping up and having to be blinked or swallowed away at the moment. It's a right pain. I turn away from her and look out of the kitchen window. The back lawn needs mowing and buttercups are scattered across the lawn. I used to dance among them as a child singing, 'Build Me Up, Buttercup'. When I think the urge to cry has passed, I face her again.

'For ten years I've gone there to sing and talk to him, to wipe the bird poo off his grave and give him seasonal flowers, which I buy in Sainsbury's on the way. And I'm sorry, Mum, but you can't take that away from me.'

'Grace.' To give her credit, her voice sounds softer. 'I've signed the form. They've got my signature.'

'But you could retract it. You could say you've changed your mind. We could talk to him together. He lost his wife; he'd understand.'

She shakes her head silently.

'No, Grace, it's different for you.'

'Why?'

'I hate thinking of that cold dark place where he is, Grace. I can't do it . . . ' She turns away. This is unprecedented. Mum never mentions my dad being dead.

'But, Mum,' I say gently. 'Come with me. Come next Saturday. It's not cold or dark. The slutty silver birch whispers to him all day. It's a beautiful place to be laid to rest. I always thought we'd be laid next to him. Please, Mum, come with me next week. You can meet Leonard and Joan.'

'Who are they?'

'I told you when I met them. Their mum is buried near Dad.'

'I didn't know you still saw them.'

'Yes, every Saturday. They're fighting the construction company, but it's not fair for them to take all the flak on their own. Len's over seventy and he has high blood pressure, and SJS Construction seem like bullies.'

'The man I met seemed like a very nice man,' she says. I might be wrong, but she looks as though she's trying to suppress a smile as she says this.

'Mum, I'm with Leonard and Joan, but it's quite hard for me to be with them when my own mum wants to sell my dad's grave. But we'll fight it and we'll win, because everyone will be on our side. They want to build a slip road, but it shouldn't be built there, Mum. Please be on our side. On Dad's side.'

'I've signed a form.'

'We'll say you've changed your mind. Don't worry about the money.'

'There is no money, Grace.'

'How do you mean?'

'We had investments and I was given money each month, but when the banks went bust we lost most of it, so I started using credit cards, and now I either sell the grave or the house.'

'Oh, shit.'

'For once I agree with you, Grace.'

'I've got money coming in, Mum. I'll sort out your debts

and I'll give you money each week. Maybe not enough to buy luxury juicers on the internet, but enough to get by. We'll work out what you need.'

'I need at least the twenty thousand pounds that he's offering.'

'I'll get you twenty thousand pounds,' I say, even though it gives me palpitations to say it. 'I'll give you twenty thousand pounds so you don't have to sell my dad's grave.'

My mum doesn't say anything, we just stare at each other. Not angrily, not frostily, but curiously, as though we've just met for the first time but look familiar.

'I'm going to open that box of letters in the study now, Mum. I'll work out how much you owe and call some of them up. Let's see if I can get a handle on your financial situation.' I walk to the door. 'And if you're making yourself a cup of tea, or thinking about a gin at any point—'

'You're very strong, Grace,' my mum says quietly, and I may be wrong but I think I detect a note of admiration in her tone.

I look at her and smile.

'I love you, Mum,' I say.

She doesn't say, 'I love you, too,' but she nods and looks at me as though I might not be as bad as she'd previously feared.

'Oh, love, that's your phone,' she gestures towards my mobile, which is vibrating on the kitchen table. I pick it up. It's a text from Danny:

Need to have a chat to Dad about something.
Getting a train to Wales. Got Monday off. Back late
Monday night. Call you later. XX

'Everything all right?' Mum asks as I pull a strange face. Danny never goes to his parents' house without me. Why didn't he call? Why tell me I'm not going to see him all weekend by text?

'Yeah, yeah, everything's fine. It's just Dan,' I say.

And as I walk into Dad's study and turn the light on, I feel I might have turned a vital mother/daughter corner. Well, maybe not actually turned the corner, this is Gracie and Rosemary Flowers after all, but at least put the indicator on. It's a start anyway. 'You're very strong, Grace,' she said. It's the nicest thing she's said to me for so long. I wish I felt it, though. Instead I feel like an emotional liability at the moment. I must be due on.

Chapter 25

It feels so weird going out without Danny, even though I'm only at the pub. You'd think I'd be more comfortable as the pub's my second home and most of the time that I'm here with Dan he's either outside smoking or droning on to other blokes about football, but I have this strange feeling I've forgotten something. It could be my handbag or my knickers, but it's actually my six-foot-three boyfriend. I've had a good evening, though. Wendy and I are sitting in the restaurant part of the Festering Carbuncle, where we treated ourselves to deep-fried Camembert because there's nothing like deep fried cheese to start off a meal. We followed it with coq au vin. It's an old recipe of Anton's French grandmother's, which is unbelievable and comes with mashed potato – after extensive research, I can comfortably say that their mash is the best in the world – then for afters we shared an apple and rhubarb crumble.

Anton's not in the kitchen as it's his night off. I was looking forward to seeing him again, but it's probably for the best that he isn't here. I dropped the picture in this afternoon after I'd visited Mum. I came over all nervous and a little sweaty, so rather than ask for him, I gave it to a member of staff, told them to pass it on and then bolted. Freddie, Anton's son, isn't here either, so Wendy and I have spent a large part of the evening talking about how Wendy wants to marry him. Wendy's obsession with Freddie is very strange. In much the same way as I walked into the Festering Carbuncle for the first time and thought, Oh yeah, this is home, I want to live here, and made an offer on my maisonette, Wendy said, 'You see that bloke there, with the freckles and a half of Guinness. He's perfect.' I do worry about Wendy, though, because although she sleeps with quite a few men and flirts outrageously with them all, she's unable to form coherent sentences around Freddie. I think that might be a problem, coherent sentences being, on the whole, a good thing when you're trying to pull.

'Mmmm,' I say, spooning the last of the ice creamy crumbly bit from the bowl. 'Shall we share some cheese now?'

Wendy doesn't answer; she just stares at me and raises her newly threaded eyebrows.

'What? Your eyebrows look amazing now the red's gone down by the way.'

'Are you up the duff or something? You never eat this much. Normally you're brilliant to share pudding with because you only have one mouthful.'

Now it's my turn to stare. I raise my monobrow at her. Mine haven't been threaded.

'What?'

'Don't say that!"

'Oh.' She giggles and shares out the end of our bottle of white wine. 'I forgot about all that. Have you not had a period?'

'No.'

'Do you feel . . . you know, preg?'

'Wend, how do I know? I've never been pregnant.'

'Oh, yeah. Well, my sister cried all the time when she was pregnant.'

Massive monobrow raise.

'I keep wanting to cry. Like everyday. And you know me, I don't cry,' I admit.

'Yeah, but with all this stuff at work and your dad's grave and you being mugged, you're bound to be emotional. And you did take a shed load of hormones.'

'Oh, Wend, man, I so don't want to be pregnant,' I say with a large sigh. But she's not looking at me; she's looking towards the door and licking her lips.

'Is it Freddie?'

'Yep, Freddie and Anton have just walked in,' she whispers.

Now normally if Wendy spots someone she knows she gets up on her seat and shouts, 'Oi, hiya, come and join us, bring us a tequila en route!' But as it's Freddie, the object of her desire, she remains seated and looks the other away. It's Anton who spots us first as he walks towards his kitchen.

'Good evening,' he says warmly.

'Anton, we had the most brilliant meal,' Wendy tells him.

'Excellent, excellent,' he says, kissing her on the cheek and then turning to me. 'Grace,' he bends down to kiss me, too, and when he gets close to my ear I hear, 'Thank you for my picture.'

I nod, blush stupidly, kiss him on both cheeks and manage to inhale a lungful of Anton's lovely smell.

'Oi, Wendy, Grace,' says Freddie. 'What are we drinking?'

'My son,' Anton says, raising his eyes to the ceiling.

'Um, really, thanks.' Wendy sounds shy, which is so not her. 'I'd like a vodka tonic, if you're sure.'

'No worries,' Freddie calls. 'Grace?'

'I quite fancy some red wine, I was going to have some cheese,'

'Cheese and red wine, a lady after my own heart. Coming up,' says Anton, striding off.

Wendy's eyes are fixed on Freddie at the bar, while mine follow Anton into the kitchen, watching how he smiles and greets each of the chefs in turn.

'He's such a magic man,' I mutter to myself.

'You what?' shrieks Wendy.

'Anton. He's such a nice man. Everything's all right when he's around.'

'My future father-in-law. And here comes my future husband.' She gazes dreamily at Freddie.

'They've called last orders, the sods.'

'No way,' say Wendy and I in unison.

'How did it get so late?' I ask.

'Nah, it's all right. We'll get a drink, but we'll have to go upstairs. Is that OK?'

Wendy smiles. Actually, she beams. In fact, I'm a bit worried she might literally beam herself up, Scotty.

'Follow me,' he says, and we both get up.

'Dad!' Freddie shouts to Anton. 'They've called last orders, so we're going up.'

'Just coming,' Anton replies.

We walk behind the bar and through a door.

'Cool.' Wendy giggles.

It is. It's cool o'clock! I've always wanted to see what the upstairs of the pub looks like. Downstairs is decorated simply and rustically, leaving the old Victorian fireplaces and corniced ceiling to speak for themselves. It's a beautiful building on the outside, so you get the feeling that the two floors above the pub will be amazing, too. Or could be, if they'd been looked after. We walk up a narrow rickety staircase and through a door.

'Oh, wow!' Wendy whispers. 'Nice pad.'

I don't say anything. I just smile to myself. It's a huge open-plan space. There's a long wooden table surrounded by chairs on one side of the room, while the other side is taken up by big brown leather sofas. It's the same simple style as the pub below, only cosier. On one wall there's an assortment of photos, all in different frames, and on another there's a huge floor-to-ceiling bookcase. Wendy walks over to look at the photos and I walk towards the bookshelves to see if I can spot *The Five Year Plan*. I know, I'm ridiculous.

'Oh, is that you, Freddie? That chubby little baby,' Wendy coos.

Freddie joins Wendy at the pictures and I watch them, open-mouthed. Wendy has just uttered a sentence with all the words in the right order in Freddie's presence. I need to give them some space. I step away from the books and head towards the kitchen. This is a great space. I'm such an estate agent. Deep kitchen units sit on one wall and there's a proper coffee maker and big copper pots. I imagine myself sitting at the table, chatting and drinking wine while Anton cooks me coq au vin. There's even a healthy-looking plant on the table. I must remember to water my plants when I go home.

'Freddie, are your bedrooms upstairs?'

'Yeah, yeah, they are.'

'Can I have a look? Sorry, estate agent urge. It's just such a lovely home.'

'Go for your life,' he says with a big smile.

I walk back to the rickety staircase and climb up the remaining stairs, which creak beneath my feet. I pass slowly along a corridor lined with three closed doors. I peek in the first one, which looks like Freddie's room as it contains shelf upon shelf of law books, a big unmade bed and a double wardrobe with lots of shirts hanging in it.

I open the next door to find a bathroom, but it's not just any bathroom, it's huge for a start, and serious money has been spent on it. There's a big free-standing bath in the middle of the room, his and hers sinks, with a vintage mirror hanging above them, and a proper power shower that's so large you could probably break dance in it if you got the urge. It's exactly how I would like my bathroom to be if money was no object.

I open the last door to find a big square room that must be Anton's bedroom. I feel as if I shouldn't be in there, but I don't want to leave. A very large bed with a wood and leather head-board, white sheets and duvet sits in the middle of the room, and there are cupboards all along one side, although they're closed. There are only three pictures on the wall. One is a huge framed picture of a pretty young woman. It's a grainy blown-up photograph with an orange tinge that makes me think it was taken in the seventies. The other is a painting of the colour red. Literally. Different shades of red and orange and a bit of purple. But the third picture is the one I gave him. He's hung it on his wall already.

My bottom starts to vibrate as my mobile phone rings. I take it out of my jeans pocket. It's 11.23 p.m. and my mum is calling.

'Mum, are you all right?'

'Oh, Grace, I had to tell you. I went to bed and as I started to doze off, there was your dad again. He spoke to me and he was very firm about it, he said, "Grace has to sing."'

'Oh,' I say sadly. I was on a bit of a high this afternoon, thinking Mum and I had broken some ice during our conversation today. Silly really, Mum's mum and this is what she's like. 'I'll bear it in mind. You go to sleep, Mum. Love you.'

'Night night, Grace. And sing, like your dad said, sing.'

I put my phone back in my pocket and sigh. What does she expect me to do, break into song suddenly now? Maybe I should see if I can get a doctor round to see Mum. Maybe she's really ill. God, I wish I had a brother or sister. I lie down on Anton's bed. I know I shouldn't, but I've had a lot of wine so I lean back on the pillows. He buys expensive pillows, not like me. Mine are like sleeping on a bag of satsumas. I turn onto my side and breathe in Anton's smell from the pillow.

'Grace, I . . .' It's Anton and he stops when he sees me curled up on his bed sniffing his pillow.

I sit up quickly.

'Sorry, sorry, it was . . . It just looked so comfy.'

He stands there all smiling and unfazed. I would clobber someone who snooped round my home and got into my bed.

'I didn't like to say in front of Freddie and Wendy, but the picture you gave me: it's beautiful, quite the most beautiful gift anyone has ever given me. Thank you.'

'It's bordering on the wet,' I say, getting off the bed.

'I don't think that at all. And anyway, what's wrong with a bit of wet? All the best songs that have ever been written are a bit wet.'

I smile. He's right, of course.

'Now then, the cheese and wine is on the table downstairs, but I've also rigged up the karaoke. I wondered if we could have a bit of a sing-song while Wendy flirts with my son.'

I stare at him and I can feel my heart pounding.

Grace, are you OK?'

'I don't sing,' I whisper.

'Oh? I thought you must have trained as a singer?'

'You what?'

'When we were singing in the car ... your voice ... it's ...'

'You what?'

'When you sang in the car ...'

'What car?'

'The Simon & Garfunkel.'

'I didn't sing.'

'Yes, you did. We sang two songs together.'

'I sang.'

'Yes, don't you remember?'

'I didn't know I was doing it.' I haven't sang anywhere except the graveyard since the summer Dad died.

'Your voice. It's. It's ...'

'Like a heavy smoking black man?' I scoff.

'Gracie Flowers,' he sounds very serious all of a sudden.

'You have one of . . . if not the most beautiful voice I've ever heard.'

'Don't be daft.'

'Grace.' He takes my hand and clasps it in his own. It feels so lovely to have my hand in his that I get a stirring in my tummy and this strange sensation that I want to kiss this man who must be twice my age, here in his bedroom, and that it would be lovely. 'I've spent most of my life around musicians. What you've got is rare.' He releases my hand and the urge to kiss him disappears, like a bubble quickly burst. 'I haven't been able to stop thinking about how you sang that night. I wish I'd known I lived over the road from Dusty Springfield . . . I could have auditioned for *Britain Sings its Heart Out* with you.'

'Did you audition for *Britain Sings its Heart Out*?'

'I did. I'm going to be on the first of the televised heats,' he says bashfully. 'With a lady friend of mine, I couldn't do it alone.'

'Oh, well done. That's great.' I smile.

I hate *Britain Sings*. Not that I've ever seen it, for much the same reason that I don't listen to the radio, but I know it's a huge live singing contest that the whole country goes potty for once a year. It started just before my dad died. People used to suggest I go on it, but there was no way on earth I would. For years my mum used to go on about me entering it. It was ridiculous, my mother, who hated me doing singing competitions when I was a child and who saw me have a breakdown at a singing competition, passionately trying to convince me to enter. It must be due to start again soon. It's fairly obvious when a new series of *Britain Sings* starts because that's all people and the newspapers go on about for months. There are loads of heats and then all the finalists have to sing live one Saturday, and from what I can gather from the papers, the winner goes on to release a couple of terrible cover versions before retiring to the Butlin's circuit. I suppose I shouldn't knock it, I well wanted to be a Butlin's entertainer when I was younger.

'So, will you come downstairs and sing with me?' Anton says, holding out his hand.

And although I want to take his hand again, I stop myself. 'No thank you, Anton, I don't want to sing.'

'Oh.' He seems taken aback. 'Just cheese and biscuits then?'

'Now you're talking.'

Chapter 26

'Oh, Wend,' I groan. 'Oh, Wend. Oh, oh, o-o-h, Wend.'

'Shuddup,' she mumbles into the pillow.

'Oh, oh, o-o-h, oh, Wend, I need you to get up and get me water . . . please.'

'Grace?'

'Hmm.'

'Shuddup!'

'Or Coca Cola, or apple juice or, or do you know what I'd really like? An Irn-Bru. Oh, o-o-h, I'd commit unspeakable acts for an Irn-Bru. And an apple juice. With ice.'

'Gracie. Is this what you do to Danny on a Sunday morning?'

'But . . . but, you don't understand, my head. I had red wine after white wine and then whisky. Oh, oh, oh-o-o-o-o-oh . . . the pain.'

'Oh, bloody buggering hell.' She sits up.

'Oh, Wend . . . '

'Will you quit this whinging!'

'Oh, but something really bad happened.'

'When?'

'Last night.'

'Oh, shhhh. We had a great evening. We all sang, except you, of course. But even you wanted to, I could tell. I snogged my future husband for the first time. Well, we kissed on the lips without tongues, but it's a bloody good start. What's the problemo?'

'I had another.'

'Oh, Grace, speak in, like, words I can understand. Another what?' She suddenly gasps. 'Huh! Oh my God, another dirty dream.'

'Yep.'

'Oh my God, about Posh Boy?'

'No.'

'Jesus, who was this one about?'

'Anton.'

'Urgh! ANTON! You with my future father-in-law. And I was in the bed with you at the time. Urgh! Gracie Flowers, I feel sullied.'

'O-o-o-oh, I'm a sexual deviant,' I moan.

'Grace, there's someone at your door.'

'I can't go. I can never see anyone again or I'm liable to lust after them in my sleep.'

'Shall I go? Who will it be?'

'No idea.'

'I'll go down and see who it is.'

'Juice, juice,' I squeak as she leaves the room.

Twenty seconds later, she comes thundering up the stairs.

'It's your wet dream!'

'John?'

'No, Anton! For God's sake, Grace, keep up. I saw him through the window.'

'Oh, hang about,' I say, finally opening my eyes. 'Did we pay for dinner last night?'

'No. Oh, shittit. I can't remember. No. No, we didn't. Whose card did we leave behind the bar?'

'Mine. Oh, I have to get up. Help me.' I proffer a limp hand to Wendy, who hauls me from the bed.

'Whoa. Oh-oh, Wend, I don't feel very well,' I whimper, clinging onto her for support.

'Don't vom on me, Flowers,' she says, pushing me away gently. I stagger down the stairs in my pyjamas.

'Hello,' I mew when I open the door.

'Sore head?' Anton asks kindly. He's dressed and clean and looks all fresh. Oh dear, I think I'm blushing: the dream is coming back to me. I squint at him.

'Hmm,' I squeak.

'Gracie, my love, do you mind signing your card here?' he hands me a plate of bacon sandwiches, with my debit card and a pen sitting on top.

'Thank you.' I start to feel tearful. It's a bacon sandwich, Gracie, hold it together. I give him a shaky signature that looks nothing like mine. 'Anton?'

'Gracie.'

I stop for a second. The sight of his hairy chest poking out from the top of his shirt is distracting me. I was running my fingers through that hair last night in my dream. My hands were all over him last night. Oh no. Oh dear.

'Anton.' My mouth is so dry. 'Do you think I could possibly give you everything I own for an apple juice?'

He chuckles.

'Come with me,' he offers me his arm.

I look down at my feet. I'm not wearing any shoes and stepping outside my door barefoot is treacherous, what with the glass shop and all.

'Here,' he says, and he lifts me up as though he's just rescued me from a fire. He does it so gently and so easily that I could be slim. Wow!

'Would you mind carrying me around all day?' I say, bobbing across the road in his arms.

'It would be my pleasure.'

He pushes open the doors to his pub and lays me on the sofa by the fire.

'One revitalising apple juice coming up,' he says, chuckling again.

'Anton?'

'My lady.'

'I don't want you to think I'm high maintenance or anything, but do you think I could have some ice, too?'

'Certainly.'

'Ice, ice, baby,' I say, because I'm a pillock.

'Stay there, Keith Moon will look after you. I'm popping downstairs to the ice machine.'

I hear Keith Moon's dog energy enter the room, all paws and sniffs.

'Hello, my friend,' I say to his pretty face as he hops on the sofa and lies next to me. I'm sure he's not allowed on the leather sofa, but I haven't got the strength for doggy discipline.

'Dad!' It's Freddie voice.

'Hello!' I call to him. 'He's getting some ice.'

'Oh right. Grace, can I ask you something?'

He stands next to me and looks down. He's up and dressed as well. All these active people are tiring me out.

'Hmm,' I muster.

'Well, I know it's a bit forward.' He's whispering now and he's crouched down next to me. Ooh, this is promising, he's going to ask me something about Wendy.

I smile.

'Can I take you out for a meal one night?'

I stare at him. I'm confused so I have a double-chin-frown face on. I wait for him to say, 'Sorry, I mean Wendy,' but he doesn't, and he really should. My double-chin frown gets bigger.

'But I'm going out with Dan,' I say.

'Oh,' he says, seemingly confused by this fact, even though he's known about it ever since he met me. 'Oh, sorry.'

'Right, ice for the reluctant songstress.' Anton's back.

'Anton, thank you very much, all my worldly possessions are now yours,' I say, getting off the sofa and walking to the bar for my juice and bacon sandwiches. I nod and smile at Anton and Keith Moon while Freddie gets just a nod, then I head for the door.

'See you later for karaoke,' calls Anton, but I don't think I'll be going to that, thank you very much.

Chapter 27

'Good morning, Lube,' I say seriously. 'Gracie, you twat, you said Lube! Come on, sort it out. This is serious. You promised your mum you'd get her twenty grand. It starts here.'

I look at my reflection and try to arrange my features into what I hope is the expression of a cool, calm and collected businesswoman who deserves a morbidly obese pay rise.

'Ken, do you have time for a word?'

I shake my head. It's wrong. It's too weak.

'Ken, can I have a word?' I shake my head again. That sounds too flippant.

'Ken, I need a word.' Whoa! I shake my head really hard this time. That sounds far too hardcore.' I think for a moment.

'Ken, I'd like to discuss something with you.' Now we're talking. 'Ken, I'd like to discuss something with you,' I repeat. 'That's it! That's brilliant.'

I'm knocked off my stride, though, by the sight of my breasts. I'm wearing my non-crease pink blouse. It's normally very prim, but today it's all gone a bit *Carry On* as I'm bursting out of it. I'm due on any second, so my boobs are massive and painful, but if I do up my normal shirt button there's a gap between the top two buttons where you can clearly see boobage. I don't know whether to keep it done up and hunch forward a bit to minimise it, or just undo the top button for a bit of cleavage. Is cleavage a good idea when asking for a pay rise? I don't know. There was no mention of boobs in the *Guardian* article about asking for a pay rise that Wendy emailed me.

'Ken, I'd like to discuss something with you. I've been thinking ...' See, the problem with doing this is that I've known Ken for years and he'll say, 'Ooh, that must have hurt. Put the kettle on will you, Grace, while I just borrow your computer to check the football scores.' I need to drive it through. Deep breath. 'Ken, I'd like to discuss something with you. I understand that you've employed that Posh Twat.' Grace! 'I understand that you've employed John Twatface.' Grace! 'John Righto Whatsit Rah Rah, My Boxster's Parked on a Red Route, Rah.' Grace, behave. Regroup, refocus. 'I understand that you've employed John and that he's Estate Agent of the Year, which if you ask me is a major travesty to the profession.' Grace! 'I think you know that I was hoping for the Head of London Sales job myself. I bring a lot to this company, in terms of time and money. No other negotiator at Make A Move brings in even half as much as me in a month, as you well know. So as a goodwill gesture to encourage me to stay here, and so that I don't feel my hard work might be more appreciated elsewhere ...'

Ken will definitely go, 'Get to the bloody point, Grace. I think one of my kids just graduated while you were talking!'

'So cutting to the chase, Ken, I'd like a pay rise.' I step back. Even I find it shocking to hear myself say that. Ken will probably fall off his chair. But it's not bad. On the whole it's not bad.

I hear my phone. It's Mum. That's a shame; I was hoping it would be Danny. He didn't call me all weekend. I texted him loads, then I called and left a message. I got nothing back, which is very un-Dan.

'Hey, Mum,' I say, taking the phone in one hand and trying to squash my boobies down with the other. 'I'm wearing pink.'

'How did you know?'

'Just knew. You OK?'

'Hmm.'

'Sure?'

'Hmm.'

'OK. I'd better go. Love you.'

'Hmm.'

I hang up. There it is again. My five year plan. Blank.

Chapter 28

'Lu—' Terrible start. I stop, freeze and try to come up with an alternative ending. 'Lu-ook!' Yes, I know. Dreadful.

'What you lu-ooking at?' asks Wendy, acting innocent. She's very good at acting is Wendy, it's in her genes, although she's sucking her cheeks in, so I know she's trying not to laugh and that's not very RSC. I'm pleased she's nearly laughing. She took it really badly when I told her that Freddie had asked me out, but I had to tell her, didn't I? I couldn't *not* have told her. Although now I've made her unhappy and I hate that. Still, at least she's enjoying my current predicament.

'Oh tell us, Grace, what you lu-ooking at?'

'Oh, just lu-ooking at the lovely day.'

Lube, Posh Boy, Wendy and I peer outside at the inarguably drizzly, grey sky.

Not today, but one day, I'm going to tell him. I'm going to say, 'Ken, we call you Lube. Have done for years. It doesn't mean that when we think of you we think of sexual organs that need to be moistened. We just call you Lube. And I can't cope with trying to cover it up in your presence any more.'

Gah! Now I've forgotten my brilliant opening line.

'Ken, I'd like a word with you . . . ' I say. I don't think that was it. That sounded too pushy. 'Please,' I add to soften it.

'Jesus, Grace,' he exclaims as soon as I have his attention. 'Have you had a boob job?'

Not a *Guardian* start. I went for cleavage and, looking down, I realise it wasn't a wise choice and do the other button up.

'Ken, do you mind if we have a quick chat?'

'I'm all yours, Gracie Flowers, except for the bits that are my wife's.'

'In private, if that's OK?'

'Whoa.'

'Where's private?' asks Posh Boy, and I hate to say it, but it's actually a very intelligent question.

'The caff or the loo,' answers Wendy.

'Righto.'

One more time. I mean it. Stapler. Tie. Desk.

Lube looks at his watch. 'No time for the caff, babe. I'm picking Rosie up from ballet at half past. Two left feet, love her, and twice the size of the other girls. That's my side of the family, that. She's got legs like my mother's, poor love. Big and don't go in at the ankles. Still, you can't stop them having hobbies, can you. Stops them nicking stuff from the paper shop like I did.'

This is so Lube. He's either orating like a Roman Emperor about to invade Byzantium – or somewhere, I didn't do my history GCSE – or he's gossiping like a girl.

'The loo then,' I say, taking his elbow and steering him towards the office toilet.

'Ooh, up close with Pammie.'

'Pammie?'

'Pammie Anderson. Big bazooms.'

There are no words. We get to the toilet, which is one cubicle and a sink, and I sit Lube on the loo and stand in front of him.

'Cor blimey, Grace, I don't know where to look.'

'Try my face, Ken, my face.'

'You all right, petal? What can I do you for? Problema?'

Ken and his wife are looking to buy a house in Spain, hence the habit of putting an 'a' on the odd English word.

'Your Spanish is coming along.'

'*Gracias.*'

'Ken, I understand that you've employed John and he's Estate Agent of the Year, which if you ask me is a major travesty to the profession.' I kept that bit in, but Lube laughs all the same. There's nothing he likes more than a bit of backstabbing rivalry in his team. 'Well, I think you know that I was hoping for the Head of London Sales job myself. I bring a lot to this company, in terms of time and money. No other negotiator at Make A Move brings in even half as much as I do in a month, as you well know. I kick arse, Ken. So as a goodwill gesture, to encourage me to stay here so I don't feel that my hard work might be more appreciated elsewhere, can I have a pay rise?'

Oh my God, I did it. I think I need a lie-down now. Lube is staring at me and blinking.

'Jeez, Grace.'

'Do you understand where I'm coming from?'

'I do, Grace, and I love you like one of my girls.'

'Thank you.'

'Come here, love,' he says, pulling me towards him for a hug. 'Big, big respect for that, Gracie.'

'Do you think I've got big balls?'

'Oh, yeah.'

'Good.'

'I'll see what I can do, Grace, but I can't do anything straight away. I've got accountants looking at the company at the moment. Give us a month, two months tops, and I promise you, Gracie, you'll be sorted out.'

I must appear devastated by his answer because he immediately stands up and takes his wallet out of his back pocket. 'Do you want to borrow some?'

I consider saying, 'Yeah, can you do me twenty grand?'

'Five hundred quid do you for now?'

I smile. 'No, you're all right, Ken. I'll sort something out.'

Debt. I'm going to have to go into evil debt. I'll probably be parking in bus lanes soon.

Chapter 29

'Righto. Are we off?'

'AGAIN! You're not going to shadow me again, are you?'

He keeps doing this. Every time I have a viewing he stands up, puts his jacket on and says righto. 'You don't need to come to every viewing with me!'

'The last time you showed this family a flat, Grace, it was what you call in the trade a cock-up, so I'm coming along. I am, after all, here to mentor you.'

Him mentor *me*. Count slowly to 6,897 now, Grace.

'Sorry, John, how many sales have you made since you started here? Oh, let me count them for you.' I stand still and raise my eyes to the ceiling for a nanosecond. 'That didn't take long. None.'

'I'm expecting an offer on a—' he blusters.

'I started here as a sales negotiator on the Monday. On the Friday morning I had my first offer accepted. And I wasn't Estate Agent of the Year before I started. I was a receptionist.'

'Well, yes, but I have . . . It's early days for me. I'm here to learn the ropes and work it all out.'

'Come along, stop polluting the silence with your voice. We've got to get to a viewing,' I say, striding to the door.

'Never, never, never have I seen balls so big on one so small,' he mutters behind me.

Now I hate, loathe and detest Posh Boy, but I *love* the comment he just made. See how my positive big-ball affirmations are working!

'They're gigantic, John!' I yelp, and then I straddle my legs and waddle out of the door, nearly crashing into a lady with a toddler on the street outside. The toddler shows excellent initiative for one so wee and walks straight between my legs. Luckily, I'm wearing leggings or it could have been damaging. I laugh, and when John comes outside he laughs, too. John and I stand on the Chamberlayne Road laughing. But let's not get too excited by this. I still think he's a twat. Suddenly he gets me in a head lock and ruffles my hair.

'I know you love me really, Flowers. Righto. Where's your car?'

I wriggle free and punch him in the tummy. It's very hard. I bet he tensed.

'Over there,' I say, pointing at Nina.

'Oh, dear God.'

'Nina is very sensitive.'

'Nina. You've named *that* Nina.'

'She's Nina the Nissan Micra.'

'Why Nina?'

'After Nina Simone, why else?'

'Which one's she?'

'Which one's she?' I say, stopping dead in my tracks.

'Come along, stop polluting the silence with your speech. We've got to get to a viewing.'

'Which one's she?' I repeat.

'Can't we go in my car?'

'No we frigging can't. No one believes a word a man under thirty says if he drives a Porsche. I'm doing this for your own good. Now, the passenger side door doesn't open so you'll have to crawl through my side.'

'Oh, dear God,' he mutters as he folds himself up to get into the car. While he's crawling across to his seat, I notice his bottom. It's not bad . . . for a twat.

My phone buzzes when I'm in the car. Danny? No. It's Bob the Builder.

'Hey, sis. Just had an appointment cancel. I'll join you at the viewing. Chat to the lady about the garden.'

That's good news, but the fact that I haven't heard from Dan isn't. Something is very wrong. It's Wednesday today and he still isn't back. I got a brief text Monday night saying he'd be a few more days in Wales. It's weird.

'You all right?' asks Posh Boy.

'Fine,' I reply, starting the engine.

We're showing my favourite family one of Bob's new super duper flats. The kids are quite excited by this one, apparently, on account of the fact that it has a hot tub.

'Nice.' Posh Boy wolf whistles when we pull up.

The family are already assembled outside and I wave.

'Yeah, Bob's stuff's always good,' I say, getting out of the car and leaving Posh Boy to make his own way out of Nina.

'Hello there, how you all doing?'

'We're fine,' says the mother, smiling.

'OK, this one's empty. I've got the key. It should be immaculate. Sorry about last time.'

'Don't worry.'

I let us in. The smell of new paint and plaster hits my nostrils straight away. I don't normally like this aroma, but funnily enough today I do.

'Oh, yes,' the mother says as I lead her into the living room where we find high white walls, a tasteful fireplace and big sash windows. Her husband stands in the middle of the room and makes a 'bah' sound. It echoes slightly in the emptiness and he starts humming to himself. Emma, his daughter, runs up to him and sings something – a word or name, I'm not sure exactly – and her dad responds. It's a song they both know and it's familiar. Suddenly I recognise where it's from. *Evita*! That's it, they're singing a duet from *Evita*. Oh, I just love this family. They sing and smile together. I watch them and it could be me and my dad, when I was fifteen and he was still alive.

I clap when they finish and then we walk through to the all-mod-cons kitchen/breakfast room with patio doors out onto the garden.

'So the garden's not as big as the last one. He's going to turf it, but he said if you wanted any areas left for flowerbeds we can discuss that. He'll be here any minute so you can discuss it with him yourself if you like.'

The mother stands there with a dreamy look in her eyes. This is going very well. This is much more like it. I lead them back into the hallway.

'Now then, this room is very important,' I say in a hushed

reverential tone. 'This, is the hot-tub room. Oh yes, with electrics for a telly as well. Are we ready?' I wait with my hand on the doorknob for a few moments to build the tension, because this bathroom really is pumping. Bob the Builder loves a hot tub at the end of a working day, so it's become his trademark.

'Yes.' The son giggles.

'Are you sure you're ready?'

'YES!'

'Absolutely sure you're ready to see the biggest hot tub in the world.'

'Hello there.' It's Bob, striding through the hall towards us. 'Has my sis been looking after you?'

'Is that your brother?' the girl asks.

'He's my chosen brother,' I tell her.

'What do you think?' he asks Mr and Mrs Hammond.

'Beautiful.'

'Yes, they've turned out well. This is my favourite room in the house, I'm a hot-tub fiend, me,' Bob explains with a smile.

'Ta da!' I say, opening the door. I don't look inside. Instead I watch their faces. Their mouths drop open, but not in delight, as I'd expected, but in horror. Bob takes a step back and looks as though he might faint. I look inside.

'OH MY GOD!' I scream. And that causes the woman sitting on the edge of the hot tub with a man's head between her legs to scream as well.

'ARGH!' we both holler.

She tries to cover herself with her hands while the man bobs his head underwater.

'Oh my God!' I shut the door. 'Oh my God, I am so sorry.'

Bob's gone. No one speaks. Whoa. That goes straight in at number one in my top crap viewings chart.

'I think we'd better go,' says the dad, and they all file out silently.

'I am so sorry. I am so sorry. I am so sorry.' I'm stuck on repeat. Jesus. This is terrible. I'll lose my favourite family. I've scarred the children for life. But that's not the worst of it, the really awful part is that the lady in the hot tub was Bob's girlfriend Stella. Bob's one of life's good guys; he doesn't deserve this. I walk back to the car, feeling sad, and find Posh Boy already seated inside.

'You all right?' he asks.

'No, I'm in shock.'

'Yeah, that was bad. Not as bad as the time a bloke had a heart attack on me.'

'No?!'

'Yeah. That's my crap viewing number one. What's yours?'

'Well, until now it was the time I walked in on a naked old man having a poo.'

'Yes, I can see how that would be unpleasant.'

'But I think this might have just pipped it to the top spot. Oh, that's my phone.' It's Dan. Finally. 'I just need to take this before we head back.'

I get out of the car and close the door.

'Hey, Welsh boyo!'

Danny doesn't say anything.

'Dan.'

He still doesn't say anything.

'Dan?'

I hear him sniff.

'Dan, are you ill?'

'No, oh . . . '

He's crying. Danny's crying! My Danny doesn't cry. He makes computer games, for God's sake. The only time I've seen him cry was a tiny tear during a particularly emotional episode of *60 Minute Makeover*.

'Danny,' I whisper. 'What's going on up there?'

'Nothing.' He sniffs again. 'I'm sorry, you're at work. I'd better go.'

He sounds devastated about something. The line goes dead, so I call back, but there's no answer. I walk back to the car and John Whatsit.

'You all right?'

'No. I, um. Very random this . . . but I need to go to Wales.'

'Right.'

'My boyfriend's there and something's happened. He's crying. I think it must be one of his parents. I think they might be ill. Like really ill.'

'Go. Wendy can cancel your appointments. It'll give the rest of us a chance to catch up with you. Just make sure you drive safely.'

'Thanks, John. Big lots of thanks and sorrys for this. I'll drop you back and then head straight off.'

I start the engine just as two figures emerge from the flat we've just viewed. One is Stella, and the other I now recognise as Bob's right-hand man, Pawel the Polish builder.

Chapter 30

It must be his mum. Danny and his mum are really close. He'd fall apart if he lost his mum. And what would his dad do? God, I don't think his dad knows where the kitchen is. We'll have to go there more often. We could go most weekends. I'll have to make lasagnes and leave them in the freezer.

Brilliant. They've still blocked off a lane of the M4 for no apparent reason again. My phone rings again. It's Dan.

'Dan.'

'Grace, no, it's his mum. It's me, Pam.'

'Oh, Pam.' My eyes fill with tears again. I've hit twenty-six and become a blubbering mess. Oh dear, not so good when driving. 'Pam, how are you? I'm on the M4. I'll only be a few hours.'

I can hear Danny in the background, sobbing!

'Grace, my love. Will you pull over at the next services and give us a call on the landline.'

'Oh, God. Yes, of course. I think Reading's coming up.'

We hang up. Jesus. Maybe his dad has died. Or maybe it's his mum and she's putting on a brave face for the boys.

'Come on Reading,' I chant. There's a sentence I never thought I'd say.

'Oh, my God,' I say aloud. 'Maybe it's Danny.'

Danny might be the one who's desperately ill. I didn't even think of that.

He hasn't been himself lately. He's been withdrawn. I think someone in his family had leukaemia at some point and went back to Wales. When people are ill they always want their mums.

'Oh, please God. I know this is a cheek because we don't have history together, but can you look out for my Dan.'

Danny is my backbone. Danny is the one thing in my life that has been fixed and constant since Dad died. He's my Dan. We're Gracie and Dan. It can't just be Gracie.

'Please, don't take Danny from me, too. Please let me keep Danny,' I whisper to the Big Man.

I finally park at Reading Services and catch my reflection in the rear-view mirror. I'm Addams Family pale. I take a deep breath.

'Grace, be strong. This isn't your crisis; it's theirs. Be strong and you can help them through it,' I whisper to myself.

I dial their number.

'Hello, Pam speaking.' She doesn't sound herself.

'Hi, Pam,' I try to make my voice sound soothing. 'I've pulled up at Reading.'

'Oh, Grace. Danny's been in a terrible state.'

I suddenly feel like an awful girlfriend. I haven't been there for him. He's been going through all this alone.

'I know, Pam. What's wrong?'

'Oh. Grace. I'm just going to come out with it.'

It's Danny in the background again. A strangulated sob. It must be his dad. That's how I cried. He probably didn't want to tell me because it would bring back memories of losing my father. Poor Dan.

'OK . . . take your time, Pam.'

'Oh Grace, you're such a lovely girl. I love you like a daughter.'

'Thanks, Pam. That means so much.'

'But he doesn't want to be in a relationship with you any more, Grace. I think he feels you've grown apart.'

I don't say anything. I just listen to Danny crying in the background.

'Grace, did you hear me?'

I did hear her, but I can't speak.

'Grace, love, he didn't know how to tell you, because he still cares so much for you. So I thought I should tell you. Was that wrong of me? Oh, love. We're all so sorry.'

I don't say anything, but I'm thinking about it. Somewhere in my mind I'm trying to formulate a sentence, a sentence that says there's too much between us to throw away, or something like that, but not so trite. But then Pam starts speaking again before I can think of one.

'He's got a new job, Grace. A terrific job. But it's in

Vancouver. And he's going to take it. He leaves on Friday. This Friday. We're going to bring a van up tomorrow and get his stuff from the flat.'

I still don't say anything. I simply turn off the phone and let it fall through my fingers. Then I gaze out of the window at Reading Services and it starts to rain.

Chapter 31

I stayed at Reading Services all night and most of the following day. I could have booked myself into the Travelodge, but I didn't want to talk to anyone. I didn't even want to say, 'Can I have a room, please?' I just sat in my car, kept my phone switched off and gazed out of the windscreen. Sometimes I opened the window. The smell of diesel was surprisingly comforting. If I needed the loo, I went inside, and at each loo stop I bought a Twister ice lolly. It occurred to me at one point that I need never leave Reading Services, and the thought didn't even strike me as worrying. I did leave, though. At five o'clock I started my engine and began the slow journey home, but when I got near I saw that Danny and his parents were still there – a white van with 'Cymru Vehicle Hire' on the side was parked outside the flat – so I did a U-turn and came to the office.

John Whatsit's still inside. I can see him squinting at his

computer so I back away from the door carefully, hoping he won't see me. I'll have to go to the cemetery, I think, heading back to my car.

'GRACE!' It's Wendy. She's rushing out of the office towards me. I quicken my step, but she's quick is Wendy. She always beats me. It's the extra three inches she's got on me. Before I reach my car she touches my shoulder.

'Oh, poppet, come here,' she says and puts her arm around me. 'Danny's mum called the office and told me. We couldn't get hold of you. I've been really worried.'

I rest my head on her shoulder.

'You know I liked Danny,' she says while we're hugging, 'but what a cock.'

I don't say anything. I don't think he's a cock. Not really. Well, maybe a bit.

'Come in the office, I'll make tea.'

I hang back. I don't mind Wendy, but I don't want to see John.

'John'll be fine. He's been really worried about you since you left yesterday. I haven't told him about Dan, though. He thinks something's happened to someone in Wales. He's fine. Come in.'

I let her lead me into Make A Move.

'Gracie,' John says, standing up. Then he realises he doesn't know what to do, so he hovers. He looks like he wants to give me a hug. Please don't, I think. And as if hearing my thoughts, he smiles and sits down again.

'Sit on the sofa,' coos Wendy. 'I'll do tea.'

Wendy scuttles out and I sit on the sofa, looking down at the brown leather.

'You had an offer,' John says in his 'I'm speaking to an under five' voice.

I glance up, hoping it's for Claire's flat.

'On that Harrow Road studio.'

I look back at the leather.

'The, um, the new penthouses are amazing.'

'Yeah, they were pumping, Grace,' Wendy calls out. 'You should see the kitchens. They're like something out of a movie. And tell her about the church we've got, John.'

'Oh, yes, there's one came on this morning that will get you going. Two mill but worth it. It's a converted church. It's unbelievable how they've done it . . . Grace, are you OK?'

'Tea!' It's Wendy back. 'So how are we doing?'

She sits next to me on the settee.

'She's not feeling that talkative, are you, Grace?' John says. I just look at him.

There's a pause.

'Oh, no,' says Wendy eventually. 'Come on, Grace, say something. Anything. Tell me to bog off if you want. *Grace.*' It's the strict Wendy voice. 'TALK TO ME NOW!'

'Wendy, she's obviously had a shock, don't shout at her.'

'That's exactly why I do need to shout at her.'

'GRACE! Oh, this is bad. I can't remember what happened last time to make her speak.'

'What?'

'She didn't speak for months one time years ago. I can't remember what happened to make her start again.'

When I was thinking about how my dad dying hadn't really messed me up, apart from me not listening to the radio any more, I forgot about this. This doesn't really happen that often, so it barely counts. Basically, when I get a sudden shock I stop speaking. I know, it's ridiculous. The most I've ever gone is two months. That was when Dad died. At the time everyone was yaking and crying. People would visit and everyone wanted to talk over the silence. I quite liked the fact that in my own head I could hear my dad talking and singing to me. No one noticed for ages, not even me. Every one was in meltdown when Dad died. Mum, their coach, their manager, other dancers, friends. It was only when the nice lady who used to live next door spoke to Mum and suggested I go to see a doctor that anyone realised I'd been mute for weeks. Mum thought I just wanted to get attention, but the nice lady took me to the doctor, who was supposed to examine me. I think she found it quite hard, though, on account of my not answering any of her questions. She was lovely that lady who used to live next door to us. She moved to Australia years ago, but we still write. She sent me Homebase vouchers when I moved into my flat, which is very canny if you think about it, her being in Australia and all.

'Has someone died?' John whispers, although it's a wasted whisper since I can hear him.

'John, maybe you should leave us alone.'

'I can if you want. But I must say, Wendy, I wouldn't speak if you were shouting at me. She's had a shock and she doesn't want to speak. We should respect that. We need to be calm, then hopefully she'll relax. Why don't we go over the road and get a pizza. We don't have to talk. We can read the *Standard*. Come on, my treat.'

That's nice of Posh Boy, I think. I look at his face and consider that maybe I've been a bit hard on him. He was kind when I was mugged and he's being kind now I'm in freak mode. Perhaps if we'd met under different circumstances, if he hadn't come waltzing in, stolen my job and annoyed me senseless, we might be friends.

Wendy shrugs and looks at me. I'm starving and he did say it was his treat, so I stand up.

'All right,' says Wendy, 'but if she hasn't spoken by the end of dinner, I'm back to shouting.'

'Come on Grace,' John says gently, holding the door open for me. 'It's actually quite odd her being here and not berating me. I almost miss the abuse. Come on fish wife,' he calls back to Wendy.

'Zip it, Posh Boy,' she says, doing an impression of me.

Chapter 32

You know that sensation you get just before you're going to be sick, when your mouth suddenly fills with gallons of hot saliva. Well, I've got that. I've had it since we walked in the restaurant. I wish I hadn't come now.

'Shall we do our usual?' asks Wendy. We always share the same pizza and salad. We get the amazing vegetarian pizza with salami and ham on it. Seriously, it's next level. But I don't want ham today. I don't know what I want. It must be because there's a funny smell in here. I'm sure it doesn't smell normal. No one else has said anything, though.

Maybe I should go to the toilets and make myself sick. No, that's mank. I'll be fine. It's probably because I've eaten nothing but ice lollies for the last twenty-four hours. I should have consumed a sandwich at some point, but it didn't occur to me.

Oh, but we're not even sitting near the toilets. They're at the back, downstairs, and I'm closer to the door. If I'm going to be sick it'll have to be outside the front door on the street.

I can't believe I'm sat here planning a path to puke. Mind you, at least it takes my mind off Dan leaving.

I don't think I'll be able to do the ham pizza. This peculiar smell is too meaty. I hold my menu out and point to a pasta dish with a spicy tomato sauce.

'Bloody hell, Grace. Pasta?' says Wendy.

'It's nice that, Grace, I've had it before. It's got a little kick.'

John flags down a waiter and orders for me and him. Wendy asks for her own veggie pizza with ham and salami.

'Grace,' he says when the waiter's gone. 'Take the rest of the week off. Don't come back until Monday. Everything will be fine.'

I think of my job and the Estate Agent of the Year competition, and I feel myself letting them go. I feel myself letting everything go. Then I remember how I haven't done my new five year plan yet. Maybe that's why everything is unravelling.

A waitress strides towards the table next door holding two plates.

'Who's having the liver special?' she asks.

That's the smell, it's liver – and it's next to me! Oh it's foul! And it's inches from my nose. More hot saliva fills my mouth as she places the dish in front of the man to my right.

'Ooh, look at that,' says the man, and he picks up his knife and cuts into it.

I try to swallow but I can't. Suddenly I'm pushing my chair away from the table. My hand is over my mouth and I'm running out of the door. I'm sick as soon as I'm outside.

'Here have some water, you poor thing.' It's John. He's holding a glass of water towards me. I take it and splash some on my shoes. then I drink the rest. It's not very cold. I wish it was. I wish it had ice in it. What I'd really like more than anything is a big personal iceberg, in cola or cherry flavour, which I could lick and lick. Oh, what's happening to me?

I look forlornly at Posh Boy. I can't speak. My boyfriend has dumped me. I've just been sick, and I hope it's caused by an overdose of ice lollies because the alternative is just … oh God, it's just too awful to contemplate.

Posh Boy opens his arms, then he walks forwards and wraps them around me. It's a very brave gesture as it presses my sicky mouth up against his shirt. It's a good hug, not limp or brief, but long and strong. I close my eyes and feel grateful for it.

'She's had a real shock, hasn't she,' he says when Wendy joins us outside.

'Yeah,' Wendy says quietly, stroking my hair. 'She's having a bit of a shocker.'

Chapter 33

'Oh! It's you, innit! Your face is well better. I've got summit for you.'

It's the young girl from the pharmacy. She reaches under the counter and pulls out my purple bag, the one that was stolen. God, that night feels like a hundred Christmases ago.

'This is it, innit. You said it were purple.'

I take it from her and open it.

'Yeah, theys took most of the stuff.'

They certainly did. All that's left inside is a battered tin of Vaseline, some tissues and odd bits of paper with random notes on them. At least I got the bag back, though. I really like this bag.

'It wasn't my brother. Not that I'm telling you who it was, you understand.'

I put the bag to my nose. I'm sniffing everything at the moment. I feel as though someone's given me a new nose and it works completely differently from my old one. Some smells make me feel nauseous, like the liver. But some smells I love, like diesel and bleach. The bag doesn't smell of anything. The girl looks at me strangely.

'I hope your nice fella is taking care of you now. He looked like that bloke in . . . what's those films called?' She looks at me hopefully. 'Oh, you must know. Like, er, like vampires or summink. Anyway, him. Fit. *Twilight* films! That's what they are. He looks like that bloke. Does everyone say that?'

I push the pregnancy test towards her across the counter and reach into my other bag for my purse. She glances at it.

'*Sh-i-i-i-t!*' she says, just as the pharmacist walks out of his Tablet Tardis.

'I hope you didn't say what I thought I heard you say,' he sings. But then he stops when he sees me.

'Hello again.' He smiles; he sees hundreds of people each week, why does he have to remember me? People often remember me, and I have a sneaky suspicion it's because I'm short. I don't want anyone to remember me today, though.

I nod at the pharmacist and turn back to the cashier girl.

'Are you all right?' says the pharmacist.

I nod.

'She's got the ump, today, hasn't said a word.'

I keep my head down, take ten quid out of my purse to pay for the pregnancy test and hold it out for her. Oh, why do I have to be so weird? Why? I don't know anyone else who this happens to. No one else has a ridiculous inability to speak when in shock. It seems crazy that I can't be polite and talk to her, but I don't have any control over it. My voice just isn't there. It's not connected to me any more. I can't do words at the moment.

'Do you . . . ?' the pharmacist starts speaking, but stops when his eyes fall on what I'm buying.

'Thanks for getting my bag back. You shouldn't have,' the girl says sarcastically as she hands me my change.

I turn away quickly. I want to be back at home. I rush to leave, but I feel a hand on my arm, and when I turn it's the pharmacist.

'You may not want to speak, and why should you? Tara over there could do with learning something about the fine art of silence. She means well, though. But this, with you, could be some form of mutism bought on by trauma, I don't know?'

I look up at him. That's what the doctor said when my voice went before. I remember him calling it selective mutism. The pharmacist smiles. 'My daughter had it when she was tiny. You don't need to speak to me, but if you need any help with the results of that test – or if you need anything for the anxiety you're feeling – you know where I am.' He sighs. 'I'm in the middle of Sainsbury's.'

I look about me. It must be strange working here, under the fluorescent lights, surrounded by groceries. I nod, then I go and locate the ice-cream section.

Chapter 34

I wanted Danny and I to be a love story. Not an 'I went out with this bloke for ten years and he got his mum to dump me' story. I wanted us to be a love story like my mum and dad were. Except without the bit where one of us dies and the other one goes mad. I wanted a love story like theirs. Theirs was proper love. The real deal. I used to love hearing about how Mum and Dad met. My mum was fifteen – the same age as I was when I met Dan, which I thought was a sign. My dad was older, though. He was nineteen. They met in Edinburgh at a ballroom dancing competition. My mum was brought up in the Highlands of Scotland, although you wouldn't know it now because she speaks with a plummy English accent. Her mum and dad were strict, humourless Catholics from what I've heard, though I never met them. They disowned my mother when she got pregnant out of wedlock by an atheist, and they've both died since.

Dad saw my mother for the first time dancing a Viennese

Waltz. He said he couldn't take his eyes off her, that she quite literally glowed and made everyone else in the room look dull and glum by comparison. It was at the end of the dance, when mum was curtsying, that she noticed my dad. She told me she saw the most beautiful man she'd ever seen and his eyes were fixed on her and he was smiling. She said she knew that he was the man she was going to love forever. They got their wires crossed for a while at the beginning, though, because my dad just wanted my mother to be his dancing partner, while my mother wanted Dad to be her *naked* dancing partner, if you know what I mean. My dad got his wish first, as Mum came down to London and started dancing with him. She moved into his family home and proceeded to throw herself upon him at every opportunity. Dad resisted Mum's advances at first because he thought she was too young, a child still, but on her seventeenth birthday they kissed for the first time. I loved that story, but I thought Danny and I had our own story. We met at school. He asked me to the prom. That's what I wanted to tell our children. I sigh. I'm still clutching the bag from the pharmacy. I haven't taken the test yet.

Danny has to come home. He can't just leave. Maybe it's a ten-year itch. He's bound to get to America and go, What the? I've forgot me Gracie. This won't do, and come home. Surely he can't bolt like this. We're Danny and Gracie. Gracie and Dan.

I'm sitting here in the lounge, alone on a Saturday night. I don't want to be in our bed upstairs. It's the extra-long bed we bought because Danny is so tall. They should have taken it. Mind you, it's probably quite tricky to check in at the airport. I keep expecting him to walk in, sit down next to me and start playing computer games, smelling of chips and beer and boy sweat. But, of course, the games have gone, and so has he. His hands, his smile, his big safe presence. It's all gone to America.

Or maybe not. I can hear something downstairs. A key in the lock. He's come back. Oh, thank you, God. I knew he couldn't just leave me like that. I run to the top of the stairs, but it's not him, it's Wendy.

'No need to look so pleased to see me!'

I gave her a set of keys to the flat, just in case I locked myself out or was away and she needed to get in for some reason.

'Gracie, I'm moving in. For as long as it takes to get you chatting, OK? I've brought the *Mad Men* box set.' She holds the cover towards me. 'Is it me or does this Don Draper fellow remind you of Anton over the road? And I've got chocolate . . . and I don't want any arguments.' She laughs. 'Not that I'll be getting any.'

She walks up the stairs.

'It's been ten years since this happened before: me chatting to you and trying to get you to let me in. You've become uber-efficient estate agent woman since then. I'd forgotten about little Gracie who didn't talk that time. I mean, when you do speak it's generally a load of old bollocks, but I do miss it. We'll get you speaking again, I promise.'

I sit back down on the sofa and pull the duvet around me. The paper bag I bought back from the pharmacy falls to the ground.

'What have you dropped?' asks Wendy, picking it up and looking inside. 'Oh,' she immediately stops flitting around, looks at me and sighs with a smile. 'Yeah, I wondered with you being sick. Do you think you might be? Oh, Grace, we'd better do the test and get it over with. It's bound to be worse not knowing. Go on.' She holds it out to me. 'Go pee on a stick.'

Who could resist such a tempting offer? Not me. I've been putting it off for hours, but I do actually need the toilet. I walk into the bathroom, shut the door and unwrap the plastic test stick. It looks a bit like a kazoo. You wouldn't want to confuse the two, I think, as I try to wee on it.

I sit it on the bathroom shelf next to the dead cactus and then I go back to Wendy in the living room.

'I reckon we do the whole first series,' she says, looking at the DVD box. If we get hungry I'll buy us sausage and mash from the pub later.'

I can't think of anything I'd like to do less than eat a sausage, except maybe be pregnant.

'I don't think you're pregnant,' Wendy starts conjecturing. 'You took the morning-after pill, and it's good, that. I've taken it. You're probably just late because of Danny 'I'm too weak to talk to my girlfriend myself, so I'll get my mum to do it' Saunders. I could kill him. Jesus. You're bound to feel awful and miss a period. Come on, how many times since we've known each other have we been here doing preg tests and they're always negative. You pay ten quid and then come on the next day. It's a conspiracy, I reckon.'

She's right. We've both done them before. I don't know how many times we've been stuck in a loo, crouched over a kazoo, waiting to see if we had a two-pink-lines situation. But this time I know I'm pregnant. It's a feeling. I know I'm carrying a baby. Well, it wouldn't be a baby yet, more like a bean. A bean of a baby. A baby bean.

I walk, incredibly slowly, back into the bathroom. I don't go straight to the test. I give the sink a spray and a wipe first, then I throw away Danny's toothbrush. I clean the mirror and pick up the bin to empty it outside. Then I freeze for a moment, holding my bathroom bin. Perhaps I'm not pregnant. Wendy could be right. We've been here before. It might be just the same as before. There could well be only one pink line, like last time. I put the bin down, close my eyes and creep towards the shelf where the pregnancy test sits waiting.

When my legs bang against the bath I know I'm within sight of the kazoo. I stand still, breathing deeply, then I open my eyes. Two unmistakable pink lines look back at me.

I'm pregnant.

Shit.

Chapter 35

Wendy has always been there for me. Always. Well, always, since the age of eleven. She went to Kensal Rise Community College with me, so I suppose we were destined to be best friends on account of the fact that my dad was a ballroom dancer and hers was an actor. When we were at school Wendy's dad was in a long-running series of commercials for Homebase. In the ads he had to dress up in a Jacobean outfit, with ballooning shorts over tights and a massive ruffle around his neck, and each ad consisted of him eulogising, whooping and screaming, 'I've never seen anything like it!' over something like a drill or a lawn mower or a barbeque. The one for the best ever bathroom sale is the most famous. It's still featured on those 'Best Ever Adverts' shows you get on Channel 4 occasionally. It was very cheesy, with Wendy's dad getting carried away by the concept of a toilet and then settling down on it to do a jobby. As you can imagine, Wendy was fodder for some pant-wettingly funny teasing. She was pursued through secondary school by teenagers doing bad impressions of her father shouting, 'I've never seen anything like it!'

The ads made him quite a bit of money, but sadly he was always known as the bloke from the Homebase ads, so he didn't get much other work, and now he teaches acting in a girls' school in Highgate. I often think Wendy is wasted at Make A Move. All through school she wanted to be a nurse. She did her A Levels and got into nursing college, and she was so excited about starting, but she passed out in the second week when she was shown some plasma. She kept at it, but it became clear by the end of the first term that she would only be able to be a nurse if she was guaranteed never to come into contact with blood or open wounds. She didn't go back after the first Christmas break. She was a bit lost for a while, like me, so as soon as I heard there was a job at Make A Move, I raved about her to Lube until she got it. But she's so caring and kind and selfless I can't help but feel there's something more for her out there somewhere.

'I thought you might need ice cream,' she says, smiling and handing me a tub of Ben & Jerry's Phish Food. See how kind she is. I sniff it. Delish. She's got her own tub of Chocolate Fudge Brownie. Wendy doesn't like Phish Food; she says it's too 'confused' a flavour. I love that Wendy takes her food so seriously.

'I don't want you to think this is terrible, Grace,' she says to me, pointing her licked spoon in my direction. She's in her familiar Freddie lookout pose, which involves moving my armchair so that she can subtly keep an eye on the pub over the road. It's not as easy as one might think, on account of the fact that we want to keep the lights on in the room and she doesn't want to be seen. So she sits on the arm of the chair and leans her head against the wall, peeking through the gap between wall and curtain. She's very good at talking to me whilst keeping a peripheral eye out for Freddie, although it must hurt her neck after a while.

'It's just an unplanned pregnancy, Grace. I bet hundreds of them happen every day. Just think of all those girls peeing on sticks across the world going, "Oh bollocks!" when they see the pink lines. And like everyone else you have two options. You don't have to have the baby, Grace. Not that it's a baby at the moment. More like a seed or a chickpea. It's just some cells, I think. Although that sounds a bit mank and medical . . .' She pulls a face. See, she so wasn't cut out to be a nurse. 'I think we'll call it a chickpea for now. Grace, you can go to the hospital and have an abortion. I think you can just take some tablets, you don't even have to have an operation. No one will ever know. Except me and I won't tell anyone. Apparently one in five women have had an abortion. I mean, that's most people. Well, not most people because it's less than half, but it's a lot. Seriously. Or, well, the other option is you let the chickpea grow into . . . what does a chickpea grow into . . . hummus? This chickpea thing is getting stupid now, but you know what I mean.

'The other option is that you have the baby. And loads of people do that, too. And I want you to know that I'm good with kids and I would babysit, so don't think you'd never get to go out again. Mind you, what with the smoking ban and those pouches you can get that cradle the baby onto your chest, you could pretty much go out with it, if you wanted. And if you're worried about the birth, I mean, I can't really help with that, but I would come with you and you could squeeze my hand. And I'd come to those meetings you have to go to where you practise breathing on the floor with your legs open. So all you need to know is that whatever you decide to do is fine. Better than fine. But you don't need to make a decision now. Take your time and see how you feel, but know that it's all going to be fine . . . Fuck me! There's Freddie and Anton getting out of a cab with . . . Oh. My. God. That must be that Pilates teacher – Fran, I think her name is – that Anton's going out with. She is proper gorgeous. Bitch. Wow! They look like they're buzzing off something.'

I quickly, but casually, saunter over to where Wendy is spying. She opens the curtain a bit wider so I can see. Anton is standing by a black cab, paying the driver, and behind him stands Freddie and a woman who looks like Uma Thurman. She's stroking Anton's back as he chats to the cabbie. There's nothing unusual about this except, like Wendy said, they are clearly buzzing about something. For some reason they're all wearing toothpaste-ad grins. Perhaps something wonderful has just happened. Maybe Anton and Uma have told Freddie they're getting married? That, as a concept, should make me feel happy, really, on account of the fact that I consider Anton a friend. It doesn't, though. If anything it makes me feel sadder. I slink back to my warm spot on the sofa.

'Freddie's wearing that blue shirt again,' Wendy says. 'I mean, the shirt's all right but he doesn't have to wear it every time he goes out. If we'd got together I was going to take him to Selfridges and dress him. You know, Danny must have told Freddie about everything. That's probably why Freddie asked you out. I know I've slept with two of his friends, but when we do end up together it'll be nice to know we find each other's mates attractive. I just wish he'd asked me out instead of you. I thought we were getting on so well that night, too. I've been trying to wean myself off him ever since then. I've started giving myself a morning mirror pep talk like you do. I repeat, "I don't fancy Freddie. He is a wanker," again and again and again. Ooh, Anton just looked up here. I hope he didn't see me spying. How cool is Anton? Now there's a man who can dress himself. He always wears nice shirts, and he changes them regularly and looks good in jeans. I think all older men should be banned from wearing jeans, except Bruce Springsteen and Anton. Anton is okey-dokey by me. And okey-dokey by you, clearly, seeing as you had a sexy dream about him. Maybe I should have gone after Anton instead of his son? Maybe I've got it wrong. Nope, Freddie's the man for me. Funny how you just know, eh? I wish he knew it, too. Hopefully, he'll turn into Anton. Anyway, Anton looks a bit loved up with model features there. Right, where was I? Greedy chops! Have you eaten that whole tub already? Impressive. Shall I put *Mad Men* on now?'

She jumps off her lookout perch and bounds towards the telly, bending down to turn the power switch on. Then suddenly she stands upright and slaps herself hard on her head.

'Oh, arse!' she screeches. 'You know what we've missed? *Britain Sings*! I can't believe I did that. I hate missing *Britain Sings*.'

She looks at me, but I can't muster much sympathy on account of the fact that I'm not speaking, I hate *Britain Sings* and I'm pregnant.

Chapter 36

I've been having sex with Danny for years. I know that sex leads to babies, so why is it a surprise to find out that one two-minute sweaty act can do this? I, Gracie Flowers, am having a baby. Except, of course, I'm not going to have a baby. How can I have a baby? I can't even raise a cactus.

'I think we should chuck that, babe,' says Wendy, gently taking the cactus from me. 'We'll throw it in the bin on our way. Are you ready?'

We're in my bathroom. Wendy has just done both of our make-up and now we're going to karaoke. I'm not that wowed about going, if truth be told. For starters I hate karaoke; for mains I'm not speaking; for a big, rich pudding my boyfriend has left me, and for coffee and after-dinner mints I'm pregnant. That's quite a meal and it's difficult to swallow, but it's hard to argue against something like going to karaoke when you're not speaking. And anyway, Wendy wants to go and she's been cooped up with me all weekend, so I owe it to her.

Wendy takes my hand. I clutch it as we head down the stairs and step over the threshold of my maisonette. She lobs the cactus in the outside bin and we walk slowly across the road, heading for the warm lights of the pub. She opens the door and looks back at me.

'You'll be fine,' she assures me.

We enter and are instantly engulfed in the hubbub. The karaoke has already started. A girl is singing a song I don't know. It's actually quite comforting to be somewhere noisy. I can just listen to the music and nod and smile, and my lack of conversation shouldn't be too noticeable. Anton is standing at the bar alone. There's no sign of Uma, which is surprising as they looked surgically attached when I saw them from the window last night. Anton looks as handsome as ever, but somehow distracted or perturbed by something. He doesn't look like his normal self. I'd love to sit next to him tonight. I've come to associate Anton with sitting in a life raft. And where's the canine Keith Moon? I look about me at people's knees to see if I can spot him, but I can't. Wendy's at the bar, talking to Freddie. I find the only two chairs in the place and sit down to wait for her. I close my eyes and listen to the girl singing. She's flat.

'Oh my God!' Wendy whoops when she returns. 'Oh. My. God. This is like more gossip than I've ever heard in my life. Anton and that woman were on *Britain Sings* last night! I can't believe we missed it. Gutted. That's why they were looking all buzzed up when we saw them, because they'd just got through to the final! You know, the big one at Christmas? But then today there was this big story in the *News of the World* about how she, Uma, real name Fran, used to be a – wait for it, massive ultra-gossip – high-class prostitute! Anyway, she's disappeared. She left a message saying she's gone to an Ashram in India and Anton can do the final without her. Right, listen, I got you a vodka, lime and soda,' she gabbles, 'but then I remembered the chickpea. But one drink tonight won't matter, I thought. Imagine you didn't do the test till tomorrow, then you wouldn't even know, so you'd still be out boozing. I reckon it's fine, but I can get you a soft drink if you'd prefer.'

I look down at the weighty vodka. What to do? Drink it, I suppose. There's no way I can have this baby. I take a gulp, then I start sucking one of the ice cubes.

'Yeah, that's what I'd do, too. Ooh, Anton's going up. He must be gutted. Wonder what he'll sing without her,' she says, shifting her chair away from me towards the karaoke stage. The music starts and we listen for a few moments.

'What the hell's this?' whispers Wendy. 'Never heard of it. He should have done a crowd pleaser.'

She doesn't recognise the music, but I do. The song is an old Patti Smith number called 'Because The Night'. It's all about the night being for sex and lust and lovers. I know it well as it was played at my parents' wedding. I haven't heard it for years.

I wish I'd been at my mum and dad's wedding. Technically I was there, but seeing as I was in a womb at the time I don't remember much. It sounds like quite a rock and roll wedding from what I've heard. Neither of their parents were present because they didn't approve, so Mum and Dad thought, Sod them, and had a wedding with just their friends. They got married in a register office in Ealing and then went to pretty Walpole Park afterwards. There were about thirty young people, and they'd all been instructed to bring a bottle, a picnic item and a party piece. Dad's party piece was first. He sang a John Denver song to my mum, called 'Annie's Song'. The lyrics are simple and beautiful, 'Come let me love you, let me give my life to you. Let me drown in your laughter, let me die in your arms.' Mum and Dad's friends used to tell me that even the blokes cried when they heard my dad sing that to my mum. After that my mum played this Patti Smith number on an old cassette player and did a bit of dirty dancing for him. It sounds like she was a right goer in her day, my mum.

I watch Anton on stage. He's good. He has a Bruce Springsteen-style growl. I'm not surprised he won. I look about me. People are nodding their heads, tapping their feet and smiling. Then I look back at him on stage and I have to say it, he's sexy. I think of lying in his bed, but this time he's in it. Oh dear, I seem to be developing a bit of a crush on Anton.

Wendy pats my knee.

'Wow! He's brilliant!'

There are huge cheers when he finishes.

'I thank you,' Anton says into his microphone. 'Now then, it's been a changeable twenty-four hours. As some of you might have heard, myself and a lady called Fran Basso entered *Britain Sings* last night and won a place in the finals.'

A deafening roar erupts in the Carbuncle.

'Yes, yes, thank you. Sadly, Fran has since decided not to do the final, which is in a few months' time, so I'm left partner-less. Now, *Britain Sings* have said I can still take my place in the final, either alone or with a new partner, and I have to say that as soon as I heard this I thought of someone. Basically, I heard this young lady sing a while back and I can't get her out of my head.'

Someone makes a wooo sound.

'Well, she's here tonight, and I'm hoping she might sing a bit of Simon & Garfunkel with me. Her voice will blow your mind. Her name's Grace and I'd like to invite her up on stage to sing with me.'

I stare at the stage. No one walks up there. How weird. Wendy elbows me in the side. Ow! I look at her. She doesn't say sorry, she just nods at me. What's up with her? I look back at the stage. Poor Anton's been stood up by this Grace person. I gaze at his kind face, but then I lock eyes with him. He's been looking at me. Me. Me. I'm the Grace. He nods as though to say come up. They can't expect me to get up there. What's going on? My mouth hangs open like a hungry dog. I glance back at Wendy. She's taking my drink from my hand and everyone's looking at me. The pub's gone quiet. Maybe I should go up there and sing. Maybe I should just sing a bit of Simon & Garfunkel. What could be wrong with that? It's just a Simon & Garfunkel song. Surely I could keep it together for that. God, I'd love to sing. Now more than ever, when it seems like my world is falling apart, I would love to take refuge in a song. I would love to take the microphone and sing. I would love to forget the world and just share my favourite songs with people. And I would love to do it with Anton.

So do it then, Gracie.

OK, then, I'll do it.

On you go, then.

I stand up, but I can't seem to move very quickly. In fact,

I can't seem to move at all. I'm going to do it, though. Gracie Flowers, ten years later. Wish me luck.

Instrumental karaoke music begins to play. Anton must have put this on to fill the silence while I make my way to the stage. I don't blame him as I'm taking for-bleeding-ever. I step around the chairs in front of me towards the stage. I can do this. I can do this. But as I'm walking and Anton is smiling at me, I recognise the music that's playing. It's 'Amazing Grace'. He's put 'Amazing Grace' on while I walk up to the stage. It's the same song Ruth Roberts was singing at the singing competition when I went mad. Anton puts his microphone to his lips. Everything is in slow motion. His lips part to sing the first line. And I scream. I start really screaming. For someone who hasn't made a sound since Wednesday I'm certainly making up for it now. I scream until my ears ring and I have to put my hands over them. But I don't stop screaming. I'm panting the screams and I'm running for the door. The whole pub is staring at me, thinking I'm a nutter, but I don't care. I just have to get away from this place. I run down the street. I can't go home. It's too close. I run and scream until I feel I'm far enough away, and when I stop I'm panting.

'Grace?' it's a man's voice. Someone from the pub has chased after me. 'Grace! Grace!' It's Freddie. I look about me to find a spot to hide, but he can't fail to miss me, seeing as Keith Moon is bounding in my direction.

'Grace. What on earth happened?'

'Oh,' I start, but then I stop. I just made a sound. My voice. That was my voice. 'Sorry,' I say, and my shoulders suddenly release, as though they've been up by my ears for days. 'Sorry,'

I say again. I'm speaking. I'm actually speaking again. Oh thank you, God! I smile. Freddie just looks at me as though I'm mental, 'Sorry. I don't sing in public. The last time I did, the same thing happened. I freaked out. I'm so sorry to scare your pub.'

'That's all right,' he says. He's looking down, his hands in his pockets, chewing the inside of his mouth. 'I was just worried about you.'

He's wearing a blue shirt. I wonder if it's the same one he had on last night. As I hug Keith Moon I look at him. Freddie is a year older than me, so that would make him twenty-seven, and he's a newly qualified lawyer. He was offered a job with a big bad-ass law firm, but he decided to work for a smaller company that specialises in human rights cases instead. Wendy, who loves the Bridget Jones books, says he's her very own Mark Darcy. Freddie's tall and broad with sandy-coloured hair and a sprinkling of freckles on his nose. He looks more like Prince Harry's older brother than William does.

'Sorry,' I repeat. Oh, it's such a relief to hear my voice.

'No, God. Don't worry. I wanted to apologise to you, Grace, for last weekend, when I asked you out. Danny had spoken to me, you see, about Canada.'

'Canada?'

'Yes.'

'I thought he was going to America.'

'He said it was a job in Vancouver.'

'Is that in Canada? I thought it was in America,' I say, then I laugh. I must be delirious.

'Oh, yeah. No. It's . . . it's in Canada.'

'I thought he'd gone to America, but it's Canada.' It's not funny so I should really stop laughing.

'Near enough. That's why I asked you out for dinner. I assumed that because he wasn't there that night you must already have broken up. But still, I should have waited. I was drunk from the night before, perhaps. Um, it's just I've always liked you, Grace. I feel very close to you. Or perhaps that's wrong. I feel as though we could be very close.'

'Freddie ...'

'Hmm?'

'As if anything could ever happen between us. Wendy's my best mate.'

'And?'

'What? Don't you know?'

'Know what?'

'That she's liked you ever since she first set eyes on you.'

'Wendy?'

'Yes.'

'As in your mate, Wendy?'

Bit slow on the uptake is our Freddie.

'Yes.'

'No.'

Oh, this is painful.

'Wendy?'

'Yes.'

I can actually see Wendy. She's left the pub and is jogging down the street towards us.

'I've hardly ever spoken to her properly.'

'That's because she really likes you,' I whisper.

'Are you sure?'

I nod.

'Wendy? I did think once she might have, you know, quite liked me, but then she slept with Martin and . . .'

'So?'

Wendy is really close now, so I make that slash-your-throat sign to tell him to shut up, but it doesn't work.

'She's a bit of a slag, isn't she, Wendy?'

Wendy stops dead in her tracks behind him and her face crumples.

'Wend!' I cry.

Freddie spins round.

'Wendy, that was unforgivable of me. I'm so sorry.'

Wendy, my lovely, mad, funny, happy friend Wendy looks so upset, but she attempts an 'isn't this awkward' smile and then turns, with dignity, and slowly walks away.

'She's the nicest person on the planet,' I hiss at Freddie, then I run after her.

Chapter 37

'Things, most definitely, are not going to plan,' I tell my reflection seriously.

My reflection, realising the gravity of the situation, nods and splutters, 'That's a frigging understatement!'

I eyeball myself.

'Right, Lady Luckless, you need to get back on track soonest. None of this four days off because your boyfriend dumps you malarkey. Regroup. Refocus. So, the plan is to sell, sell and sell some more. And sort out the . . . you know . . . the thingy quickly. Go to the pharmacist and get the tablets Wendy was talking about and get on with your life.'

I walk over to the stereo on my cactus-less windowsill. I need a song for today. A song that will make things better. A song of hope. I put the loo seat down and sit on it because I'm clueless as to what this miracle song should be. What would Dad play? Probably 'I Will Survive' loudly for a laugh. But I don't have that on CD, and anyway, there's nothing worse than a cast-aside woman humming Gloria Gaynor through her tears as she leaves for work. Although maybe that's the look I should be going for. Danny and his parents would have been loading that van for hours. The whole street would have seen. Perhaps I should just throw open my front door and perform a rousing rendition of the just-been-dumped classic, complete with sequinned boob-tube dress and a half-drunk bottle of gin. Maybe that's the way to do it. People would say, 'Isn't that the girl who had a screaming fit in the pub last night? Her boyfriend moved out last week. She's got a good pair of lungs on her.' I wonder whether the old Gracie, the one who used to sing all the time, would do that. She probably would, too. She once sang the whole of a Grace Jones song called 'Pull Up To The Bumper' a cappella on the street in Brighton while her school outing coach driver made about twenty-seven failed attempts to reverse park his coach.

My dad and I used to sing everywhere. Literally everywhere. He would dance, too. I didn't. I was always too embarrassed. I can dance, though. I can do a basic waltz, rumba and probably most other dance steps because I was weaned on ballroom dancing and went to dance classes from the moment I could walk. I loved dancing as a child, but then I found music, and from then on my instinct was always to sing. I was never too embarrassed to sing.

Songs. God, they can be perfect. A simple song. Three and a half minutes of instruments and voices, generally that's all it is. Yet those three and a half minutes can show you the world in all its horror or glory; it can move you to tears or make you dance in the kitchen in your slippers. It can capture a feeling you didn't know you had, or a yearning somewhere deep inside of you. I know I sound like a plonker, but I've spent too many hours listening wide-eyed in wonder as I played the same song over and over not to sound like a plonker when it comes to music.

Dad and I listened to hundreds of songs in the bathroom during our mornings together, and I always experienced the same feeling of breathless anticipation between the moment the inch-wide button on the cassette recorder was pressed downwards until the song began. How would it start? With a guitar? A voice? A beat?

I must be careful not to spend too long in here. I'm used to Dan's bladder curtailing my morning natter, but now there's nothing to stop me blathering my way to being late for work. I close my eyes in the hope it will give me a musical brainwave. It doesn't. Instead I hear someone knocking on my front door. I stay put, eyes closed, slumped forward on the toilet, wondering whether to answer it. Knowing that, with my hilarious luck, it will be someone saying, 'Hello, so sorry to trouble you, but is that your Nissan Micra I've just smashed my car repeatedly into?'

'Grace,' I say sternly. 'Answer the door. It may not be all doomage and gloomage. You have to believe good things will happen again.' I gasp. 'It might be Danny back!' I run down the stairs.

When I'm at the front door, I remind myself that the odds of Danny being there are marginally more than nil. I arrange my features into an 'ill, vague and baffled' expression before opening the door – useful for dealing with people trying to sell, canvass or collect stuff.

'Grace.'

My features relax into a smile. It may not be Danny Saunders, but it's still one of my favourite people. Anton.

'I'm so sorry about last night.'

'No. No. No. I'm here to apologise. I put you on the spot. I, er, are you all right now?'

'Fine. I just had a bit of a freak-out. It's a long story. I'm so sorry.'

He smiles. I smile. I love this man.

'So, by way of an apology,' he says, handing me a plate, upon which sits a bacon sandwich.

'Oh, thank you!'

'Pleasure.'

'Do you have a bacon sandwich every morning?' I ask.

'No, but I'd like to. If I get up and walk Keith early then I allow myself one as a treat.'

'Well, thank you, and what's this?' I say, picking up a CD in a soft sleeve which is wedged between the two sandwich halves.

'It's another apology present. I was thinking about you not listening to the radio, because of its randomness, and I know you like the classics like I do, but I thought you might not have heard some modern music that's just as great, so I made you a CD. I've called it "Modern Classics". I wrote down the tracks and artists so it wouldn't feel too random for you.'

He's given me songs. The perfect gift. I stare at the CD.

'Was that wrong of me?'

I don't answer.

'Do you mind me doing that?'

I look up at him and blink.

'Er . . . ' I swallow. 'It's the nicest gift I've received.' I can't say 'ever', but I can confidently say, 'For at least ten years,' so I do.

'Good,' he smiles. 'Enjoy.'

I watch him walk back to the pub. He's such a special man. It's almost as though he sensed me sitting up there in the bathroom searching for a song.

Chapter 38

Dad liked singing Queen in Sainsbury's, particularly 'Don't Stop Me Now'. If my life wasn't currently in freefall without a parachute I would smile as I imagine him doing his Freddie Mercury routine under this very roof.

'Oh, it's you innit?'

'Hi. I'm so sorry about the other day.'

'S'cool.'

'I brought you these, to thank you for getting my bag back,' I say, handing her the bulging carrier bag I'm holding.

'Sh-i-i-i-t!' she says, smiling as she opens it. 'Cheers.'

It contains ten big bags of Haribo.

'Enjoy.'

'What was up with ya?'

'Oh.' I sigh, then I shrug. 'Oh, the usual. My boyfriend dumped me. You know the guy you met who looks like the bloke from the *Twilight* films.'

'Sh-i-i-t.'

'Actually, he didn't do the dumping. His mum did it for him.'

'Sh-i-i-t.'

'And now he's moved to Canada.'

'Sh-i-i-t.'

'Yeah.' I nod. 'And I'm pregnant.'

'Sh-i-i-i-t.'

'Yeah, that is a bit sh-i-i-i-t.'

'Don't have it,' she says, shaking her head.

I think the EU might have something to say about her pharmacy etiquette.

'No, I don't think I should, either.'

'Like my mate, Daz, right, she had a kid in February. Oh, man. It screams, like, all day. Screams. It's mad.'

'I thought I'd talk to him.' I nod towards the Tablet Tardis. 'Is he in there?'

'Yeah.'

I knock on the pharmacist's door, which he opens quickly.

'Hello,' I say, pulling a box of Ferrero Rocher out of my bag and handing it to him. 'These are a little thank you for being so kind the other day when I wasn't speaking. I wasn't being rude. Like you said, I go a bit mute sometimes when things are bad. I'm a freak. Sorry.'

'This is too kind,' he says, taking the chocolates. 'Not at all. What made you speak again?'

'Oh, I heard a song and it made me scream, and after that I spoke.'

'Must have been a powerful song.'

I almost laugh.

'You could say that. Also, I'm pregnant. I want to have a … you know … a thingy. Can you help me?'

'You have to go to the doctor.

'Oh, I thought you could take a pill and it would cause a … you know.'

'A thingy?'

'Yes. Sorry, I don't like the other word.'

'You can take a pill that would lead to that, but first you have to go to your GP, then he or she will refer you to a clinic and they will schedule a time to administer it.'

I stare at him. I so don't want this to be happening.

'Can't you give it to me?' He shakes his head.

'Who's your GP?'

'Dr McGovern.'

'She's a lovely woman.'

'I know.' I sigh. Dr McGovern's almost too lovely. She's known me since I was a baby and I don't want her to know I'm in this situation.

'Do you want to use my phone to make an appointment?'

So many appointments. So much time off work. So much talking about it.

'No, no, I'll do it. Thank you, though.'

'Take these,' he says, handing me some pamphlets. The top one is titled 'Terminating a Pregnancy'. I stare at it sadly. There's not much to love about a pregnancy termination pamphlet.

I walk out of the Tablet Tardis and Tara Innit makes a loud hissing sound for my attention.

'You've got a stalker,' she says.

'Probably,' I say, with a casual shrug. 'It would be about the level of my luck.'

'He's over there, behind the kitchen towels, watching you. He was watching yous when we were talking, then he bought summink, and now he's stood there waiting for ya. He's fit.'

Now, I raise my eyebrows. The odds could work for me having a stalker, but he wouldn't be fit. More likely, he would be homicidal and smell of tooth decay. No, it's bound to be someone from work who's caught me skiving and is taking a mobile phone photo as evidence.

'What's he like?'

'He's fit.'

'Anything else?'

'He's posh.'

I turn round. It's Posh Boy, the dastardly destroyer of my professional life, and he's standing behind a tower of special-offer ultra-absorbent kitchen towels.

'Oi, Posh Boy, what are you doing here?' I shout while folding up the pamphlets in my hand so they're as small as possible.

He doesn't respond in time so Tara shouts, 'He was getting some athlete's foot stuff.'

Posh Boy reddens.

'With all that badminton they must pong.'

'I could ask you the same question,' he counters.

'I was just discussing whether now is a good time to sell a house with the pharmacist.'

'I'm sure you were, Grace Flowers, I'm sure you were. Now, as we've caught each other in Sainsbury's during office hours, shall we get a coffee?'

Chapter 39

Danny and I stopped talking during our relationship. It wasn't like we sat there in stony silence, wildly gesturing when we couldn't find the remote; words did leave our mouths, but our conversations tended to focus on dinner arrangements or the perils of parking. If someone put me on the spot, not that they would, and asked me to name a memorable conversation I'd had with my boyfriend of ten years, I would be embarrassingly stumped. Looking back I realise we simply recycled the same non conversations day after day after day.

'What we doing for dinner?'

'Dunno. What d'you fancy?'

'Dunno. Indian*?'

'Cool.'

'I'll pick up the usual on the way home.'

'Cool.'

*Replace with Chinese, kebab, pizza, Maccy D's.

I knew all the stories he would trot out in company, because I was either in them or had heard them a hundred times. There was the time when Anthony Hopkins was at his work doing a voice-over for a computer game and Danny made him a cup of coffee. He said it was one of the greatest cups of coffee he'd ever had, and then he did his *Silence of the Lambs* tongue flick. And there was the time we were making a star to go on our Christmas tree and he ran off for a lightning wee and superglued his thumb to his foreskin. Those were the sorts of tales he told, but he'd never reveal anything about his feelings. He would never *really* talk.

That's something that definitely couldn't be said for Posh Boy. He wouldn't know a pregnant pause if it picked his nose.

'Oi, foot rot, do you ever shut up?'

'Oi, cavern stomach. Do you ever stop eating?'

I interrupt the important job of wiping baked-bean juice from my plate with toast to give him some rather good, if I do say so myself, evils. I wasn't planning to join him for a coffee. I was rather keen to get back in my car and listen to an amazing song by someone called Adele on Anton's CD, but then we walked past the café on the way out of Sainsbury's and I spied their four-foot poster for an all-day breakfast for £4.95 and changed my mind.

'You had a fry-up, too.'

'I went for the more civilised five-item option. Not the eight.'

'Ah ha, but you missed out on the fried bread. Grave error.'

'When was the last time you ate?'

I must look like a starving midnight-diet breaker, but I had Anton's bacon sandwich only an hour and a half ago.

'I've been meaning to talk to you about something.'

'What?'

'You know that day . . .'

'Oh, yeah, that one. I remember it well.' I roll my eyes. 'You might want to narrow it down.'

'You were stood on the street calling a man who'd parked on a red route a bastard.'

'Even that doesn't narrow it down to be honest.'

'Big car. Logo on the side.'

'Yeah, I know what you're on about.'

'You don't have to tell me, I'm just looking out for you. If anyone's giving you trouble, maybe I can help. I would have asked you before but you've been in Wales etc.'

'Oh, right, thanks,' I push my plate away. 'This company is planning to build a housing and retail development near here. They want to build a slip road to it, which means snipping a corner off the big graveyard there, but my dad is buried in the graveyard and it means digging up his grave.'

'Are you serious? People want to build on your dad's grave! That's awful.'

'Yes, John, it is.'

'I don't believe it.'

'Well, it's true. They're bribing everyone with thousands of pounds. Even my mother has said yes. But there's a lovely old couple who won't back down, and I think I've made my mother see sense, too. Well, as much as it's possible for my mother to see sense.'

'Right. What? Don't they need the money?'

'No,' I say, looking at him as though he's stupid. 'Some things are more important than money.'

'Sorry, Grace. I didn't mean to—'

'No, well, it's horrible. Horrible.'

'Some people don't see beyond profit, sadly.'

'I know.' I sigh.

'Oh, Grace. I'm sorry,' he says kindly. 'I lost my mum, too. I don't know what I'd do if someone wanted to build on her grave.'

I nod, but leave it at that. Best not to get into one of those riotous dead-parent chats.

John smiles as though he understands, and I smile back. I don't even want to say anything mean to him. He leans across the table and takes my hand in his. It's like the hug he gave me after I'd hurled up outside the Italian. There's something about his big, posh, badminton-playing hands and arms holding me that isn't as repulsive as I would have expected. Although, if truth be told, Posh Boy doesn't look that wowed by my touch. In fact, he's turning his nose up, and now he's pulled his hand from mine and is wiping it on a serviette.

'Oh, sorry, was there bean goo on my hands?'

'Urgh!' He nods. 'I can't stand baked beans.'

'How can you not like beans?'

'I'm just not a bean man, although I am partial to a chick-pea.'

'Oh,' I say flatly, remembering my predicament. 'I'm not that fond of chickpeas at the moment.'

Chapter 40

I'm going to miss loads of time at work because of this thingy. I've been out of the office for fifty minutes already this morning, most of which has been spent in the doctor's surgery staring at a poster for chlamydia. I'm on a bogus viewing. A bogus viewing is a useful tool in the estate-agency profession.

'I'm just going to show Chetwynd Road,' you say, and promptly drive to the chemist to buy some Tampax. Not that I need those at the moment because of this almighty cock-up – in the depressingly literal sense. And anyway, bogus viewings haven't been great for me since I accidentally told Lube about the gambling afternoons the boys in another branch were running. It was a very unfortunate incident, but when Lube launched an inquiry into why there was a property boom and his Notting Hill branch seemed to be sleeping through it, I thought he knew about the gambling syndicate the boys in the office there had going at William Hill. I assumed they were all in on it. 'Look at the tits on that, put down a fiver each way for me,' sort of thing. But that wasn't the case and Lube went ballistic when I mentioned it. Now I don't get many favours from the Make A Move lads.

Dr McGovern's just come out of her office. Please let it be my turn. I promise I now know all there is to know about chlamydia.

'Grace Flowers.' She smiles at me. The pharmacist was right. Dr McGovern's a lovely woman. She's tall, and not just by my standards, but officially so, like a man. You could most definitely rely on her to get a mug from the top cupboard. She never wears make-up or tries to look glam, but she smiles all the time, and somehow that makes her beautiful. I should correct that, she doesn't smile all the time; she wouldn't smile if you were telling her about your thrush symptoms or bowel cancer. She listens attentively to ailments and then she smiles the rest of the time.

The irony of all this is that for the last few years I've only ever needed to see her for my contraceptive pill prescriptions.

She leads me into her office, where there's another chlamydia poster on the wall.

'I was so pleased to see your name here. Well, not pleased that you're ill, of course,' she says, gesturing to a plastic chair for me to sit upon.

'I was at a dinner last week with some other doctors. There was a group of us, we trained together and now we're all coming up to retirement together and we were reminiscing about our more memorable appointments over the years. I told them about your mum and dad when they came to see me, pregnant with you.'

'Why? What happened?'

'Well, she was nervous. Your mum was quite young, wasn't she?'

'Eighteen,' I say, and it suddenly hits me how young that was. I'm twenty-six and I feel too young to have this baby. Mum must have been bricking it.

'Eighteen, my goodness.'

'And my dad came, too?' I ask, surprised.

'He did. He was jumping off the walls with excitement.'

'About me?'

'Oh, yes. I nearly asked him to step outside. I thought he'd have something over, like your mother! But then he calmed down, and as I was examining your mum, he took her hand and he sang to you – well, to your mother's tummy.'

'My dad sang in here.'

'Yes. In all my years as a doctor, no one else has ever sung in here. And it was beautiful, that's what I was telling my colleagues.'

'What did he sing?'

'Oh, what was it? Oh, I'm sorry, Grace. That, I can't remember.'

I must look disappointed because she says sorry two more times.

'Um,' I whisper. I need to get to the point, but suddenly I don't want to. Come on, Grace, you have to get back to work. 'I'm pregnant, but I can't have this baby,' I whisper.

'Are you sure?'

'Well, yes. I mean. I work all the time and there's no money unless I work!'

'Sorry, Grace, I meant are you sure you're pregnant.'

'Oh right. Yes, I did a test. But also I know. I feel pregnant, sick, my boobs are killing me. I'm craving ice lollies. And there was an accident . . . '

Dr McGovern waits to see if I'll continue. But I don't.

'So it was an accident.'

'Yeah, I forgot I'd run out of pills, because I was working really hard to get this promotion and then we accidentally, you know . . . Then I took the morning-after pill but it didn't work.'

'Hmm.' She smiles, not an 'I'm so happy' smile, more of an 'It'll be all right' smile. 'And what are your thoughts about this pregnancy?'

I sigh a deep sigh. It's a sigh that goes right into the dusty corners of the issue, making my chin quiver and my eyes prick with tears. I've already told her I can't have a baby, why does she have to dwell on this? I look down at my lap. There's a crusty Twister lolly stain on my leggings, which I pick at.

'I've got ice cream on my leggings.'

'Have you told your mum, Grace?'

I shake my head. I've made the ice-cream stain bigger. Bugger.

'Are you in a relationship at the moment, Grace?'

I keep my head down and shake it from side to side. I can feel a tear forming in the corner of my eye and I don't want it to drop, although if it landed on the Twister crust it might remove the stain. Despite its potential stain-removing properties, I wipe it away with my tear-swiping finger. I mustn't cry.

I hear a phoof-phoof sound and then see Dr McGovern's hand brandishing two tissues under my face. I take them and wipe my eyes and nose.

'Well, Grace, if you want this baby, you just need to look

after yourself for the time being and then I'll see you again in a few weeks' time . . . '

She lets the words settle. She waits a long time for me to respond, but I don't. I can't even look at her. I've already told her I can't have it. Why is she doing this?

'But if that's not what's best for you, then I can book you an appointment at St Mary's and they will talk to you about the other options.'

I was born in St Mary's. I slowly raise my eyes to meet hers and swallow. No words are spoken, she just turns efficiently to her computer screen. I listen to the clop clop of the keys as her fingers pat them. When she's finished she passes me a sheet of paper with a date and time printed on it, then she points to a telephone number.

'That's a twenty-four-hour unit. If you have any trouble, you can go there or call them at any time.'

I stand up.

'You'll be all right, Grace.'

I nod again.

'Send my regards to your mum.'

I nod again and walk out through the waiting room.

'Grace!' It's Dr McGovern calling me back. 'It was – oh, hang on – something about fish; it's a famous song. I had it for a moment there.' She puts her hand to her forehead, closes her eyes and starts humming.

'"Summertime",' I say.

She looks at me blankly, so I quietly sing the first few lines for her.

'Yes! Yes!' she squeals. 'Oh, Grace, you do have a lovely voice.'

Chapter 41

My mother craved oranges when she was pregnant with me. Oranges! That is so my mother: nutritious, low calorie and too fiddly to binge on. She says that's why I've got nice skin. She may be right, because I certainly don't have much in the way of a skincare routine. I'm a pretty rubbish woman if truth be told, as is evidenced by my pregnancy cravings, which are ice cream and pork-based breakfast products with ketchup. If I had this baby, I wonder whether it would have horrible skin. I keep doing this! I know I can't have the baby, but I find myself constantly imagining what it would be like if I did. Gracie Flowers, you've got to stop the baby daydreams!

The worst thing about being pregnant is how pregnant I feel. I'm about a million times more tired than usual for a start. This is my first day of the week without any bogus pregnancy-related viewings, but I'm sorely tempted to tell Posh Boy I'm off to show a property and go home to bed for half an hour. It's very hard to stop my mind compiling fantasy fried breakfast combos; I'd eat a scabby horse if it came with ketchup, and I think my breasts are in danger of exploding. They're massive and they seem to get a little bit bigger every day. Even my big-bazooka due-on bra is tight. And my boobs hurt, too. If I bend down they hurt; if I touch them they hurt; if I lie on my tummy at night they hurt. Normally I can forget I have breasts on a day-to-day basis and get on with my life, but not at the moment. There's barely a breast-free nano-second. Today, breast discomfort has taken a surprising turn for the weird. My nipples itch. But it's not a normal itch that you deal with by way of a quick scratch, because if I cop a sneaky boob scratch when no one's looking, they don't feel any less itchy. In fact, they burn even more. Itchy boobs. Who'd have thought?

Having itchy boobs is a particular nuisance today, because it's just me and Posh Boy in the office, and he looks annoyingly handsome. He's wearing a pink shirt and, because it's hot, he's taken off his tie and undone the top two buttons so you can see a bit of dark chest hair. Not that I care, of course, but it's hardly ideal that he's sat across the office looking as fit as a box of Ironman triathlon runners while I sit here touching my breasts.

'Looking forward to paintballing?''

'I've just wet myself,' I say. Actually, it's not a million miles from the truth as I've been needing the loo all morning.

'I love having a run-around.'

I shake my head with a pained expression. Having a run-around. Do people really still say that?

'Do you work out?'

'I work out how much commission I make,' I scoff. 'Sorry,' I add quickly. 'That wasn't a joke, it was an abortion.' I tense as soon as it's out of my mouth. It's such a hideous word.

Gah! It's my nipples again. They're so tingly. I press them against my desk in the hope of some slight relief. Nothing. I've just made my nipples erect. I notice John glancing at them and give him a stony 'pervert' look.

Out of the corner of my eye I see someone approaching the window. John is still looking at my boobs so he hasn't noticed the potential client. Result. I jump up, lick my lips and head to the door to poke my head out.

'Hi, I'm Grace, do you need any help?' I sing, but I stop as soon as I set eyes on this fella. Except he's not a fella; he's far too exotic to be called that. He's a man, and not just any man, but a man who's obviously been made in Italy, Spain or somewhere hot like that. And as if that isn't enough, he looks ludicrously wealthy. I can tell by his shoes.

'Oh, 'ello, Grace, Ricardo. Or Richard eef you want. My mother call me Richard. She was Eeenglish, and 'er last name was Burton. She call me Richard Burton after ze actor. She love eem.'

He holds a hand out in my direction and I take it. Normally, I would make some joke regarding Richard Burton's alcoholic, philandering ways, but I can't jest with this man for so many reasons. He sounds like Antonio Banderas, for a start, and then there's the fact that he's as tanned as Peter Andre, but with more of a six o'clock shadow. Also, he's not too tall. His head is much closer to mine than the majority of the men I meet when vertical. We're still holding hands and I'm gazing at him. 'Yeaas, I need 'elp. I need an apartment. Beautiful, like a – what the word – penthouse, for myself. But I also want a house – comfortable for . . . '

'For a lady?' I say and instantly feel like a hussy. It's the accent.

'No, no.' He laughs shyly. He's got a dimple in his chin. Oh, dimple in chin joy. 'No, for my mother and my seeester.'

For his mother and sister! Oh, bless him!

'Fantastic, follow me inside and I'll ask you a few questions.'

'I am beesy now, but I am free later. Possible I take you to deeener? I only 'av tonight before I fly back to Roma. But I free tonight . . . '

'Did you say Roma?'

He nods. I sigh. Roma is Rome. I've been to Rome. My best ever day happened in Rome.

'Um.' It's not completely out of the ordinary. I've had lunches with clients to discuss properties, so I could have supper with him. Although I haven't had complete confidence in my dinner performances since the liver incident. However, I think that was because I hadn't eaten for ages. I find myself less likely to vomit when I eat little and often. But what if we walk into a restaurant and the chef is frying liver or kidney? Oh dear, hot saliva is starting to flow just thinking about it. But he did say Rome, and Rome is my favourite place in the whole world. 'Um, er, well, yes. Good idea. Tonight, seven-thirty at The Paradise.' I write the address and time on the back of a business card.

I've chosen a local institution, a big old gastro pub large enough for the frying of liver not to make me gag.

'Paradise. I meeet you in Paradise,' he says.

I don't say anything; I just watch him walk away. I'm thinking about Rome. I'd give anything to have another day like the one I had in Rome.

As I daydream a lady approaches me. She's small and hunched and she's fishing something out of her bag.

'Do you need help?' I ask her.

'We all need help.'

'True.'

'The Lord's help.'

Oh, Jesus. God people are always after me.

'I need to get back to work. Nice to meet you.'

'Will you take the good news,' she says, holding a tiny booklet out towards me.

'Thank you,' I say, taking it with a smile, then she scurries away. I flick through it and it sticks open on a page. I peer at it. It's a picture of a pink baby curled up in a womb. Tiny fingers, tiny toes and a tiny ear. The baby looks as though it's sucking its thumb. My baby might suck its thumb. I did when I was little.

The caption below the picture says just three words: 'Life not death.'

Chapter 42

My best ever day was in Rome. It was magical. So much so I sometimes wonder if it actually happened to me. It feels as if the young woman in my memory was someone else entirely. I was fifteen and I'd travelled there with Mum and Dad because the World Ballroom Dancing Championships were being held there. I didn't normally go with them, but this time was different. I was given time off school and everything because I'd been asked to sing. The organisers wanted me to sing at the prize-giving ceremony. So I did. I sang 'Mr Bojangles'. But I wasn't alone; my dad sang with me.

I try not to hark back to when he was alive too often, but sometimes I can't help it. It often feels as though my life was in colour when he was here, but turned to black and white after his death. He didn't really sing much of the song, it was mainly me, but he acted Mr Bojangles. Mr Bojangles is an old soft-shoe dancer who travelled around dancing with his dog for drinks and tips. My dad sang in some bits and danced in others, while I sang the whole song. I wasn't nervous. We sang 'Mr Bojangles' for fun at home. I was really excited and Mum made me a dress. God, it was beautiful, like something Sophia Loren or Marilyn Monroe would have worn. It was blue satin with a bodice top and it was fitted over my hips to my knees, causing me to walk like I was in a beanbag race, but it looked wonderful when I stood still. After we sang, the audience clapped and we bowed – but they didn't stop clapping. There were over two thousand people in the auditorium and they just wouldn't stop clapping. I walked, well, wiggled off stage, but the clapping still continued, so I had to go back out and bow again. The organisers said that we performed for five minutes and they clapped for seven. That wasn't even the best bit, though. The best bit happened later.

Our hotel was in a piazza, surrounded by ancient buildings, and that night there was a band playing, consisting of a guitarist, a double bassist and a man who played the accordion. Me, Mum and Dad sat in a café in the piazza listening to the band after the award ceremony. We drank Prosecco and danced in our chairs. Suddenly Dad ran up to the band and told them I was a singer and they invited me to join them. I sang with them for hours and they made lots of money that night and wanted to share it with me. I didn't want the money, though, I just felt so happy to be doing something I loved and that other people enjoyed too. Everyone was smiling. When I remember that day, that's what I see: smiling faces. I was so excited about becoming a singer. When I went to bed that night I daydreamed that if I didn't win the Sony contract singing competition I'd come back to

Rome and sing with this band in this square for the rest of my life.

Ricardo is smiling at me. He's been smiling at me all night. The memory of Rome is so lovely that I've been managing to smile back, even though we're sitting at the table Danny and I used to call 'our table'. Danny and I used to come to The Paradise a lot when I still lived at home with Mum. Pretty much once a week he'd treat me to dinner here and we liked this table. Me, because it was near the fairy lights; him, because he said it was easy to get the bar guy's attention when he wanted another pint; both of us, because it was away from the crowds and suitable for snogging.

'We 'av a saying in Etaly. You no do two theengs at the same time, or you get sheet on your shoes,' Ricardo said when I sat down. Whatever it means made absolutely no sense to me, but it's his reason for refusing to talk business until we've finished eating.

As a result, he knows far more about me than any other client I've ever had. I even told him about the brutal Danny dumping. An elementary error, as since he's learned that piece of information he keeps touching my leg or arm every time he speaks to me.

'So, are you from London?' he says, stroking my shoulder.

'Yes, I grew up round here actually.'

'And your family. They live here steel.'

'Er, well, yes. But it's only my mum.'

'Ah, ees she beautiful, like you?'

Perv. But he's put his knife and fork together, so at last I can be an estate agent again.

'She's far more beautiful than me,' I say quickly, and I

wriggle free from his embrace to get out my A4 notebook and start getting down to business. 'Now, let me ask you a few questions about what you're looking for?'

'Grace, I need a house and an apartment. I want them to be beautiful. I have no budget. That ees all you need to know.'

I'm blinking quickly like there's a bug in my eye. Never, ever, ever, ever, have I heard the words, 'I have no budget.' Ever. Ever. What do you say to them?

'Oh, that's nice,' is all I can think of.

He smiles and nods. This is unprecedented. This is many, many, many, many, many, many, money.

'So, tell me about yourself?' he says, stroking my knee this time.

'Um,' I start. I don't want to tell him anything except 'Please get your blinking hands off me', but the words 'no budget' and the thought of the commission and Posh Boy's face when he knows I've landed a dream client mean that I smile, instead, and say, 'So, what would you like to know?'

Chapter 43

Now, I admit, I've been a little smug about bagging a 'show me the money' client, but that is a void on a blank bit of nothing in comparison to the way Posh Boy has been going on today.

His one and only contribution to our esteemed agency is the paintballing team-building event. Yet, far from hanging his head in shame or repeatedly banging it against the corner of a shelf, he's strutting about like he's created world peace. I fear he'll be bitterly disappointed if he's hoping for some staff bonding from us lot. We haven't even had a Christmas do since the year of the Super Hero-themed party. Lube's wife came as Wonder Woman and, unfortunately, was sick all down herself and most of the Cricklewood Sales team. Chunder Woman we called her. Lube organised a Christmas meal the following year, but he banned booze and only four people turned up.

'Yah, yah, paintballing. Dislocated my shoulder one time. Wasn't supposed to tackle my opponent. Ha!' and other hilarious anecdotes have been pouring poshly from him all day as he prances about like a prat. I have ignored him and left Wendy to feign interest, which she's doing so realistically that I think she might actually be looking forward to tomorrow. I can forgive her, though, because she doesn't get out of the office much.

'I hope they've got lots of ammo!' he exclaims.

But Wendy isn't looking at John this time. Something outside the window has caught her eye. 'Fuckeroony,' she's muttering. I turn to see what warrants her favourite profanity.

'Oh.' I smile, standing up. 'That's Ricardo. My client with no budget. Oi, Fungus Foot, did I mention that I have a client with no budget who wants me to find him not one, but two properties?'

'That's Ricardo?' Wendy sighs. 'Oh, you cow of all the prized cow herds in the land. You went for dinner with him. Why didn't you go back to his hotel and shag him?'

'Did he ask you to shag him?' asks John.

'Yes, and she didn't. Are you mad?'

'What did he say? Will you shag me?'

'No! He's Italian! He said, will you come back to my room?'

I didn't like that bit at all. He insisted he wanted to pay for dinner, so he asked for the bill. Then he said, 'Please, do me ze honour of accompanying me back to my hotel,' and I said, 'No, sorry, we'd best keep this business.' Having been blown out, when the bill came he didn't seem quite so thrilled about paying it. He said he thought he had more cash on him than he did and was very reluctant to put it on a credit card. I could see that he wanted me to cough up, but I didn't to serve him damn well right. Mind you, I can understand it, credit cards are the work of the devil.

'Is he that attractive?' asks Posh Boy.

'John, that is ... what can I say? He is ... wow!' says Wendy.

'Wend, close your mouth,' I hiss. 'He's coming in.'

Ricardo enters. He greets us all with a small nod of his head. He's looking slick. His black pressed trousers fit him perfectly, his black V-neck jumper has no fluff on it and his brown shoes are so polished you could probably squeeze your blackheads in them if you fancied. He stands at a polite distance and smiles at Wendy and then John.

'Good afternoon.'

He walks towards me and kisses me on both cheeks. Out of the corner of my eye, I spot Wendy pretending to fall off her chair. I nod towards the door and we both start walking. Ricardo puts an arm around me. It's not actually touching me, he just holds it away from me like you do when a toddler is learning to walk. I feel my mobile vibrating in my pocket. I pull it out. It's my mum. I don't answer it.

'Please,' says Ricardo, gesturing towards the phone.

'No, we have to find you your future home.'

We carry on walking towards the door in our strange embrace.

'Er, Grace, your mum's on line two,' shouts Wendy.

'Can you tell her ... ?'

Wendy shakes her head and gives me the 'your mum's being a bit of a fruit cake' look. I need to take the call so I walk back to my desk.

'Hi, Mum,' I say into the receiver.

'Grace.' She's sobbing.

'Mum.'

'Oh, Grace. I need that money.'

Of course she does. I haven't even tried to take out the loan I promised her yet. Partly because the thought makes me shudder, but also because I've been going through a lot, what with Dan leaving me with such a complicated parting gift. I notice John watching me with interest.

'I'll pop round. I can't talk here. Love you.'

I join Ricardo outside.

'Trouble?'

'It was my mum.'

'Oh, your beautiful mother. How is she?'

'Well, in a bit of a state. Do you mind if I just run in and speak to her for thirty seconds? I'm normally much more professional than this, but it is on the way to our first property and we've got loads of time. Do you mind?'

'Grace. Your mother is more important than your job or my house. All we 'av ees family,' he says and then he tries to open the passenger-side door to my car.

'You're a star. Sorry, but I'm afraid you need to crawl into the car through my side. That door doesn't work. I really need to get it fixed.'

I wish I could say that I didn't look at Ricardo's bottom as he crawled into the passenger seat, but I can't.

As I tear off with Ricardo next to me, I open the window to combat the effects of aftershave in the confined space of a Nissan Micra on an easily nauseous woman.

I park the car in the driveway and quickly run up to Mum's house, leaving Ricardo in the passenger seat.

'Mildred, what's been happening here, eh?' I exclaim as I open the door.

'Oh Grace!' Mum calls from the kitchen. I run in there to find her seated at the table clutching a gin. She stands up. 'Do you want one?'

'No, Mum, I'm working. I've got a client in the car. Are you OK?'

I look at her. She looks different. She's slightly flushed in the face and her eyes are blotchy, but it's not that. She looks nice. My mother always looks nice, but now I see what the difference is, today she looks sexy nice. She's wearing her mid-calf black pedal pushers, a black T-shirt and a pink neck scarf. She looks like a character from *Grease* that puts out!

'That nice man from the construction company came here again and he was so kind. We spoke for a long time. Oh, Grace. It's a lot of money.'

'Mum!'

'Grace, he was ever so nice.'

'Ever so nice! Ever so nice! Please don't do this to me,' I say in panic.

'But Grace, I need the money. He said he'd give me twenty-five thousand, just like that.'

'Mum, I'm sorry. I've been a bit distracted but I will get it for you.'

'I don't want to take your money.'

'But I'm family, it's what families do. What they don't do is sell their graves.'

She looks down at her feet.

'Mum, promise me you won't change your mind. Promise me. I don't know if I could speak to you again if you sold the grave. I just don't.'

Her eyes remain fixed on the floor.

'Look, I've got to go. It will be all right. I'll go to the bank and sort out this loan. The guy I'm showing property to today is minted, and that means loads of commission. Don't worry, Mum. We'll sort this.'

She finally looks up and offers a pathetic smile. It'll have to do because I have to go.

'I'm so sorry,' I say as I get back into the car.

'Grace,' Ricardo turns to me and takes my hand. 'Family is everything, please don't apologise. Do you want to talk to me?'

'No, we need to show you some houses.'

'Your mother she has a beautiful home. Where is your father?'

'Oh, he died,' I say.

'Oh, Grace, I am sorry. He would be very proud of you.'

I nod, but the thing is I don't think my dad would be proud. I mean, he'd still love me, but he would be alarmed to see me now. The me I am now was not the me I should have become if you'd known me as a child.

'Hmm.'

'So your mother ees alone and she ees sad.'

'Yeah. And there are money troubles. It's complicated.'

'But your mother, if she 'as money worries, she could sell 'er house. And you could help 'er find another smaller one. That house would be worth how much?'

'Oh, God knows. Well over a million now, though, definitely. It's listed and the garden's quite big, so I could see it going for crazy money actually. But we don't want to sell the house. It was in Dad's family for years.'

'But she owns it.'

'Yes.'

'So she should just borrow money against the house. People do it all the time.'

'Hmm, maybe. Please, Ricardo, you're very kind, but we have work to do.'

'To infinity and beyond!' he exclaims for some reason.

'Yes.' I laugh. 'Infinity and beyond. Or maybe just Notting Hill.'

Chapter 44

Doctor's appointments, paintballing, bank-manager meetings – when am I supposed to get any work done? Bob's fallen off the radar since the hot-tub fiasco and I still haven't managed to sell Claire's flat. I'm starting to worry that my hormones are interfering with the old Gracie sales magic. I'm still doing well, just not well enough. I'm about to fiscally fry myself for my mother by taking out this loan, so I need to be making sales. I've got everything crossed to the point of discomfort that the bank will give me a loan today. Although I'm not just relying on luck, that would be foolish, I'm prepared. too. I'm a big fan of the six 'P's: 'Perfect Preparation Prevents Piss Poor Performance.'

Wendy helped me. She sent me lots of articles about how to successfully nail your bank-loan meeting. She's a bit obsessive when it comes to online articles. She can barely blow her nose without consulting one. If chicken fillets are on offer in Sainsbury's, she'll be stood there typing, 'Easy delicious chicken fillet recipe,' into her phone. If she buys a red top, she'll go online and tap in something like, 'How to look gorgeous in red,' and if that doesn't work she'll try, 'Sexy hot in red,' although that would lead to porn, which would make her start shrieking. The articles she sent me about bank-loan strategy were brilliant, though, and I now have the lingo, the jargon, the strut. Basically, I'm Alan Sugar in a slightly overworked pencil skirt.

The main point they all railed on about was that you have to look smart. Hence, I am wearing heels and there's goo in my hair. The goo is supposed to make me look officious and not like, as Wendy said I am prone to resembling, a defiled farm girl. I'm not convinced as I think it looks greasy and it feels like I've wiped my hair on a battered cod. My favourite piece of advice was that you have to walk into the room from a position of power. Wend and I got quite excited by this and agreed that the ultimate powerful entry would be to abseil in dressed as Wonder Woman. But there's never time to learn to abseil when you need it, is there? Anyway, now that I'm here there's no window to abseil through, so I'm standing very straight and trying not to look apologetic. It's actually quite hard to keep all this up, because although the door is open and I can see the man I need to speak to, standing in my way is a lady with a buggy. She's just left the room and her toddler is yelling, so she's trying to get him or her to drink some Irn-Bru out of a plastic bottle, whilst muttering to the bank manager man who is looking awkward.

'Thanks for nothing,' the woman eventually says, so that half of West London can hear her, and strides off pushing the buggy with venom.

'Grace Flowers,' the man says with relief.

'Yes, very pleased to meet you. Thank you for taking the time to see me today,' I say, shaking his hand and sitting on the seat he proffers. A very impressive start, as I think all my online articles would agree.

'Well, Grace, I must say, you're a rarity as a client. You've never been in debt.'

'Thank you,' I say with a smile. 'I like to keep my finances in order.'

'I can see that,' he replies.

'Now,' I say, leaning forward and clasping my hands together on the desk. 'I'd like, if I may, to put a motion on the table.'

Businesslike, formal, brilliant, if I do say so myself. I've been working on my business jargon and it has paid off.

'Oh, ho, I'd rather you didn't, we have toilet facilities for that.'

I stare at him. He laughs. It takes some time for it to dawn on me that he's referring to a bowel motion – I definitely wasn't planning on putting one of those on the desk. I start to blush. I can feel the hotness in my cheeks spreading and I know, I just know, that I now look like a red edible fruit rather than a sleek businesswoman and it's all gone to pot.

'Um, what I meant – oh, gosh – well, I mean.'

He's still laughing.

'Can I take out a loan?'

Still he laughs.

'Please.'

Now he's choking. I hope he doesn't die.

'A loan,' he says, finally pulling himself together. 'I'm sure we can arrange that with your impeccable history. How much did you want to borrow?'

'Twenty thousand.'

'Grace!' he chokes with surprise. 'You're supposed to bank with us. Not us bank with you.'

'Um.'

He's laughing again. I think it was a joke. I smile. This is nothing like the *Guardian* article.

'I've completed the paperwork,' I say, sliding over the forms I'd neatly filled in.

'Right, now, you're a home owner, is that right?'

'I am,' I say proudly. 'I have a maisonette.'

He looks like he might laugh again but holds it in.

'Well, to borrow a sum of that scope we would need some collateral from you, i.e. your home.'

'Yes,' I swallow.

'And how quickly do you want to repay the loan?'

'Very quickly.'

'Good. Say forty-eight months at nine point nine per cent interest and the repayments on this loan would be five hundred and six pounds, twenty five pence a month.'

The blush has gone and I feel like I'm turning pale. The words, loan, interest, and five hundred quid a month can do that.

'Yes,' I say, but I feel a bit sick.

'You have to be sure you can make these repayments, Grace, or you could be forced to sell your maisonette to cover them.'

'Yes,' I say again.

'Well, let me take those forms. You'll hear from us in about a week whether we've approved it, but I shouldn't think it will be a problem.'

'Really? You really think it won't be a problem?'

'I really think it won't be a problem. The money should be in your account soon, but you must keep up the repayments. Or it can get . . . messy.'

'I don't want messy.'

'I'm sure you don't.'

'Thank you,' I say and I get up.

'Thank you,' he says. 'A motion on the table! Haven't laughed like that in years.'

I wish I could smile back, but the thought of borrowing twenty grand makes it hard. Banging my head repeatedly on a table whilst howling the word 'arse' would be easy, but smiling's hard. It's just so much money. I will do this for Mum, though, I think as I stand up on shaking legs, but this has to be the last and only time.

Chapter 45

I think my bladder's shrunk. Seriously, in all the times I drove to Wales with Danny I never once needed to stop for a wee, and sometimes we were stuck on the M4 for hours. Mine has always been a bladder of steel, but not any more. I only went an hour ago and now I need to go again. Like really, really need to go. I'm not sure what the protocol is when you're paintballing. How am I supposed to indicate a ceasefire in a war zone? As predicted I haven't taken to paintballing. I don't know why it's called team building as I've never hated my work colleagues more. I couldn't care less whether we get the other team's flag, and I hate guns even if they're only firing paint.

I'm not even on the same team as Wendy as she's on Lube's Green Team. The Green Dream he called it when he gave them their rallying address, complete with *A Team* theme-tune der der ders. I am on John's Blue Team. Although I look terrible in green, so perhaps there's a positive about being on the blue side. John gave me a cushy job – probably because I'm a girl – but I refrained from doing a feminist rant because I really don't want to be running around on account of the fact that it poured with rain last night, so every time you step into the 'combat zone' you go arse over tit in the mud!

I'm currently crouched in a wooden hut, ready to fire at anyone from the other team who comes near our flag. Maybe I should just pull my overalls down and wee in here. No one will come in. There's grass beneath me so it should disappear into the ground, and if there's a smell of wee I'll just blame it on a boy. I'm going to have to do it. We're out here until someone gets the other team's flag and that could be hours yet. I take off my Darth Vader hood – oh, that's so much better – unbutton my overalls – my boobs look gigumbous in this vest. I feel as though I'm in someone else's body at the moment – pull down the trousers, then my leggings. Oh damn, there's someone outside; I can hear them running. Talk about timing! Shit, I'd better defend the flag. I pick up my paint gun and follow the figure with it. I fire, I yelp, I miss. I shuffle to a better position – it's not easy to move, though, as my leggings are around my ankles – and fire again. I miss again. Oh God, he's charging towards me, so I just keep firing. He comes right at me into my hut.

'Argh!' I scream, scrambling to pull up my trousers, but stumbling over into the mud. I slide around as I try to haul my leggings up, but before I can the figure lurches into the hut and dives on top of me.

'Don't shoot, it's me, I'm on your team!' the figure pants. It's John. I hadn't noticed he was wearing blue as well.

'Whoops. Sorry. Get off me, you bugger.'

We appear to be lying down in the hut. That's not really the odd part, though. The really 'is this paintballing etiquette' weird point is that we seem to be entwined – I believe spooning is the technical term – and my trousers are around my ankles. John's gripping me and I can't get out of his embrace. Well, perhaps I could if I tried, but it's not unpleasant being held in strong arms, although it would be preferable if my bottom wasn't out, my bladder wasn't full and it wasn't Posh Boy whose arms I was being held in. I attempt to wiggle free and pull up my leggings, but he grips me even harder. I hear his breath in my ear. My heart is thumping, which is strange because I've done absolutely nothing cardiovascular. He keeps one arm firmly around me, and with the other he pulls off his Darth Vader helmet. His hand is resting on my tummy, on the baby. There are three of us here at the moment. If Danny had stayed, would he have held me and his baby like this? I close my eyes and imagine for a moment that he did.

Posh Boy lobs his helmet on the ground and gently pushes me back to the floor. I'm very pleased I didn't wee in there. He leans over me. His breathing is quick, too, but then he has actually been doing some running. He moves my hair from my face and touches the skin on my cheek. He's stroking it and looking at me, and I know I'm panting, too. My chest is heaving up and down, which is quite unnerving considering the current size of it. He slowly moves his fingers from my cheek to my lips and ever so tenderly he touches my lips with his finger. And – oh feckeroony – he's leaning down with his lips slightly parted. His lips land on mine. My boss is kissing me, but that isn't the worse part; the worse part is that I'm kissing him back. This so isn't Estate Agent of the Year behaviour. His lips are warm and soft and gentle. After heavy paintball combat in freezing conditions this feels as warm and comforting as a cup of tea. Fruity tea. He stops for a second and looks at me again, making an odd little groaning sound.

'Grace,' he murmurs. 'Grace, I can't stop thinking about you.' Then his hands are in my hair and his lips are on mine again and it's urgent. It's like we're in a war zone and this may be the only kiss we'll have before we're bombed into extinction. Although that could be the screaming and paint firing going on outside. I feel like a Bond Girl. The world's shortest Bond Girl with a very full bladder. But John could easily be James Bond if he was an actor and not an estate agent. He's tall, handsome and looks delicious in a suit.

'Grace,' he pants in my ear. This is full-on movie-star kissing. I've never kissed anyone other than Danny, and I'm beginning to think he wasn't much cop. My insides are all excited, but then suddenly I remember that the man I'm kissing is John, Bain of my Life, Twat of the Year, and the realisation causes me to pull away from his kiss and knee him in the gonad area. It's more a case of two knees to gonad area, on account of the fact that my leggings are still around my ankles, so both knees move together.

'Argh!' screams Posh Boy, although he doesn't look quite so posh rolling on the floor and clutching his groin. There's a loud sound of cheering outside.

'I think they just got the flag.' I giggle. 'We'd better move,' I say, deftly pulling my trousers back on and standing back up.

'What the hell did you do that for?' he cries. His eyes are watering.

'We work together, that was bad . . .'

'No. We *work* together, you and I, Grace. Or we could work really well together if you'd be a bit kinder to my manhood. Now,' he says, getting up. 'Act along with me. I'm going to pretend my trainer came undone, and I just popped in here to do it up, away from the paint fire. And if you're nice to me I'll refrain from telling the team that I found you in here with your trousers round your ankles!'

And with that he walks out of the hut.

Chapter 46

I have a cunning plan regarding Posh Boy. It involves ignoring him forever. Snogging him put me off my post-paintballing ploughman's lunch. I didn't think anything could put me off a ploughman's. The pairing of Branston pickle and Cheddar has never in my whole life let me down, until today when I just couldn't swallow it. I did manage a selection of home-made ice creams afterwards, though, so thankfully it wasn't all silent starvation. At lunch, I made sure I sat as far away from John as was humanly possible without being in the toilet. And now that we're on the coach, I'm sat next to Wendy and he's at the back with Lube. I haven't told Wendy yet about the snoggage because I know she'll make loud whooping noises.

'Wend, I'm going to say something in a second, and I need you to put your hand over your mouth as I say it, and promise me you won't make a sound.'

'Why?'

'Just do it.'

She does.

'Now promise me no screaming or whooping.'

She nods.

'I'm serious!'

She nods again.

'Posh Boy came into my hut during the paintballing and we snogged.'

She gasps.

'HAND!'

We sit for a little while until Wendy has processed the information.

'That is so cool,' Wendy hisses at me eventually. 'Was it good?'

'NO!' I exclaim. 'I kneed him in the goolies afterwards.'

'Seriously? I always thought he'd be a good kisser!' Wendy exclaims.

'Wend, voice down.'

'What a waste. I thought his lips had kissing potential. He's got good full lips for a bloke.'

'Well,' I humph. 'He was all right.'

'Admit it, Flowers. He was a good snog.'

I shrug. 'Quite.'

'I knew you loved him really,'

'Oh pur-lease.'

'We have to do the Love Test.'

'No, Wend. We definitely don't need to . . .'

'Close your eyes.'

'No.'

'Do it!'

'No!'

'Please, please, I am your best friend in the whole world. Please, please.'

'OK. But this is the most wasted Love Test ever.'

'Ooh, I love, love, love doing the Love Test.'

'Wend, keep your voice down, if the blokes hear this it will be Mick Take Nation.'

'Sorry,' she whispers. 'OK, right.'

She sits up, straightens her back and coughs. Wendy takes the Love Test very seriously.

'OK, are you relaxed?'

I roll my eyes, then nod.

'Now, close your eyes.'

I close my eyes.

'Very good. Now, take three deep breaths.'

I roll my eyes again, but take the breaths to appease her.

'Very good. Now, I'm going to ask you to visualise various things. I want you to listen very carefully to what I am about to say, and take your time. We'll take it nice and slow.'

Wendy has modelled her Love-Test voice on Paul McKenna's hypnosis CDs. She speaks in an American accent, as though she's underwater.

'So, first of all, I want you to imagine his face. Start with his hair, then his eyes and his nose. Now, his mouth. Imagine his lips. His teeth. He's smiling at you. Blimey, Grace, you're doing a gooey smile already.'

Damn. I forgotten that part of Wendy's comprehensive scoring system takes into consideration how much you smile. I try to straighten my mouth, but it's hard, because in my head he's smiling at me, and he does have a nice smile.

'Now, enjoy his face in front of you for a little while longer.

OK, he's still in front of you, but now he's not alone, he's with another girl. She's pretty, this girl, and she looks nice. And he's kissing her. A real "I love you" kiss. They're really into each other. Ooh, ooh, there might even be a bit of hand on boob. How do you feel?'

'Um.' I swallow. 'I just hope she's worthy, really.'

'Now, get rid of the girl. Throw her away. It's just him again, but he's old. He's like eighty. He's got old hands and an old, crotchety face and maybe a mole with a hair coming out of it.'

'Wend! I'd tweezer the mole hair for him.'

'Shh. So he's old and wrinkly. Now, I want you to imagine kissing him. Whoa, Grace. You've still got that sappy smile on.'

I straighten my face again.

'Right, now it's your wedding. Everyone is there. Me, looking absolutely stunning with Freddie, who's changed his shirt. OK, now it's your first dance as man and wife. What's the song?'

'"Annie's Song".'

'"Annie's Song", as in the one your dad sang to your mum that made grown men blub.'

'Yep,' I open my eyes. 'Funny thing, but with Dan, the first dance was always an issue in my head. I mean, the only song he ever really got pash about was Guns N' Roses' "Welcome To The Jungle".'

'Yeah, well that says it all.'

'You know what, Wend? I don't miss him any more.'

'No, I bet you don't.'

'Why do you say that?'

'Well, he was never really there, was he, Danny?'

'How do you mean?'

'Well, he was always there somewhere – on the computer or in the pub or watching telly – but he was never really there, was he? Never really present. He didn't bring much to the table.'

'Oh, I don't know.'

'The thing is, some women like to have a man like that – a quiet bloke who's just there – but I don't think that's you really, deep down. I think you want a man to rock your world. Like your dad did.'

'Hmm, like Anton.'

'No, like Posh Boy. You just got full "I love Posh Boy" marks in the test.'

'It wasn't Posh Boy I was imagining when you said all that stuff.'

'You what?'

'It was Anton.'

'What, those big smiles and "Annie's Song" were for Anton?'

'Totally.'

'Grace, he's like twice your age.'

'He's about the same age as George Clooney,' I say, affronted.

She laughs as though I'm joking.

'Can I interest you in a Freddie update?'

'Yes. In depth, please.'

'Well, Freddie is being very nice to me. As he frigging should be after be called me a slut.'

'He didn't call you a slut.'

'Slag then, whatever, the meaning was clear, even though

he's been with far more girls than I have blokes since we've known him. Obviously, it's fine for him to put it about, but not me. So, anyway, he's being lovely now. Kind, sweet, attentive.'

'And?'

'And I'm ignoring him.'

'Oh no, Wend. Don't play games, that's so not you.'

'Hang on, not proper ignoring him. I'm *politely* ignoring him. I smile and nod and respond if he says something, then I say, "Nice to see you, Freddie, but will you excuse me while I just go and talk to so and so."'

'And?'

'And it hurts to say it, but he's sniffing around me like I'm a dog's arse. Years I've spent lobbing myself at men – I'm getting a bit of a tennis metaphor going here. Right, so I'm the tennis ball. Bouncy, bouncy. Wendy of old used to hurl herself forcefully at a man, but New Wendy is a tennis ball that bounces across the ground and is impossible for a man to catch. When he tries the ball falls out of his hand and he stumbles about like a pillock. You know what I mean, don't you? You can't catch.'

I smile at her.

'Yes. Wendy, I know exactly what you mean.'

Chapter 47

'Hallelujah! Hallelujah!' I scream, dancing about the office. Finally, something positive has happened. I've just got an offer on Claire's flat. 'Who's the daddy?' I scream.

'What is she doing?' Posh Boy asks Wendy.

'That flat with the sanitary-towel child. She's got an offer. Asking price.'

'Oh.'

'Hallelujah! I'm going to tell Claire in person,' I say, grabbing my keys from my desk.

'I'll come, too.'

I freeze. What if he tries to kiss me in the car? What if he thinks I'll be doing office nooky from now on?

'No, you're all right, I'll go.'

'No, I'd like to.'

'Um, but . . . '

'Come on, stop polluting the silence with your voice.'

'You should really think about getting your own lines.'

'Come on, stop dithering. We should get going.'

'Righto,' I say, grabbing my keys. GAH! Shoot me now. I just said 'Righto'!

'You should really think about getting your own lines,' he taunts proudly, following me as I power walk to the car. I get there speedily, but then have to wait for him. If he's going to come along he'll have to climb in my side. Eventually we belt up and I start the engine.

He waits until we're at the first set of traffic lights before he speaks.

'You, er . . . ' he starts.

'I couldn't have put it better myself,' I say, pretending to concentrate on the road.

'I, er . . .'

'Absolutely.'

'Grace.' He puts his hand on my knee.

'Don't, please.'

'No?'

'No. Absolutely not.'

'Oh, absolutely not?'

'Hmm.'

'That's a shame.'

'Well, it's not a good idea. It's a really, really bad time for me and we work together.'

'I thought we were made to kiss each other.'

I'm parked now, but I don't look at him; I undo my seat-belt. He puts his hand on mine.

'It's a really, really bad time for me.'

He strokes my hand and I look up, and suddenly we're

kissing again. Oh, damn! It takes a moment for my brain to catch up with my mouth, then I push him away.

'See, made to kiss each other,' he says softly.

I have to admit that the kissing's good, but there's more to it all than kissing. I wouldn't want to sing to Posh Boy. I wouldn't want to lie in his arms all night. I wouldn't want to wake up next to him for the rest of my life. I know that. Although the kissing is good. The kissing is really rather lovely, actually.

'Let's get back to the constant abuse and me outselling you eight to one without the snogging, OK?'

'I'm not choosing to have this crush on you, Flowers, believe me! I'd much rather have a crush on someone who was nice to me. Someone who offered me the odd kind word or look. I'm not choosing to have a crush on Big Balls Woman who's made my life a living hell since I took this job and kneed me in my own big balls.' He sighs. 'How about we have one night of passion to get it out of our systems.'

'I've got nothing in my system to get rid of,' I tell him. There's a knock on the window on my side. It's Claire, so I open the door.

'I wondered who was in my spot, then I saw it was you two,' she says, a tiny baby propped on her shoulder. She's not crying, which is positive. 'The twins are at Tumble Tots, do you want to come in for a cuppa?'

I look at John to see if we've got time.

'Do you have biscuits?' he enquires formally.

'Freddie the Frogs and Hungry Caterpillars.'

'Sold.'

'We've got good news,' I say, getting out of the car.

'Oh?'

'An offer. Asking price. This morning. Banker. No chain. He's been renting, so should be quick.'

'Oh.' She looks so happy she might cry.

'Shall I take the wee one?' I say, holding out my arms for the baby.

'Thank you,' she says.

She places the tiny warm bundle into my arms.

'Oh, you're so precious,' I whisper into the baby's head. 'Oh you're so precious,' I say again. 'How old is she?'

'Two and a half months.'

'Look at you, broody,' Posh Boy says, having finally extricated himself from the car.

'Grace'll make a lovely mum,' Claire says warmly.

'I think so,' agrees Posh Boy.

'Just don't leave it too late.'

I don't say anything. I just sniff the tiny baby's head and imagine how it would feel if she was mine.

Chapter 48

My loan has been approved! Mum will have the money in her bank account by the end of next week. I've come round tonight to tell her. She doesn't know the good news yet, but she's already in a peculiarly good mood. I'm watching her closely. She's making cauliflower cheese. Now in essence this is a wonderful spectacle, because I love cauliflower cheese, but my mother has never made it before. The main problem with cauliflower cheese, for my mother, has always been the cheese. My mother doesn't encourage cheese in the house. Occasional tubs of Philadelphia Light might make an appearance once a month, and there has been one lone sighting of some feta, but Cheddar! Not on your nelly. She didn't even make it for Danny, and she loved Danny.

'Is Danny working late?' she chirps from the cooker as though she's been reading my mind.

Do I tell her now? Do I risk trampling on her rarely spotted mirth? Yes, I suppose I have to. At least I have good news about the loan to chase it with.

'Mum, we split up.'

She spins round. She was always very good at turns. Her mother spotted her turns as a toddler and took her straight to dance classes.

'Oh, Grace.' Her face has fallen. 'Oh, Grace, how are you?'

'Oh.' I hadn't expected her concern. 'I don't know really.'

'Do you want to talk to me about it?' This is so odd. This is normal mother behaviour.

'Um, well, I dunno. He's moved to Canada for a job.'

'Oh, Grace,' she says. 'Oh, Grace.'

She places her hand on my back as I sit on the table. It's physical contact from my mother. I close my eyes. We stand still like this, as though a painter is before us doing a mother and daughter tableau, until Mum screeches the word, 'Bugger!' and rushes back to the cauliflower cheese.

'Ew, it's stuck to the pan,' she says, stirring it furiously.

'Never mind, the crunchy bits are nice.'

I'm in a daze. I've fantasised about having girly chats like this with my mum for a decade.

'I haven't had this for years,' she says, peering inside the saucepan with a clenched jaw before continuing. 'I never thought he was good enough for you.'

'But you doted on Danny.'

'Because he was there. He's always been there, and that counted for something. But if I think of you, I see you with someone stronger, more creative, someone more like your dad. Mind you, I never would have thought you'd be an estate agent, Grace. I thought you'd be a singer. I thought me and your dad would have been at Ronnie Scott's listening to you by now.'

'Yeah, well, we both know why that didn't work out.'

'Do we? Anyway, I don't want to upset you. I have some good news, which is why I wanted to cook you something nice,' she says, wincing at the cauliflower cheese. 'Our money troubles are over. I took some advice and borrowed some money. A loan.'

'Oh, but that's my news. I got you a loan. It was approved today.'

'Well, I don't need your loan; I got my own. I waited until it was in my bank account to tell you.'

'But you have to pay loans back.'

'Grace, I'm not completely stupid. I've been on the planet a lot longer than you.'

'But—'

'It's fine. I'm sure I don't need all the money I've borrowed. I shall pay off all the debts and I'll still have enough to live on, and then I'll get a job.'

'What sort of job?'

'Something I can do online.'

'Like what?'

'Don't say it like that, Grace. I thought I could make and sell dresses on eBay.'

'Well.' I wonder what to say. I'm so used to sniping at my mother that I find myself searching for something negative to say, but actually it's a good idea. Ricardo mentioned borrowing money against the house, that must have been what she's done and he's obviously very good with cash. Mum can make amazing dresses, she could do very well. Best of all, it means she doesn't need the graveyard money. It also means I don't need to borrow twenty grand. 'Well done, Mum. That's a brilliant idea.'

'I thank you,' she smiles and does a perfect curtsy.

I smile.

I put my hand on my tummy and look out of the window. Someone has mowed my mother's lawn. I don't ask her who because I'm thinking about something else entirely. If I no longer have to support my mother, could I support a child? It's a ridiculous question to ask myself really, as I've got an appointment at the hospital tomorrow to organise the thingy.

Chapter 49

I wonder whether you can have an abortion and put it away in a box in the corner of your mind? Or does it come back to haunt you in every baby's face you see? Wendy says that one in five women have them. Do they all feel sad? I expect so. It's hardly laugh-a-minute stuff. You don't hear many girls saying, 'What are you up to today?' 'I'm off to Topshop. You?' 'Having an abortion.' 'Oh, wicked!'

I'm having a scan to check my dates and so I can see it. I'm lying down on a gurney in the clinic, my tummy is covered in slime and I can see with my own eyes what's going on in my tummy. It's being shown on a screen next to me. There really is something there. I can see a tiny, growing, moving thing, a little him or her. I wish Dan was here, holding my hand, and that we were discussing names. Not that I'd let him have a say, Camilla for a girl, Camille for a boy, although I'd shorten it to Cam so he didn't have the total mick taken out of him at school.

They've told me to come back in a week's time. That's when they'll do the procedure.

'Excuse me?' I say to the Chinese-looking lady doctor.

'Yes.'

'Do you mind if I do something a bit weird?'

'Um . . .'

'I wondered if you'd mind me singing.'

'Oh no, not at all.'

Perhaps it's certifiable to do what I'm going to do, but I feel that even though I'm not going to have this baby, I should offer it some love. So I sing. I sing 'Summertime', like my dad sang to me. But when I get to the lines, 'One of these mornings, You're going to rise up singing,' my voice starts to crack and I have to stop and look up at the ceiling. I don't want to break down, not here. I so want to sing the next lines – 'Then you'll spread your wings and you'll take to the sky' – but there's a lump in my throat and I can't. I lay back, close my eyes and try to think of a small good thing to cling on to, but there's nothing. I'm sure there's something, but I can't get beyond the fact that there's a heartbeat inside me that could grow into a person. I could love it, laugh with it, play it music. All I've wanted for years is family, yet here I am destroying the opportunity. I feel as though I came here today to arrange a swift abortion, but doubt put on a boxing glove and punched me in the face. I've been trying so hard not to think about it. Foolish really, we all know that if you push things to the back of your mind, sooner or later they come back and bite you on the bum.

When I open my eyes, the doctor is staring at me. Oh, dear, she might actually certify me.

'Are you a singer?' she asks.

'No, I'm an estate agent on the Chamberlayne Road,' I reply, though I don't say it as proudly as I normally do.

She looks disappointed.

'You know what you should do?'

'What?' I ask, but I have a feeling I know what she's about to say.

'Enter *Britain Sings its Heart Out*.'

See. I knew.

'Oh, no,' I say automatically, but then I stop. Suddenly I'm not sure of anything any more.

Chapter 50

I have had the worst week. I thought I would just be able to have the thingy and it would be easy, but it's not. I haven't slept for days. Every time I close my eyes I see the picture in the booklet that the God lady gave me. But that's not all. The strangest part is that I don't feel alone at the moment. I lie awake at night feeling that I, or we – baby and me – are a little team. I didn't expect to feel like this. Tomorrow at 11 a.m. I go into hospital, and when I come out it will just be me again. I feel wretched. I don't want to do it. I violently don't want to do it. But I know that I have to. Don't I?

Why is it that whenever you feel really, properly dreadful, you are obliged to go to a soirée and pretend you feel fine?

I'm at one of Bob's 'Wet the New Development's Head' parties. When he finishes a new development he always holds an opening party in the show flat for any bigwigs who've helped him along the way – planners, architects, local councillors and business owners, people from the local paper, that sort of thing. I come and wander around, introducing myself to people and giving out my business cards. I usually quite enjoy them, although it did take some practice. At my first one, the thought of people walking on the brand-new carpets was too much for me, so I stood at the door and made everyone show me the soles of their shoes, and then instructed them to 'enter', 'wipe' or 'remove' accordingly.

This is the plushest party Bob's hosted yet and the apartment looks luscious. An agency has done the canapés, but sadly they're the sort that look marvellous but taste revolting. After each circle of the room, I've treated myself to a little rest by a barely-touched-because-they're-truly-disgusting tray of posh mini Scotch eggs. The bite I had and spat out into a napkin was the first thing I'd eaten all day. There's also a pop-up cocktail barman, who I will be visiting very shortly. Posh Boy is here. I keep catching sight of him shaking suited men's hands and patting them on the back. He thinks he's at the G20 summit.

Bob looks as miserable as I feel. He's walking towards me now and I just want to cuddle him up in bed with a box set of *Friends* and a bowl of chicken soup.

'Hi, Bob, how you doing?'

He tries to smile.

'Oh, Grace. It's not been good.'

'I'm sorry, Bob.'

'Mini Scotch egg? Don't mind if I do.'

'I wouldn't,' I advise.

'Urgh!' he says as he bites into it.

'I tried to warn you.'

I hand him a napkin.

'Sorry I haven't been in touch. I've been trying to get a new foreman, so I'm laying off the acquisitions for the moment, and I didn't want to burden you with my "stuff".'

'Bob. Burden me with your stuff. Lay it on me, bro.'

'Thanks, sis.'

'How have things been?'

'Oh, Grace, it was awful. They'd been at it for months and I didn't have a clue.'

'How are things now?'

'Well, she's left and I sacked him. I think they might be together.'

'I'm sorry.'

'Nah, it's for the best. She wasn't the girl I thought she was. You know me, I had her down for an angel. But . . .' He slumps forward and rests his head in his hands.

I rub my hand up and down his back and say, 'It will get better.'

'Yeah, I know it will. But before she left she told me this thing, Grace, and I can't get it out of my head.'

'Do you want to talk about it?'

'There's not really much to say. She was pregnant a year ago. It was mine – or so she said – but she wasn't happy and she got rid of it.'

'Oh, Bob.'

'I tell you, Grace, I can't stop thinking about it.'

'Oh, Bob.'

'You know me, I've always wanted to have kids. And there was a child, my child – sorry, our child – and she did that. It's stupid, but I just can't get it out of my head. I went to see QPR on Saturday and they sell these babygro things there and I stood in front of them wiping my eyes. Sorry, Grace, I'm not much company.'

I don't speak; I just stroke his back.

'I keep thinking about all the love I could have given it,' Bob says and his voice cracks.

I can't offer any painkilling words.

'All that love.'

I nod. That's all I can do. I stand there next to him, nodding and thinking of the extra heartbeat inside of me that won't be there tomorrow.

'Can I buy you dinner after?' he offers.

'Oh.' I pause. I love Bob, but much as I want to comfort him, I can't be a sympathetic ear tonight. I can't hear about the baby he would have loved. 'I'm really sorry but I can't.'

I should have dinner, though. I haven't eaten a proper meal for days. God, I haven't eaten, I haven't slept, I haven't taken care of myself at all. I know why. It's because I hate myself for what I'm going to do tomorrow.

Chapter 51

Posh Boy finds me later, sitting on the bed in the master bedroom, draining a margarita and staring out of the window. He's carrying two drinks: a margarita and clear-looking drink in a martini glass. He holds the margarita towards me.

'You looked like you could use another.'

I take it and place my empty glass on the bedside unit.

'Thank you.'

I sip it and wince.

'Yeah, I think the barman's taken a shine to you. He asked if this was for you, and when I said yes, he had a very free hand with the tequila.'

'Oh,' I say vaguely.

'What's up with you?'

'Nothing. Why?'

'Grace, you look like you're contemplating suicide.'

'No, just murder.'

'Mine, I suppose.'

'Always.'

'Blimey, was that a smile.'

'Just a little one.'

'It was a nice smile, too.'

'Yeah, well, don't get too used it.'

'I've been thinking.'

'Don't be ridiculous, John, that would involve having a brain.'

'I know you love me really, and that's why I've been thinking that you and I should really have one night of passion, you know, to get rid of this sexual tension between us.'

He's standing at the end of the bed and he's taken off his suit jacket. He's wearing his black suit trousers and they fit him perfectly. They must sit just below the belly button on his flat tummy, and whereas some blokes buy shirts way too large, he doesn't, so you can decipher his shape. Broad at the shoulders, tapering in at the waist and, although I haven't seen his bare arms, I've felt them round me and I know they're wide and muscly at the top. Badminton, who'd have thought?

'Are you mentally undressing me?'

'No, John, I am not.'

'Shame. You can whenever you like.'

'Thanks, very kind of you.'

'Righto,' he says, knocking back his drink. 'Gotta get out of here.'

'Yeah, I'll see you tomorrow.'

'Why don't we go for another drink?'

'Because you'll jump me.'

'Oh ho, aren't we full of ourselves. I won't jump you. I might try to find out the secret of your sales success, because it's quite unprecedented, but I promise not to jump you. I did it once and it still brings tears to my eyes.'

I smile at the memory and then I think about the offer of a drink. Why not have another drink? The one in my hand hasn't done nearly enough anaesthetising for my liking. What else would I do? Go home alone and lie awake, wrapped in a blanket of sadness. Anything to stave that off, even a drink with Posh Boy.

'Go on,' he says, as if reading my mind. 'You won't be seeing me for a while now, I'm doing a stint at the Cricklewood branch. What do you reckon?'

'You're buying.'

'Of course, highly independent, feminist woman, except when it comes to being bought drinks by men.'

'No, but when posh blokes appear from nowhere and nick the job I've been working towards for five years, then yes, I let them buy me a drink.'

'Oh, now we're getting to the point. Did you really want Head of London Sales?'

'Did I really want Head of London Sales? Er, no. I wanted it to go to you, a bloke who appeared from nowhere, doesn't know the company and can't sell as much property as I can.'

'You will be—' He stops.

'Will be what?'

'You will—' he stops again. 'You'll be OK. I know you'll be rewarded.'

'What are you on about?'

'Nothing, I just, um, I think Ken has something lined up for you, that's all.'

'What?'

'I can't say.'

'Hopefully he'll sack you and I'll get your job.'

'Could be.'

I don't know what Posh Boy's going on about, and at this particular moment in time, I don't know if I care.

'So what did you make of my offer?'

'What offer?'

'The one night of passion.'

'Oh, please.'

'Is that please, oh, oh, oh, John, yes, *please*,' he pants orgasmically, and it's quite funny, so I laugh.

Much later on, we're in a hotel bar. We hadn't planned to come in here, but he was walking me home and I needed the toilet. So we came into the hotel and when I emerged from the toilet he'd ordered me a drink. Now he's just got me another, although I don't remember saying I wanted one. He's carrying my fifth or possibly sixth margarita when he asks again, 'What do you reckon? One night of passion? Well, there can be more than one, but I thought I'd try to sell just one first.'

As he puts my drink down in front of me I reach out and touch the muscles on his upper arms, just because I want to feel them. He lets me trace the contour of his muscles with my fingers for a few moments, then he scoops me up and sits me on his lap, and there's something about his strength that makes me feel as though I'm being lifted away from my problems. Super quickly his lips are upon mine, and the idea of one night of passion suddenly doesn't seem so bad.

'Come back to mine. My dad's away,' he whispers urgently in my ear.

'You live with your dad! You're such a shuttlecock!' I screech. But I go home with him anyway, because I don't want to go home alone to another sleepless night, because I want to block out tomorrow, and because even though they're not the exact arms I want, I'd like to feel them around me, just for one night.

Chapter 52

'Oh dear, Gracie,' I say, slowly banging my head on the landing wall as the night before comes back to me. I'm creeping out of John's house. John has already gone. Oh God, I shagged my boss. I bang my head on the wall again.

'Why, Gracie? Why?' I whimper. 'It was the tequila-based cocktails, your honour, I can't take them. I'm short.'

'Good afternoon,' says an oriental female voice. I keep my forehead on the wall as it's easing the dull ache inside, and turn my face to see a small Filipino woman in a salmon-coloured dress standing a foot away from me.

I thought John had a housekeeper. His bed was made hotel taut and you practically needed a crowbar to get in it. Not that we did get in it for ages. We had sex as soon as we were through the door. He's very strong and he kept lifting me up and moving me from cupboard top to wall. I repeatedly felt his arms and shouted shuttlecock, and he kept shh-ing me by kissing me. It was over very quickly. At least the first time was, but then there was a second time and a half-hearted third attempt, which I think I might have fallen asleep during. Still, at least I got some sleep. At least I didn't lie awake thinking about what I have to do today.

'You make the beds beautifully,' I mewl. 'Good afternoon to you, too.'

Slowly – really very slowly considering – I realise something. 'Afternoon?' I say quietly. 'What time is it?'

She turns her tiny wrist so I can see her watch.

'One twenty?'

She nods, smiles and walks away.

One twenty in the afternoon! I, Gracie Flowers, have slept until one twenty in the afternoon! I never oversleep. The trains always wake me up at home. Why didn't Posh Boy wake me? What's he playing at? One twenty! I've missed my appointment! I've missed the thingy!

Shit! Shit!

Or is it?

Is it a sign? Should I have this baby?

I have never been so confused. Ever.

Chapter 53

'Dad, I need to talk to you,' I came here early, so it's just me and him, like the old days in the bathroom. 'I'm pregnant.'

Normally when I talk to Dad the words flow and I drench the poor man with a power shower of language, but today there's barely a dribble. I pause before I speak again.

'I've got a baby inside me,' I say eventually. But again I just leave the words hanging there, lonely. I can't find them any friends. I don't know what to say. I'm sitting cross-legged on the dirty old cushion that I've kept for years in the boot of my car, facing Dad's gravestone. I reach forward and wipe a bit of wet leafy goo from it.

'Baby,' I say, looking down at my tummy. 'This is my dad. He was very cool. He always knew what to do.'

If I had this baby, he or she would never meet my dad. They'd never experience his amazing hugs. They'd never know what all that love felt like. But this baby feels connected to my dad somehow. People tell me that I look like my father.

Perhaps this baby will, too. It would be a little bit of him living on. I sigh.

'Oh, Dad, can I do it alone? It won't have a daddy.' But, Grace, I remind myself, it would have a daddy.

'I need to talk to Danny, don't I?' I say suddenly.

'Dad, should I have this baby?'

The problem with dead people and gravestones is they don't answer back when you need them to.

'Dad, a baby was so not in the plan. Nowhere near it.'

I trace his name on the stone with my finger. Camille Flowers.

'I've even named it, Dad, which was probably a silly thing to do. They don't recommend it in the abortion leaflet. Camille for a boy, Camilla for a girl. Oh, Dad, why did I name it? I should have kept it at chickpea. How can I abort it now I know its name? What should I do, Dad?'

I sit and wait for a sign – a something – but there's nothing. For a moment the sun nearly breaks through the clouds, but there's nothing celestial about it. I hear a train in the distance, but there's nothing about a train that helps me make the decision whether or not to bring a baby into the world. I feel three spots of rain and a bird rustles in a tree. It's all as it always is, and perhaps that's the sign. Perhaps that's what Dad is trying to say, that life goes on. That no one can make this decision but me.

'But it's so hard, Dad.' I sigh and I know he agrees. 'Of course you can't give me a sign. I'm sorry, I always do this to you.'

Leonard and Joan arrive a few moments later and I can sense their pace slowing as they spot me sitting here morosely. I turn round to smile at them so they feel free to approach.

'Look who we found,' Joan says very gently, but I've already seen. My mother is with them. Rosemary Flowers, who hasn't left the house for nearly three years and hasn't visited this spot for ten, is walking between Leonard and Joan. She looks ashen, as though she might faint. We stare at each other for a moment.

'Your dad thought I should come today. He was very insistent,' she whispers.

'Oh, Mum,' I gasp.

She leaves Leonard and Joan and walks unsteadily towards me on her own until she's standing above me.

'Mum, I'm pregnant,' I whisper.

She bends down and kneels on the ground by her husband's grave and she puts her arms around me. It's a hug. It's the hug from my mother that I've been longing for.

'Oh, Mum, I want to have the baby.'

We don't move; we just stay there, hugging each other, next to Dad's grave. Neither of us notices when Leonard and Joan quietly leave us. I don't know the time, but I'm sure we're there for nearly half an hour.

Eventually it starts to rain and Mum stands up and holds out her hand for me. We walk back to my car and drive home.

Chapter 54

After Dad died, Mum and I lived together like two loco ladies. Mum started to spend a great deal of time in bed and I sat in Dad's study, playing every single one of his vinyl records. The hours were only punctuated by Danny popping round, me going to the shops or cemetery, or Mum randomly suggesting I enter *Britain Sings its Heart Out.* At first it was as though we were waiting for him to come back, for an envoy from the afterlife to drop by and say, 'Terribly sorry about all this, we didn't mean to take Camille; he's on his way, he'll be home for tea.' For ages afterwards letters would come for him or the phone would ring and a voice would ask to speak to him, and there was always a second, a fabulous fleeting second, when he seemed to still be there and life seemed normal. 'Oh, yes, I'll just get him for you,' I would say, and I'd lay down the receiver and be just about to holler, 'Dad!' when I'd remember. It was like learning the most awful truth, but having to keep on relearning it.

Life was going on about us but we were stuck in limbo, unable to move on. Then one day the telephone rang. It was a man called Sidney who worked in publishing and he asked if we knew how Dad had been getting on with his *Five Year Plan* book when he'd died. We'd forgotten about Dad's book idea and the interest he'd had in publishing it. I went on Dad's computer and found lots of files. He had numbered each folder and it was clear that each number held notes, which were intended to be structured into a chapter. I showed them to Mum and we agreed we should tidy them up, make them into a book and see if they still wanted to publish it, so that's what we did. It was definitely a good thing as it gave us a purpose.

Every afternoon we would sit in Dad's dark study, fathoming his notes and trying to draft them into a narrative. For me it was like being hypnotised. Every day I learned about the benefits of a five year plan, so perhaps it's no surprise that I eventually made my own five year plan and became evangelical about it. I thought it was working on Mum, too, as she started to leave the house more. Nowhere too rock and roll, just the hairdresser's and the gym, but for a few months she seemed stronger.

Then we received another phone call. A female Scottish voice told me to pass on a message to my mother. 'Tell her that her father died,' was all the voice said. If my mother had been buttoned up before, she became stitched in after that. I can't be sure exactly, but I don't think she's left the house since that phone call.

She left the house today, though, to come to me. That's something, isn't it? That's something else.

*

I'm still at Mum's. I've been here all day. Now it's late and I'm sitting up in my childhood single bed with the lamp on. I did a terrible job of moving out when I did. I shouldn't blame Mum for the clutter in the house when I left an entire bedroom full of stuff. It's funny, as I remember moving into my flat and feeling so free from baggage, when really I'd just loaded it all on my poor mother. I even found Dad's old Ramones T-shirt under the bed. I'm wearing it now.

There's a torn poster of Nina Simone on one wall, the desk I was sitting at the last time I saw Dad is still where it's always been and the wardrobe is full of Mum's old ballroom dancing clothes. I turn to my bedside table and open the top drawer. It's full of cheap make-up and Topshop labels with buttons attached to them. I open the next drawer down – more crap and some truly disgusting jewellery. I open the third – yep, more crap. But I feel around more thoroughly in this one and my hand finds what it was looking for. I squeeze the soft cover of my old diary, wondering whether to pull it out or just leave the past there in the bottom drawer. Curiosity beats caution, though, and out it comes. It's a very ugly diary. I wonder why I bought it. It's orange with garish green flowers all over it, and it's furry. Not posh teddy furry, more like a cheap toy you'd win at the fair.

I open the diary. I only wrote it for a few weeks and then Dad died, so I stopped.

> I AM GOING TO WRITE A DIARY!!!!! IT WILL CHART ME LEAVING SCHOOL (FINALLY!!! RELIEF!!!) AND GETTING A LUCRATIVE RECORDING CONTRACT WITH SONY.

I stare at the capital letters on the page. It's as though my confident younger self is bellowing at me. I don't know whether I can keep on reading. I don't know whether I can take any more of this positivity. But, of course, I don't stop reading. I turn the page and am instantly drawn in.

> I GOT ASKED TO THE PROM!!!! Feel bad though, 'cos Wend and I were going to go together dressed as the Blues Brothers. It's her dad's favourite film and he said he'd hire the costumes for us. Oh God, he'll be disappointed, too. Anyway, to the point! Danny Saunders asked me out. And he is well fit!!!!! AND he was wearing a Ramones T-shirt. I told Dad and he said, 'Good man, good man.' Then he went on and on about how he was going to speak to Danny and tell him a few things. 1) That I am not allowed to have sex until I'm forty!!! 2) That he may be a ballroom dancer but he's quite capable of hospitalising sixteen-year-old boys who hurt his daughter. Obviously Danny is NEVER allowed to meet my dad. It was funny, though. I couldn't stop laughing. Dad's in a really good mood because ITV want to meet him to discuss a ballroom dancing programme for the telly. V.V.V. exciting!!! Mum made – wait for it – MACARONI CHEESE!!!! Yep, her period must be due. Excellent. Dad whispered, 'Time of the month' when we sat down at the table, and I laughed and Mum copped a strop, so I reckon it's true. Did bloody geography revision all night. Like, literally nearly all night. I bloody HATE geography, remind me again why I picked it? Oh yeah,

so I'll know where I am when I go on tour with my bestselling album! Must hold that thought. Night. Knackered.

I'm sucked in. I can't close the book on all these capital letters and exclamation marks now.

> OK. Weird day. Had small break with Danny Saunders. And YES he is fit. Ultimate fitness boot camp getting up at 6a.m. to run up a mountain with a heavy backpack on fit, BUT he is well quiet. Like, really, really quiet. Like, pretty much silent. So I had to keep talking to make up for it. I spoke a ridiculous amount of rubbish. I even told him what Dad said!!!! I must never talk to a fit bloke again. But I was nervous and he just sat there with his chocolate milk, so I had to say something and out that came. I hope he starts talking soon. Maybe blokes just talk less than girls, although that can't be true because my dad never shuts up. Like NEVER!!! Still, at least he's fit. Danny Saunders, I mean, not my dad. And I want to kiss him. FIRST PROPER SNOG!!!!! (I'm not counting Julian from the youth club disco last year, 'cos that was RANK!!!) First kiss reserved for Danny 'Silent but Deadly' Saunders.

I close the diary. That's enough for now. It's impossible to read the name Danny Saunders and not think about an awkward fact. I am not going to have an abortion. I am going to have his baby. Danny is the father. I have to tell him tomorrow.

Chapter 55

'Do you want a small gin while you do it?'

'I don't think pregnant people are supposed to drink gin at eleven in the morning.'

'Oh no!' my mother clasps her hand to her mouth and starts giggling like a twelve-year-old child at the mention of the word willy. I watch her and smile. My baby is bringing us together. I wonder if it will last. I don't wonder about it for long, though, because I'm distracted by the telephone in front of me and the Welsh telephone number lying next to it.

'Tea!' my mother says shrilly. 'I'll make you a nice cup of tea and then I'll step out of the room so you can make the call.'

I've been psyching myself up to call Danny's mum for the last half an hour. I don't have a contact for Danny in Canada, so his mother will once again have to act as envoy.

'No, I'll just do it,' I say, stabbing the telephone keypad quickly before I can find a new method of procrastination.

It rings for a long time. It gets to the point where you think,

Is this rude now? Should I hang up? But then you think, A few more rings, which in this case turns into about forty. They might have gone to Vancouver to visit Danny. What if, right now, they're eating pancakes with bacon and syrup, or something equally wrong, and he's introducing them to his new, really tall girlfriend? It wouldn't surprise me if Danny had a new girlfriend already. He's the sort of bloke who'll always find someone to look after him.

'Hello!' It's Danny's mum and she's very out of breath. Either she's just run across acres of their land to get to the phone, or more likely she's been doing one of those keep-fit videos she likes to buy from the charity shop in Carnarvon. Maybe Beverley Callard's, or Lorraine Kelly's. Actually, I'm not sure Lorraine Kelly has a workout video. And I'm not sure I should be having these ridiculous thoughts at the moment.

'Hello?' she repeats.

I look at Mum. I don't know what I'm expecting her to do. I'm on the phone and she's over by the kettle.

'Er, Mrs Saunders?' I finally manage to say.

'Yes.'

'It's Grace.'

'Oh.'

She could at least make an effort to sound pleased. Ten years I've spent picking up her son's socks. Well, not so much picking them up, more kicking them into a pile under the bed. She said she loved me like a daughter, but now I'm cast aside like an unwanted IKEA CD rack.

'Um, I need to get in touch with Danny about, er, something.'

'Why's that, love?'

'Er, just . . . '

'If it's not urgent, Grace, then I don't think the two of you should be contacting each other.'

'Um, well . . . '

'I know it's hard, Grace, and you know I'm not a fan of cliché, but the two of you need to move on.'

'It's urgent, Mrs Saunders.'

'Are you sure, Grace?'

'Well, I think being pregnant with his baby is pretty urgent.'

BIG PAUSE.

'Are you sure it's his?'

I really, really, *really* want to say, 'I'd only ever slept with your stinking son, Mrs Saunders,' or, 'Not really, Mrs Saunders, I haven't stopped shagging randoms since you dumped me on your son's behalf.' But that's not me and this isn't *The Jeremy Kyle Show*, so I don't. I make do with, 'Yes.'

There's another very long pause, so I think she must believe me.

'Right. How are you, Grace?'

'Oh. I've been quite sick and tired actually, but I feel OK today. I'm with Mum. We . . . I . . . um. Originally I wasn't planning to, you know, what with Danny leaving, I didn't think I could manage. But what I'm trying to say is, I was booked in at the hospital. I mean, I was booked in at the hospital to have a thingy, but I don't want to do that. Mum's being great and we think we can manage.' Mum and I bust some soppy team-baby smiles at each other. 'So, obviously Danny needs to know, but I don't need anything from him and I'm not asking for anything from him.'

'Right. Well. Gosh.'

Poor lady. She's probably got a nice roast dinner planned and I've sabotaged it. They should go out for lunch. She shouldn't be dealing with her Aga when her mind is on other things. That's how accidents happen. Still, at least there are some nice pubs in the countryside. She could pop into the Boots in Carnarvon while she's there and tell the pharmacist there's a baby on its way for her to look after, as promised.

'So shall I leave you to tell Danny then?'

'Oh, er . . . '

'Or you can give me his number and I'll do it.'

'No, no. I'll do it.'

'Right, bye then.'

I nearly add 'Granny' for a laugh.

'Whoa,' I say when I put down the phone.

'Well?' asks Mum, putting my tea in front of me on the table.

'Poor woman. It was a bit of a shock.'

'What did she say?'

'Oh, er, "gosh" mainly. She definitely didn't have an orgasm about it.'

'Grace!'

I look down at my tummy.

'Poor little thing,' I say. 'Granny in Wales isn't as excited about you as Granny in London. Don't you worry, though, we'll get her back with crap smellies at Christmas and all your rubbish drawings. I can take you to stay with her when you're teething, potty train you in their posh lounge, that sort of thing.'

'Oh, Grace,' my mother tuts. She's trying to admonish my

Granny-in-Wales-is-mean tirade, but it's not working because she's beaming and clearly thrilled about her role as nice Granny.

'Poor, Danny. He so won't be expecting this.'

'At least the baby has a chance of being tall.'

'Hello! Are you a giant child in there?'

The phone has started to ring. I stop breathing and Mum touches my shoulder.

'That was quick.'

'OK, Baby Bean. This might be Daddy,' I whisper before I pick up the phone. 'Hello?'

'Grace.' It isn't Baby Bean's Daddy, it's Granny in Wales. 'I meant to say, Grace, that if you need anything, anything at all, you have our number and you know where we are.'

'Thank you.'

'I'll be keeping in touch.'

'Thank you.'

We hang up and I pat Baby Bean.

'Watch out, Granny in London, Granny in Wales is catching up!'

Chapter 56

I gave Wendy the shock of her life when I called earlier.

'Come to karaoke with me?' I asked eagerly.

She didn't reply for a long time.

'Wendy?'

'Is this a piss-take?'

'Nope.'

'Karaoke?'

'At the Carbuncle.'

'Wha . . . ?'

'Just say you'll come.'

'I'll come.'

I could tell she wasn't expecting me to go through with it. She thought I'd cry off and we'd file the episode under 'mental insanity', an already bulky folder, but go through with it I did.

Although Wendy keeps looking at me as though she doesn't quite believe I am who I say I am.

'But,' she says, shaking her head, 'we're not even sitting by the door for a quick getaway.'

'I know.' I smile smugly.

'But . . .'

'The thing is, Wendy. Everything makes perfect sense now.'

'If there's one thing you're not making, Gracie Flowers, it's perfect sense.'

'Think about it. I didn't get Head of London Sales. It felt like the end of the world, but actually, now I'm having the baby, it's a bonus that I didn't get the job. I'd have been on my knees with work and Danny leaving. That felt disastrous, as though I'd wasted ten years of my life, but we made a baby together. How awesome is that? Even me shagging Posh Boy led me to miss the abortion and face up to the fact that I wanted to have the baby. And Mum and I are bonding over it all. Do you see? Everything makes sense now.'

My attention drifts away from Wendy as Anton steps up onto the small stage, holding a microphone. He looks like Cary Grant tonight.

'*Willkommen*, howdy, hello. Here we are,' Anton starts. Then stops and coughs. He looks slightly nervous; it's very sweet. 'Welcome,' he says, in case we haven't got the message. 'Now then, there should be song sheets on every table, but if you can't see one then there are plenty more behind the bar. I've marked my favourite songs with asterisks, and I must warn you, as these are my favourites and it's my pub, I reserve the right to stop any of you if I consider what you're doing to be a criminal act against these songs. Harsh but fair, I feel. You have been warned. Also, while I have your partially rapt attention, I would like to ask a favour of you. Many of you already know that I have a place in the final of *Britain Sings its Heart Out*, but I'm looking for a lady to sing with. The organisers said I could still enter if I can find a new partner, so if you know of anyone, or you're interested yourself, please grab me later. I beg you.'

Then he starts singing his first song. It's 'What A Wonderful World'. I sit back and smile, glad that Baby Bean is listening to this. It's important to start his or her musical education early.

I watch Anton. Why is it that every time I see Anton, and even when I'm not near him, I imagine him undressed? Not in a crude way, but I like to picture us curled up in his big bed, naked under the covers. In my mind now we're naked and spooning, and his hands are resting gently on my belly, cupping Baby Bean, and he's singing this song to us.

'Who's next?' he calls once the applause has died down. I raise my hand. Anton scans the room and stops short when he sees me. I try to reassure him with a smile.

'Gracie Flowers.'

He says my name quietly, as though to himself, but he has the microphone next to his lips, so everyone hears.

I walk up to the stage. I'm not frozen with fear this time. I feel light, cheeky and confident. I want to sing a song for this baby. I want to give it music, like my dad gave music to me. I don't want this poor child to have my hang-ups.

'What would you like to sing?'

Now, it must be noted that Anton doesn't sound at all light and cheeky. If truth be told he sounds petrified. I suspect he thinks I'll flee his establishment squawking again.

'"Summertime".'

He sort of smiles and nods, as though to say, 'Of course you do.'

'I have the Sam Cooke version on backing track.'

'Perfect. Not that I don't like the Gershwin.'

'Gracie Flowers, you do know your classics.'

'My dad sang this to me when I was in the womb,' I tell him for no other reason than that I want to tell this man everything. Every memory, every batty thought. Oh, dear God. I pray for his sake that I don't.

I hop up on stage and take the microphone. I haven't had a microphone in my hand for many years. It feels much heavier than it used to. Anton starts the track and steps back. I'm breathing quickly now. I close my eyes. I don't want to see the faces of the people in the pub. I want to sing this song to my baby.

After the first verse I open my eyes and smile at the drinkers and then I carry on. When I finish, there's quite a lot of whooping, mostly from Wendy, who's going bonkers. I smile, do a quick bob for a curtsy and turn to give Anton back the microphone.

'Are you crying?' I blurt.

'That was beautiful.'

'Soft.' I smile.

'Do *Britain Sings* with me, Gracie?' he asks.

'OK,' I answer.

'Really?'

'Really.'

'I've found my partner for *Britain Sings*!' Anton shouts, pointing at me. The pub erupts and I think of my dad. I hope he's watching.

See! See, how it all comes good in the end.

Chapter 57

After Danny Saunders asked me to the shit prom thing my dad gave me a talk about love.

'Grace, my darling, I think it's time we spoke about a crazy little thing called love,' he said. He definitely said that, because then I did my Elvis impression. It wasn't a great impression and when I stopped he said, 'So, Grace Flowers, with love, as with all things, you need to think big and aim high.'

I know he said that, too. I remember it clearly, but I can't recall the rest of the conversation in the detail I'd like. He described love for me and what it felt like, and I remember him saying, 'You'll know it's love when all your songs are for him.' I wish I had a recording of that conversation, or better still that Dad were here so I could ask him to repeat it. I haven't thought of it for a long time, perhaps that's why it's gone from my mind; memories fade if you don't use them. My songs were never for Danny. I stopped singing almost as soon as we got together and I haven't sung for ten years. But now I want to sing again. I want to sing for this baby. I want this child to love music like I did. I want my house to be full of songs again. But it's not the baby that's made me think of the 'crazy little thing called love' conversation. It's Anton. I don't even think it's a crush I've got. I think I'm in love with him.

I wonder what it's like with older people. Not the nooky mechanics – which I imagine are exactly the same – I mean asking people out. I don't think older people get paralytically drunk and snog each other like my generation do. I doubt he did that with Fran Uma Prostitute Woman. I bet she sauntered into the pub one afternoon for a sparkling mineral water, he spotted her leading-lady looks, she clocked his fine hairy torso, he checked his breath on his hand and she smiled. Then they probably started casually chatting, and one of them mentioned a great photographic exhibition and the other one said, 'Oh yes, I was thinking of going to that,' and they arranged to meet there and have tea afterwards. She was probably upstairs in the Festering Carbuncle by dinnertime, demonstrating her amazing pelvic floor muscles.

It's strange. I'm here with Wendy and Freddie and I'm involved in the conversation, nodding and saying the odd word, but all the while I know exactly where Anton is in the room and what he's doing. Earlier he took beers to all his kitchen staff and had a toast with them, and he just caught a young man doing coke in the toilets and asked him to leave. Now he's telling people to 'start drinking up now, please'. Basically, I've spent the whole evening thinking about Anton.

Uh oh. Wendy's crying. I reach over to place a hand on hers. If Freddie's upset her again, I'll twat him.

'Are you OK?' I ask.

She nods tearfully.

'Freddie just told me this awful story about a fourteen-year-old girl who was abducted from her home and forced to become a prostitute.'

Blimey. It's a bit like watching *Comic Relief* when you've been laughing away – ha, ha, ha – and then suddenly they show some footage of African babies dying of AIDS.

She tells me the sombre story and I listen, feeling sad. When she finishes we both sit for a moment, thinking about the lives of these poor women, but then I get this all-consuming craving for a roast chicken sandwich. I try to kick it from my mind, because the plight of trafficked Eastern Europeans is definitely more important than me wanting a sarnie, but it's still languishing there, all granary bread, thick butter and a spot of pickle. It's winking at me. Maybe Baby Bean needs protein, or maybe I'm just greedy. Where am I going to find roast chicken at half past ten on a Sunday night? I probably need to drive to the Edgware Road. There's definitely a bonus to not drinking.

'Penny.' It's Anton. He's standing in front of me with a tower of beer glasses leaning against his shoulders.

'You want to spend a penny?' I ask.

'No.' He laughs. 'Penny for your thoughts.'

'Oh, sad to say, I was thinking of a roast chicken sandwich.'

'If you stick around, that can be arranged.' He smiles. 'Pickle or mayonnaise?'

'Oh,' I say, dribble forming in my mouth. 'Pickle, please.'

'A very good idea,' he says and waltzes off with the glasses.

'Freddie has just asked me if I want to go upstairs and have a drink,' Wendy whispers in my ear.

'This is very good news,' I whisper back.

'I do not fancy Freddie. He is a wanker,' she chants.

'Oh, so did you say no, then.'

'Course not. I'm going upstairs with him.'

I watch Wendy and Freddie take a bottle of wine upstairs. Then I spot two glasses on the floor, pick them up and take them to the bar. The bar staff, who had been quite lacklustre all evening, are now hurtling around trying to get cleared up and out the door as soon as possible. I pick up a wet cloth from the bar and use it to wipe down the sticky tables while Anton carries the karaoke equipment upstairs. He looks very strong and not at all old. When he comes downstairs again he says goodnight to the staff and locks the door behind them. He turns the majority of the lights off so the only illumination comes from a few bar lights and the street lamps outside. I suddenly feel very black and white movie, circa 1950. Or as black and white movie, circa 1950, as it's possible to feel while wearing leggings.

'Right, chicken and pickle. Follow me, Gracie Flowers. You're on buttering duty.'

I trail him into the kitchen and wash my hands in the small sink behind the door.

'A natural.' He nods to me.

I don't speak, I just smile contentedly as he opens and closes stainless-steel doors and fridges, assembling ingredients. He thickly slices a granary loaf and hands me a knife and butter.

'As my gran used to say, I like to taste the butter,' he instructs me.

'Excellent, I love butter!'

He's slicing the chicken now and holding me out a slice. I take it. Not in my mouth, though. I take it with my fingers. I must not throw myself at this man just because I want to spend the rest of my days with him.

'I'm glad I've got you,' he says after the sandwiches are made. My stomach flutters again, as if it's full of daddy-long-legs. 'I'm seducing you with chicken sandwiches,' he says, smiling and licking a bit of pickle off his thumb. Poor Baby Bean, it must feel like there's a birds of prey convention assembling in my tummy at the moment.

'I just wanted to say that I am pretty much the happiest man alive knowing that we'll be doing *Britain Sings* together. We'll have fun.'

I nod and smile.

'Shall we take these upstairs?'

I nod and smile again, then follow him through the bar and up the stairs. The karaoke is all set up, as it was when I was last here, but there's no sign of Wendy and Freddie. They must be in his room.

We sit on the sofa and I take the first bite of my roast chicken sandwich.

'Unbelievable,' I exclaim. 'Chicken sandwich heaven.'

'Hmm,' says Anton, biting into his.

I sit and eat half my sandwich, exploring the lounge with my eyes. It's such a comfortable room. I cast my eyes over all the photos, then I inch myself forwards on the sofa to get a good vantage point. I might be here a little while as I'm going to do my usual bookshelf search and there are lots of books to canvass.

'Gracie Flowers, what are you doing?' Anton asks.

'I'm just checking out your bookshelf.'

'Are you the bookshelf police?'

'Actually, I am. I'm chief of the . . . Oh. My. Goodness.'

'What?'

'Oh. My. Goodness.'

'Grace?'

'Is that . . . ? That's not . . . ? It's not *The Five Year Plan*, is it?'

'Ah, yes. Guilty. That book made me buy this pub.'

'No?'

'Yes. I wanted my own gastro pub, so I bought the book, wrote my plan, followed the tasks and bought the pub.'

'It made me buy my maisonette,' I whisper.

I stare at him, willing him to say, 'How strange, your plan and my plan brought us together. It must be fate.' I wait but he doesn't say anything. He just sits and eats his sandwich. People never say what you want them to say, do they?

I take the book from the shelf.

'It's a bit dog-eared.'

I hold the book with the cover away from me and walk towards Anton. I hold it out for him to see and he gives me a puzzled smile.

'What?'

'Read the cover.'

'Why? *The Five Year Plan: Making the Most of Your Life.*'

'No, but who's it by?'

'Camille Flowers.'

'Keep reading.'

'Camille Flowers, with Rosemary and Grace Flowers.'

'Yes.'

'Grace Flowers. But . . . you're Grace Flowers. Gracie Flowers.'

'Yes.'

'You wrote this book?'

'Yes, well, no. My dad wrote most of it. It was on his computer, and when we died, my mum and I put it together for the publishers.'

'Grace Flowers. I've known you all this time and it never occurred to me.'

'Why would it?'

'Because you look like him.'

'My mum always says that.'

'I met your dad once.'

'When?'

'I was going to do a photo shoot with him for *Vanity Fair*.'

'Oh, the *Vanity Fair* shoot.'

'But obviously it didn't happen.'

'No.'

The *Vanity Fair* shoot didn't happen because my father died a few weeks before it was supposed to take place.

'Oh, Grace, I'm so sorry.'

'Don't be.'

'I met him before, though. We took some test shots.'

'Did you?'

'Yes. I have them upstairs if you'd like to look at them.'

'I'd love to.'

The amazing chicken sandwich is eclipsed. We leave our half-empty plates and walk up the next flight of stairs. I can hear Wendy and Freddie talking behind the closed door.

I follow Anton into his bedroom and breathe in its calm. He slides one of the huge fitted cupboards open. It's deeper than I would have thought. One set of floor-to-ceiling shelves holds vinyl records, another books and the other holds boxes, each labelled with a year on the side. He pulls down the box marked 2001: the year my dad died. He puts the box on the bed and deftly fingers through cardboard sleeves until he pulls one out. Then he puts the box on the floor and sits on the bed. I sit next to him.

'We got on very well, your dad and I. I was in the States when he passed away and I felt as though I'd just made a new friend and then lost him straight away. I only found out after the funeral or I would have come back for it.'

'I sang "Mr Bojangles" at his funeral,' I say quietly. 'It was his favourite song.'

Anton opens the cardboard sleeve to reveal a contact sheet – one large sheet of photographic paper with twenty-four miniature pictures on it – and there is my dad. My dad, ten years ago. My dad, as I remember him. He's dancing in a room at Pineapple Studios, wearing his jeans and his Ramones T-shirt. Dad always made dancing look so free and easy. He's spinning in some of the photos and leaping in others, and there are close-ups of his laughing face. The pictures capture him perfectly. Often, when I look at photos of Dad, they don't look like the father I remember; he just looks like a dancer caught in a move. But these really show him; the man I love and remember. They've caught his charm and the twinkle in his eye.

I scroll down the tiny thumbnail pictures, wishing they were bigger.

'We can enlarge whatever you want. These are yours now, Grace.'

'I like them being here.'

I can't take my eyes off the pictures I'm holding.

'Whatever you prefer.'

'He looks so alive,' I whisper. My dad was so vibrant. He completely inhabited each moment and when you were with him you did, too. He gave me so many wonderful moments.

'We had a great afternoon.'

'What did you talk about?'

'Oh, it was quite deep.'

'In what way?'

'Well, he started off wanting to know all about my photography and how it all started.'

I smile. That's so my dad: he loved to get to the bottom of people, to find out what they did and what they loved. He loved people and their stories.

'So I told him about my days on the road, and that led to quite a big discussion about music. He really knew his music. And then I told him I'd always taken photos, and one day I plucked up the courage to show them to some people who knew about photography. That paid off and led me on the route to becoming a photographer. We discussed how to live a true life you have to believe in every moment, and often that involves taking risks. You don't meet many people where those conversations are possible. Conversations about life and how to live it well. He was a special man, Grace.'

I put the contact sheet carefully back in the envelope.

'I'm so glad you met him,' I say as I hand it back to him.

'Shall we go downstairs and sing?' Anton says, standing up. 'It's just the two of us.'

I stand up, too, but I shake my head, then I look into Anton's eyes and start to unbutton my shirt. My hands are shaky. I've never done this before and I don't want him to think I'm a slapper. I just want him to know that I am all his. Not just for now, but for always, if he wants. I let my shirt fall to the floor behind me. It's so quiet. It feels as though the whole of London is holding its breath for me. I'm not sure what to do now. I'm wearing leggings. They should come off next, but that will definitely look ungainly. Perhaps I should undo his shirt? I'm so longing to touch his chest, his flesh. Or should I take off my bra? I keep my eyes fixed on his, and take another step towards him. I wonder whether I should undo the buttons on his shirt. I start to reach up towards his top button, but change my mind and take hold of his hand instead and steer him towards the bed. He lets me lead him and sits down, placing the envelope of photographs behind him on the bed. My breathing is very shallow. I don't know where to start with this man, but I want it to be perfect. I am such a short arse that with him sitting and me standing our faces are almost level. Our eyes are still locked when I lean towards him and kiss him softly on the mouth. I close my eyes and feel my whole body literally aching to press against his. His rough chin brushes against mine. I put my hand gently to his cheek and feel his hands, big and strong on my shoulders. I am adrift. Softly his hands push me away from him.

'Grace, this isn't a good idea.'

It takes a moment for his words to register. It certainly feels like a good idea to me. He reaches to the floor, picks up my shirt and holds it out for me.

'I'm a lot older than you are.'

'George Clooney is about your age,' I say, forever clearing up any doubts anyone might have about whether or not I'm a complete imbecile.

He chuckles sadly. I can't laugh or even smile.

'My whole body is on fire for you,' I whisper, because it's true.

I wrap my shirt around me and walk to the door.

'Stay, please, Grace, I just don't think it would be right to—'

'I have to go.'

'I'll see you out.'

He follows me out of the room and lets me out of his pub, but I don't look at him.

Chapter 58

'Oh, BB, what's Granny in London been buying now?' I shriek as soon as I step into the hall. 'Jeez.'

BB doesn't answer and neither does mother. That's because mother's on her new treadmill. I can tell by the pounding, whirring sounds coming from what used to be the dining room. She's paid off all her debts and has decided to turn it into a gym. So far we have a treadmill, a cross trainer and an exercise ball in there, and this huge package appears to be a bench press. It's enough to make you tired.

I open the door slowly and peak into her fitness emporium. I don't want to give her a fright that might hurl her from a piece of moving machinery. She looks ever so sweet in her pink shorts and sports bra, with a little sweatband round her head. She waves when she sees me, and then presses a button until her moving walkway slows down.

'Phew!' she says when she's down to a fast walking pace. 'How are you both?'

I smile back. I haven't seen her since the weekend and I was worried I might have imagined our lovely closeness.

'Good,' I say, balancing my bottom on the exercise ball.

'You look tired. I had trouble sleeping when I was expecting you.'

I don't tell her that it's not Baby Bean who's keeping me awake. It's the fact that I stood before a fifty-year-old man on Sunday night in my bra, and his face as he handed me back my shirt keeps haunting me every time I close my eyes.

'Hmm.'

'You OK?'

'Hmm.'

'You sure?'

'Yes, I've just got a break between viewings, so I thought I'd pop in.'

'That's nice. Grace, darling, what's the matter?'

'I just feel so guilty. Poor little Camille or Camilla. Do you think it will scar him or her, the fact that for a brief period they weren't wanted?'

'Grace, that's ridiculous. This baby is going to be very, very loved.'

'Hmm. I just feel bad.'

'Well, don't.'

'But I'm so scared. I want to be a good mother, but I'm worried I'll mess it all up.'

'Grace, I'm the last person to ask.'

'You were a good mother.'

'No, Grace. I wasn't. I haven't been.'

She was a good mother, I think. I know I adored her

when I was little. When I met Wendy at secondary school, she would come and play after school and we would ask Mum if we could look at her dresses. We'd wash our hands until they were pink because we didn't want to mark them, and I would show Wendy not just the dresses, but photos of my mum dancing in them. Mum would let us try on her jewellery sometimes, too. We'd sit down to tea bedecked in jewellery and my dad would go, 'Cor blimey, it's two Liz Taylors!' Once, when Mum and Dad were performing in Blackpool, they invited Wendy, too. And Mum let us come backstage, where we watched her doing her make-up. Wendy still does her eye make-up like Mum did hers that day. I never once thought she was a bad mother when I was growing up. I knew she wasn't keen on my singing competitions, because she'd say things like 'Oh, not another one!' when I told her about them, but looking back, having a child who insisted on going to places like Wolverhampton and Milton Keynes most weekends would be trying. And she did used to tell me she loved me. It's only since Dad died that she stopped.

'You were a good mother,' I tell her.

'I am pleased with my new treadmill,' she says, changing the subject and giving it a little pony pat as she gets off. 'Now, will you help me unwrap my new bench press?'

'OK. How much did all this stuff cost?'

'Oh, it was rather dear, but I'll use it, so it's worth it.'

'Cool. But you are sorted now, money wise, aren't you?'

'I'm fine.'

'Because you'll have to start paying back the loan soon.'

'I know all this, Grace. I've bought lots of books on starting up my own business, and my wonderful new sewing machine is arriving next week.'

'OK. As long as you're cool.'

'Grace.' I can tell by her tone that she's getting vexed. 'It's fine.'

Chapter 59

'Dad, thank you,' I whisper. I went to town and bought a ballerina bunch of flowers today and laid them at his grave. They're peonies. I can't remember whether he liked peonies, but I do. 'These are from me and BB. BB stands for Baby Bean, not *Big Brother*, by the way. Do you remember that show? It's finished now. No, BB is your grandchild. So far you'll be pleased to hear that BB is a very well-behaved little thing.

Mum's being amazing. Whatever you said to her, she's different. Much, much stronger. Loving. Happy. I think the money has really helped, and the fact that she sorted it out herself and didn't need me. Anyway, she's started a dressmaking business. Good, eh? Or at least it will be when she starts actually making some dresses, instead of fannying about deciding on the company's name. And you're still here under the silver birch. You're not covered in tarmac. And – I hope you'll like this – I'm going to enter a big singing competition and be on TV. It's called *Britain Sings its Heart Out.*'

I hear Leonard and Joan approaching, so I lean forward towards the tombstone and whisper, 'Love you.' Then I stand. 'Hello, you two,' I say, spinning round. 'I've got some—' I was going to say good news, but I stop. Leonard doesn't look right. He's the wrong colour. Normally he has a rosy glow, but today his skin looks sky-before-rain grey.

'Hello, Grace,' Joan says with a smile that I can see takes effort.

'You not feeling well, Len?' I say, going over to take his other arm. He's walking slowly and I can hear his breathing. He's puffing as though he's exhausted, but he's only come from the car. This isn't Leonard at all. Leonard has been known to skip from the car.

'He's had a bad week, haven't you?' Joan says.

He nods as we settle him on Alfred George. We stand back and look at him.

'Have you been to the doctors?'

'We've been referred to a specialist at the hospital. His blood pressure has been going through the roof.'

'Well, that's something the specialist should be able to sort out. No?'

'Two and a half weeks we have to wait till the appointment. It never used to be this bad. I don't remember Mum having to wait so long. And Elaine in Dorset, a similar thing happened to her a few years ago and she was seen the next day! London's not what it was. It's the overcrowding; we'd be better served outside London. Still, we'll be all right, won't we, Len? He's on some drugs to keep his blood pressure down, but just the smallest activity takes it out of him.'

'Oh, you poor thing,' I say, giving him a kiss on the cheek.

'See, still got it.' He winks at me.

'You certainly have. Now then, I have some good news, and as two of my favourite people in the whole world, I'd like you to be amongst the first to know. I am pregnant!'

'Oh, Grace,' whispers Joan. 'Are you, love?'

I nod.

'Oh my. You'll be a lovely mother.'

'And I would very much like you two to be godparents!'

'Oh.'

Oh dear. I think Len might have a tear. Oh blimey, I think I might have one, too. Regroup. Refocus.

'Now then, you handsome devil, what song are you having?'

'Oh. We were talking about this in the car. We've been watching that talent show, *Britain Sings its Heart Out*. Did you see it, Grace?'

'No, I don't watch it.'

'Well, we think you should enter it. With your voice, Grace, you'd wipe the floor with them.'

'Funny that—' I start. I'm just about to tell them about going on *Britain Sings* when Joan carries on speaking over me.

'There was a girl on there, pretty thing. Must be your age. She sang "Amazing Grace". She got through to the final. She was by far the best of the bunch, but we both said, "She's good, but she's nothing on our Grace." So we wanted to ask you to sing that.'

'"Amazing Grace",' Len croaks.

Oh, no. Oh, please, no. I would give Leonard and Joan anything – anything in the whole world – but not that. I can't sing that song. I can't even *hear* that song.

'I'm so sorry, I can't sing that. I don't know it,' I say quickly. 'What about a bit of Leonard's favourite? A Fred Astaire number.' And before they have time to protest I start singing 'Cheek To Cheek'.

Chapter 60

I'm standing outside the Carbuncle with a letter in my hand. The letter is addressed to Anton. I don't want to give it to him, but I have to.

Dear Anton,
I am so, so, so incredibly sorry. Not just for embarrassing myself in your presence on Sunday, for which I am mortified. Hopefully, at some point in the future I will be able to look you in the eye again, but it might take a while. Please pretend it never happened.

I am also sorry to tell you that I won't be able to perform with you in the *Britain Sings* final. My reasons are not because of the other night. It's because I recently learned that a woman will be singing 'Amazing Grace' in the final and, as you may have realised, I have an adverse reaction to that song, so I think it's wiser all round if I decline your offer.

I am truly sorry, Anton, and I wish you the best of the best of luck.

Yours, Gracie.

I swallow and enter the pub, where I lean on the bar, waiting for the young chap to finish serving a customer. I can't see Anton, and I will the universe to keep it that way. A copy of the *Daily Mirror* lies folded on the counter nearby. I pick it up and open it to find out what's going on in the world. The headline says, 'AMAZING RUTH. Bookies' favourite to win *Britain Sings*, Ruth Roberts, hits out against US record deal rumours.' And there's a photo of her, ten years on. She looks the same really, except her features seem sharper and she has bigger boobs. It's unmistakably Ruth Roberts, though. I haven't seen her since I was carried screaming from the stage she stood upon, and just seeing her face again gives me that same panicky feeling in my chest.

I push the newspaper away from me. Thank God for Leonard and Joan and for me seeing that newspaper. It's most definitely a sign.

The barman smiles.

'You all right, love?'

'Yes, thank you. Please give this to Anton for me,' I say, handing him the letter. 'It's very urgent.'

Chapter 61

'Help! Help! Help!'

I'm not having a good day at work, so I'm banging my head against my desk repeatedly. There's nothing else for it. The buyer for Claire's flat has just pulled out because he's lost his job.

'Help! Help! Help!' I repeat, giving my head another good bang.

'You should have your hard hat on.'

It's Bob.

'Where did you come from?'

'Just walked in!'

'I'm not even keeping an eye on the door. I've fallen apart,' I tell him dramatically, but then I smile. 'Nice to see you, I was going to call you later. I wanted to tell you something.'

'Pawel's at the yard, clearing out his stuff, so I thought I'd escape rather than punch him. Can you get out for a coffee?'

'Yeah, but I have to deliver some bad news to someone first.'

'Shall I come for the ride?'

'Yeah. Can you pretend to be interested in her flat?'

'Anything for you, sis.'

We pull up outside Claire's flat in Bob's van, because like so many others he refuses to travel in Nina. I sigh. I so don't want to do this. Claire deserves some luck. It's long overdue. So where is it? What's stopping it, eh?

'Excuse me!' calls Claire from the front door.

'You all right, love?' Bob calls to her.

'You can't park there. It's my spot.'

Patrick suddenly whizzes from between her legs out onto the drive. Bob, like the Bruce Willis lookalike he is, darts out of the van and catches him, tucks him under his arm and walks him back to Claire.

'I believe this is yours,' he says with a smile.

Claire laughs, and I realise I haven't seen her laugh for a long time.

'What have you got on your head, mate?' Bob asks, pulling off the sanitary towel. Claire reddens.

'Sorry. I'm, um. It's a phase.'

'You don't want one of these on your head, mate,' Bob tells Patrick as he places him gently back on the ground by his mum. 'See, it looks stupid,' he says, putting it on his own head. 'Nah, you don't want to do that. Shall we give it to Mummy to put in the rubbish?'

Patrick nods and Claire takes the sanitary towel, smiling shyly. I remain sitting in the van, mesmerised by the whole thing.

'I'll move the van,' Bob says, walking back.

'No, he's with me!' I call, finally waking up. 'Claire, this is Bob, he's going to look at the flat.' I walk up to her. 'We lost that other buyer. I'm so sorry.'

Her big eyes water and her bottom lip starts to go.

'Let's see what we've got here, shall we?' Bob says buoyantly. 'It might be my lucky day. This looks like just what I'm after, and it's got a parking space.'

We walk into the lounge to find it moderately tidy and the curtains open. And there's not a potty or wet puddle to be seen.

'There's another one!' Bob shouts, pointing to Daisy sitting on the sofa watching telly. Patrick sits at his feet staring up at him. 'Is that your sister, mate? Good work.' Patrick nods. 'This is my sis,' Bob says, pointing at me.

'Really?' asks Claire.

'Well, I've chosen him as my brother.'

'I don't blame you,' Claire mouths to me while Bob walks over to Daisy, with Patrick trailing behind. We watch him as he sits down on the sofa with the two of them. '*Come Dine With Me*! A classic. Are you the new Delia?'

'Would you like a tea or coffee, Bob?'

'I would love a tea,' he says. 'If it's not too much trouble.'

'No, no trouble.'

It's starting to feel like an electricity showroom in here. I feel I should pop outside.

'Where's the wee one?' I ask Claire.

'In the bedroom.'

'Can I have a peep?'

''Course.'

I creep into Claire's bedroom and over to the crib. Baby Ruby lies awake on her back, her little white babygroed body laying in a comfortable sprawl. Her eyes are wide and her lips open and close contentedly. I gaze at her, at the wonder of it all, and I touch my belly. Soon, I'll have a baby lying like this in my room. I reach my finger through the wooden crib bars and feel Ruby's tiny digits wrap themselves around it. I smile at her and a tune comes into my head. It's vague at first, and I don't know why it's coming to me. I hear a few guitar chords and suddenly I'm singing. I'm singing to baby Ruby, but also to my baby, to little Camilla or Cam. It's a Bob Dylan song and I can't remember the last time I heard it, but it's perfect and true. I remember now, it's a blessing he wrote for a child. It's called 'Forever Young'. I turn away from Ruby and close my eyes as I try to remember the words. I probably end up making most of them up, but I don't care. I'm singing to my baby. I'm going to give it music just like my dad gave me. See, it all comes good in the end.

'What CD's this?' Claire says, bursting in.

'Oh, sorry,' I say, opening my eyes. 'I got carried away.'

'Was that you?'

'Yes.' I laugh.

'I didn't know you could sing.'

'I haven't for years.'

'You should never stop.'

'You've got another one,' Bob whispers, tiptoeing over to the crib.

'Guys, I'm pregnant. I'm having a baby. I wanted you to know.'

'Oh, Grace,' says Claire, looking overcome.

Bob just stares.

'Are you, Gracie Flowers?' he asks, as though he doesn't believe it.

I nod.

'Can I be Uncle Bob,' he whispers.

I nod and he grabs me into a hug.

'Right, Grace, promise me he or she will be QPR through and through. Don't let those Arsenal swines get him. You've got to promise me on this.'

'I shall leave the baby's football education entirely down to you.'

He kisses my head.

'Good on you, sis. And if you need anything, I'm your man.'

'Thanks.'

'Right, we'd best get back. Claire, it's been a pleasure. And I'd like to put an offer in of five grand over the asking price.'

I stare at him.

'But, but . . . ' Claire stammers. 'You haven't seen the bathroom.'

'A bathroom's a bathroom,' he says casually.

As we're walking back to the van, I whisper to him, 'You were only supposed to act interested.'

'What is the asking price by the way?'

'Seven nine five.'

He whistles. I run in front of him and indicate that he should stop moving. We're standing face to face but I can't wait any longer.

'Will you be the godfather?' I blurt out.

'For real?'

'Yep.'

'You'll set me off!'

'Is that a yes?' I ask keenly.

'Is it . . . ? Course!'

I gasp, thrilled. Cam or Camilla will have the coolest godparents. Leonard and Joan, Wendy and Bob. I don't think babies usually have this many godparents, but my baby won't have a christening in the Christian sense. He or she will have a naming ceremony, like I did, where close friends are invited to make wishes for the baby. A bit like in *Sleeping Beauty*, but without the bad witch turning up and cursing the child.

'I can't believe you offered on her flat,' I say, stunned.

'Neither can I.'

I gasp.

'I've got an idea. There's this lovely family, and they saw the flat when it was in a right state. If we could give the place a good old clean, I could get them round to see it again, and I just have a feeling they'll take it.'

'Gracie Flowers, you're dynamite. I'll pay for some industrial cleaners to go in there, that should do the trick.'

'Brilliant!' I whoop.

'Maybe I could take Claire and the kids to the zoo while they're cleaning,' he adds dreamily.

Chapter 62

My baby is so loved already. Not just by me, but by everyone I tell. Today is the biggie, though. Lube. He might not be so thrilled.

'Oh, Grace, love, I'll gag if I have to go in there,' he says, stepping away from the toilet door. 'Spray the air freshener, will you, and open a window?' he asks.

'Oh, yeah,' I say, walking into the office loo. 'I see your point.'

I do what he asks. 'OK,' I sniff. 'It's relatively safe now.'

He nods, enters and sits on the toilet with the seat down.

'You have to keep this brief, Grace, I've got a plane to catch, darling. Now, what is it you wanted to talk about?'

'Maternity packages,' I say, but I'm not very good at talking about anything baby-related without breaking into a smile.

Lube doesn't smile.

'Ken?' I say, peering down into his face.

'Did you say maternity packages?'

'Yes.'

'Are you planning . . . ?'

'No, I am.'

'You are! Well, well, well, blow me down. Little Gracie Flowers with a babby. Oh, I feel as though I'm about to become a granddad. Oh, Grace, I might cry.'

'Do you want a tissue?'

'No. No, love, it was just a moment. So how are you feeling?'

'Happy, Ken. I feel so happy.'

'You look it. I'm dead proud, me. Best thing I've ever done having me kids.'

I smile. Then I stop smiling.

'But how will it work? I mean, can I work? I want to work, obviously, and I'll get childcare and Mum wants to help, but I'll need time off to have it and it won't be so easy for me to work all the frigging time, like I do now.'

'As far as I'm concerned, Grace, you're the best in the biz. What you want, you get. I'll do my best to make it work for you. We'll draw something up, don't you worry.'

'Seriously?'

'Too right. I knew we'd have this conversation one day. There was never a question. You have to have kids. We need more Gracie Flowers in this world.'

'Oh, now I think you'll make me cry!'

'Come here,' he says, giving me a hug. I love Lube hugs. He's short for a man, so I come up to his chest. It can get a bit uncomfortable when I hug really tall men and find myself pressed against their belt area.

'GRACE!' It's Wendy shouting from outside. 'GRACE!

Come here now! GRACE! It's your mum!'

'Sorry, Mum on the phone. I'd best go.' I walk out of the toilet to find Wendy standing at her desk.

'GRACE! GRACE! YOUR MUM'S HERE!'

'Wendy, I'm here. What line's she on?'

'No, Grace, she's here. Like there.' And she points to the road outside. I turn my head.

'Oh. My. God.'

My mum is being carried across the Chamberlayne Road by evil SJS Construction man.

'What the . . . ?'

And it looks like they're coming in here. I run to meet them at the door, and it's then that I see the state of my mum. She's clinging to him. I can see her fists as they grip onto the fabric of his shirt. Her face is turned into his chest and her shoulders are shaking. Her whole body's quivering.

'Grace? It's Grace, isn't it?' the man pants as he swoops my mother into the office and lays her on the sofa. She doesn't let him go. She's sobbing in loud, irregular shudders. I can't go to her yet. I haven't seen her like this since she broke down at the hospital when I was having my freak-out, and I couldn't go to her then.

'I found her on the side of the road,' the man says as I stare at him.

'She said she was on her way to the bank. She was in a terrible state.'

This doesn't make sense. My mum doesn't go to the bank. She does everything online. She doesn't need cash because she doesn't leave the house.

Her sobs get quieter.

'Mum, mum,' I say, finally walking towards her.

She's still clinging to the man. I rub her back and shoulders slowly and rhythmically until eventually she relaxes. Her breathing returns to normal, but she doesn't show her face. She must be embarrassed.

'It's all right, Mum. You're all right. You're safe,' I whisper.

'I'm going to take her back to my house,' the man says. 'I thought I should let you know first.'

Who does he think he is?

'No! I'll look after her now,' I tell him coolly. 'I'll take her home.'

He looks down, as though he's disappointed by my answer or hurt by my tone. What was he expecting? I'm hardly going to allow this man, who wants to build on my dad's grave, to look after my mum.

Chapter 63

'Hello, Mildred, m'dear. How are you? Have you missed us?' I whisper as we cross the threshold into the house.

Mum's still weak and distant, like the old mum from the dark years, not the mum I've been spending time with recently. It's heartbreaking. She walks silently into the hall and I follow her.

'Why don't you go upstairs and have a bath?' I suggest.

She looks at me. It's a pitiful look and I don't know what her big searching eyes are asking me.

'You'll be fine,' I chipper. 'Next time you want to go out somewhere, we'll go together, then if it gets tough you can hold on to me. But it was good you tried, no? And good that the evil graveyard destroyer found you.'

She nods.

'Even if he is an ogre.'

Suddenly she flinches. I put my hand on her shoulder and find she's trembling.

'Mum, what's the matter?'

'I heard something.'

'Just something outside. Footsteps on gravel. It's bound to be someone kindly dropping off an advert for a kebab shop.'

'Come upstairs,' she whispers urgently and darts up the stairs two at time.

'Mum, no, what's the—'

I hear a loud, strong knock on the door. My mum crouches on the stairs.

'Don't get it, Grace!'

'Mum?'

I haven't seen my mum this bad for years. She's literally bricking it about a knock on the door.

'Grace, come up,' she whispers, beckoning me to follow her up the stairs.It's the door again, louder than before.

'Jesus,' I mutter. 'That's a Victorian knocker. Have some respect!' I'm walking towards the door, on my way to open it, when suddenly there's an explosion. Well, it's not an actual explosion, but it sounds like one. I shield my face as glass flies towards me, and I hear a thud. Something's been thrown through the window into the house. It's a brick. There's a brick lying on the floor in the hallway. It's broken the coloured glass in the hallway window. It could have hit me. This isn't the worst of it, though. The worst part, the scariest part, is that a man is shouting. I can't see him through the hole in the window, but I can hear him.

'Rosemary, you can't keep ignoring us. Let us in or we'll break all the windows. If you haven't got what we need, you know the deal, we'll take what we want.'

Mum looks as though she's having a panic attack on the

stairs. Loud irregular breaths are making her body quiver. I stride to the door.

'Hello? What's the matter?' I shout as I slowly open the front door.

A huge man is standing in the middle of the drive, holding a brick as though he's about to hurl it at another window.

'What's . . . ?' My heart is hammering so much I can hear it. 'What's going on? I'm Rosemary's daughter,' I say, desperately trying to sound more confident than I feel.

The man relaxes the hand holding the brick and drops it to his side. He stares at me menacingly as another man appears around the side of the house. They're both huge. Heavies, you'd call them. They look like they've served time for ABH and do a bit of work as bouncers or debt collectors. Debt collectors! Of course. This is something to do with Mum's debt. Oh God, she hasn't got a dodgy loan from some crooks, has she?

'Does she owe something?'

The man with the brick laughs.

'Yes, she owes us four thousand pounds cash. We should have had it Tuesday. We've given her two days and now we've stopped playing nice.'

'Four grand?'

'Very good, darling. Very good.'

'OK. I'll get it for you.'

'Now we're talking. We'll be back in an hour. You've got one hour. He looks at his watch. I'll be back at nine. That's an hour and five minutes. Don't say I haven't got a heart.'

Chapter 64

I don't know about him having a heart, but I definitely have one and I can feel it beating. It's like there's an angry man in there trying to get out. I've never known anything like it. It's literally thrashing around in my chest. I'm down to fifty-seven minutes and there are still three people ahead of me in the cashpoint queue. I would tell them that some heavies have given me a time frame in which to get my hands on four grand, but they'll just think I'm a London crazy, tut and tell me to wait in line. These brick-throwing blokes can't be legal. I mean, this isn't a Ray Winstone film. I'll have to talk to whatever company they work for. We must be due some compensation. I've never been so scared in all my life.

Finally I reach the cashpoint. My hands shake as I type in my pin, select 'other amount' and tap in 4000. There's a small pause, then, 'Sorry. £300 maximum withdrawal today.'

I stare at the screen. I try the whole transaction again. It must be a computer error. It's my money, why can't I get it out?

Still no luck and my watch now says 8.11 p.m. I withdraw £300. Under normal circumstances that would be a lot of money, but today it isn't even ten per cent of what I need. I step away from the cashpoint and call Wendy.

'Hey, babe,' she sings.

'Wend. I'm really in it. Mum's in trouble. These violent men came round. Seriously massive, throwing bricks through the windows and everything. I need to give them four grand by nine o'clock tonight or they'll wreck the house.'

'What?'

'Sorry, I'll give it back tomorrow, but I need whatever money you've got. I haven't got time to explain now. You just have to just trust me.'

'Yeah, yeah, cool. Shit. Right. I'll get all I can and meet you at your mum's. Is that OK?'

'Yeah, thanks. I'm going to try Bob and Lube, but get as much as you can. I'll see you there.'

I dial Lube's mobile number.

'Gracie Flowers, *mi amiga*, is everything all right with you?'

'Lu— Ken, where are you?'

'Stansted, darlin'. We're on our way to Spain.' He's shouting against the sound of a plane. 'You must come out with us for a trip, you'd—'

NO!

'Thanks,' I sing quickly. 'Have a lovely time.'

I hang up. Heart, calm down. It can't be healthy for it to beat this hard. It feels like it might explode. I dial Bob the Builder's number. I don't know why I bothered with Lube. Bob's always about.

'Please leave a message after the tone.'

NO!

'Beep.'

'Bob, Bob. It's Gracie, Bob. Can you call me? I'm in a spot of bother. Call me, please.'

I hang up. Spot of bother?! I'm starting to sound to sound like Posh Boy. Posh Boy! Could I? Should I? Yes, Grace. You haven't got a lot of options here.

I call him. It rings once, it rings twice.

'Please, Posh Boy. Please, please. I'll do anything.'

It rings a third time, then clicks onto voicemail. I don't leave a message. I'm too busy racing back to Nina. I'm going to go to Bob the Builder's yard. Bob always works late, so he's bound to be there. My car clock says it's eight twenty-seven. The roads are heaving and I break all my time-honoured driving rules to get to Bob's yard by eight thirty-four, but there are no lights on and no Land Rover parked outside. I knock on the door just in case, but there's no answer. I've just wasted seven minutes! Heart, please, please, stop it. I slam the car door shut and start the engine again. Stupid idea, Gracie. Stupid. THINK!

'Someone, somewhere, help me, please,' I whisper. And then it comes to me. I know who'll help. I should have gone there first. The Festering Carbuncle. I make it in six minutes. I double park and don't even lock my car before racing inside the pub.

'Anton. Where's Anton?' I gasp to the young guy serving.

'Haven't seen him.' He shrugs.

'What?' I pant.

'He's not here.'

'What?'

'He's out.'

'Freddie? What about Freddie?'

'I don't think he's home yet.'

My watch says eight forty-two. No one has called my phone. My brain says nothing. I always thought I was resourceful, but I can't think of any way to get this money. All I can think of is the £120 I keep in the drawer in the kitchen for emergencies. I run and get it from the flat and am back in the car by eight forty-five.

I'll have to beg them to give me a few more hours until the banks open in the morning. That's what I'll have to do. Beg.

I let myself back into Mum's house. I don't even acknowledge Mildred. There are voices coming from the kitchen, so I walk towards them. It's Wendy and Freddie. They're sitting round the kitchen table with Mum. I can't look at Mum. I've failed her.

'I . . . I . . . I couldn't get it,' I tell them.

'Grace, there's four grand in here,' Freddie says, standing up. 'From Dad.'

He hands me a big soft envelope, squidgy with notes, and as if on cue the big brass Victorian door knocker slams three times against our front door.

'I'm coming with you,' Freddie says.

'Thank you,' I whisper.

We walk to the front door, avoiding the glass debris and the brick.

'What you got for us?' Brick Man asks.

'Four thousand,' I say, holding out the envelope.

'Now that's more like it.' He smiles.

'Tell me,' says Freddie. 'Who do you work for?'

'Who don't we work for?' he grunts.

'Well, you're acting outside the law with your methods of extracting payment.'

'Acting outside the law.' Brick Man laughs. 'The lady inside took out a loan. She knows the terms. See you next week,' he says, before smiling and turning away.

I watch him go. I feel faint, my head is thumping and my tummy hurts.

Chapter 65

'Is Anton here now?' I ask the young barman again.

'Yeah, you just missed him earlier. He's upstairs.' He nods, then squints at me. 'You all right?'

'Yeah. Fine, thanks.'

'Sure? You want a drink of water or anything?'

'No, thank you.'

'Just go up.'

'Is that OK?'

'Yeah. Knock when you get to the top, though. Yeah?'

'I will.'

I walk behind the bar. I don't feel at all well, to be honest. I feel a bit other-worldly and unsteady on my feet. I need to eat. I can't remember when I last ate. That awful hour took it out of me. I owe Freddie and Wendy something expensive. They're still with Mum now. And Anton. I really owe him. He saved the day. Again.

I tiptoe up the creaky stairs. The door is open at the top

and it sounds as though Anton is listening to music. I creep nearer and nearer, but when I get to the doorway I stop. I hover on the top step and watch Anton. He's sitting on a leather sofa, crouched over a guitar. He's not listening to music, he's playing music. It sounds as though he's trying to learn a song. He plays a chord or two, then stops and tuts and tries again or moves on. He's deep in concentration. I lean my head on the door frame and close my eyes. I know this song. Whatever song it is, it's a song I love. A song that's meant a lot to me at some point. If he could just play a bit more I know I could remember it.

'Argh!' I scream. My foot slips and I topple back for a moment. I manage to steady myself on the banister, then I scream again. It's my stomach. It feels as though someone's punching me.

'Argh!'

Jesus, it hurts! My fingers turn white as I clutch the banister.

'Grace!' Anton runs to my side.

I'm doubled over on the stairs.

'Urgh!' I bawl again.

Oh, no. Don't be. Please, please. Don't be what I think this is. 'No!' I scream.

'Grace, let's bring you up here to sit down.'

I shake my head and grimace as another wave of pain comes.

'Right, let's get you to hospital,' Anton says suddenly. He doesn't even go back upstairs to get his coat or drop off his guitar. He just leads me downstairs and outside to his car.

Chapter 66

'She's lost the baby. I'm so sorry,' the nurse tells Anton. He remains still for a few seconds, then he nods and turns back to face me. I don't move. I'm curled up in a hospital bed. It's late now. It's all over.

Anton stays with me all night. We don't say a word, but I do cry. I let out the tears I've been holding back for nearly ten years. There are so many of them it takes all night for me to rid myself of them. Anton strokes my hair and sometimes he holds my hand. He changes my tissue when it gets soggy and he plays his guitar very quietly. After a while I recognise the song. It's 'Annie's Song'. The song my dad sang to my mum on their wedding day. The song that made all the guests cry.

At about 6 a.m., when the sun starts to rise, Anton masters the tune and starts to sing the words, but he gets them wrong. Not really wrong, but pretty wrong. I know because I learned this song when I was ten and I remember it like my five times tables. He stumbles over the lines. He knows they're wrong but he doesn't know what he should be singing.

I lie and wait for him to play the song again on the guitar, and then I start to sing. I sing the whole song for him. I sing the same words that my dad sang to my mum before I was born. 'Let me lay down beside you, let me always be with you. Come let me love you.' I sing them to him because I love this man. Amazing, magical Anton, who's far too old for me and doesn't even love me back. But that doesn't matter, because I mean the words and I want to sing them to him, so that he knows. Because we only have now, and because life's far too short.

By the time I finish the tears have stopped. I lie still. I'm breathing normally for the first time in hours. Anton gets up, leans over me and presses his lips to my forehead. He keeps them there in a kiss. After that I fall asleep and when I wake up he's gone.

'Hey,' says Wendy when she sees my eyes open. I tip the corners of my mouth up to see her, but it's not a smile, because my brow is furrowed and my eyes are sad.

'Hey,' I mouth back.

'Anton called me,' she whispers. 'He thought you might need the girls.'

Over Wendy's shoulder I see my mum getting up from the hospital chair and walking towards me. I start to push myself up in the bed, but she lightly presses my shoulder back, as if to say, 'Lie where you were.' So I lie down again. Wendy steps back and Mum perches on the bed and takes my hand. I just gaze at her, amazed and grateful that she's there.

Chapter 67

It's one of those days that knows there's been a trauma: still, grey, solicitous. I'm at the graveyard because life goes on. Well, not for the little one that never was, and not for the bodies lying here, but for me.

I don't know much about anything really, but I know that when bad big things happen in life you have to appreciate the good little things. Otherwise the bad spreads to every corner of everything and all you can see is pain. That's what happened when Dad died and Mum started hating me. There was no good in anything for a long time. But slowly – and it really was ever so slowly – I started to find the good stuff again. But I had to look for it. A Saturday job at an estate agent was a good thing, Danny Saunders wanting to go out with me was a good thing, my five year plan was a good thing and coming to the graveyard every week was a good thing. That's why I didn't want to miss today. I could have lain in bed, but I didn't. I got up because I didn't want to let the bad take over.

I bought extra flowers, a bunch for Dad and a bunch for my baby. I don't know what I'll sing today. Not 'Tears In Heaven'. Not 'Tears In Heaven'. Well, maybe 'Tears In Heaven', but only after Leonard and Joan have gone. I don't want them to see me cry.

I walk to silver birch corner. At least I still have this. I'll always be able to come here, and that's something. I can see Joan standing in front of her mother's tombstone. I hang back for a moment. She looks older than I've ever seen her. She's seventy now. She must be, because Leonard's seventy-four. I step closer. There's no sign of Len.

'Afternoon,' I call, trying to sound upbeat and normal.

'Oh, Grace, hello.'

She turns and I see her face, lined and without make-up. I've never seen Joan without make-up. I feel like I can see her skeleton under the skin.

'How are you?'

'I'm fine, love, but poor Len's in the hospital.'

'Oh no. Why?'

'He had a stroke late last night, love.'

'Oh, Joan.'

'I just wanted to let you know.'

'Thank you. Where is he?'

'St Mary's.'

I was there last night, too.

'Can I visit?'

'I'd give it a week.'

'Is it bad?'

'I think so, pet. I think so.'

'I'm so sorry.'

'Well, we knew it was on the cards, what with his blood pressure.'

'Oh, Joan.'

'It wasn't helped by a visit from a young man from SJS Construction. He made the old chap look like Ghandi.'

'Jesus! What happened?'

'Len wasn't doing well, as you know, and then the other morning a young man came round to try to persuade us to sell the grave again. Blackmail, I'd call it. I'd better get back to him, I just didn't want you to worry.'

'What's it like at St Mary's for him?'

'Oh, you know, it's a big, busy city hospital.' She offers a resigned smile. 'It's fine.'

She comes towards me and we hug.

'Will I see you here next week?'

'I'll try, but don't be worried if I'm not.'

'OK. Bye. Send Len my love.'

I watch her as she walks away.

'Joan!'

She turns.

'Joan, maybe you should take the money the construction company is offering and go to Dorset with Len. That's where he should be, in the fresh air, with the sea views. That's what your mum would want. And my dad, I know, and Alfred with his syphilis here. I'll tell Mum to take the money, too.'

She stares through me for what seems like a lifetime.

'I couldn't do that to you.'

'But I'd like you to. These bastards have ruined enough, so we may as well take their money.'

'Let me think about it, Grace. Thank you.'

Chapter 68

I thought fighting the graveyard was a no-brainer. Destroying part of the graveyard was wrong. Saving it was right. Surely? But now look. If I'd just let Mum take the money she wouldn't be in this state, and Len only started to get ill because of the stress of it all. Maybe I'd have been able to keep the baby, too, if I hadn't run around that night trying to get that money. I was the catalyst for this disaster. Me. Maybe the SJS Construction man was right and I've been selfish.

I park outside the flat. I'm going to lie in bed for the rest of the day. Mum wanted to stay with me. She found strength neither of us knew she had today by coming to the hospital and being so calm and caring. I didn't like to say 'no' to her, but I just need to be on my own for a little while, away from people, away from any chance of me causing yet more disaster. I need a little time on my own to grieve and then I'll get up and write my new five year plan. I'll really do it this time and I'll stick to it – I'm determined to feel the control I used to have over my life. It will all be well again soon. It will.

I unlock my front door and push it open, bending down to pick up today's pile of free pamphlets and dump them straight in the recycling.

'Grace!' It's Anton running out of the pub. 'How are you?' he mouths. He's crossing the road, holding a large brown envelope. I smile to see him.

'Grace!' calls another voice to the side of me.

I know the voice, but it can't be who it sounds like. I turn to my right. It is him. Danny Saunders steps out of the chippy holding an open bag of chips with a battered sausage laid on the top and comes towards me.

Anton freezes in the middle of the street.

'Anton!' I scream, because a car is coming. Anton shakes himself and races across the remainder of the road towards me.

'All right, mate,' says Danny and offers him a chip. Anton ignores the offer.

'These are for you, Grace. I had copies done. I thought you'd like them. They're the photos we spoke about. I was just checking you were OK.'

'Thank you, Anton,' I say, but my voice is tiny.

'I'd best be getting back,' he says and crosses back to the pub.

I turn to face Danny, who offers me a chip. I don't even bother to shake my head. I can't think of a single word I want to say to him.

'How are you?'

I shake my head. Where do I start?

'I mean, have you got morning sickness and stuff? You look the same. Bit tired maybe. I know how you feel. My flight got in this morning and I haven't slept.'

I feel nothing. I thought that if Danny came back I'd beg him to stay or I'd be angry, furious at him for the way he left, but as it is there's nothing. Just disbelief. Disbelief at the nothingness. Ten years and now diddly-squat.

'We need to talk, Grace, about the baby, money and stuff. Mum says we should start talking about things now. That's why I came back, to do it face to face. I fly back tomorrow. I just got a long weekend break. So . . . ' he picks up the battered sausage, then drops it again. It must be hot.

'So . . . ' I say finally.

'Do you want to talk inside or in the pub. If we go over there I'll have to finish my chips first.'

I shrug.

'I'm really sorry about, you know, how I went. I, you know . . . I was really upset, too. I just, um . . . Canada's great, Grace. You ought to go. Really big portions and you don't have to show your ticket on the tube.'

'I lost the baby last night.'

'You what?'

'Don't ask me to say it again.'

'Oh, did you have a whatsit. Abortion. I thought you might.'

'No, I had a miscarriage, last night.'

'Oh, right,' he says and he leaves his chips alone for the first time in our exchange. 'Well.' He sighs. 'It's probably for the best, isn't it?'

I don't answer.

Another sigh. 'Listen, I'll be off, Grace. I don't think you want me here. I mean, I'll stay for a while if you want me to. Do you?'

'No. Just go, Dan.'

Chapter 69

'Hey, Mildred,' I say, stepping on her, but then I stop suddenly and peer down at the gravestone. 'Have you been scrubbed?'

I walk into Mum's house. I've had twenty-four hours on my own, but I feel so empty I think it might be better to have someone there. Wendy offered, but actually I'd prefer to be here with Mum. I hope she doesn't mind.

'Mum! Mum!' I call, but then I stop again. 'Whoa! What did you do with all the stuff that was in the hall?'

'Oh, hello,' my mum says, walking out of the kitchen and closing the door behind her.

'What the . . . ?' I'm speechless. I hold my arms out wide and slowly spin 360 degrees. 'Where's all the stuff gone?'

'I had a bit of a tidy.'

'*A bit!* Even demolition clearance would have called that a big job.'

'How are you feeling, love?' She walks towards me and strokes my arm.

'Sad.'

She nods as though she knows.

'Can we drink gin?' I ask, leading her into the kitchen. 'Ah!' I cry as I open the kitchen door.

The evil SJS Construction man is sitting at Mum's kitchen table. I blink at the scene. He's wearing a pressed shirt and she's laid out biscuits on a plate. They're proper biscuits, luxury, chunky cookie-type things that look well over a hundred calories each. The only biscuits I've ever seen in this house are Jaffa Cakes, because they're only forty-six calories each. And the biscuits are on a plate! The few times we've had Jaffa Cakes they've always been fished straight out of the packet. Never on a plate. I can't take it all in. A teapot stands next to the plate of biscuits. I didn't even know we had a teapot. We're a dunk-in-the-bag household, always have been. All this suggests that this is an arranged tea.

He stands.

'Grace, a pleasure.' He holds out a big, rough hand. 'I'm John, I don't think I've ever introduced myself properly.' I think about Len in the hospital and Dad's grave and I shake my head at his hand. Then I leave the room and walk upstairs. I want my childhood diary. I want to read about a time when I was happy, because I'm certainly not happy now. I find it in my bedside cupboard and take it downstairs, I'm passing the kitchen on the way to the front door, when I hear SJS Construction man say, 'He sounded Italian to you? So we have a smooth-talking Italian man in expensive shoes and two thugs, but nothing more.'

I hover in the hallway for a moment, wondering whether or not to leave. Then I decide to quickly poke my head round the kitchen door and ask them what they're talking about.

'Oh, I'm sorry, Grace,' SJS man says, standing up again when he sees me. 'I was trying to see if I could get a handle on this loan shark your mother had dealings with.'

'I was just telling John that he looked a bit like that chap off the telly.' She tuts. 'What's his name?' She giggles like a girl. She's got the hots for SJS Construction man. I'm sure of it. 'Oh, you know, um, er, ooh,' she whitters and blushes. See! She's lost it completely in his presence. 'He looked like the one Jordan got together with on that jungle programme. He looked like him.'

I feel my eyes getting wider and wider as mum's words sink in.

'An Italian man who looks like Peter Andre?'

'Peter Andre! Thank you, Grace.' My mum giggles again in Evil John's direction. But he's looking at me now. He's noticed something in my expression.

'Do you think you've come into contact with him?' he asks.

I stand still in the doorway and put my hands over my face. 'What was his name?' I gasp behind my hands.

'Laurence,' my mum says.

'Oh,' I say. I'd thought it was my Italian client, Ricardo, for a moment then. I thought I'd led the swindler right to my mother's door. At least that's one disaster I wasn't personally responsible for.

'Laurence Olivier he was called. His mother was British and she loved the actor apparently.'

'Say that again.'

'His mum loved Laurence Olivier, so he was named after him. You remember him? Old actor?'

'Oh, Mum.'

'Grace, what's the matter?'

'He's my client. He told me he was called Ricardo – or Richard – Burton because his mum loved the actor. He was charming. Oh God, I'm so sorry.'

'I don't understand. Did you tell him to offer me a loan?'

'No, but I . . . God, I told him you had money troubles.'

'Oh, Grace. Why on earth . . . ?'

'Oh, God. I'm so sorry! John, when you came to see Mum about the graveyard situation, she was upset when you left and she called me. But Richard – Olivier whatever-he's-called – was with me. I was helping him find some bloody house for his mother and his "seester". Anyway, on the way to the viewing I dropped in here, and I left him in the car as I ran in to see Mum. When I got back in the car, I was really flustered and I spoke to him about it. He asked me how much the house was worth and stuff. Oh, God!'

'Oh, Grace, it's not your fault. I took the loan because I was too pathetic to walk half a mile to the bank. That's what's done it.'

'Rosemary, don't blame yourself. You have kept this house together all on your own,' he says, touching her on the shoulder. And she smiles and suddenly I remember the mysterious fresh flowers and the mown lawn and my mother dressing sexily, and I seriously wonder whether something is going on between them.

'Oh, God, but he took me out for dinner. I told him much more than I ever usually tell people, and all because he was from Rome.'

'Where did you have dinner?'

'At The Paradise.'

'Did he pay? This is a long shot, but did he pay by credit card by any chance?'

'Um, I can't remember. Yes. YES! He did and he seemed freaked out by it, actually.'

'Right, Grace, perhaps you could come with me. They should have the credit card receipt. And perhaps he gave you a telephone number?'

'Funnily enough, he didn't, and he's completely disappeared since. I've been cursing myself for that.'

'Don't curse yourself, these people are pros. Right, Grace, take me to Paradise. Oh good grief,' he says. 'I didn't mean it like that.'

My mother, of course, thinks this is the funniest thing she's ever heard.

'Until tomorrow,' John says, and he bows his head, takes my mum's hand and kisses it.

My mother giggles for too long and then fiddles with her hair.

Chapter 70

I just can't make sense of it at all. I would have loved that baby so much. Why did it have to happen? Why? That's all I seem to be asking myself at the moment. Why? Why? Why? There's an ache inside of me that knows the answer: You didn't want the child at first, it says. You didn't deserve it.

I need something good to cling to, but they're thin on the ground at the moment. All I can think of is that The Paradise had a credit card receipt of Ricardo's. That will have to do for the time being.

'Grace,' Wendy calls from her desk. 'Can I have a word?' It's just the two of us.

'Hmm,' I say, staring sadly at the computer screen.

'Um, it's quite important,' says Wendy.

'Wha—?' I look up and Wendy's face looks worried.

'Oh, no. What have I done?' I ask anxiously.

'Nothing. Why do you say that?'

'I feel like a walking curse at the moment. I just thought I might have ruined your life in someway accidentally.'

'Grace. No. You make my life better. That's why this it's so hard.'

'Oh my God, Anton's getting married.'

'No! Are you still pining for Anton?'

'Hmm. But, you know, I'm used to it.'

'Oh, Grace, it will get better. Why don't you have another bit of Posh Boy to take your mind off things?'

I scrunch my face up. I haven't seen Posh Boy since that drunken night when we did the shaggy shaggy. He's been at the Cricklewood branch. He's due back today.

'What is it you want to tell me?'

'Well, you know when Freddie was telling me about the trafficked women.'

'Uh, huh.'

'Well, he mentioned this charity that helps women who've been exploited. And when I got home I went online and looked it up. You know, just because I was interested. And, well, they were advertising a job. Just doing what I do now, but for the charity. And it felt like a sign, so I applied.'

'Oh my God, Wend, that's brilliant.'

'And I had the interview.'

'Oh my God! How did it go?'

'I got the job!'

'That's amazing.'

'Do you think?'

'Of course, don't you?'

'Yeah, but I thought you might miss me. And I feel bad because I know you're low at the minute and I don't like to leave you. Listen, I could stay here an extra month or two to be with you, if you wanted. Just until things aren't so raw for you.'

'Wend, of course I'll miss you, but this is great news. Great news! You have to start as soon as possible. This is a big good thing.'

'I know, and they've actually given me a better job. Oh, Grace, they really liked me. They want me to be involved in, like, some PR and stuff. They said they were impressed by my enthusiasm and empathy. And they're really excited about me starting.'

'Oh, I feel like a proud mother.'

'Ooh, Posh Boy alert.'

'Where?'

'Coming in.'

We jump apart and sit back in front of our respective computers. I open my emails, and am just putting on my 'I am working very hard' face when I notice that I have one new email from an unexpected email address: anton@carbunkle.co.uk. I smile just to see his name on my computer screen. I open it and find a link to YouTube, which I click on. I hear Posh Boy walk into the office, but I can't take my eyes off the screen in front of me.

It's the strangest thing. The sound is tinny and the picture is blurry, but it's a video of me singing in Rome with my dad. My favourite day is here in front of me. My breath deepens and my hand reaches towards the screen. There I am in the blue dress I could barely move in. It really was me that day. My dad is next to me doing dance steps in a spotlight, and when he finishes he turns to me and smiles. It's a lovely smile, but I didn't see it at the time because I'd already started to sing to the audience. I've seen it now, though. I smile back, over ten years too late. I sound good, too. I look like I was born to be up there. But if I was born to be up there, then what am I doing here? Before I can get dragged down by that notion, I have a happier thought. Anton must have Googled me!

'What is that?' asks John as he walks behind my desk, puts a hand on my shoulder and watches with me.

'Bloody hell, Grace, it's you singing?' Wendy shrieks, joining us.

We watch the video the whole way through.

'Grace, that's . . . ' John says when it's finished. 'You're like a superstar.'

'She is a superstar.'

'We could get her to do a Make A Move jingle.'

I let them talk behind me. I can't speak. I feel emotional and foggy and I wish I was back there.

'Oh. My. God. Grace, read the comments below it. Jeez.'

I skim down to see what people have written. There are fifty-six comments in total, and on the whole they're positive:

'She's amaze.'

'Who is this girl?'

'Where is she now?'

'I love this song. Is there a recording of this somewhere?'

Although some are from men stating, in rather crude ways, that they want to boff me. And one is from a man who speculates on what it would be like to boff my dad.

I exit YouTube and click on Anton's email again. All he has written is this:

> Grace, I hope you're feeling better. I am thinking of you. Often. I'd love to sing this song with you. Forgive me for trying to persuade you again. Please sing with me in the *Britain Sings* Contest. We would have fun, and I think you might need some of that at the moment. Go on. Why not? X

Why not indeed? Oh, Anton, it's a very long story.

'Grace,' John whispers once Wendy is back at her desk. 'Grace, I've missed you. Can I take you out at the weekend? You know, catch up on some abuse and insults. Can you do Sunday evening? I'm sorting some things out with Lube on Saturday.'

That shakes me free of my reverie.

'What things?'

'Oh.' He looks a bit taken aback that I've asked. 'Oh, he just wants to catch up with me.'

I raise my eyebrows. That doesn't sound like Lube to me.

'So, can I take you out on Sunday?'

'You won't jump me?'

'Promise.'

'Really promise? I'm not up for nooky.'

'I really promise.'

'OK.'

'Great. Listen, I'll come up with something good for us to do and I'll text you where to meet. Is that good?'

'Yeah. Perfect.'

He smiles. I think back to kissing him. All that lovely kissing. And I smile, too. Then I turn back to my computer screen and press replay on the YouTube clip.

Chapter 71

John was so pleased with himself.

You will love this! he texted me.

Graice Flowers, I have the perfect thing for us, he boasted.

Karaoke! How about 7.30? @ the Festering Carbuncle. Nice pub. Does food. Do you know it?

'I thought with your voice and my Elton John impression we'd wipe the floor with them,' he told me excitedly when we met.

I said very little. In actual fact, it hasn't been as disastrous as it could have been. No one has sung 'Amazing Grace' for a start, I've hardly seen Anton and John hasn't done his Elton John impression, although that's largely because he's been outside on the phone for most of the night. He's having a big old barney with his dad by the sounds of things. He's outside now and I can see him, arms waving, striding up and down the pavement by the smokers. Here's Anton coming up to the stage.

'So I'm singing alone tonight. I, er, still haven't found a partner for the *Britain Sings* final.' He looks in my direction. I wasn't sure whether he knew I was here or not as he hasn't been over to say hello. I pull an apologetic face. Much as I love this man. I could never, ever, enter the final of that competition next week. 'If I could ask you all to spread the word. If you know any ladies who might want to sing with me, please tell them about my plight. It's urgent as the final is only six days away. Thank you.'

Anton looks sadder than usual. I can tell by his eyes, which normally sparkle. Anton's eyes were the first thing I noticed when I walked into this pub two years ago. I thought they were the kindest eyes I'd ever seen. They seemed to say, 'Look through my soul, you won't find any hatred or darkness there.' I walked into this pub and looked into those eyes and something inside me said, 'Yes, this is where you should be.' Anton's eyes were probably the reason I purchased the noisiest maisonette in the United Kingdom.

Today his lips are smiling but his eyes aren't. I want to go up there and hold his hand, or clutch his head to my chest and stroke his hair, or sing a song to make him smile.

'If you'll excuse my mistakes, I'm going to play this one on the guitar.'

He picks up his acoustic guitar, puts the strap around his neck and holds the plectrum in his teeth as he settles himself on a bar stool. Then he takes the plectrum out of his mouth and looks at me.

'This is "Annie's Song",' he says and he starts to play.

As he starts to sing he's still looking at me. Our eyes are locked. I couldn't look away if I tried. I can't remember having seen or heard anything so beautiful in all my life.

A figure walks right in front of me and practically straddles me, blocking my view. It's Posh Boy, climbing over me to get to the seat next to me.

'Babe, sorry about that,' he pants loudly. I can't believe he's speaking over this song. He puts his arm around me and pulls me towards him in a headlock, then he lurches his face down and kisses me with a bit of tongue. It's just a quick kiss, but then he keeps his arm around me and starts to stroke my arm, catching the side of my breast with his hand. I try to ignore him as my favourite bit of the song is coming up.

I get back to watching Anton, but he's lost his way in the song. He stumbles over some words and then repeats a line from earlier in the song. I want to go up there and sing with him, and I think about doing just that. I could stand up and walk over there and sing him through to the end, but I don't, and Anton finishes the song sooner than he should. He still gets a big cheer, though. I spy Freddie wiping a tear from his eye as he claps. Posh Boy isn't crying; he isn't even clapping.

'He cocked that up,' he says, leaning in for another kiss.

'No, he didn't,' I say quietly. 'It was beautiful.'

I avoid the kiss and look for Anton, but he's left the stage already and I can't see him any more.

Chapter 72

It's strange. I don't feel as though all my songs are for him, although that might come. He doesn't make me want to sing, but that's probably a good thing. Perhaps he'll help me get back to the Gracie Flowers Overachieving Estate Agent that I was. I am simply fond of him. Nothing dramatic. Nothing all-consuming. I just feel fond of him and grateful to him and protected in his big, strong, badminton-playing arms. The 'yah' and 'righto' will have to be binned straight off, but I'm beginning to think, like he said at paintballing, that we could work. We didn't do anything physical last night as I'd made it clear I didn't want to. We just had a kiss and a cuddle. He was the perfect gentleman. Well, he did try to get into my knickers twice, but that's men for you.

It's early now and I'm watching him sleep. Yes, I'm a sap but I like sleeping men. They're so nice and quiet. He's got more stubble than I've ever seen him with and it's sexy.

There's also a scar on his cheek that I've never noticed before. Chicken pox maybe, or the remains of a teenage zit. I feel it with my finger. There's a tiny ball of yellow wax nestling in the nook of his ear. That's mank. I won't be touching that. I kiss his lips softly. He stirs and mumbles, opens one eye and smiles. I get a whiff of morning breath. Bloody hell.

'Morning gorgeous.'

Clean air! I need clean air!

'Have you got any gum?'

'Hmm. Somewhere.'

'Please, it's an emergency.'

He climbs out of bed and I watch him pad around the room in his pants. He's so much bigger than Dan. I mean, Dan was tall, but he was super skinny, like a disappointing drumstick. Posh Boy's broad and muscly and tall. Dan's a gangly kid in comparison. Posh Boy's a man. A man who wears good-quality suits and probably has matching luggage. So different to Dan. Dan had a Chelsea bag and a rucksack he used for the Duke of Edinburgh Award he failed.

'How old are you?'

He stops rummaging in the pocket of a pair of jeans.

'Why?'

'Just wondered.'

'Thirty.'

'You?'

'Twenty-six.'

A four-year age difference. The same as my mum and dad had. That's a good sign.

'Come back to bed,' I say, smiling. He moves towards me and bends down for a kiss.

'GUM!'

'I don't think I have any.'

'Well, anything would do. Anything at all. A sweet? An old mint? A festering satsuma?'

'I've got some Quality Street somewhere.'

'Perfect.'

He opens a desk drawer and pulls out a box.

'Ta da!' he cries. So incredibly posh. He bounces back into bed with them, lies down and pours them onto his chest.

'Colour?'

'Purple.'

'I knew it.'

'I love purple,' I say, but then I remember my dad's odd anti-purple stance.

'What's up?' Posh Boy asks, unwrapping a purple chocolate for me.

'Nothing. I was just thinking about my dad. Sorry.'

'Don't be.'

'Do you think about your mum a lot?'

'All the time.'

I take the sweet, clear a space on his chest and lay down amidst the assorted chocolates. I can hear his heartbeat and his tummy gurgling like a drain. All I smell is cocoa and I feel content.

Suddenly there's a loud bang on the door.

'Shit!' says Posh Boy quietly, but with an awful lot of feeling.

Posh Boy's heart rate gets quicker and louder. He doesn't say anything, but he puts his finger to his lips to indicate that I shouldn't make a sound.

'JOHN! JOHN!' the voice shouts.

The knocking continues. Posh Boy's heart drums away. His finger rests on his lips. I suck on my caramel centre. I'm taking this keeping-quiet thing so seriously I won't even risk crunching the hazelnut. Whoever is knocking very much wants to come in. I haven't heard knocking like this since the night of the heavies.

Eventually it stops, and for a baby second I think that we've been left in peace, but then the door flies open. Now I've heard the expression 'a door flies open' before and really it's nonsense, a door can't fly, it's on a bleeding hinge. But this door gets pretty close to busting its hinges and soaring off into Hyde Park. If anyone treated my doors like that I would break their neck. We both sit up quickly. No, this can't be right. In walks John, the evil old bloke from SJS Construction.

'DAD!' shouts Posh Boy aggressively.

'DAD?!' I repeat in higher register. 'He's your dad!' I screech again. I furrow my brow and stare at him, as if he were an algebra problem I can't get my head around. SJS Construction Man is Posh Boy's Dad! 'He's your dad,' I whisper.

But the two men aren't taking any notice of me. They're glaring at one another, like boxers before a match.

'I wrote you a note!'

'Oh, yes, a note telling me not to disturb you because you have a lady friend staying.' SJS Construction man looks at me now. He stops and squints. 'Grace Flowers,' he says, sounding bizarrely polite after the earbashing he's just given Posh Boy. 'Do send my regards to your mother.'

'But … but … you're not posh …' is all I can muster by way of a response.

'No, unlike my son, who had tens of thousands of pounds spent on his education!'

SJS Construction man is Posh Boy's dad! But I told Posh Boy all about the graveyard situation and SJS Construction and he never mentioned it. SJS! St John Smythe!

'And as for you, young man. I tell you, I've wanted to kill you. I've calmed down now and I'll make do with just disowning you, but anger me any more and I'll raise my fist to you, believe me!'

If this is him calmed down, I'd hate to see the revved-up version.

'DAD!'

'Don't "Dad" me! I'm telling you now, just leave those plans alone. Touch them again and our little agreement, which we go public with in an hour's time, is off. Off, I tell you.'

'But—'

'That graveyard stays as it is. It was a stupid idea of yours, I don't know how I agreed to it, but we leave those people's graves alone from now on, do you hear me?'

'You lose thirty-six units by moving the slip road, Dad,' Posh Boy says in a cold voice. 'Thirty-six. I don't need to tell you what a difference that will make to the profit figures.'

'WHAT?' I suddenly holler. 'What?!'

'Damn!' Posh sighs.

'Damn! Damn! Yep, damn you! All that …' I stop as it comes back to me. 'All that, "I don't know what I'd do if someone wanted to build on my mum's grave." Urgh!' The sex. I had sex with him. 'Urgh!' I say again. 'Urgh!'

'Grace,' he starts, and he looks quite pitiful, it has to be said. I shake my head, then I look at his dad.

'I would thank you for backing down, but my friend, Leonard Barry, who you were pressuring, had a stroke from all the stress it caused him, so I can't thank you. But I'm pleased about your decision.'

He nods.

'I'm terribly sorry about your friend.'

'Yeah,' I say, and I pick up my leggings and babydoll dress and leave the room with them. It's unfortunate that my bra is in there somewhere too, but it didn't seem the moment to go rummaging around for it.

I change on the landing, leaving Posh's shirt on the floor, then I pad my way down the stairs and across the spacious hallway to the front door. As rotten-luck patches go, this one is quite extensive.

'John!' shouts a lady's voice and a head pops out of a closed door to my right. 'Oh, sorry, I thought you were John.' She smiles.

She's an attractive older woman. Her hair is rolled up in those big Velcro curlers and covered with a pink silk scarf.

'No, sorry,' I say.

'I couldn't just ask you a favour.'

'OK.'

'Can you open this?' She holds up a jar of honey.

'Oh, honey's always a nightmare to open,' I say sympathetically, 'but I'll have a go.'

She pads into the hallway and offers me the honey. I take it and open it straight off, because I'm surprisingly good at opening tricky things. It's one of my powers. I hand it back.

'Marvellous. I can't have my tea without honey.'

'No,' I say. 'Well, cheerio, enjoy your tea.'

None of this is good. SJS Construction man, who my mum is smitten with, has clearly got a woman. He must have. Why else would there be an incompletely dressed woman is his house at seven forty-five in the morning?

Chapter 73

I don't want to go to work. I don't want to go to work. I don't want to go to work. Why's that then, Grace? Because you slept with your boss and he turned out to be the devil!

I came back to the flat and had the longest shower of my life. I still feel dirty, though. Now, I'm giving myself a good telling off before I have to go to work and face him again.

'Grace. Oh, Grace. Oh, oh, oh, Grace! You fool. I mean, Jesus, I knew he was posh, I knew he was annoying, but I didn't think he was sly! I didn't think he was evil! I thought he was all right. All that 'I don't know what I'd do if someone wanted to build on my mum's grave'! I mean, this couldn't be on many more levels of awfulness. I work with the bloke. Maybe I should tell Lube what he's like. But John just wants money above everything else, what's Lube not going to like about that? This is all wrong. How did I get here? The plan!

I look at the wall. It's still there. Blank. But I don't want to look at that one. I want to look at the one I followed religiously. The one I breathed for five years. The one that led me here. I squint at it. 'This is where you got me! Was that what it was all about? Was I just supposed to find out that people are evil? That they'll take your body, the graves of the dead, anything if they think it will make them some wonga? If they think they can put some self-contained apartments on it?! Oh, Grace! GRACE!'

I'm really shouting at my reflection now. 'THIS IS ALL WRONG!'

I sit on the loo.

'Calm down, Grace, put a track on. Chill out. I look through my CDs, but there's no song that would help. A song would be too good for this situation. A song would be like introducing something pure to something that's rotten. I just need to go to work. Ignore Posh Boy and work harder. I make my way to the door. When I get there, though, I turn back.

'Calm down, Grace,' I say to my reflection. 'Calm down.'

And I walk back to the toilet and sit down. This time I close my eyes and wait until his voice comes to me, then I sit and listen to my dad singing to me until it calms me.

Afterwards I get up and finish getting ready. But I still don't want to go to work.

Chapter 74

It's eight forty-five and Lube and Posh Boy are already in the office.

'What's going on here?' I ask Lube as I walk to my desk and turn on my computer. I will never, ever speak to Posh Boy again.

'Gracie Flowers, don't take your coat off. We're taking you out.'

'Why? To see a property?' I say directly to Lube.

'No.'

'What then? Oh please, not another team-building exercise.'

'A celebration.'

'What for? Where?'

'Grace, just shut up and follow me to my car. Fifty questions, that's what women are like,' Lube says, holding the door open for me. I walk back out onto the street. I haven't looked at Posh Boy once, and I'm not going to either.

We get into Lube's Audi and he drives us to a fancy hotel on Park Lane.

'What on earth are we doing here?' I protest. I don't want to be anywhere near Posh Boy this morning, or any morning, in fact. Let alone off on some jolly celebratory threesome with him and Lube.

'Champagne breakfast, my darling.'

'Champagne? Why? I can't drink champagne at 9a.m. I'll be asleep by ten.'

'That's all right by us today, isn't it, John?'

'Certainly is, Ken. It's your day,' chimes in Posh Boy.

'Please don't talk to me,' I mutter.

'Children,' chides Lube.

'Are you two pissed?'

I'm ushered into a lift that takes us to the top floor of the hotel, and when I get out I'm faced with a floor-to-ceiling window. The whole of London is at my feet. I can see Hyde Park, Marble Arch and beyond to the streets of houses I've been selling for the last five years.

'Wow! What a view,' I say.

'London Town, eh. Isn't she a beauty?' Ken sighs, sidling up to me. 'The streets are paved with gold down there, eh, Grace.'

I scrunch my face up because Lube is being a freak this morning.

'Paved with gob and fried chicken wrappers more like.'

'Grace Flowers?' a waitress asks, approaching me with a glass of Buck's Fizz. 'Congratulations.'

'What have I done?' I ask. 'Oh my God, am I Estate Agent of the Year?' I gasp.

'She thinks she's Estate Agent of the Year.' Lube laughs to John.

'Oh,' I say, disappointed. 'I'm so confused.'

'She probably will be,' chirps Posh Boy.

'I'm starting to feel sick.'

'What with the height?' Lube says.

'No, with you two fruitcakes being so weird! What's going on?'

'Come through, come through.'

I'm led into a meeting room, again with a floor-to-ceiling window, and this time I can see Buckingham Palace. There's a big glass table in the middle, around which sit four people. A woman in her mid-forties, who looks very expensively coiffed, two middle-aged men who I don't recognise and SJS Construction man, Posh Boy's dad. I stare at them. I'm completely baffled now, so I may as well drink this Buck's Fizz. The three people I don't recognise get up as soon as I walk in and hold out their hands to congratulate me.

'What's this about?' I ask.

'This is it, Grace Flowers,' Lube says. 'I'm so proud of my girl.' His voice cracks and he hugs me.

'Grace,' John St John Smythe Senior says. 'Let me explain. Sit down everyone. Top Grace's drink up please, son.'

I still don't acknowledge John, lest I be tempted to throw my Buck's Fizz over his head.

'Now, this is the board of John St John Enterprises, minus two others who have some business in the Cayman Islands. John St John Enterprises owns SJS Construction, which is the fourth largest commercial housing construction company in the UK. We also own Smiths Estate Agents.

My eyes open wide.

'We lost the "y" and the "e" to make us feel friendlier as a brand,' he explains. 'We have various other ventures, but these are our largest and the ones which will affect you.'

'Sorry? How?'

'We will be merging Make A Move with Smiths and we want you to head up the new company, which will be known as Smiths Make A Move, so as to maintain the two strong brand identities. My son John has been working in the company undercover for the last few months while the deal went through, in order to learn the ropes and see if, as Ken here suggested, you were the woman to front the venture. And you impressed him hands down. He said you were the best female estate agent in the country.' I shake my head at the word 'female'. 'So it's a big job, but one we know you can do. John will head up the construction side of things and Ken Bradbury, your old mentor, will sit on our board while the transition takes place. We're tripling your salary and we'll throw in a five per cent share of the company. You'll also be paid a generous commission if each branch hits its target. It's the big time, Grace, Well done.'

I stand there blinking at them all. I'm not smiling. I'm thinking, I'll be tied to them. This will be my life. Do I want this? Deep down inside, Gracie Flowers, is this what you really want?

'I'm sorry. I can't. I thought this was what I wanted, but, I'm sorry. I've got to go.' And I walk back to the lift and out of the hotel. It's not until I'm in the middle of Hyde Park and have taken off my shoes, felt the damp grass under my toes, hurled my mobile phone at a tree, downed my Buck's Fizz in one and burped that it dawns on me I've just quit my job. I don't care, though. I want to feel fifteen again, before all the bad stuff. I fling my coat down under a tree and rummage in my bag for my old diary. I want to read it and find that girl again, that Gracie Flowers. The one who loved to sing. I want to meet her again. I settle down under a tree and I start to read:

> I won! I didn't think I would. This means I've won every competition this year. Now I start my parent-imposed singing break while I do my GCSEs, then it's the biggie. The National Under 16s. Apparently I'm the favourite. I don't want to get too excited. It's not the be-all and end-all. Sometimes people get record deals and they're horrible. I mean, what if they wanted me to record shit pop and be on the cover in me pants. So not me. I need to not get too worked up. What will be will be.
>
> So, song choices. I haven't really worked them out yet. I talked about it with Dad in the car. I have to do a hymn or gospel and I have no idea. I blame Dad for bringing me up such a non-believer! Dad said I should do 'Amazing Grace' just to piss Ruth off! So cruel. Maybe I'll do 'Kumbaya' or 'Little Donkey'! I'd like to do a Nina, maybe 'Feeling Good', because I'll definitely be feeling good to have finished my GCSEs. Anyway there's loads of time.
>
> We had a funny journey home. Dad was in a good mood. He'd finished the opening chapter intro thingy for his book. He said I'd like it. Then! Then! Oh my God!!! I got a love talk. It was well soppy! I assume it was inspired by Danny Saunders asking me out.

Apparently, I'll know when I've met the right man because I'll be shy and weird around him, like I'll behave strangely and stuff and probably embarrass myself in his presence. Because I won't be able to stop thinking about him. Because all I'll want to do is kiss him and touch him. Because he'll make me want to be a better person. Because I'll want to sing for him. Because all my songs will be for him. Phew! Sounds exhausting! I think there was more that I've forgotten, but even when I feel all this I'm not allowed to have sex with him for twenty years. What's he like?!

I scroll back up the page. Something is very not right. When Mum and I compiled *The Five Year Plan* after Dad's death, there was no opening chapter intro on the computer. Our biggest problem with doing the book was the start. Chapter One never felt like it was the first chapter. It felt as though something should have gone before it, so we ended up writing an intro about Dad.

I close the book and get up, then I catch the bus to my mum's house.

Chapter 75

'Oh Mildred, what am I doing?' I say, dancing over her and letting myself in. 'Mum? Mum!' I call. 'Mum!'

'Grace, good grief, what are you doing here?' She's coming out of the kitchen, holding a bowl and a wooden spoon. The sight stops me in my tracks.

'Are you making a cake?'

'Yes.'

'A cake?'

'Why aren't you at work?'

'Mum, listen to this. I was reading my old diary. And there's another chapter. Dad wrote a chapter – a foreword – to *The Five Year Plan*. It's in the diary. Look,' I turn to the relevant page. '"Dad was in a good mood. He'd finished the opening chapter intro thingy for his book." He wrote a chapter but we never saw it. It wasn't on the computer. The computer notes started with how to write the plan, so there must be a chapter somewhere that we missed. I haven't been able to write my new plan, and I need to know, Mum, because I've just quit my job. I need to find this chapter.' When I stop speaking I'm panting.

'You quit your what?! But I thought you were being offered a new job.'

'How do you know?'

'John told me.'

I raise my eyes and shake my head. I hate this friendship between Posh Boy's dad and my mum.

'Mum, where would it be? Where should I look?'

'Grace!' she shouts. The hand clutching the wooden spoon tenses and jolts. I jump. 'The book's done,' she says, a touch more quietly. 'Please, love, let's leave it. I want to talk to you about something.'

'But, I—'

'Grace!'

'Why are you shouting?'

'Because you're not letting me finish.'

'Sorry.'

'I want to talk to you about my friend John, the man from SJS Construction. We're spending a lot of time together and we thought we should tell you that our feelings are develop—'

'No, Mum. No, no, no! He's not nice, and it's not just the fact that he tried to buy your husband's grave. I—' I stop and swallow. 'Mum, I hate to say this, but he's a player. I know he spent the night with another woman.'

'When? No, don't be silly, Grace. Neither of us . . . we've spoken—'

'I saw her, Mum. I saw her at his house. She was in curlers, opening honey. It was definitely his bird.'

'When?'

'This morning.'

'What?'

I nod.

'Why were you at his house?'

'I stayed over with his son. Please don't ask. I wish I hadn't. When I was leaving there, I saw her.'

Mum doesn't look at me for ages, she just stands there, stirring the cake and glaring into the bowl as the stirring gets more and more and fierce.

'Mum, talk to me,' I say quietly.

'NO!' she screams. Literally screams. It's the most painful sound. 'URGH!' she hurls the bowl in my direction. It misses but showers me with chocolate dough mixture. 'Why do you have to ruin everything, Grace?' She's retching the words. 'EVERYTHING! You ruined my relationship with your father. You ruined—'

'What? How?'

'I was eighteen! I didn't want a baby. I wanted to be with him!'

'But—'

'And then … and then,' she's crouching now and sobbing. 'And then we argued about you. YOU! We were arguing about you the night before he died, and I never said goodbye in the morning. I never said goodbye.'

She's on the floor now, curled up in a ball.

'Why?' I ask, taking a step away from her.

'He told me he wanted to enter that *Britain Sings* competition with you, the one on the telly, and do that song you performed in Rome. And I didn't want him to, because then it would have been all about you two. I was jealous. I was jealous of the two of you!'

She sobs like an abandoned child, but I don't go to her. Instead, I walk into Dad's study and open the blinds. The dust from them makes me cough. I start in one corner of the office and I work methodically, searching and searching for the lost chapter. I go through everything until I find it, and when I come out Mum's not there. I don't call out. I just leave.

Chapter 76

I've been in Wendy's lookout position, spying, all night. Anton's light is still on upstairs. It's midnight now and I know he's alone. I saw everyone leave the pub. I watched him say good night and lock the door. He looked weary, defeated almost. I know Freddie is staying with Wendy tonight – I think tonight's the night for them. Tonight's the night for me, too, though in a different way. A very different way. I pick up my dad's journal and hug it to my chest, then I turn my light off and leave my maisonette.

I hurry across the road and press the buzzer. I wonder whether he'll answer. He might think I'm a drunk person trying to cadge one last whisky.

'Hello?'

'Anton, it's Grace.'

'Grace.'

'Hmm.'

'Are you all right?'

'Yes, I was wondering if you still need a singer for the *Britain Sings* competition tomorrow.'

'Sorry?'

'If you need someone to sing with you tomorrow, then I'll sing with you, Anton. I'm sorry this is so last minute, but things have been happening and I just . . . '

I'm still talking into the intercom, but Anton is in the bar downstairs now. I can see him through the window. I wait while he unlocks the door.

'Come in,' he says.

'Thank you.'

I wait while he locks the door behind us. I watch his arms and his back and I want to step into him. I want to step into his space forever. But of course I just hang back, hugging my dad's book until he turns round.

'Are you sure?' he says eventually.

'Yes.'

'You're sure, you're sure.'

'Hmm.'

'Why now?'

'I, er, I suppose I've just realised that I had it all wrong.'

'I'm not following you, Grace.'

Of course he doesn't follow me. I'm not making any sense. It's quite understandable that he should look baffled.

'I found this,' I say, and I pass him the journal. 'Read it. Please read it.'

Anton takes the book, turns on a freestanding lamp and sits on the sofa by the fireplace. I watch him read my father's words.

*

First Chapter

This is a book about achieving your dreams by breaking those dreams down into doable chunks. It's a book about carving out the life you daydream about. It's about making your life amazing. But before we start developing our five year plan, and talking about the skills we'll need to implement it, we must look at the most important thing of all. Choosing your dream. How do you choose your dream? I am lucky to do what I love. When I started my first five year plan, my aim at the end of it was to win the World Championships in Ballroom Dancing with my wife at my side. For five years, every day I knew what I was aiming for and I achieved it. I knew that in order for me to do that I would have to succeed in many qualifying rounds. I would need sponsorship. I would need to train with the best teachers and choreographers. I knew where I wanted to be. Not all of us know. Some of us do jobs we hate because we are too afraid to follow our real passions. We make the most of those lives, but what if we found the courage to pursue the thing that made us happiest, that we daydreamed about as children. That is what I want you to get from this book. Don't write a five year plan to get ahead in your corporate job if what you really want is to own a tea shop on the Northumberland coast. Life is short, so follow your heart. If you follow your heart, you're always going the right way.

Let me use my daughter, Gracie, as an example. Now Gracie is fifteen. Ever since she was three she has known what she wanted to be. She wants to be a singer. And she is blessed with a talent that I know will blow you away. She sings from the moment she wakes up to the moment she goes to sleep. I even heard her once singing in her sleep. She wins singing competitions across the country and I have no doubt that she will achieve her dream. Why do I know this? Because she has no fear. None at all. She never has. When she was eight she started doing singing competitions. She was always smaller than the other children and she would stand on stage and look so tiny that I would want to run up there and hold her hand. And I would have done, too, but she didn't need me, because she had no fear. And I pray that nothing ever makes her fearful. I pray that she continues to love and use her gift. And that is what I hope for you, too. I urge you to find your love, your gift, and never be afraid.

When Anton is finished he looks up.

'I've been afraid to sing. I've been afraid of music since he died and that's the last thing my dad would have wanted.'

'But are you sure you'll be OK?'

'I probably won't be the most emotionally stable contestant, but I promise I won't scream or leave.'

'What shall we sing?'

'"Mr Bojangles"?'

'I think I've learned it already from the YouTube video, I've watched it so many times.'

'See, it all works out.'

'Do you want to practise now?'

No, I just want to walk into your arms and stay there, really.

'I think we're both too exhausted. Tomorrow.'

'I'll pick you up at two thirty.'

'OK.'

We move towards the door.

'Oh,' Anton says, suddenly remembering something, 'don't wear purple.'

'What?'

'Don't wear purple.'

I spin round and stare at him.

'Did you just say don't wear purple?'

'Yes.'

'Why?' I ask very quietly.

'They tell you that, the organisers of *Britain Sings*. The set is purple, I believe, so they suggest you don't wear the same colour.'

Chapter 77

'Gracie Flowers,' Wendy whispers. 'What's the hell's going on? Lube's here. He's in a well weird mood. He said you turned down the job of a lifetime or something. Why didn't you call me?'

'It's a long story.'

'It's my last day as well. I thought we'd glue everything to Posh Boy's desk and then get pissed. This is crap. It's just me and Lube.'

'Wendy, I need your help. I need you to dress me.'

'Ooh. Is it fancy dress? Do you want my bee suit?'

'No.' I laugh. 'Although that would be funny.'

'What are you up to?'

'I'm doing *Britain Sings* with Anton today.'

'*What?*'

'I'm doing *Britain Sings* with Anton.'

'Today?'

'Yes.'

'Jeez!'

'I know.'

'You're messing me.'

'I'm not.'

'You don't sing for years and then go and enter the biggest singing competition in the country.'

'Yeah.'

'This is awesome.'

'I need your help.'

'You don't need my help. You need to borrow one of your mum's old dancing dresses.'

'I can't.'

'Oh, come on, Grace, your bum's not that big. I'm sure you'll be able to squeeze into one of them.'

'No, I can't ask her. We're not speaking.'

'Shit!'

'What do I do?'

'You have to go and talk to her.'

'I can't.'

'Grace, you can. Go now. I'll meet you there with make-up and stuff.'

'But it's your last day.'

'Well, they can't sack me.'

'Wend, we had a stinking great row. You don't understand. It was next level.'

'We all have stinking great rows with the people we love, Grace. It's how we deal with it afterwards that matters. Go and talk to her. She'd want to lend you a dress. I would if I had a daughter and she was about to do this, and so would you and so would she. Just get a bloody move on.'

'OK. Ooh, Wend.'

'Yeah.'

'I was supposed to be showing my favourite family Claire's flat today. Can you call them and ask them to do the viewing without me? And call Bob and get him to go over and help Claire.'

'Yep. Will do.'

'And will you tell Lube I'm sorry.'

''Course.'

'And Wendy.'

'Yeah.'

'I need magic knickers.'

'Where will I get them?'

'I don't know, but it's desperate.'

'OK. And Grace?'

'Yeah.'

'I think this is bloody brilliant news.'

Chapter 78

'Hey, Mildred.'

I put the key in the lock and slowly push the door open. There's a light on in the kitchen and I walk towards it.

'Mum, it's me,' I say softly as I enter. A figure is standing by the kettle. The figure is wearing my mum's pink satin dressing gown. However, the figure is definitely not my mother. This figure is at least a foot taller and at least a foot wider and has never had a lower-leg-waxing session. It looks suspiciously like John St John Smythe Senior.

'Oh, no,' I say with feeling.

'Grace, is that you?' he says, still with his back to me.

'Yes.'

'Now, Grace, your mother is a tiny woman. A tiny woman, Grace. And this dressing gown doesn't do up at the front on me.'

'Oh, urgh!'

'I quite agree. This is most uncomfortable. If I could ask

you to look away while I go up and tell your mother you're here.'

'It's all right, John, I saw her car.' It's my mum walking up behind me and into the room. Thankfully, she's wearing a tracksuit.

'Good morning, Grace.'

'Morning.'

'I don't want us to row,' she says calmly. 'Just let me clear something up. The woman you saw in John's house was his PA. She starts at seven thirty every morning. She's been working for him for years and feels very at home there.'

'Yes, Grace, not a . . . not a . . . you know. There wasn't anything untoward going on.' John Senior says, with his back still to us.

'John came round last night. He's been helping to find the crooks who lent me the money. He even hired a private investigator to see if he could track down the Italian man.'

'Oh. Did they find anything?'

'As a matter of fact, they did.' Mum smiles.

'We handed it all over to the police and I came round last night to tell Rosemary. Then this morning we had a call to say they've caught the syndicate. They arrested them in the early hours.'

'Oh, wow!' I say to John's pink satin back.

'And I'm so terribly sorry, Grace,' Mum says softly. 'About what I said. I'm so terribly sorry.'

'Me, too.'

'No, you shouldn't be sorry.'

'Well, I am.'

She walks towards me and takes my hand.

'I . . . ' she starts, but then she stops and closes her eyes. 'I didn't want to hurt you, Grace. I don't mean to hurt you.'

'In a strange way, I'm glad you told me all that. I mean, it was horrible, but at least things make sense now.'

'Can we move on?'

I catch sight of the clock. I haven't really got time for chit-chat.

''Course, Mum. One other thing, I'm . . . um. This is quite weird as things go. I'm entering the *Britain Sings* competition tonight with a chap called Anton who runs the pub over the road and I was wondering if I could borrow a dress.'

There's a pause.

'Is that the singing show on the telly?' pipes up John Senior.

'Yes, John. Yes, it is,' my mum says quietly, and as she walks towards me I see tears in her eyes. 'Oh, Grace, what will you sing?'

'"Mr Bojangles".'

She just nods at me, while her chin quivers and tears escape her eyes.

'Come upstairs,' she says with a sniff. 'We'll make you look beautiful.'

As we leave the room, John Senior calls out, 'So can I turn round now?'

Chapter 79

'Where is she?' shrieks Wendy. 'Magic knickers delivery!'

'We're up here,' Mum and I call out.

'In my old room,' I add.

'Rosemary Flowers, is that your beau who let me in?' Wendy says, bounding into the room. 'Oh!' She stops suddenly. 'Oh!' she repeats, dropping her Selfridges bag on the ground and slumping onto the bed. 'Oh!' she says again.

She's struck dumb because I am wearing the Death Dress.

'Where did the dress come from?' she whispers.

'It's Gracie's dress,' my mum says, oblivious. 'I made it for her years ago. I always thought she should enter *Britain Sings*, and I tried and tried to persuade her, but she always said no. I'd given up hope of ever seeing her in it, to be honest. This dress and I have been waiting for a long time.'

All that paracetamol we chucked away and it was my dress

after all. Perhaps I should have guessed. It's the same pattern as the one I wore in Rome, but in black velvet. Mum felt the pale blue was too girly and this was more fitting for a young woman.

'I always thought that dress would be too big on the hips for you, Rosemary.'

'What do you think?' asks Mum, cheerfully. 'Do you think she looks like a beautiful young woman with a huge talent who's going to knock everyone's socks off when she gets on that stage tonight.'

'That's exactly what she looks like, Rosemary.'

I peer in the mirror. I know one thing, I don't look like Gracie Flowers. Gracie Flowers wears leggings, dirty ballet pumps and ponytails. The girl in the mirror is squeezed into a fitted black cocktail dress, high black shoes and her hair is swept up in a French pleat.

'So will you do her make-up, Wendy?'

'Really, Mrs F, you are the master. You taught me all I know.'

Mum can't suppress a smile.

'Well, you start on some smoky eyes and I'll pop downstairs to see how John's doing.'

'Knock knock!' shouts John from behind the door. 'Are you ladies decent?'

'I was just coming down to check on you,' my mum says, opening the door and beaming.

I don't beam because standing next to John Senior is his foul offspring, Posh Boy. I scowl at him.

'Grace,' John Senior says, walking towards me and taking one of my hands, 'you look ravishing.'

'Thank you.'

'Gracie Flowers, you look hot,' Posh Boy says.

I silence him with a well-placed middle finger.

'Grace,' my mother admonishes.

'Now, we have a few announcements,' John Senior says. 'The first is that I've been on the phone all morning and managed to get four tickets for a certain *Britain Sings its Heart Out* live final tonight.'

'Oh my God, how much did they set you back?' Wendy asks.

'Oh my God is quite right, Wendy. But it's money thoroughly well spent, I feel. Now, John here can't go, Rosemary and I will obviously take two of the tickets, but we wondered whether you and your helpful lawyer friend would like to join us, Wendy?'

'YES!' Wendy jumps up. 'YES! YES! Thank you, thank you.' She throws her arms around John Senior, who looks tickled pink if truth be told.

When Wendy lets him go, he takes my mum's hand tenderly in his own. 'There's something else we wanted to say, which is why I asked John here to join us this morning. I proposed to Rosemary last night and she's made me the happiest man alive by saying yes.'

'Ah,' Wendy cries. 'Congratulations.'

'Good work,' says Posh Boy, shaking his dad by the hand and kissing my mum on the cheek.

I walk out of the room and onto the landing. I can't get my head around all this. Wendy follows me: 'What's wrong?' she whispers.

'But my mum's a fruit loop, she can't get married!' I hiss.

'Don't speak about your mother like that.' It's John Senior, my stepfather-to-be, and he's telling me off already. He walks onto the landing and closes the door behind him.

'You hardly know her!' I protest.

'Grace, I've known her for some months now. From the first time I popped round and met her, I have been spending time here and getting to know her. Yes, she's delicate. I am aware of that. But I for one have seen huge improvements. Huge. I want to help her. Both our eyes are very open, Grace.'

Part of me wants to fight back, but he's right. Mum has been much better. When she came to the hospital after my miscarriage, she was the strong one, and even though the loan was disastrous, at least she made an active decision, which is something she hasn't done for years. I nod at him.

'Sorry.'

'No need for apologies. It must be quite a shock.'

'Yes.'

He comes towards me with his arms open – oh dear, I'm not sure I'm ready for this – and gives me a hug. And surprisingly, because I certainly wasn't expecting it, I like it. It's not too bearlike or too chummy. It's careful and kind and it makes me feel protected.

'Grace,' he says as he holds me, and there's something in the soft way he says my name that reminds me that his first wife, Posh Boy's mum, was called Grace, too. I hope she's smiling down on us today.

When we release each other, he opens the door to my old room for me enter. Mum looks up expectantly, and I can see how much she wants my approval, how much it means to her. I grin, and it's not forced. It's actually rather easy to smile because I know that this big rich man with the calloused hands will worship my mother, and that's all I want.

The word champagne is mentioned and we all move downstairs, where Posh Boy sidles up to me.

'All my life I've wanted a brother, and I get you,' I hiss.

'I shagged my stepsister.' He smiles. 'That is very cool.'

Chapter 80

'Right, Ruthie Roberts singing "Amazing Grace", ready to go in two minutes,' the studio manager shouts.

'Anton, I whisper. We're sitting side by side in the wings of the huge stage.

'Are you all right?'

'Yes, but do you mind if I hold your hand?'

He shakes his head and smiles as he takes my hand. I squeeze it tightly and close my eyes.

On the morning of my Geography GCSE, the morning my dad died, I was sitting at my desk with the lamp on when Dad knocked on my door.

'How you feeling, Amazing Grace?'

'I'm going to fail,' I wailed because I was a dramatic teenager. He just sat on the edge of the bed. He didn't say anything at first, and neither did I. I was so wrapped up in a world where getting below a C in my geography exam was a national disaster. So we sat in the lamp light, him on the bed, me at the desk, and he opened his mouth and started to sing. He sang me the whole of 'Amazing Grace', softly and beautifully.

Amazing Grace, how sweet the sound
That saved a wretch like me.
I once was lost, but now I'm found,
Was blind, but now I see.

'Twas Grace that taught my heart to fear,
And Grace my fears relieved.
How precious did that Grace appear
The hour I first believed.

At the end I felt so calm. Dad's voice played in my head as I walked to school that day and it played in my head as I sat in the exam hall and read through the paper. It played in my head when I travelled to the hospital and it played in my head when I didn't speak for two whole months. I was able to block out the world and listen to him singing me 'Amazing Grace'.

Then one day I went to a big singing competition in Manchester and Ruth Roberts stood on the stage and was about to sing this song. And I couldn't let her, or rather I couldn't let myself hear it. Because then maybe, just maybe, I wouldn't hear Dad's voice in my head any more singing 'Amazing Grace'. I would hear Ruth Roberts instead. Then I would have lost him. So I screamed and screamed and screamed to block it out. That's why I haven't listened to the radio for years, just in case there was the slightest chance I'd hear someone else singing this song. That's why I once had to run out of a cinema screaming, and it's why I ran screaming out of the karaoke. It's why I've become so afraid of music.

I'm going to let that go now. I'm going to hear this song and I'm going to sing again, because I know that's what Dad would want.

Chapter 81

'Are you ready?' Anton whispers.

'Yes, are you?'

'Yes.' He smiles. Then he looks at his shaking hand. 'Well. Ish.'

I take the shaking hand and I hold it in my own.

'And three, two, one,' the stage manager mouths energetically.

Over the sound system an upbeat male voice announces, 'And now . . . Mr Anton James and Miss Gracie Flowers.'

The stage manager puts a hand in the small of each of our backs to launch us onto the stage. The live theatre audience clap and whistle. We have to walk to our two microphones, which are set a few feet apart in the middle of the stage. I look at the floor as I walk. Anton gets to his microphone first and we release hands. I still can't look up. When I get to my mic, I clutch it for support with both hands and hope no one can see my knees shaking beneath my dress. My hands are trembling, too, and it's making the microphone wobble. I put my hands down and hold them against my sides instead. A panel of six judges sit at a long table towards the front of the stage. Rod Stewart is one of them, and the rest are all music bigwigs. I can't look at them, so I keep my eyes fixed on the floor.

'Anton,' a voice calls from the judges' table. 'Very good to have you back.'

'Thank you for having me back.'

There are quite a few wolf whistles from the audience.

'And you have a new partner, tonight.'

'Yes, Gracie Flowers.'

I know I should look up, but I'm too terrified.

'Hello, Grace.' A woman's voice comes from the judges' table. I keep my head down and raise my eyes towards where her voice is coming from.

'Hello,' I say. My timid, terrified voice goes through the microphone and comes out sounding like a small child who's just wet herself. The audience laugh.

I look back down at my toes. They're still laughing.

'Grace Flowers.' It's a man talking to me now. I peep up at him and the audience laugh again.

'Camille and Rosemary Flowers' daughter?'

'Er, yes, sir.'

Suddenly there's a cheer from the audience for my mum and dad. I look up now at the vague shadowy figures in the auditorium who are cheering my mum and dad, and I smile. The buggers laugh at me again.

'I was hoping I'd hear you sing one day, Grace,' the man says. I don't know who he is and I don't know why he's saying this.

'Thank you,' I mumble into the microphone.

'So, Anton, what song are you going to sing for us?'

'We're going to sing "Mr Bojangles",' he answers.

There are a few whoops and yet more wolf whistles.

'It was Gracie's father's favourite song.'

I glance quickly at Anton, who's smiling at me.

'When you're ready?' the female judge says.

Oh, dear, I have to nod us in. Oh, bloody hell, my knees, my hands, I don't want to look up. I never used to be like this. I take a deep breath and I nod. It's my signal for the backing track to begin. It starts, but so quickly. I nodded it, I called it, but when the music starts I miss the note to sing on. I start breathing really quickly. I've missed the opening. I look at Anton and he's wincing at me. I wonder whether to jump to the next verse. I can't miss the first verse, though. It's a story, and everyone knows the song.

'Um, sorry.' I put my hand up to the music person. 'I'm sorry. I missed my cue. My fault. I'm so sorry.'

The audience's mad wolf whistling and laughing has vanished and they're as quiet as a jury now.

I look at Anton and mouth the word, 'Sorry.' That's it, I've blown it.

'Would you like another try, Grace?' one of the judges asks.

Even if I have another try, I don't think I can do it. I've never been so scared in my life. I'm shaking. I stare at him. I don't know what to do?

I close my eyes and look at the floor as I blink back a tear, and then I hear a voice. A faint voice. My father's voice: 'Just lay the song at their ears, Amazing Grace.'

Someone has taken hold of my hand. I look towards Anton,

but he's still too far away from me. There's no one near me. I know this is stupid, but I think my dad is holding my hand.

'It's your time to shine, my girl,' he whispers. 'Sing your song. Lay it at their ears.'

'Yes, please,' I say.

I look out at the crowd.

'Yes, please, may I try again.'

The audience whoop and I smile with them, then I stand for a moment before I nod to the music man. This time I come in at the right moment. I don't know whether I'm in Rome, in the garden of my childhood home, at a singing competition in Milton Keynes or at the London Palladium. I don't know whether I'm singing with Dad or with Anton. All I know is that I'm singing. I, Gracie Flowers, am singing.

At the end, when the audience is screaming, I feel the hand I've been clutching throughout the song release me. I gasp and look about me, but my eyes meet Anton's and he takes my hand. I smile at him and we bow together.

Chapter 82

I'm sitting backstage with my head on Anton's shoulder and we're listening to the other acts over the tannoy. I feel so light, as though I might float out of my seat at any moment and have to be pulled back down to earth.

'How you doing?' Anton whispers.

'I feel on top of the world. I think someone must have slipped something in the water.'

'We might win, you know.'

'Oh,' I hadn't even thought of winning. I'd forgotten it was a competition. I was too busy thinking about how completely right I feel. 'I'm not really bothered about that.'

'The money might come in handy.'

'Do you win money?'

'A hundred thousand. Gracie Flowers, don't you watch the telly?'

'I've never seen *Britain Sings.*'

'The show could have been made for you.'

'I will now, though.'

'And you get a recording contract to make an album.'

'No?'

'Yep. Would you like that?'

'Would I like to record an album with you?'

'Yes.'

'Yes, although not rubbish pop where we'd have to be on the cover in our pants.'

'No.' He laughs. 'I, er . . . oh, God, Grace.'

He starts fiddling with his bottom on the seat.

'What's the matter? Have you got piles?'

'No.' He laughs. 'This is just something I put down on paper. Read it. I'm an old fool.'

I take the folded-up piece of paper he's holding.

'You're my favourite old fool,' I tell him, but he just looks down at his lap uncomfortably.

I open the paper.

Grace, I don't know where to start. I can't say it in words. I've tried, but I lose the ability to form coherent sentences around you. I couldn't even do it in a song.

Oh, Grace, I've been dazzled by you since the moment you first walked into the pub that lunchtime. Dazzled by this tiny young woman with long blonde hair who was buying a house over the road from me. I suppose what dazzled me was your spirit. A kind spirit, a fighting spirit, a smiling spirit. I don't know to explain it and my words are falling short. I tried John Denver's words and I even messed those up. But really, you'll find everything I want to say to you in the words of 'Annie's Song'.

Grace, I may well be the same age as George Clooney (thirteen months younger actually!), but I am still a lot older than you and I'm at a different point in my life. You're at the beginning, while I'm in the middle. And when we had a moment that night, I froze. I remembered your father. I respected him, Grace, and I wanted to do the right thing by you, for you and by your dad. I didn't want to take what I shouldn't. I've given it a lot of thought, though, and no matter how much I think about it, I am always led back to a fact that's bigger than all the questions and doubts, the fact that I am completely in love with you, Grace. When I sing songs, when I play songs, they are all for you.

Now, I just want you to know this: that I am over the road, thinking of you and wanting above all else for you to be happy.

Yours, an old fool and an admirer.

Anton xx

'I'm going to keep this forever,' I whisper, and I look into his eyes and smile. 'I'll keep it in a little box under our bed.'

'Grace.'

Talk about interruption of the decade. It's Ruth Rogers. Wow! She's smiling at me. She certainly wasn't doing that the last time we met.

'Hello, Ruth.'

'Hello, Gracie. I loved your song. I used to be so jealous of your voice, but it was nice to hear it again. I'd missed it.'

'Thank you. And I'm pleased I heard you sing "Amazing Grace" again. It was beautiful.'

I look at her for a second, wondering whether to apologise for that incident ten years ago, but the frantic *Britain Sings its Heart Out* floor manager takes the decision out of my hands by storming into the room and shouting, 'All acts in line: they're ready to announce the winner!'

Ruth rushes back to her place and I stand up beside Anton, who steadies me as I fall off my high heels. I take his hand and everything, every little thing feels right in the world.

Chapter 83

In other parts of London, people aren't quite as relaxed as Gracie Flowers.

'Oh, Len, I can't bear it!' Joan says, lying next to her brother in his hospital bed at St Mary's Hospital.

It's an hour past the end of visiting time, but the nurses understood when she told them that the pretty blonde girl with the amazing voice is like family to her, so she has to stay until the end. Of course they understand. This is the final of *Britain Sings its Heart Out* after all. They are all seated in Len's private room, watching it together.

Len was moved into a private room a few days ago. It's been paid for by an anonymous donor, although Joan has a feeling it might have something to with a cheque from SJS Construction, which landed on her doormat the very same day.

Joan has kicked her shoes off onto the floor and is squeezing her brother's hand, the one that can squeeze hers back.

'Oh, why do they always do this? Take so long to announce the winner. I can't bear it! What did you say, love?'

As Joan moves her ear closer to her brother's mouth she notices a tear in his eye.

'Yes,' she says, agreeing with him. 'That's our girl.'

'Put the telly on!' Gracie's favourite family scream as they enter the living room.

'They're about to announce the winner! We've missed all the singing. I can't believe I had to go to your stupid school play,' Emma Hammond shrieks, kicking her brother in the shin as they sit on the sofa. 'This is my favourite programme!'

The camera on the telly slowly focuses on all the contestants one by one.

'There's the "Amazing Grace" girl. I love her,' she says seriously.

'She was rubbish,' her brother chimes.

'Shh,' she instructs her brother.

'Ooh, that's the handsome man who won the first show,' Mrs Hammond whoops. Her husband squeezes her waist. 'Not as handsome as you, darling, and I'm sure he doesn't sing "Don't Cry For Me Argentina" as well as you, either.'

'No one sings "Don't Cry For Me Argentina" as well as I do. Now then, shall we have a glass of something to celebrate my son's stellar performance in *Wind in the Willows* and finally finding our new home today?'

'That blonde girl looks like . . .'

'Oh, my God, it's her! It's Gracie! That's Grace!' Emma Hammond shrieks.

'Ah,' they all gasp in unison as the camera zooms in on a radiant Gracie beaming up at Anton.

'It was singing,' Emma Hammond whispers to herself. The thing that Gracie loved doing most of all was singing. Emma smiles. She knew Gracie wasn't telling the truth when she said it was being an estate agent.

'*SH-i-i-i-i-i-t!*' says Tara, her mouth crackling from the popping candy she is eating. She's sitting on her brother's bed watching the new Sony widescreen TV that he mysteriously came home with this afternoon.

'What?'

'It's her, innit?'

'What the . . .?'

'The one you nicked the bag off. I told you. She got pregnant. I gave her the bag back.'

'Shit! You should've kept the bag. If she wins we could've sold it on eBay.'

Tara opens her mouth so it pops and fizzes in her brother's face, then she twats him hard on the leg with her fist.

'Oh shit! What d'you hit me for?'

''Cos, you're a dick, innit. I well want her to win.'

'Oh, Bob!' Claire says, swigging some Moët & Chandon out of the bottle. 'I can't bear it. She's got to win it. I wish they'd just come out with it! It's torture!'

Bob is walking around Claire's multi-purpose living area with a twin under each arm, as he's found it's the only way he can stop them walking up to the screen and dribbling the word 'Gracie' all over it.

'Gracie Flowers, come on, sis. Come on, sis,' he chants.

'Bob, sit down. I think I need to cling on to you.'

Bob perches next to Claire on the settee and can't help but grin as she clutches his leg.

Lube is just pouring out the last of the bottle of Rioja when his mobile rings. It's his daughters and they're screaming.

'What's going on? What's happened at the sleepover?' Bob says, jumping up like the concerned father he is. 'What? My Gracie? On the telly?'

Rushing up to the TV, he turns it on, only to see the face of Gracie Flowers, the best female estate agent in London, filling the whole of his widescreen plasma television.

'Well, I'll be blown.' He sighs. 'Well, I'll be blown.'

John St John Smythe Senior sits in the dress circle of the London Palladium, holding his beautiful wife-to-be's tiny hand and hoping that all the screaming hasn't harmed his hearing. Rosemary Flowers sits next to him, beaming. It's been quite a night for Rosemary: she's been asked for her autograph seventeen times and she's heard her only daughter sing for the first time in ten years. John Senior has never seen her look so beautiful, he thinks, as he bends down to kiss her on the cheek.

Freddie, who is sitting next to Rosemary, is paying close attention to the goings-on on stage. Unable to hold it in any longer, he turns to his new girlfriend.

'Wendy,' he whispers.

'Yes,' Wendy croaks back. She's almost lost her voice from screaming, 'GRACIE!' all night.

'Do my dad and Grace look like more than just good friends to you?'

Wendy scrutinises her best friend down there on the stage. She notes the way Grace's hand is wrapped around Anton's waist, how her head leans into his chest and how Anton is smiling proudly down at her. And being an expert on love and the creator of the hugely successful Love Test, she turns to Freddie in his new shirt – purchased this morning in Selfridges, along with the most magic of knickers – and says, with conviction, 'Yes, Freddie. Yes, it does.'

'Blimey.' Freddie sighs.

'Is that weird for you?'

'Yes,' he says, 'but in a good weird way.'

'Ooh. Shh . . . they're going to announce the winners.'

Chapter 84

Down on the stage, Gracie Flowers is getting a bit bored with this presenter leaving a sixty-second gap before he says anything. She wants him to hurry the hell up and announce the winner, so that she can do things like gaze into Anton's eyes and play with his hair and kiss him oh so softly on the lips. She smiles up at him and wonders whether she could kiss him now. No one would notice as there are loads of contestants on the stage. I'll just steal a quick one, she thinks, and she pulls herself up as high as her five-foot frame allows and puckers up. She feels the warmth of Anton's face coming towards her own.

'Er, Grace,' he whispers. 'I think the camera's on us. They just said we won.'

'You what?' she yelps, quickly opening her eyes and turning towards the presenter she'd forgotten all about.

The audience, who are becoming very fond of this funny, nervy, short person called Grace, laugh and cheer. Grace stands there with her mouth open until Anton takes hold of her hand

and steers her towards centre stage. They now have to say a few words to the presenter and the nation.

'How do you feel?'

'Great,' says Anton, and he turns to the crowd and the judges, smiles bashfully and says, 'Thank you.'

'And, Grace, how are you feeling?'

Grace still has her mouth open.

'Um, a bit strange,' she whispers.

And this time she's not surprised when the audience laugh.

'So are you ready to sing again?'

'Do we have to sing again?' she asks, shocked.

'Yes.'

'Oh,' says Grace, seemingly baffled by the whole event. But then she smiles and whispers something to Anton, who nods and gives her a thumbs-up sign.

'Excuse me, sir,' Gracie asks. 'Are we allowed to sing a different song?'

'Er, well, I'm not sure, we'd need to have the music.'

'We don't need a backing track.'

'Er, well then, I believe that's fine.'

'Excellent.'

'So, what would you like to sing?'

'"Feeling Good" by Nina Simone.'

Gracie looks up at Anton's smiling face and thinks, Sod it. Then she stands on tiptoes and reaches up to kiss him softly on the lips.

Next they take their microphones and face the audience at the London Palladium. As they wait for the whoops to quieten down, Gracie has this one thought: Today is the best day of my life.

Songs for the one and only – thank goodness! – Gracie Flowers

Adele – Make You Feel My Love (I normally feel strong surges of violence towards people who cover songs that were perfect to begin with . . . but not in this case . . . listen . . . wow).

Ellie Goulding – Your Song (ditto . . .).

Laura Marling – Ghosts (lovely – very young singer songwriter).

Florence + the Machine – Dog Days Are Over (quite something this . . . she's very good live. Always a strange expression, as though she might be good dead – I'll keep an ear out, perhaps we could see her in concert).

Lily Allen – Smile (hope it makes you).

Alicia Keys – Fallin'

(American – amazing).

As you might have noticed, they're all by women. All talented but, and I mean this Gracie Flowers, none of them is a patch on you.

Norah Jones –

Come Away With Me (lovely).

Corinne Bailey Rae – Like A Star (ditto).

Katie Melua – Nine Million Bicycles (very cute – this CD isn't making me sound very masculine, is it?).

Paloma Faith – Upside Down

(I think you'll like her!).

Songs for the handsome devil who's rocking my world

The First Time Ever I Saw Your Face – Roberta Flack (I remember it well . . . it's a very nice face xx).

Feeling Good – Nina Simone (yes, indeedy, yes, I most certainly am!).

Song for the Asking – Simon & Garfunkel

Make It With You – Bread

Let's Stay Together – Al Green (well, I'm up for it if you are?).

(As you might have noticed the majority of these are unashamedly slushy love songs . . . and they're all for you . . . xxxxxxxxxxxxx)

Let's Get It On – Marvin Gaye
(ditto!).

Annie's Song – John Denver
(my dad sang this to my mum at their wedding – apparently it made grown men weep).

Summertime – Louis Armstrong and Ella Fitzgerald.

Mr Bojangles – Sammy Davis Jr.

Amazing Grace – Ray Charles
(it's lovely to hear this again).

SHIIIIIT – bloody Wendy just hijacked my mixtape . . . she put on Madonna's 'Like A Virgin'!!! . . . We've just been dancing around the room singing it . . . I haven't done that for years . . . THANK YOU . . . I'm going to give you all my love boy x

Acknowledgements

An especially huge and heartfelt thank you goes to my dad. One day, some time ago, I called him up and said, 'Dad, I've got an idea for a story,' and told him the bones of the Gracie Flowers tale. At the end he was silent. Oh bugger, I thought, I've bored him to sleep. But then he sniffed and confessed to me that his eyes had welled up. Since that moment he's constantly been there listening to me rabbit on about it, offering me advice and encouragement and reading rambling drafts. I am so grateful and I love you lots. Huge thanks to my mum too. I was a very lucky girl when they were giving out parents.

I realised whilst writing this book that the act of writing could be done anywhere as long as I had my laptop. I therefore owe huge thanks to people who let me cadge in on their holidays (Mum and Dad, Mexico; Gail and Mick, Spain), invite myself to their homes (Jane and Martial Zohoungbogbo, Ghana), gave me homemade flapjacks and whisky in their B & Bs (Charles and

Barbara, Bamburgh), and most of all the man who continually whisked me away (Paul – Italy, Canada, California!).

I was also a very lucky girl when they were dishing out agents and publishers. A massive thank you to the amazing and gorgeous and lovely Rowan Lawton, and her estimable sidekick, Juliet. Also to Rachel Mills and Alexandra Cliff and all at PFD. And to my lovely, brilliant editor Rebecca Saunders. I have so loved working with you on this. And the dream team that is Sphere's fiction department: Manpreet Grewal; Charlie 'The' King; Emma Williams; Shauna Bartlett.

Find Lucy on f at:
Lucy-Anne Holmes Author

Follow Lucy on t at:
@lucyanneholmes

Discover how Gracie would spend her perfect day off, where she would go on a girls' night out and even her tips for selling a house; plus playlists, competitions, audition song videos and news of upcoming books at:

www.lucyanneholmes.co.uk